Rodanthe's Gift

YVONNE PAYNE

First published 2018 by Black Bay Publishing
E-Mail – Blackbaypublishing@gmail.com

Copyright © Yvonne Payne 2018

The right of Yvonne Payne to be identified as the author of this work has been asserted by her in accordance with the Copyright, Designs and Patents Act 1988.

ISBN-13: 978-1727291391
ISBN-10: 1727291395

British Library Cataloguing in Publication Data
A CIP catalogue record for this book is available from the British Library

Set in Sabon LT Roman by Black Bay Publishing

Front Cover by WorkingType – www.workingtype.com.au

Printed on environmentally responsible sourced paper

Introduction

Yvonne Payne has enjoyed a home in Kritsa, Crete, since 2001. This has provided her with time to explore the area, absorb local culture and develop a keen interest in Greek history.

In her first novel, *Kritsotopoula: Girl of Kritsa*, Yvonne drew on the true story of Rodanthe, the Kritsa woman who fought alongside rebels disguised as a young man, under the leadership of Captain Kazanis. An epic poem, handed down orally over generations, acted as her guide to supplement information and experience gained walking in and around Kritsa, visiting museums, and academic research. Yvonne included most of the key points from the poem in her first novel, except for addressing how a rich *pappas* – priest – happened to be in Kritsa the day Rodanthe was born, when he gifted her one hundred gold napoleon coins.

Once Yvonne caught the research bug, she became aware of further hardship, bravery and atrocities suffered by Cretans during the long fight for freedom from Turk rule. This would probably have stayed background information, had she not discovered that Captain Kazanis fought on the mainland during the siege of Missolonghi.

As Yvonne pondered over the rich priest being in Kritsa for Rodanthe's birth, and Captain Kazanis travelling from Crete to Missolonghi, this novel, *Rodanthe's Gift*, took shape.

Praise for Rodanthe's Gift

'Yvonne Payne has managed to weave many of the major events in the battle for Greek independence into this rip-roaring historical adventure. Her novel reaches epic proportions as the struggle for freedom shifts between the island of Crete and mainland Greece. The author is a great storyteller, and this, in harness with her great attention to historical detail, makes Rodanthe's Gift a terrific read.'

Richard Clark, acclaimed author of *Eastern Crete – A Notebook* and other Greek travel guides

In memory of my grandmother, Olive Goodwin

KEY LOCATIONS IN RODANTHE'S GIFT

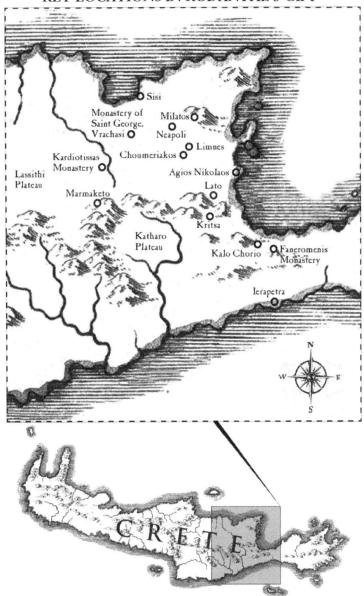

Sisi

Monastery of Saint George, Vrachasi

Milatos

Neapoli

Kardiotissas Monastery

Choumeriakos

Limnes

Lassithi Plateau

Agios Nikolaos

Marmaketo

Lato

Kritsa

Katharo Plateau

Kalo Chorio

Faneromenis Monastery

Ierapetra

N
W · E
S

CRETE

Part 1

Reflection

1

The Egyptian, Hassan Pasha

Hassan Pasha clenched his knees against heaving, blood-smeared flanks and tightened his one-handed grip on the reins. His maniacal screams passed unnoticed amid the din of battle as he hauled hard to turn his favourite stallion. This extra momentum allowed his other arm to tug his sabre free of its latest victim. Clashing steel, gunfire, frightened horses and screaming hoards drowned the man's dying shriek. Without a second glance, the Egyptian leader of a combined Arab and Turk force galloped towards slaves bearing waterskins at the edge of the action. Under a common mask of sweat, blood and soot, he halted by an officer in his command.

'In Allah's name, what will stop these crazy Christians?' He wiped his mouth on the back of his leather gauntlet without acknowledging the lack of reply, 'Don't they realise we'll keep killing?'

Again, his Arab officer avoided opinion, 'Lord, dusk spreads its dingy blanket. Will you signal withdrawal? Our Turk brothers are already turning.'

With no sign that he'd heard, the pasha tossed the waterskin aside and reached forward to pet the ears of his steed.

'Now, my beauty, you are without doubt the best weapon in my army. Know my thanks. Your skill and tenacity kept me whole today as much as Allah's grace.'

Not for the first time, he marvelled to see the animal wriggle his ears, appreciating a quiet word while ignoring the chaos of fighting. From his place on the sideline, he recognised that the funnel-shaped gully benefited the infidel. He sensed his army falling back, so stood tall in his stirrups to see further. Yes, they knew the muezzin's call to prayer was imminent. To regain the initiative, he flashed his sabre over the once-white turban with its signature trailing silk now streaked by flying gore and gun smoke. Certain he'd gained the attention of those nearby, he galloped towards the fields below Kritsa. Depleted after a day of battle, Hassan Pasha's force retired to camp with no thought to their fallen comrades strewn across the mired battleground. If these men had died well, they were already enjoying paradise; and if not, their eternal fate was not worth concern.

Within an hour, the haughty Arab luxuriated in a tin bath full of hot, rose-scented water, paying no attention to his body servant who was busy laying out fresh robes. In time for prayers, he stepped out, allowing the servant to drape a thick, snow-white Egyptian sheet over his shoulders. Refreshed, and devotions complete, he strode to the ornate goatskin marquee which served as the mess for high-ranking officers.

A boy opened the flap to allow his master access, then fell in behind him to walk alongside trestle tables groaning under the weight of food, scenting the marquee with mingling aromas. In anticipation he tugged his moustaches and licked his lips, watching the boy taste each chosen dish. Once he was on his divan, two slaves lowered trays laden with golden roast chicken, stewed goat with glistening fat, heaped rice pilaf flavoured with spices, mutton stew, mixed vegetables, and fresh oranges, sliced open to add their zest to the exotic air.

Ravenous and aroused, he rubbed his swelling crotch while passing up a silent prayer of thanks that his entourage included perfumed girls. His head eunuch was at his heel the second after he'd clicked his fingers.

'An experienced girl tonight. My hunger needs an expert touch. No need to collect her until morning.'

*

Drowsy and replete, Hassan Pasha smiled, fascinated by fingers of early sunlight reaching between branches to paint dappled shapes on the hide roof. Voices outside his scented, lamp-lit campaign tent spoilt his reverie. A moment later coded knocks on the taut leather door flap had him on his feet. Still tying his wrap, he shouted, 'Enter,' disregarding the squeal from his bed. Unseen arms thrust a dishevelled Turk scout inside to cower where he fell.

'Praise be to Allah. Blessings of peace be upon the Messenger of Allah.'

'Get on with it. It must be important if my guards allow you to disturb me.'

Blurted out in a rush, the scout's message failed to gain response, increasing his fear with each heartbeat of silence. Prone on the ground, the scout observed hairy legs stride up and down a short length of elaborate blue silk carpet, then he blinked as dainty, slippered feet stepped from the canopied bed to disappear behind a curtain. Tent walls, lined with woollen blankets to keep heat in, provided scant barrier against the sound of running men, their swords clinking. Outside, a shout brought a squad to attention, sending vibrations along the prostrate man's length.

'Gone! In the name of Allah, how can an army disappear overnight? Come in and explain.'

Now the miserable man counted three pairs of expensive black boots march inside the tent. Their muddied heels clicked to attention. Scared witless, he flinched, sensing a static charge as the commander's furious gaze swept over his officers.

'Why did they flee? They held us at bay.'

No officer risked an opinion.

'Do you imagine my illustrious cousin, Mehmet Ali, leader of all Egypt, thought for one moment I'd not cow tiresome Christians?' Spittle sprayed as he seethed. 'Now infidels live to fight another battle, they'll celebrate as if they are victors. Do you know the worst thing?'

None answered.

'If the curs don't fear us, I can't control them.' He stamped the ground to accentuate each word. 'They. Must. Feel. Fear!'

He poked the terrified wretch with his bare foot, and hissed,

'Will my fearful reputation subdue them and deliver order?'

From his awkward position, the trembling messenger didn't see the maddened pasha seize his polished sabre from its hook next to tomorrow's freshly pressed cavalry uniform. As the honed blade swished through the air, the scout screamed in horrible anticipation.

2

Farewell Rodanthe

Christian rebel Captain Kazanis hefted the shrouded body across his shoulder, wincing from the sharp pain shooting up his arm from his injured hand. Despite the January chill, he felt a film of sweat drench his face. When he turned to see his exhausted son slumped under trees, his throat constricted – he'd give anything to send Petros out of harm's way. Instead, he towered over the lad.

'Scout ahead, Son. Stay on this cobbled path, it leads to the village graveyard. Double back if you see anyone.'

Without a word Petros rose, and hunched in misery, set off to do as bid. Anxiety gnawed at Kazanis. Watching his son pass from sight, he swallowed hard and patted his sad load, 'Time for us to go.'

Nearby, two injured men – his cousin Kostas and Pappas Mathaios – aided each other to stand, sparking a flash of anger at his soft decision to help them. How he wished he'd not allowed compassion to cloud his judgement. He barked, 'Follow me,' and strode away.

Clamour from the joint Turk and Arab force striking camp in fields below Kritsa carried on a light breeze. Snorts and whinnies rose from hundreds of cavalry horses, each welcoming their rider. While resting against a tree, Kazanis imagined a multitude of slaves loading tents, kitchens and supplies on droves of braying mules and donkeys. Metallic notes signalled artillerymen fastening helmets, guns and bayonets. It was time to move.

Kazanis grunted as he adjusted the body slung over his shoulder. 'We'll honour you with a proper burial, once the mongrels move.'

*

Deep in a hide of tangled undergrowth, Petros wept until distracted by movement on the far side of the Christian cemetery. As his sobs reduced to sniffles, he watched his pa rest the shrouded remains under trees and then massage his shoulder with his good hand. Moments later an overloud click signalled he'd primed a pistol to start a systematic search of the graveyard. Petros wriggled back; he dreaded his pa taunting his tears. When thorns bit his neck, he didn't care, as the physical pain seemed easier to bear than choking grief.

At the smashed door to the small graveyard church, Kazanis kicked out at the wreckage and desecration, then risked a low call.

'Petros, show yourself.'

Rustling in nearby shrubbery brought a rush of annoyance; this was no time to test his patience. He shook the bush, and as his harsh, 'Petros!' left his lips he felt sorry; his lad had endured so much. He crouched down, reaching to deliver an awkward hug. 'Well done, Son! Bloody Turks and their cronies must be cocksure not to have set patrols.'

In the close confines, Kazanis knocked his roughly bandaged hand, drawing a gasp of pain, 'Sorry, Pa!'

'It wasn't your fault. You can replace this tatty rag later. I'll admit the bastard's javelin damaged my hand more than I realised. Move closer. I'll use my other hand to rub your chills away.'

Had his son realised this day marked his thirteenth year, he'd have thought the rare embrace a birthday treat. Together they watched the ragged one-armed cleric enter the graveyard. Without hesitation, Pappas Mathaios went to the body, sat, lifted the head to his lap and talked to the corpse as he stroked the shroud.

Sounds from the oppressor's army faded as the hated force headed towards yesterday's battlefield. Tranquil at last, a gentle morning hymn soothed those in the graveyard. A fluting blackbird sentinel in a tall cypress tree accompanied cheery chirrups from a concealed robin wintering on the southerly island. Overhead, melodious crested larks flew high. A sudden blast startled them.

'Bravo! Freedom or death!' bellowed Kazanis, 'Our brave

rearguard delivered a hot reception.' He nudged his son then pointed towards a man struggling on rudimentary crutches, 'Cousin Kostas will need a mount to get back up the mountain.'

He called to Kostas, 'Those bastards now enjoy an early paradise. Have you any *raki*?'

After fumbling in his tattered, mired tunic, Kostas produced a small flask. Warmth from the potent colourless spirit hit the back of Kazanis' throat. After smacking his lips together in appreciation, he returned the flask, 'Take a draught, Kostas. Toast our fine *palikars*, rebels. The old heroes sacrificed themselves. I've left enough to wet your tongue.'

'Pah, it was only noise. Their casualties will be minimal.'

'Our benefit comes from the time those bastards spend clearing debris at the narrow pass. Every hour of delay gives more Christians the chance of escape. Now, let's get this done.'

Kazanis towered over the pappas, 'Show me your wife's tomb. Petros will help me prise it open.'

Despite enduring the gore and stench of battle, vile tomb corruption sent the pair reeling. Petros unwound the loosely woven black turban cloth from around his head to fashion a mask in a futile attempt to conquer the stink. Kazanis grabbed two fistfuls of his matted beard and tied its length across his mouth and nose to create a barrier against evil decomposition. When they'd hauled away the marble lid to reveal the stained wrap below, Kazanis said, 'Gather leaves from under those trees. Cover what's left of his wife. No point in making it worse than it need be.'

Kostas shuffled to Kazanis, 'Be proud of your Petros. He's seen enough death and bloodshed these past two days to last a lifetime.'

'I'm hoping him witnessing the burial of this brave rebel will help. Ah, here he comes …'

*

Stood around the stinking grave, none knew how to respond to the heartbroken cleric's wail: 'I can't do it.' He knelt, 'It was hard enough burying my murdered wife. I never imagined burying my sweet child.'

Kazanis sought to galvanise the distraught man and pointed at the body, 'I'd come to admire the lad we called Spanos. I feel your loss. Had I realised he was a lass I'd never have deployed him,' he shook his head, 'but then, without her pluck and ingenuity I'd be grieving the death of my son. Now I implore you, commit her body, the day races.'

The stricken man stared up at the hirsute, dishevelled and blood-spattered hulk bristling with an array of arms harvested from fallen foe. Petros knelt to lift Pappas Mathaios' hand to his throat.

'Feel my scar. I'd have died in a noose had Spanos not tricked a felon to save me. She was my older brother. I'm bereft, but we have to do this.'

Kostas rested a hand on the pappas' shoulder, 'I loved her. I realised too late.' Overwhelmed by a loss he could no longer contain, Kostas wept.

Not bothering to wipe his eyes, Pappas Mathaios said, 'Bless you for loving my daughter. I'm amazed you knew her as a brave lad. How she maintained such a disguise is a mystery. I shudder to imagine her ordeals. Yes, I'll withstand this final deed for her.' Pappas Mathaios looked skyward to cry, 'God help me,' then, in a whisper, 'Forgive me Rodanthe. I loved you so much.' Pain seared his chest to take his breath. Sweat drenched his back, and too dizzy to stand, he dropped to his knees. 'Dear God, how did it come to this?'

Closing his eyes on the brink of unconsciousness, he smiled, hearing friendly voices from his past. Memories jostled with images dancing in his mind's eye. Then he sighed, imagining himself back in the security of his monastery schoolroom. His last words before he fainted were, 'Yes, that is where it all started.'

3

Rising Stars

While Mathaios' body lay slumped in the graveyard, his mind tricked him to believe he sat next to his close friend Nikolaos in the monastery's schoolroom.

Reverend Abbot was in his element, delivering extra tuition to prepare his two star pupils for ordination as deacons. Engrossed in a complex explanation, it appeared their teacher was oblivious of the supper bell. When Nikolaos nudged his friend and mimed hunger, Mathaios looked away to stifle giggles.

A knock on the attic schoolroom's door brought sighs of relief from the hungry youths.

'Enter.'

'Sorry to disturb you, Reverend Abbot. Tinker waits in your office.'

All thoughts of supper vanished as his pupils gasped, both wondering what would bring a visitor after dark.

Owl-like, their tutor blinked several times, seeming to take a moment to comprehend.

'Thank you, Brother Michalis. Tell him I'm on my way.' As the monk scuttled off, Reverend Abbot turned to his students. 'I'm sorry for the interruption. Go to your supper.'

❊

Apprehension tempered the abbot's curiosity so much he was in no mind to take his usual glass of wine with his itinerant friend, Tinker. It was as if the letter delivered from the bishop in far-off Megalo Kastro burnt his hand.

'Thank you, Tinker. It's not long since the supper bell rang. Get yourself down to the refectory for a meal and ask Brother Michalis to bunk you in the guest bed above the gatehouse.'

As he pushed the door shut with his foot, his fingers tore at the seal. A fast read-through had him punching the air in glee before falling to his knees in thankful prayer. After rising with an arthritic groan, he took the letter to the window to read it aloud for clarity.

The blessing of the Lord to the Very Reverend Abbot of Faneromenis.

With joy I share news from our sister church in Russia. A group of their clergy aim to see how the Hellenic people fare under the Ottoman yoke. Once on Crete this band of eight, all bound for high office, will split to cover our island. When they arrive, I will ask our mutual friend Tinker to guide a pair around the east before visiting you for hospitality and recuperation. They will return to us in Megalo Kastro for a month, before sailing to experience life among the blessed monks on Mount Athos.

May the Lord bless you.

Kissing your hand, the Right Reverend Bishop, Megalo Kastro.

On opening his office door Reverend Abbot tripped over Brother Michalis.

'How strange you've chosen this evening to scrub the floor. I doubt you've cleaned this patch since the last time Tinker brought me a message. No, don't get up, Brother. Clean my chamber while the mood is upon you.'

*

As usual, when he wasn't labouring on the monastery smallholding, Mathaios spent the morning in the empty schoolroom engaged in private study. When the door opened unexpectedly he hid his surprise by kneeling.

'Bless me, Your Reverence.'

After kissing the abbot's hand, he remained on his knees for the expected response.

'May the Lord bless you.'

Still on his knees, Mathaios felt nervous. Why did this senior monk seek him?

'Come, my son, let's walk downhill to take lunch with your

aunt.'

A resounding thump behind them signalled that the huge fortified monastery gate had slammed shut. Intrigued to learn the reason for their unexpected outing, Mathaios offered his arm to steady his mentor along the initial part of the steep slope, pointing out jutting rocks and loose scree. Where the path wound across an open pasture, the abbot invited Mathaios to rest on a sun-warmed rock, smooth from centuries of similar use. With their heads moving in unison from west to east, they gazed over the magnificent view – the majestic Dikti Mountains to the left, the azure Mirabello Bay in front and the nearby rounded tops of the Thripti Mountains to the right.

While the abbot focused on the horizon, where blue sea and bright sky merged, apprehension threatened to choke Mathaios. Desperate to calm the pounding in his chest, he concentrated on breathing in the heady scents of purple thyme, white oregano and sun-warmed grass. When he heard bells tinkling in the distance, he guessed his uncle herded goats to new pasture.

A mewing buzzard took the abbots attention.

'You remind me of that bird. You need to soar on a thermal of learning far greater than we can offer. With the right tutors, I'd say unlimited heights stretch before you. Only God knows how high you can fly.'

Mathaios sought the bird, now a tiny fleck in the cloudless sky, 'He flies to the height atmospheric conditions and his skills allow.'

'Yes, but if someone, no matter how kind the intention, kept him in a cage from a young age, he'd never know the purpose of his wings, never experience the thrill of viewing the world from a different perspective.'

Mathaios studied the abbot's kind face and realised his innocuous words held a deep message. His stomach churned. What answer did Reverend Abbot want?

'If he had food, light, and the company of those who wished him well, he'd thrive. If he'd experienced nothing else, he'd be well content.'

'Breeze might reach through his well-intentioned bars to ruffle his feathers until his instinct made him beat his wings in a frenzy. Imagine the poor fellow, injured and over-dependent on the hand who fed him. Even if someone left the cage open, he'd continue to sit confined.'

Another mewing buzzard brought the first one swooping to greet her, and they weaved mesmeric patterns together before gliding out of sight. With the abbot's gentle arm around his shoulder, Mathaios heard of their visitors.

Excited questions tumbled. How long will these guests stay? How much time could they spend with monks and students? Could he act as their servant?

In measured tones, Reverend Abbot answered expected questions. After a brief pause, he hugged his protégé.

'When our guests leave, go with them.' He ignored the stunned, slack-jawed face staring back at him to continue, 'You'll gain experience travelling before a Russian career.'

Even in the initial flush of astonished excitement, Mathaios felt torn; he owed the abbot so much.

'You've directed me towards ordination. I'll consider myself fortunate to become a deacon before I take monastic vows. With humility I admit my ambitions reached to having my brothers call me Pappas. Are you sure you don't want me to stay?'

'Pride blinds you. Another novice has competence to fill that future role.'

'Of course! Nikolaos.'

Now the abbot laughed to see the young man jump for joy. It was obvious his brain sped through unimagined experiences ahead of him.

'You gambol more than a spring lamb. Come back and give me your hand, I need to stand. Let's go to your aunt where you must find words to tell her you're travelling to serve God in Russia.'

4

Faneromenis Festival

Two months later Brother Michalis stood at his favourite vantage point, at the high gatehouse window of the fortified monastery, willing his failing sight to penetrate the dark cloak of night. He anticipated the first pinpricks of light from oil lamps heralding women from villages as far away as Kritsa.

First to appear around midnight were those from the nearby hamlet below the monastery. These hostesses had justifiable pride in the feast they'd prepared to feed pilgrims after the service held that very morning, on the fifteenth of August, to celebrate the Dormition of the Panagia when Mary, Mother of God, fell asleep. The previous two-week fast banning meat, poultry, milk, cheese, eggs, fish, oil and wine produced an abundance of ingredients for their baking and making. Local menfolk never attended this service out of respect for the many women craving an opportunity to kiss the monastery's miraculous icon of the Panagia, Mother of God. Despite this, cheerful men set prime hogs to roast, in certain knowledge they'd make short work of the leftovers. Brother Michalis sniffed the air. Yes, there was a faint aroma proving the fat porker was above the firepit. His belly rumbled as he remembered the youthful hours he'd spent turning the spit, and he rubbed his arms as if the memory pained him. Sandals slapping on stone steps made him smile.

'Might have guessed you two would join me. Ever since you realised visitors brought cakes and pastries you've been too excited to rest between services.'

As he stepped back from the window, Brother Michalis feigned protests.

'I'd have thought soon-to-be deacons above hugs and kisses.'

Instead of gaining cheer from the easy familiarity, Mathaios felt tears prickle and moved to peer from the window. He wondered if this was the right time to tell these dear people his news. One stood instead of a papa and the other as his adopted brother. As he swallowed the lump in his throat he decided not to spoil the festival, reminding himself there was time to spare as he'd assured the abbot he'd tell them before September. In a cheery voice, he masked his emotions.

'Lamplights head this way. Come, Nikolaos, let's greet them.'

The distance between women of the Kritsa group belied the fact they'd set out as a closely formed unit full of chatter and anticipation. Those unable to face the final steep climb until first light took advantage of hospitality in the nearby hamlet of monastery servants. One spurning rest was Irini, and as she crested the last mound her weariness evaporated at the sight of lamps with dancing flames set along the monastery's steep steps. With her arms sweeping, she spun.

'God is so near. Those stars invite us to touch the heavens. Since we passed our village sentries, I've felt free as a bird, and enjoyed every step of our trek.' Giddy, she clutched her friend Katerina by the arm, 'Our pilgrimage is more enjoyable for having you to walk with.'

'How could I refuse when you explained about kissing the icon famed for aiding women?'

Sad in an instant, Irini hugged Katerina.

'Your plea is an easy guess. Two stillborn boys is unbearable.'

'Place your palm here. Can you feel it? My prayer is for a girl babe.'

'No wonder you agreed so fast when I suggested we wear our looser white cotton smocks without aprons and take waistcoats for church instead.'

'Your gift of a long white scarf kept the worst of the sun off me and felt more comfortable than our usual face-binding kerchiefs.'

'You'll see more women wear them tomorrow for the service. So many women wear the constant black of mourning, I was surprised the first time I saw Grandma wear a white scarf at the monastery. Of more importance, does my cousin know about the baby?'

'I'll tell him when we return.' As superstitious as most local folk, Katerina made the sign against the evil eye. Frightened by speaking her dream aloud, she changed the subject, 'Lights head our way.'

'I expect it's the lads. It's two years since our last pilgrimage from Kritsa, and I've missed them.'

With an ease forged in childhood, Irini kissed the tubby youth, Nikolaos. Not expecting Mathaios to have grown so tall, Irini blushed, grateful for the cover of darkness as she took his proffered hand. In her confusion Irini forgot to let go and failed to make introductions.

'Hello, I'm Katerina. I married Irini's cousin and settled in Kritsa.'

A group of six including Irini's mama drew near and Nikolaos called out to attract their attention. Puffed from exertion, they flung themselves on the brittle remains of sunburnt grass, clamouring for the water flasks the thoughtful youths carried. When the rested group walked on, none noticed how a young pair lagged, chatting in quiet voices with tinkles of laughter.

Reverend Abbot, twenty monks, five novices and eight pupils of the secret school filed to stand in front of the small church in the cleft of the rock. The congregation took it in turns to enter the church to kiss the revered icon after the monastic population had paid their due respects. On their return to the courtyard, the audience sought shade from the hot sun. Settled under the soothing tones of melodic chanting, Katerina risked a whisper.

'I made my special prayer when kissing the Panagia.'

Irini delivered a hug. There was no chance to answer as the crowd hushed to see the icon placed on a bier decorated with dried flowers and grasses. Carried aloft by monks, it toured the monastery precincts. When visitors filed behind monks, novices and schoolboys, Irini's mama realised there'd been a muddle because Mathaios was out of his rightful place, walking with her daughter at the rear of the procession.

Later, as they sat digesting an amazing array of food, Irini's mama said, 'Shall we take our leave, Katerina? Distance seems greater on our tired trek home.'

'Not yet. Irini says schoolboys and novices plan to sing *mantinades*: rhyming couplets to commemorate brave rebels who plotted against ruling Venetians, long before Ottoman oppressors took control of Crete.'

Irini saw her mama's eyebrows arch, and nodded.

'Mathaios told me. A recent earth tremor dislodged stones behind the refectory to reveal pots of hidden verse written on fine goatskin.'

Flushed cheeks and sparkling eyes didn't escape sharp eyes.

'Tsk, retire behind the female rest screens. Don't return until you've retied your dishevelled scarf – your hair is showing.'

As Irini rose, those nearby resumed gossiping, pretending they'd not witnessed her chastisement.

Performers bowed low to signal the recitation's end, and as applause fell away, Irini whispered, 'Today's men should heed those words. It's time to resist the Turks.'

'You've been listening to your papa resenting paying bail to guarantee our return. Did you think it worth it, Katerina?'

'It was everything promised, and more. How can we thank the monks and the generous folk who've treated us so well?'

'Let's sing a chorus to repay their kindness.'

Although proud of her daughter's voice, Irini's mama was aghast that she'd dared to perform a soft lullaby outside family confines. Desperate to hide the indiscretion, she rose and stretched out her hands to her neighbours. 'Come, let everyone sing thanks.'

*

Once the monastery's great studded gate thudded shut, the women set off, chattering and laughing until caution on the steep path kept them quiet as far as the hamlet. Safe here, they milled to bid a proper farewell to friends and family they might not see again until their next trip. While waiting for a Kritsa grandma to deliver a matchmaking message, Irini noticed her friend hunched over and pacing. A second glance took in the tears.

'Are you too hot? Shall I fetch water?'

'*Panagia Mou*, Mother of God, help me. My prayer passed unnoticed among the many. This babe doesn't want my love.'

*

Happy to toil in the hot courtyard Mathaios pushed his broom around in a daze, not noticing busy hands had already completed the task. In an uncharacteristic moment of idleness, he watched a cat crouch, stare fixed on a small bird enjoying his trilling. 'Ah, cat. Sweet Irini has a voice to put songbirds to shame.'

After speaking her name aloud, it fixed in his head. Such a lively girl, not giggling and silly. He sighed. No doubt she'd make some lucky man a wonderful wife.

'Ouch, that thought hurt.'

'Hey, are you talking to yourself?'

'Sorry, Nikolaos. What shall we do next?'

'Help me stack planks used as food trestles.'

Midway through the task Mathaios discovered a large basket under bushes.

'This must be Aunt's. My bed cushion, a gift from her, has the same embroidered design as this cloth cover.'

'Is anything important in there?'

'Ha ha! I should have guessed. There's enough food here to keep my uncle going for two days. I'll take it down for them, the walk will do me good. Tell Brother Michalis I'll stay overnight and be back in time for matins.'

Ahead of him a multihued sea with bands of turquoise, azure, cobalt and cerulean stretched to the grey-lined horizon. Whenever he walked to his aunt's he stood mesmerised on this jutting rock above the five dome-roofed stone dwellings of the monastery servants and shepherds. From his elevated position he could see the ever-changing scene among the bays created by the headlands known as the Five Fingers. This late afternoon, white foaming waves surged into the bays at differing speeds and angles and, to the far right, slapped the foot of the rounded Thripti Mountains, now caressed by a pink hue of the reflected setting sun. In the stillness he heard a distressed whimper beneath his rock ledge.

'Irini? Whatever is wrong? Why are you here?'

In her wretchedness she clung to him without realising her scarf lie by her side. Instinct had him caressing her back, his hand under her long tresses, soothing her until her sobs ceased.

'If it's true God manages everything, I don't understand.' At his gentle squeeze she continued, 'Katerina wants a baby. Is that too much to ask?'

Lost for words, he didn't answer; whatever the issue, he wanted to continue holding her.

'Mama fears for her life. Blood loss was disproportionate for the tiny babe, another boy.'

Not registering Mathaios held her. She accepted his hemmed and pristine white cotton square.

'Who knows what God plans for us? My mama died in childbirth, leaving Aunt to care for me among her brood until I was old enough to join the monastery boys.'

Despite her words – 'I shouldn't sit here with you, someone may see,' – she moved closer, resting against his arm which embraced her shoulders, 'Trouble is, there's nowhere else I want to be.'

Not trusting his emotions, he kept quiet, eyes closed, enjoying her closeness. With a start he realised they needed to move.

'Night falls and I fear you'll slip. Let me escort you downhill.'

'Whatever will people say?'

'I carry Aunt's basket of food. No one will comment, if you replace your scarf.'

*

By unspoken agreement they met in the same place the next evening, where she gave him the best news.

'Mama and I are staying to nurse Katerina. Other Kritsa women left to bid her husband bring his mule.'

Mathaios almost thanked God when her voice faltered, giving him an excuse to hold her again.

'Let's not sit here in sadness. I'll walk you the long way down to my aunt's.'

*

Pattern set, the next few evenings passed with accelerated speed, although both found the days between overlong. On the fifth morning, Irini wore a practical kerchief as she helped Mathaios' aunt milk her goats. Safe in the knowledge this kerchief hid her blush, she tested what the future might hold.

'I've enjoyed chatting to your nephew while I've been here. How long do you think he'll stay at Faneromenis?'

Caught unawares by the question, the proud lady presumed Mathaios had taken their spirited visitor into his confidence and gave the girl a conspiratorial wink.

'I think there'll be a significant announcement before the end of the year.'

'Do you think he'll visit Papa soon?'

'Why? Oh, a man on a mule. It must be poor Katerina's husband.'

*

That evening, Irini followed her established pattern. She waited until out of sight of prying eyes before removing her kerchief, shaking her hair loose and lightly covering it with her trailing white scarf. Her final preparation was to rub her cheeks and lips to bring a rosy glow.

Arm in arm the pair strolled, chatting without pause, until they reached the long, flat rock that provided a seat overlooking the bay and mountains. Here, as usual, the pair fell quiet, lost in their own thoughts as the blue sea turned dark and the reflected sunset bathed the Thripti Mountains in pink. When the creeping grey shadow climbed halfway up the mountains, Mathaios knew nightfall would soon cover their path.

He rose to offer Irini his hand. Although Mathaios expected his treasured walks to end soon, it didn't lessen the jolt when she said, 'Katerina's husband has arrived. We leave tomorrow.'

'So soon? Although I'm glad Katerina is going home, our strolls and chats have been delightful.'

Love shone from his smile. In unconscious anticipation of a kiss, she took a step forward. Coy under his fond gaze she blushed, then fished. 'Tell me your plans after ordination.'

In the pause, buzzards mewed, distant goat bells tinkled and thick, heat-scented air clogged her constricted throat. Joy soared at his delayed answer.

'Um, my path takes me away from here.'

Confusion hit as he frowned.

'Thank you for your company. Excuse me for not escorting you this evening.'

Open-mouthed, she watched him bolt uphill as if chased by Lucifer.

*

Back in Kritsa a week later, Irini flared in a rare temper.

'Mama, I never agreed to marry Fanis. You assumed I'd be a pliant bride to Papa's cousin. Why do you think he's called Sly Fanis? No, I'll stay unmarried, thank you!'

'Hush. The neighbours will hear. A few whispered moments on hot August afternoons are not enough to throw away your whole life. Don't pretend shock, I saw how you gazed at Mathaios. And you always wore a dreamy-eyed flush after your evening walks. If I hadn't been so busy nursing Katerina, you'd not have gone out alone.'

'I wasn't alone.'

Her mama rolled her eyes, 'My point entirely. Thank goodness there were no neighbours to see you.'

'But you don't understand.'

'Believe me, he's wedded to a career within the church. Only clergy content with lower office may marry. If you decline Fanis, we'll lose face. Do you want to embarrass your papa?'

'Please, Papa. You must want my happiness. I'm not actually betrothed, am I?'

Forced to decide, he looked first at his flushed youngest daughter, and then his thin-lipped wife. Both willing him to find in their favour, he tested with, 'Sly Fanis is a cruel childhood name. After six months of marriage you'll wonder why you worried.'

His wife opened her mouth to agree, but before she could say a word her sister dashed into the house.

'The deacon is dead.'

Faced with satisfying blank faces, their visitor continued, 'Poor man. A wall collapsed to crush him. With the amount our men are taxed there's no excuse for the head Turk not to maintain safe garden walls.'

Her sister, brother-in-law and niece stood as statues.

'What is it? Are you all deaf?'

Now her aunt had broken the flow, Irini realised she'd not change her papa's mind. In defeat she slumped on the sofa.

Her papa, Nikos, leapt up, grabbed his sister-in-law and planted a kiss on her cheek.

'Thank God for your visit!' Next, he clasped his wife's shoulders and kissed her, 'Your sister has the answer. Pass my condolences to the deacon's wife. Tell everyone my shock is so great I've gone to Faneromenis.'

5

Mathaios in Turmoil

Brother Michalis peered inside the tiny chapel cut into the high rock face. Distressed to see the prostrate figure knelt before the iconostasis, separating the nave from the sanctuary, the monk shook his head. No sound came from the still figure, although frenzied fingers threatened to tear his prayer rope. With a sigh, the worried monk recognised the child of his heart was beyond aid.

As he stepped back into daylight, he met Nikolaos and ushered him away. At the unspoken question, he shrugged – nothing had changed.

'Are you certain I shouldn't go in, Brother? I've been doing so at intervals throughout the day. I knelt beside Mathaios in prayer and hoped my presence aided him.'

'May God bless you, Nikolaos. His torment is beyond our support at present. When I asked Reverend Abbot for advice, he said Mathaios had requested release from duties to resolve a personal turmoil. Reverend Abbot advised me not to pry. He's convinced prayer will bring resolution. Ah, there's the supper bell. You go on, I'll check on Mathaios.'

Instead of disturbing the prone figure, Brother Michalis lit a candle to illuminate the miraculous icon of the Panagia, Mother of God.

'Holy Panagia, you know the name of our beloved monastery Faneromenis means "revealed". I can guess about the issue causing my boy such distress. My prayer is for him, I beg you to intercede with God to reveal the right solution.'

With a chuckle, the monk remembered Mathaios recounting the miraculous story to each recruit to their secret school. In his mind he remembered the piping voice:

A shepherd from these parts lost his prize ram every afternoon, but it always reappeared before the flock moved for the evening. One day the shepherd followed the ram to find him drinking sweet water flowing from a cave. This astounded the shepherd, who had always grazed the area without discovering the cave. When the shepherd stooped to sup he staggered backwards, shocked to see a glowing icon of the Panagia hanging over a pool inside the cave. Impressed, the shepherd took the icon home to display it on the wall of his humble kitchen, disappointed at its dull appearance. For the next three afternoons, the ram remained with the flock.

On the fourth morning the icon disappeared, and once again the ram returned to drink in the cave. Here the shepherd found the icon restored to its rightful place, once again glowing bright. Moved by the revelation, this thankful man founded the monastery and promised an eternal flame in front of the icon.

With due reverence Brother Michalis kissed the icon before heading for the exit and, feigning a stumble, he cried out, falling to the rock floor. Jolted from his prayers, Mathaios stared at the crumpled heap. It took a few seconds before realisation hit.

'Oh! Let me help you.' He hauled his surrogate papa to his feet then assisted him to the side, 'Take a seat. Are you ill?'

'I've bruised my knees. I rushed when the supper bell rang. Will you help me to the kitchen?'

After supper, Brother Michalis followed Mathaios. To divert him from climbing the church steps, he called, 'Mathaios, wait. Give me your arm. It's my turn to stand watch in the gatehouse.'

'Go to your bed, Brother. I'll take your shift.'

'Your arm will give me confidence, and I always find the gatehouse comfortable.'

Once in the nook above the gatehouse, Mathaios flung open the west-facing shutters to inhale the hot evening scent of pine and enjoy the cooling breeze from the coast. A gibbous moon outlined the Thripti Mountains to the east and cast a silvery path over the sea towards the small port of Agios Nikolaos. Careful not to intrude on the young man's thoughts, Brother Michalis sat on the narrow bed sometimes used when isolating contagious patients.

Boys assembled for lessons in the schoolroom a floor below them and their murmurs fell silent, signalling the tutor's entrance. As always, Brother Michalis was in awe, wondering how young heads could hold such learning. He remembered acknowledging the sin of pride when *his* Mathaios always scored highest in exams. When the boys recited mathematical tables, the monk judged the rise and fall of their chants cloaked enough sound to risk a conversation.

'Are you trying to glimpse a light on the mountainside from Kritsa?'

'Oh, you know me too well. Can I dare to dream she'd look in my direction?'

'You only had eyes for each other. Talk to the abbot.'

'It's complicated. Since he took me in, with no wealth behind me, I assumed I'd spend my life here. Reverend Abbot has clarified his ambitions for me. How can I spurn his wishes?'

As the chanting below ceased, the listeners heard, 'Now we'll have an hour of grammar. Afterwards, I'll try to knock mathematical formula into your skulls.'

Mathaios slumped on the mattress. Brother Michalis sat next to him, 'Tell me.'

'While everyone in the monastery has been cleaning and preparing for our distinguished Russian visitors, my focus has been on them leaving.'

'I'm proud you and Nikolaos will join their party to travel to Megalo Kastro for ordination as deacons.'

'There is amazing news I've been trying to pluck up courage to tell you. I will leave Crete to travel with them.' He ignored the pained gasp to continue, 'It's a wonderful opportunity. I'll journey across Greece before proceeding to Russia for the rest of my career.'

Brother Michalis forgot his feigned injury and jumped up to pace the small room, 'Oh my, what a shock. You'll see sights beyond your wildest dreams. Even to embark on the lengthy journey to the bishop's seat is amazing.'

To hide his tears, the monk pretended to study the view from the window. Not bothering to hide his own distress, Mathaios hugged the hunched shoulders, 'You're right, Brother. I'll put my foolish thoughts aside and rekindle my motivation for what lies ahead. I mustn't spoil the opportunity for Nikolaos, it's his ordination too.'

'I want what's best for you. I'm sure Reverend Abbot would say the same. Talk to him.'

Although Mathaios had towered over Brother Michalis since he turned eleven years old, it didn't stop the elderly man from clutching him close.

'Remember, you've not yet taken vows. You can make a free choice. May God help you.'

Mathaios' answer came through a constricted throat, 'At least Nikolaos will return brimming with tales of city life. He's beside himself with excitement.'

Those were his final words before he rose to gaze out to the starlit heavens and, settling himself on the mattress, Brother Michalis resolved to keep vigil with Mathaios.

'Wake up, Brother. A traveller comes.'

Without a lamp a man had almost reached the Roman-arched gatehouse before Mathaios saw him. Now their visitor thumped the vast wooden door between its protective sheath of metal studs. Brother Michalis leaned out to glimpse a lone figure.

'Help me open the door. If he's not lost, he'll have an important message.'

'My name is Nikos from Kritsa. I need urgent words with Reverend Abbot.'

'Mathaios, take our guest upstairs and I'll inform the abbot when matins finishes.'

The exhausted visitor collapsed, not caring the mattress still held the warm indentation of its recent occupant. He woke delighted to find he had time to talk to the young man.

With the first grey light of dawn, the old monk hurried up the gatehouse stairs, energised by curiosity. He carried bread, olives and water for the guest to break his fast before meeting Reverend Abbot. Low, murmuring voices ceased the moment he opened the door. As if scalded, Mathaios jumped up from his seat on the mattress next to their guest. He raced through the door, calling back, 'I must tell our abbot the purpose of this man's visit.'

At least an hour had passed since Nikos entered the abbot's office. Since then Mathaios had sat in the corridor, fidgeting on an exquisitely carved, uncomfortable chair in sight of the closed door. When sweat stung his eyes, he wiped it away with the back of a sticky hand. Two of the youngest schoolboys walked past, and Mathaios couldn't help his mouth creasing at a giggled, 'Ooh, I wonder what he's done to earn a summons to Reverend Abbot?'

As the boys turned towards the kitchen, the abbot opened his door to invite Mathaios to join him and his guest, Nikos. After the three men had chatted for a few minutes the abbot held up his hand, winked at Mathaios and in a loud voice said, 'You may as well come in, Brother Michalis, I doubt that patch of floor needs washing again.'

'You wanted me, Very Reverend Abbot? Bless me.'

After delivering the customary blessing, the abbot spoke with a twinkle in his eye, 'You can congratulate Mathaios on his betrothal. His ordination as deacon continues as planned, but now he'll marry first. I'll send a message to Right Reverend Bishop to recommend him for the vacant post in Kritsa. As a pragmatic man, His Eminence is unlikely to disagree or move him to a different parish. Rest assured, Mathaios knows his decision puts high office out of reach.'

Despite Brother Michalis entangling him in an enthusiastic embrace, Mathaios peered over the monk's shoulder to face the abbot.

'What of Nikolaos? Could he take my place with the Russians?'

'You're a genius! Go. Tell him the news.'

6

Nikolaos

On the eve of him leaving the monastery, Nikolaos climbed the steps to the rock chapel. As he prayed, light from a flickering candle before the remarkable icon of the Panagia held his eyes. Mesmerised by its dancing glow, his mind wandered through times he'd enjoyed with his boyhood friend. From the moment he regained consciousness they'd been inseparable. Many years had passed since Nikolaos thought of his scant history.

*

Older boys took young Mathaios down to the coast to teach him to swim. When he realised the lesson entailed dropping him into a deep pool, he'd scampered along the beach in fear. Mathaios hid behind a rock, then screamed in terror at the gruesome washed-up remains.

In response to his scream, the lads dashed to pull three male bodies onto dry shingle. The eldest returned to assist Mathaios, who stared in horror at a naked boy still clutching a wooden chest.

With his gaze fixed on the corpse, Mathaios pointed.

'Fish ate his privates!' In horrible fascination he reached out to stroke the bruised shoulder. At his touch, eyelashes flickered, 'Help him, he's rousing.'

For the long uphill slog, the older boys paired up to take turns carrying the boy on a rough stretcher of driftwood and blouses, while closing their ears to his frequent cries of pain in a foreign tongue. Mathaios lagged behind carrying the small chest, so heavy compared to its size.

Brother Michalis nursed the strange child, and after a few days updated his abbot.

'Apart from a few bruises, he's fine.' With his face showing disgust, the brother added, 'A barbarian cut him. It's not a new injury. He squats to pee through a healed wound where his manhood should be.'

'I've heard tale of such things. Poor soul. A servant to women in the harem, or a plaything for deviants. We'll give thanks Saint Nikolaos, patron saint of seafarers, saved him.'

Without realising it, Brother Michalis suppressed a shudder.

'Our Mathaios has been comforting him. He tells me the little pagan's name is Ibrahim.'

'Ah, it's a good thing Muslims venerate Saint Nikolaos too. Don't be harsh on him, Brother. Although Turks murdered your family, this frightened child needs our compassion.'

'Somehow Mathaios understands his heathen jabbering enough to tell me his needs. Shall I tell him to stay away?'

'Of course not. Children need to play together. In time God will send a solution, I'll pray to recognise it. Tell Mathaios to act as a Samaritan to help ...'

'Ibrahim.'

'Yes, Ibrahim. It feels so alien to my tongue and makes me realise how difficult it must be for the child.'

Within days the boys bonded and Mathaios spoke for them both while teaching Ibrahim Greek, the language used within the monastery. Within weeks the boys adopted the Turk tongue as their private code for plotting and laughing, frustrating brothers and peers.

*

Five years later Reverend Abbot summonsed Ibrahim to his study, and as the lad rushed to the meeting he tried to recall any recent misdemeanours. After formal greetings the plump lad accepted a seat.

'We need a difficult conversation. You've reached the age where I speak to lads, to help them understand the tricks their bodies play. My custom is to bestow a prayer rope to keep fingers busy and discuss their future path.'

As if punctured by these kind words, Ibrahim fell forward in his chair, then to his knees.

'Please, Reverend Abbot, don't send me away. What life will I lead? I'll work for my keep.'

Distracted from his intended course, Reverend Abbot said, 'Come, sit by me. No need for tears. It's time to learn your wishes. A man must make his own choices, taking responsibility for his actions. Yours are more ... complicated.'

Through tears Ibrahim struggled for composure. His mouth fell open, matching his widening eyes to see the abbot holding forth a chest full of jewels.

'These belong to you, Ibrahim. The box was in your arms when my lads found you on the beach. You'll make a good life with this fortune. My suggestion is, start with an Islamic education. I've been remiss in that quarter.'

Relief flooded the lad's face.

'This is all mine? I can walk from here and never look back?'

'Yes, my son. Not today – consider your options. When you're ready, I'll ask Tinker to guide you to a town or port, as you wish.'

'Forgive me, Reverend Abbot, I've never voiced my preferences. Now I'm not dependent on your charity, I beg you to baptise me. I only want to stay among your monks. If you let me keep a place alongside my brothers, I'll deem these trinkets well spent.'

To be fair, the abbot gave the lad half a year to be sure, and then, on a day of joyful celebration, baptised him Nikolaos. His tutors agreed he was an able student, overshadowed only by the brilliance of Mathaios.

Now aged around twenty, the two prospective deacons spent every spare minute at their studies, and until recently had teased each other they'd become abbot in due course. Tonight, Nikolaos prayed for strength in front of the Panagia's icon. The church door creaked to announce someone entering. Nikolaos watched his friend light his candle and kiss the icon, before whispering, 'I'm missing you even before we leave here'.

'We'll be together in God's sight, Nikolaos. Both enjoying a life we never expected.'

'Will your new family travel to Megalo Kastro to see us ordained?'

'Only Irini's pa. I expect he's testing whether I'm decent enough for his daughter. It's been such a whirlwind. We leave within hours of our wedding, and ... um ... I must abstain from marital relations until after ordination.'

Nikolaos laughed and punched his friend's arm, 'Ha, it's a shame for you my ordination must be before I travel with the Russians. Otherwise you'd have enjoyed time together first.'

'True, but it will be worth it. With God's Grace we'll have a long life to get to know each other, and a family of six children before I rise to become pappas.'

'With so many children Irini won't have time for duties as the deacon's wife.'

This time Mathaios punched Nikolaos, their giggles masking the door's next creak. A scolding voice interrupted them.

'Thank the Lord I'm to lose you two. No more listening to you chattering in heathen tongues. Walk with me. Let us take one last supper together.'

To mimic their childhood, the friends chorused, 'Sorry, Brother Michalis. We promise to behave tomorrow.'

Both remained kneeling and laughed anew as their favourite monk tweaked each of them by an ear.

'Panagia Mou, Mother of God, help me. What can we do with them?' With a loud sigh he stalked out in mock anger.

Had he looked back he'd have seen the young men embrace, fighting back choking tears, each distraught at losing the one they loved as a brother.

7

Bride and Groom

Despite the early hour, Irini felt stifled by the crush of women in her home and seized an opportunity to fetch water. Hands full with two jugs, she paused outside Katerina's home.

'My bridal party has started. Come with me when I've collected water.'

'Look at you. In the street without a kerchief.'

'Oh, surrounded by women I didn't think. There's no one about. I'll be quick.'

'I've taken our milk goats uphill to graze. We can't have you stepping in droppings. I'll shovel this pile and sluice the cobbles before you return.'

Lack of hens, goats, dogs and midden piles showed other neighbours had taken similar kind action to make sure nothing marred this perfect September day.

*

'Such a surprise to see you, Irini.'

An icy chill rushed down her back. Without turning away from the carved cedar spout delivering crisp mountain water, she gripped the jug handles until her knuckles showed white.

'I'd have expected the blushing bride to stay indoors. Look at your fine locks begging a stroke.'

'A bare head does not equal an invitation.'

'I feel entitled, you were betrothed to me. Are you not afraid I'll snatch you away?'

'Go away, Fanis. Grandma explained to your pa, there was no betrothal.'

His filthy hand wrenched her around to face him, 'Guess you thought you could sneak off to marry while I was with other men on Katharo.'

Forced against the rim of the fountain's rock-hewn bowl, Irini bluffed a calmness she didn't feel.

'There's no sneaking. The aga is the head Turk in the village and he gave permission for the pappas to conduct our wedding at the woodland church of Panagia Kera. You're invited, and as a goodwill gesture the aga's authorisation means you need not pay surety to leave the village today.'

'Ah, so I could bundle you away without a Turk sentry expecting a backhander?'

Angry now, Irini pulled free to walk away. Fanis darted to block her progress.

'I'll take my chance to tumble you.'

'You're too much a coward to risk the ire of Kritsa's men.'

Pinned against the wall, his rank breath proved his bravery came from brandy.

'What men? My guess is only herdsmen of your close family will entrust their flock to other shepherds. Most men will stay on Katharo for another few weeks.'

'Let her go.'

'Oh, it's Katerina. My friend's barren wife thinks to save you.'

'Since you cheated him, he wants nothing to do with you. Unless you want to start a vendetta you're not man enough to finish, let her go.'

Not waiting for a response, Katerina grabbed a water jug from Irini, clasped her arm and hurried away, ignoring juvenile threats and catcalls behind them.

When Katerina realised her friend was trembling she pulled her to a halt.

'Did he defile you?'

On the edge of tears, Irini shook her head.

'Say nothing, or Papa will seek him out. That cur is not worth an upset. Come, Mama is serving lemonade and *soumada*.'

'Mmm, soumada. Your mama's almond cordial is the best I've

tasted.'

Irini's grandpa arranged borrowed benches and chairs in the space between the end house, his gift to the newlyweds, and the church of Afentis Christos. He'd had a message to say Irini's male relatives were descending from Katharo, and a mound of fresh bread stood ready to serve with the cheeses they'd bring with them. His wife, plus her two cousins, had left home at dawn to walk to the seldom-used Byzantine Church of Panagia Kera. Escorted by the pappas, they'd gone to ready the church and tend fires under two huge *kazani*, the local name for cauldrons. His stomach rumbled at the thought of stewed goat, and he knew his wife had a sack of rice to add to the fragrant broth. He'd enjoyed responsibility for logistics and was pleased with his scheme to station boys at key points to relay news of the groomsmen passing the mountain's narrow checkpoint. Satisfied with his arrangements, Grandpa thought it best to test the bread and raki.

If anyone noticed Irini's delay, her reappearance on Katerina's arm gave proper reason, and her pinched white face proclaimed nothing more than wedding day nerves. Good-natured teasing gave way to traditional songs of good wishes for a fertile union.

Bathed, scented and hair shining, Irini stood pliant in the centre of the kitchen while her proud mama dressed her in the finery stored for this occasion. A white smock fell past her knees to cover her white cotton ankle-length pantaloons. At the back, antique red silk swathed her skirt from her waist down, and a white apron, woven with red and black threads in a complex geometric pattern, covered the front. Her black jacket had delicate flower motifs traced in gold wires, evidence of her embroidery skills, and small splits set in the fabric at her wrists allowed the smock's long sleeves to create a frill. A black silk kerchief edged with tiny coins from her scant dowry was her mama's design.

Faint from standing so long in an overhot room, Irini wobbled. Caught by her aunt, she laughed and said, 'Oh dear, I'm intoxicated by happiness.'

'Step outside for air.'

Queasiness hit in case Fanis was still nearby, 'No, I'm fine now.'

Despite protests the aunt bustled her niece to the alley and then used an overloud voice, 'Oh, can you hear music?'

Her mama beamed, proving something was afoot. As cheery tunes became louder her aunt squeezed her arm.

'Grandpa made you a sumptuous bed, but it's not sufficient to make a home.'

For the first time she realised Mama, two other aunts and a cousin held trays of *xerotigana*, coiled pastry, fried and coated in honey syrup.

'When did you cook this?'

No one answered as heads swung to watch the crowd funnelling towards them, two lyre players in the lead. Mama raised her voice above the nearing babble, 'Every Christian in Kritsa wants to use this special period of unfettered movement to wish you well. Most men brought their herds down a week or two earlier than usual.'

'Ha, I bet folk are keen to taste Grandma's goat stew and spot their new deacon among his Russian companions.'

Musicians halted to play a traditional song proclaiming the bride's beauty, accompanied by the joyful crowd. Once Irini emerged to take up her position behind the lyre players, they led the few paces further up the alley to her new home. Pastry carriers dashed ahead, determined to greet well-wishers with a sweet treat. Grandpa heard the commotion and signalled for the men of the family to join his proud moment. Yes, he thought, I'm a great organiser.

Outside the house the crush of people was so dense they needed to pass their gifts along, hand to hand or over the heads of others. Irini squealed in joy as each item filled her small kitchen. A table in two pieces for Grandpa to fit together, a chair with a new woven seat, a three-legged stool, kazani pots for the fire and six assorted plates. Generous neighbours and kin brought a pail, various-shaped glasses, two coffee cups with saucers lifted from Turk coffee houses known as *kafenions*, an ornate handwoven basket, a broom, a sharp kitchen knife, an upholstered armchair, three oil lamps, a pot of lamp oil and a huge jar of olive oil. Irini's papa, Nikos, saw a flagon of raki pass inside the house and nudged the man next to him.

'Did you see that? My new son-in-law has the means to lubricate our get-to-know-each-other sessions.'

Thrilled and overwhelmed, Irini looked forward to sorting through her bounty. Discussions on how to replace the rat-chewed cushions of the elegant carved sofa had just brought offers of help from industrious aunts when a boy hurtled to the door.

'The bridegroom and his party have passed the checkpoint in the village below ours. Be at the church an hour before noon.'

Her proud parents flanked Irini during the parade to the woodland glade. Instead of the Christians' usual steep, rocky route down to the fields below Kritsa, the musicians led towards the main street. Red blankets fluttered from most doorways and those who could afford carpets had generously laid them across the path. As the carnival continued, commerce halted. Now the baker knew why he'd worked since midnight to fulfil a large order. In the knifemaker's workshop his spinning grindstone slowed as he lifted his foot off the treadle. With lips clamped on nails, the carpenter stopped his hammering. Two uniformed guards outside the aga's house stomped to attention. Above balconies, hidden women twitched curtains. Fez-wearing waiters in both kafenions paused, trays in mid-air, while their customers gawped, not noticing the tiny cups sloshing the contents onto their elegant jackets. In the butcher's shop, a cat snatched trimmings from the block as the distracted man turned to view the street. Customers in various shops left their soap, spices, chestnuts and leather boots to stand at the roadside, joined by a barber and his frothy-faced client. A day's free movement gave Christian men extra verve for their songs. Kerchiefed women tried but failed to keep their inquisitive eyes demure, and squealing children chased each other, enjoying every moment.

At a wide bend with three forking tracks, the musicians faltered: they'd not ventured beyond this point. Proud Grandpa took the lead down the cobbled road. This route afforded a wonderful view of countryside sweeping towards the distant azure sea and the backdrop of the grey domes of the Thripti Mountains. As the track levelled out by the vineyards, Grandpa turned right and, back on a familiar dusty track, the musicians led with renewed confidence. Laden olive boughs hung low, lush grasses sprouted by recent rains fringed the track, and bushes of vibrant pink geraniums edged huge vineyards abuzz with wasps on ripe grapes. Once in the clearing, women emptied their heavy baskets of crockery, wine flagons and food to supplement the feast.

The bridegroom's attendants were his best man, Nikolaos, Brother Michalis, enjoying the adventure of his life, Reverend Abbot, and four men from the hamlet below Faneromenis. Their guide, Tinker, waved, pleased to see the local pappas and three women awaiting their arrival with water to rinse away the dust of travel. Reverend Abbot renewed his acquaintance with the pappas of Kritsa and introduced him to a very nervous Mathaios. Sensitive to the other cleric's feelings, Reverend Abbot insisted the local pappas was to marry the couple, adding, 'Nikolaos will represent the monastery as best man. Mathaios thinks Tinker will provide tin rings and allow him to pay off the cost over the next few years. I'm looking forward to seeing his face when he realises Nikolaos swapped them for gold bands.'

'Why is this cloistered youth special? Can one not yet blessed by His Eminence give me adequate support?'

If Reverend Abbot felt affronted, he didn't show it. 'Believe me, he'll add great value.'

Musicians clambered onto the low wall in front of the distinctive buttressed church, famous for its colourful frescoes. Strings of flags and colourful pennants fluttered between shady trees and the Panagia's icon stood on a flower-decked easel next to the outdoor altar. Nikos greeted his almost-son-in-law, 'Where are the Russians?

I swear our numbers swelled at the chance of glimpsing them.'

'By the coast. A boat will take us to Megalo Kastro. You'll meet them tomorrow. But now,' – he made a self-conscious cough – 'can I greet my bride?'

Irini and her mama rested under trees a few paces from the mêlée. With a squeal of delight, she ran to her groom's arms, relishing his kiss.

'Dear Irini, I never had the chance to ask. Will you be my wife?'

'Oh, my love, I will. Now the day is here, I'm sad you'll leave without even visiting our home.'

Mathaios kissed his bride. 'We'll have a lifetime together. What's a few weeks?'

*

After listening to opening prayers on behalf of the bride and groom, Nikolaos stepped forward to produce a white silk pillow bearing gold rings for blessing. He winked at Mathaios' open mouth.

'My wedding present to you both.' Awkward in case the extravagance embarrassed his friend, he added, 'From the treasure chest I carried when you rescued me from the waves.'

Irini was still admiring her ring when she realised the pappas waited to hand over lit candles to gift them "Light of the World" for their life together.

Next came the highlight of the service. Nikolaos displayed the two exquisite wedding crowns made with loving care by Katerina. She'd woven daisies and jasmine around pliable lengths of mulberry, tied them in hoops and then joined them with silk ribbon taken from a gown she'd once intended as a christening robe. Now the pappas blessed the bridal pair and positioned the crowns on their heads. Puffed with pride, Nikolaos stepped forward to interchange the crowns three times to seal the union. Next, he took the wine goblet from the pappas for the now husband and wife to sip from, three times each to signal they would share whatever the cup of life had in store for them. As the service continued, the congregation fidgeted, stirred by delicious aromas of stewed goat filling the glade.

A communal sigh of relief was audible when the pappas reached the familiar ending: 'Through the prayers of our Holy Fathers, Lord Jesus Christ Our God, have mercy on us and save us.'

*

Neither bride nor groom ate a morsel. Swept from person to person, all keen to deliver best wishes, they snatched moments to exchange news of wedding gifts and plans for the ordination trip. At last they slipped behind the church to kiss their temporary goodbyes.

'Wife, why giggle while I try to kiss you?'

'Well, Husband, I've realised that by the time you and Papa return to Kritsa, you'll know him better than me.'

8

Spanos

Marriage proved a blissful delight to Mathaios, but village life was purgatory. In his cloistered upbringing, each person had responsibility and activities allocated by hierarchy, age and career plan. He'd never considered how many people lived in a village. Constant noise drove him to distraction. Men used loud voices, flamboyant gestures and wild guffaws. Shrill mothers chastised laughing children, dogs barked, donkeys brayed and goats seemed to bleat without pause for breath. Walks along alleyways proved hazardous; he often stepped in something horrible while shooing a hen intent on pecking the rim of his vestments. Irini smothered her laughter one night when she overheard his prayers.

'... and, Dear Lord, as well as the noise there's the overwhelming smell of food, animals, middens and too many people. Give me strength to bear it. Amen.'

With a smile, Irini caressed his neck as she passed him to climb the four steps to their high bed. She threw the cover back in invitation, 'Life here will become familiar and comfortable. We'll clamber up Kritsa Gorge to enjoy clean, crisp autumn air and colours, where you'll meet more of my relatives. They descended from the original *klephts*. Do you know the word? It means thieves, and our ancestors stole livestock to set up secret herds and flocks. Papa's great-grandpa lives there.'

'Why sound proud? May God forgive them.'

'Don't be pompous, Mathaios. It began under Venetian rule, and I've heard many tales of klephts keeping Kritsa folk from starvation. Now, come here. At least the blanket of village noise gives us privacy.'

'Mmmmm, I've almost forgotten your papa and uncles sit

outside our window drinking raki. What they need is a kafenion to match those of the Turks in the middle of Kritsa.' Determined to end the discussion, Irini delivered light tickling kisses, soon answered by a deep passionate kiss. Mathaios murmured, 'I'll try harder to fit in with village life. Oh, I forgot to tell you, I'm to meet the pappas tomorrow at Saint George's church, by the large cisterns next to an uphill track.'

'Mathaios!'

'What?'

'Leave church thoughts for a while.'

*

He left the house bright and early, sparing a glance for the church dedicated to Afentis Christos, the Transfiguration, the oldest in Kritsa. What a shame the pappas made it clear it was his domain. Disappointed at his lukewarm reception, Mathaios had begged for more stretching work. While he strode the distance along Kritsa's main street, he pondered on the remarkable differences between churches. Saint Titus in Megalo Kastro had overawed him – he'd never imagined such a magnificent building. He planned to return to enjoy Panagia Kera in its tranquil woodland. As his wedding was outside the church, he hadn't seen the renowned frescoes. On his way home from ordination, Nikos had suggested going inside to give thanks for surviving their rough sea trip from Megalo Kastro to the port of Agios Nikolaos. Mathaios grinned, remembering he'd said, 'Yes, Nikos, we must thank God for our safe return. If you don't mind I'll pray in Kritsa, I'm keen to greet my wife.'

Now, hurrying to pass bustling Turk shops, he wondered why he'd had an invitation to a church beyond the Turk quarter. At the last shop, a general store selling everything imaginable, plus more, he asked the owner if he was on the right path for the cisterns. The Turk pointed, and in the dialect of most Kritsa-born folk said, 'Turn left under the arch and along the cobbled path. Pass by the harem and don't look up at their balconies.'

'Is it far?'

With a shrug, the trader said, 'I've seldom had reason to go there.' The Turk's surprise at a Christian cleric addressing him was nothing to him voicing thanks with formal terms, 'May Allah reward you with blessings.'

Oblivious to his impact, Mathaios rushed off, wishing he'd checked the distance before leaving home. Dismayed, he glimpsed his superior's cassock disappearing inside the small domed Church of Saint George.

'You'll allow me responsibility for this church?'

'You'll not have a congregation. Unless you hold services by the cisterns opposite for the slaves washing heathen sheets.'

Excited, Mathaios resolved to excel at his unexpected opportunity.

'Thank you, Pappas, I'll take each service as if this special place is full to brimming.'

Business concluded, his superior turned to withdraw.

'How will I start and end without you? People may seek a blessing and I'm not qualified.'

'You know the services; state when you speak parts on my behalf. Say you relay the words I'm using in my church. If anyone wants a blessing, the strenuous walk will increase the value.' With a kick at windblown debris, the pappas added, 'Tidy this mess first.'

*

In his first six months, his only congregation was an itinerant group of lepers sheltering from rain. Mathaios interpreted this as a message from God and opened a refuge for those in need. Most days he used quiet hours to continue private study towards the day he might become a pappas. One bright morning, after chanting matins for an inquisitive pigeon, Mathaios took the uphill track. On reaching the checkpoint, he realised he'd not obtained a pass from the *kardi*, the administrator who authorised exit. Recent tax increases for Christians had fuelled angry scenes, and he didn't want to hand the kardi an opportunity to score against him by refusing a pass. No matter; a stroll through the olive grove suited his mood.

While kneeling on a grassy knoll, he marvelled at the carpet of spring flowers and music of countless birds and insects. A fragrant breeze played through the trees and tuneful distant goat bells soothed him. On recognising soft mews from a nearby nest of kittens, he remembered boyhood when Brother Michalis gave him an orphaned kitten. Memories of his kitten's antics had him chuckling as he searched in nearby long, lush grass. He stopped at an area squashed flat and bent to touch fresh, bright blood. A smeared trail led him behind a rocky outcrop.

'Whatever happened? I mistook your distress as a kitten.' No answer came from the beaten man. Mathaios knelt. At his gentle touch, the man cried out, curling his body in defence.

'Shall I leave you to run for help, or aid you to walk?' He felt the hunched shoulder, 'Can you stand?' Not gaining an answer, he rolled the man on his back then eased him to a sitting position, 'I'll not hurt you. Let me help.'

Dishevelled robes took his attention, and he stared at a cut like that of his childhood friend. In an attempt at reassurance, Mathaios spoke the tongue of Turks. This brought fresh sobs from the wretch who clutched at his tattered garments.

'Pull your clothing straight and lean on me. There's a spring nearby. I'll wash your wounds, then assist you to your home.'

Anyone listening to the crying man, groaning anew with every step, would think Deacon Mathaios tortured him as he led him to the spring-fed cisterns. Women busy laundering sheets from the nearby harem stood in confusion watching the odd pair approach. To reassure them, Mathaios called out in the language of high-born Turks. As slaves to nobles from birth, the women understood the cleric's plea and shrank backwards.

'This man wears remnants of fine silk. I guess he's a harem servant. He needs help.'

One of the veiled group said, 'Despite your Christian robes, I'll tend his wounds.'

Timorous associates tutted at her boldness. She ignored them to tear a holed cotton sheet as bandages, explaining, 'This one is only fit for rags.'

Assured the man's wounds were not life-threatening, Mathaios bowed and turned. With her shrill voice full of fear, she said, 'You can't leave him, he's not from the harem.' To underline it was her last word, she lifted her bundle of wet sheets and followed the hurrying women.

Once alone, the injured man spoke, sounding coherent for the first time.

'I use local and high-born language, and I'm a free man,' – pain from his forced laugh made him pant – 'if you can call me such. I've spent most of my life between the silk sheets of the brothel.'

'Good Lord! A brothel. Is it nearby?'

'In a confiscated church, near the place you found me. My patron, a retired Turk officer, died last evening. He'd used me since I was a boy. With his last breaths he proclaimed me free and gifted me his rich red leather purse.'

'Who robbed you?'

'A Christian visiting the girls must have overheard. He followed me, left me for dead and stole my inheritance. I'll not last long without means of support, but it's better than degradation. I relish those brief moments of freedom.'

'Come with me. Rest in the church across the track until you're fit. It's seldom used. Don't worry, I'll return with food and bedding. I'm Deacon Mathaios. What do men call you?'

'Whatever they want.'

'Oh. What shall I call you?'

'As a child I had an imaginary friend called Michalis, he saw me through difficult times. I'll use the same name.'

'Very well. Shake my hand, Michalis. Although I must warn you, ah … oh …' he coughed, his face reddening in embarrassment. 'Because of your condition, men hereabouts will name you Spanos. It means beardless.'

*

Loud, drunken laughter outside a Turk kafenion claimed Mathaios' attention, and he heard the shout aimed at youths hauling brushwood.

'Come, lads. Take a drink with Fanis. I've had a windfall and I'll share my joy.'

The braggart ignored the disdainful looks of the waiter to urge, 'This Turk will serve us.' He tossed a leather pouch in the air, catching it with a flourish, 'My coin is a passport to fragrant coffee and raki. See, I've even bought a pipe. Will you take a puff?'

Indecision flashed across the young faces. Although drawn by the offer, they didn't want to associate with Fanis.

Fuelled by a rush of fury, Deacon Mathaios strode to grab a filthy hand.

'I see you've bloodied your knuckles, Fanis.' As if stung he dropped the hand and snatched the pouch, 'Ah, praise be to God. You've found my friend's purse. I'll take it.'

After a few paces, Mathaios turned on his heels to dash back to where the loudmouth still sat open-mouthed while the waiter hovered near his unwelcome customer. Stunned, Fanis leant back from the deacon's raging hot breath, 'God will forgive you, he always does. But can you live with yourself?'

Without waiting for a reply, Mathaios rushed away. Christian lads sped in the opposite direction to share exciting news: the deacon had bested Sly Fanis.

For the next six mornings, Mathaios took Spanos a huge bag of bread, sweetmeats and fruit purchased from Turk stores using coins from the purse.

'Here, no wonder you're on the mend. There's a feast in this parcel.' While shaking his head to refuse the offer of a huge cheese pie, Mathaios continued, 'Nikos, my pa-in-law, has a building he'll sell at a fair price. It's on the edge of the Christian sector, with an easy downhill walk to Turk shops. Nikos knows people to make your furniture and thinks they'll grab the opportunity to earn money instead of barter.'

'I don't know how to thank you.'

Intending it as a humorous remark, Mathaios said, 'Save my sanity. Keep noisy men away from my door. Open a kafenion.'

'Would customers come to one such as me?'

One look at the excitement on his friend's still swollen face was enough.

'If I can persuade my pa-in-law, other men will follow. Keep a tally and let men pay when they can. It might only be once a year, after the olive harvest.'

9

Epiphany

Saint George became a night shelter for outcasts. Deacon Mathaios turned none away and always offered a breakfast of bread, paid for by Spanos as a token of his gratitude. Although the pappas did not encourage use of the church as a refuge, he never visited it so could pretend ignorance. Over time, the senior cleric came to rely on his deacon's support and enjoyed joining him for meals prepared by Irini.

A day after Christmas, Mathaios invited his pappas for supper. In a lull between dishes, the pappas voiced concern over disruptive youths who spoilt services. Busy serving, Irini agreed, 'I noticed fidgeting and play-fighting during Christmas Day matins.'

With a cup of savoury broth midway to his mouth, the pappas said, 'I've seen similar behaviour. Boys reach an age where approbation of their peers gains more power than a furious parental frown.'

Mathaios felt helpless. Even the unruliest schoolboys behaved during monastery services. 'It's hard to know what to do. Shall I talk to them before Epiphany?'

Irini placed a chipped plate of dried figs and cheese on the table. 'What they need is something so enjoyable they'll not risk losing it with bad behaviour. I've topped up the raki flask. I'm going next door to see my sister.' Unable to disguise the longing in her voice, she added, 'She'll be glad of my company; the next addition to her brood is imminent.'

*

The week between Saint Basil's feast at New Year and Epiphany on the sixth of January brought cloudbursts. Sheltered in the doorway of his home, Mathaios watched rainwater gush through the alley in a torrent. Mesmerised by swirls and foam, he'd been there for ages. Irritated by the puddle forming on their beaten earth floor, Irini said, 'Can you help me put sandbags by our entrance?'

Deaf to her plea, he hitched his cassock high, retied the belt to keep it in place, kicked off his clogs and went barefoot in the flow.

Irini ran to the door clutching his hooded cloak. She shook her head at the sight of him wading towards the nearby church of Afentis Christos, oblivious to her call. She sighed and pulled her door shut, guessing he worried about water damaging the frescoes. It must have proven a big leak as for three days her husband returned home in the evenings with mud-caked legs, arms and clothes, and slumped in his armchair.

Epiphany morning dawned grey. More rain threatened while the pappas and his deacon watched desultory worshippers amble towards them. Neither cleric sensed much enthusiasm for the planned service to retell the story of Christ's baptism in the River Jordan. At the end of the service, Mathaios led a procession that traditionally passed three times around the church courtyard. Next came altar boys, flanking the pappas who used his censor to waft pungent frankincense over the trailing congregation.

As expected, the deacon made his first circuit of the churchyard before shocking everyone with a right turn onto an uphill path leading towards an area of open ground, with the surprised assembly and an angry pappas snaking behind him. Mathaios passed several rabbit breeding hutches and halted beside a new pool of muddy water which had formed where the run-off from a seasonal stream diverted to a rectangular pit. A tall man could have lain along each side of this pond and folk would soon discover it had a similar depth. The crowd fanned around the pool, making it impossible to continue without comment.

Smiling with more confidence than he felt, Deacon Mathaios took a deep breath, 'Pappas, I've never forgotten Epiphany services by the sea with an extra special element for youths of a certain age. As you celebrate the baptism of Jesus, we can bid chosen lads to recommit to Christ by washing away past sins and promising to carry their faith demurely in church for the forthcoming year.'

At first the pappas frowned, but then gave a slow smile of comprehension as he held his precious crucifix up to bless the water. When Mathaios saw the pappas' hand waver, he nodded encouragement. Now fully engaged, the pappas dropped the holy symbol in the pool, then laughed to hear his congregation exclaim. Rapt attention brought silence as suspended mud rendered the revered silver invisible.

Deacon Mathaios stepped forward.

'Attention, you five boys aged eleven. I want volunteers to compete for the honour of retrieving the blessed cross.'

Within seconds loud squeals confirmed the water originated in the snowy mountain peaks high above the village. A happy mêlée churned the water, increasing viscosity to a mud bath. Championed by their families and friends, the lads came up spluttering. Each grinned, gulped air and dived for another try.

When a youngster brandished the crucifix, willing hands hauled the drenched and sludge-caked boys out. All hailed the winner the hero of the hour, and the pappas declared he'd have good luck for the entire year. By throwing the crucifix in the pond twice more, lads aged twelve and thirteen competed for triumph. This ingenious move engaged disruptive adolescents and left younger children busy calculating how many years needed to pass before they would have their opportunity to dive for glory.

*

Over the following decade, Mathaios relished the way church festivals blended with the rituals of the seasons, setting the rhythm of village life. He joined shepherds on their annual trek up ancient cobbled paths to the rich pastures of Katharo Plateau, and each autumn climbed Kritsa Gorge with Irini to enjoy a meal with her relatives. He visited Spanos for a daily chat and enjoyed the occasional raki with the growing number of men using his kafenion. Each month he took coffee with the imam, a Muslim cleric. This allowed him to use the language of his childhood while the pair discussed theology, marvelling at the similarities of their faiths and bemoaning how it divided people. If God had blessed Irini with a child, he'd deem his contentment complete.

10

Pappas

A perfect, warm January day allowed the extended family to work together harvesting fat olives. Later, they crammed inside the kitchen of Irini's mama to enjoy one of her famous mutton pilafs. One diner joked that the fragrant aroma had called him from the olive grove. Demure kerchiefed granddaughters and nieces cleared away while the celebrated cook accepted due praise. Imagine her affront to see Mathaios sat before an untouched plate of food. At her raised eyebrows, Mathaios explained, 'Oh, I've eaten more than my fair share. This plateful is for the pappas, he's so ill. Although he enjoys eating, he shrinks before my eyes.'

'Does he have excessive thirst?'

Amazed at her foresight, Mathaios nodded, 'Even when feeling faint, he tries not to make a fuss. You may have noticed my larger role in services these past few weeks.'

He blushed when she said, 'Does he have pain passing water?'

Focused on his fingernails, Mathaios said, 'We've not discussed it, but I believe I've overheard difficulty.'

To amplify his discomfort, the other men crowded around the dinner table fell quiet when she said, 'Suggest he spills a drop of water next to a splash of pee. If ants ignore the water to feed on his pee, I'd say the honey disease strikes again.'

Irini overheard and wavered in her task of refilling wine flasks.

'Poor man. Many local people suffer and there's no cure. Although I've noticed his weight loss, I thought he'd not been eating properly since his wife died.'

Diners were peeling fresh oranges to end their meal when a breathless boy hurtled to the open door, 'Pappas is unconscious on the floor of his church.'

Mathaios rushed to scoop him up, Irini at his heels.

'Under this cassock there's only skin and bone. God help him, see how he's turning blue struggling to get air in his lungs.'

Irini recognised the guttural rattle.

'His nephews live nearby, I'll fetch them.'

At the end of the afternoon, Mathaios went to the kardi to seek permission to bury the pappas and requested a travel pass to report his death to the bishop in Megalo Kastro. The kardi agreed, recognising how well a pappas controlled Christians; only Allah knew how much trouble they'd cause otherwise.

'Travel with the olives bound for the soap factory. It's the fastest route, down to the port at Agios Nikolaos and then by boat to Megalo Kastro. If your business doesn't take long, you can travel back the same way; they make several trips.'

With a low bow, Mathaios gave his thanks.

'Tell your bishop I want you as Pappas. My preference is to deal with someone who uses proper language.'

'I appreciate your confidence, Kardi, and confirm I intend to apply for the post. However, His Eminence is bound to appoint someone with more experience.'

*

Four weeks later, he climbed the steep track to wave his travel permit at the mountain pass checkpoint. At noon Mathaios paused at Panagia Kera to thank God for his safe return and seek help for the challenges ahead, promising God to serve him well as First Pappas of Kritsa.

'Such a high-sounding title, Lord. In fact, I'm the only cleric until a new deacon arrives. This woodland church is a haven of peace. I'll bide a while to appreciate the bright frescoes.'

Mid-afternoon, Mathaios returned to his knees.

'I can't deceive you, Lord, I'm delaying the moment of truth. My best approach is to trust You to show me the way.'

He remained knelt in prayer at dusk when the church caretaker entered to tend the lamps. She smiled to see a new cassock, only lightly soiled by travel, and crept away to leave him at prayer.

After spending the night at his prayers, Pappas Mathaios strode along the track, weaving through the olive grove accompanied by cheerful tunes of the dawn chorus. At the steep cobbled path to Kritsa he ascended with ease, giving his new hat of office a self-conscious pat to stop it falling.

*

Spanos pushed his broom in circles around a pristine yard, his thoughts on the church caretaker's news. By the time Mathaios reached the kafenion, his red face beaded with perspiration gave Spanos his cue. 'Ah, Mathaios, my friend. Sit, drink cool water and regain your breath to enjoy the last part of your walk refreshed. No, not there. Please come inside, I'd like to share an idea while you sip.'

Although keen to reach home, Mathaios followed Spanos.

'What's on your mind?'

'Will you baptise me Christian?'

Mathaios embraced his portly friend.

'Oh, how wonderful. God bless you! A fantastic start to my new life as a pappas. Let's discuss it tomorrow. Now, I must hurry.'

*

News of Pappas Mathaios' return spread faster than wildfire. Amid a clamouring crowd, folk dropped for a blessing and many stuffed a congratulatory gift of food, raki or a small coin in one of his carrying sacks. It took an age for the delighted pappas to pass along the congested alley. The crowd thinned out near his own house, and after his greetings elsewhere Mathaios acknowledged his disappointment with a sigh.

Behind him, the procession of noisy people fell silent. Bemused, Mathaios turned to look, shrugged, and lifted his hand to find his door latch covered with grey, gritty dust. Confused, he touched the powder, rubbed his fingers and hesitated, sensing the watching people hold their collective breath. He glanced up, then beamed with joy to admire a fine cross etched in his door lintel. On entering, cheers from the alley masked those of the reception committee crushed inside his home.

With one arm hugging Irini, he shook hands with his pa-in-law.

'Thank you, Nikos. You've put your chisel to good use.'

'We don't want people knocking on our door by mistake when they seek your aid!'

*

After wolfing his celebratory breakfast, Mathaios related every detail of the ceremony to Irini, proud to show his precious texts and guidance from the bishop. When his excited chatter slowed, his patient wife craved information about city life. This sent him rummaging in his rucksack.

'Such products arrive in Megalo Kastro! There's no limit to the range of things available if you've coin. Even this fine bottle of French wine.'

'How marvellous. I think you'll soon find a good time to savour it.' Not noticing her wink, he delved in his bag to produce an exquisite, ornate silver knife, 'This is for you, the betrothal gift you never had ten years ago. Here, let me tuck it in your waistband in the traditional way, a permanent token of my love.'

'Thank you, I'll treasure it.' She laid her hands across her stomac,. 'Although there comes a time when I'll feel more comfortable leaving it in my trousseau box under our bed.'

His heart somersaulted.

'Do you mean what I pray you mean?'

Tender hands cupped his face. 'Yes, my love. God has decided you should be a papa.'

11

The Sultan

Excited Turk boys followed the procession of six strangers riding four horses and two mules up through Kritsa. Fez-wearing men, enjoying habitual mid-morning coffee in kafenions, stared at the odd group, each observer unaware their tiny coffee cup hovered before their gawping mouth. Two guards outside the aga's long, grey dwelling stomped to attention and then shrugged in confusion as the cavalcade passed. Black-clad Christian women gossiping in the baker's queue fell silent, eyebrows arched in astonishment above their covered faces. Inquisitive eyes raked their companions in case one of their number had advance knowledge of these travellers. Curiosity won the day, as most forgot their need for bread to follow behind the group, albeit at a safe distance.

The lead rider reined to a halt at the top of the cobbled street, and after a quick discussion led his party via a rough alley to the Christian quarter. Indecision held the boys – should they follow? Pragmatism won when they decided not to venture further in case infidels ate them for breakfast.

In a clearing by a spring two grooms dismounted from mules. One secured their mounts under shady eucalyptus trees while the other held the reins of the portly man's stoic mare. Awkward while dismounting, the rider exposed a chunky, white, hairless knee above its booted calf. A slight breeze ruffled the black silk length flowing from the back of his tall black hat; its elaborate gold thread cross matched one hanging from a thick gold chain around his neck. In a quick movement, he clamped the hat in place with one hand, using the other to smooth his dark silk gown. With a satisfied glance he saw the sun gleaming off his apparel with a blue-black iridescence to match the understated beauty of a rock thrush. Satisfied with his neat attire, the beardless man looked up to notice a terrified girl filling a jug at the spring. Oblivious to overflowing water soaking her bare feet, she appeared frozen until the great man took a step forward. Her clay vessel smashed on the ground as she fled screaming, 'Sultan! The sultan from Constantinople is here.'

Most doorsteps in the narrow thoroughfare served as a seat, and on this warm day, industrious folk filled them. Mamas cut vegetables or worked their crochet in elaborate patterns. Men carved clogs or resoled worn boots. Children cracked mounds of almonds, teased kittens or tended younger siblings. All craned forward to glimpse the girl shrieking that the sultan was in Kritsa. Most stood in her wake, checking what they'd heard with neighbours. Speculation was cut short as folk shrank back to allow the exalted retinue to pass before crowding the alley, keen to witness the momentous event.

Roused from a nap by a panicking girl calling his name, Mathaios opened his door to a breathless messenger who threw herself at his feet to wheeze incoherent babble. Before he could make sense of her words, an odd procession headed by a rotund, rosy-cheeked man wearing exquisite robes halted in front of him. After aiding the girl to her feet, he gripped her arm for reassurance, hoping she'd not detect his tremble. He gulped, delivered a brief pat on her shoulder and stepped forward with stomach contracting, mouth drying and sweat drenching his back.

Villagers within earshot deemed it no surprise that their pappas' polite greeting evoked no reaction. An evil smirk formed on the sultan's puffy face as he used the hated Turk tongue.

'Hello, Pappas Mathaios. Will you invite a fellow pappas and my colleagues into your home?'

Unable to comprehend, Mathaios stood as if petrified.

'I've journeyed a long way to embrace you.'

With a shriek of joy Mathaios hurled himself towards the outstretched arms. As the two men exchanged kisses, wonder zigzagged through the crowd wearing cocked eyebrows, open mouths or frowns.

After a hurried exchange in foreign words, Pappas Mathaios switched to the local dialect.

'Good Kritsa folk, I'm honoured to welcome my school friend Pappas Nikolaos. During the past ten years he's travelled far and wide with members of his adopted Eastern Orthodox Church, and in two months he leaves for Russia. Imagine my pride to learn he's chosen to devote a few days as my guest. Go in peace, and may God bless you.'

As Mathaios led Nikolaos and his aides inside – a deacon and two novices – he blushed, ashamed at the lack of furniture, and bustled more than a newlywed girl confronted with her first guests.

'No, Nikolaos. Not on the stool, it needs mending. Have the armchair by our fireside. Now, you two, I'm sure you'll find Irini's sofa comfortable.'

A creaking rear door caught Nikolaos' attention. Irini peeped out, white-faced with fear.

'My apologies, we've disturbed your wife.'

'Oh yes, come out my dear. This is Nikolaos, from Faneromenis.'

Irini stepped forward, tugging her kerchief for propriety. In an automatic gesture Nikolaos held out his hand, 'How lovely to see you again.'

She tried without success to bend down far enough to kiss his ring of office.

'Oh, God bless you – now I see why you were at rest.'

'Um, yes, we've needed patience for our first child. My sister had no such problems. Her latest boy is a few months old, a playmate for our babe. Excuse me, I forget my manners. Mathaios, please go next door to borrow chairs while I blow on the charcoal to brew coffee.'

Relieved Irini had taken charge, Mathaios rushed to do as bid.

Not standing on ceremony, Nikolaos helped his companions push the kitchen table aside to make room for the chairs Nikos and a son-in-law delivered. Nikos pumped Nikolaos's hand.

'Welcome. I'm Irini's pa. You've set the whole village agog. Thanks to you I'll sip free raki for weeks as men clamour to hear your news.'

With easy laughter the men settled to swap stories, while despite great discomfort Irini brewed coffee, two at a time in tiny tin pots. With everyone served to her satisfaction, Irini patted her husband's shoulder. 'I'm going to Grandma's, don't expect me back tonight. Mama will prepare supper for your guests.'

Mathaios assured her she should stay, then he noticed her maternity basket. At the doorstep he clasped her close.

'Today? I'll walk with you.'

'Enjoy your visitors. At least it gives you a spare bed for Nikolaos. You can use the sofa. Widowed aunts will offer hospitality to a religious traveller and enjoy a lifetime telling others of their important visitor. You'll get a message when I'm respectable. Now, kiss me and I'll go.'

Distracted by chatter, the hours flew. Nikolaos explained his role of interpreter – working for the bishop attached to the Russian embassy in Athens had him roving across Europe. He assured his enthralled listeners that senior eastern orthodox clergy travelled without restriction as the sultan feared rousing the Russian bear and allowed unrestricted access. Proud of his friend, Mathaios listened, entranced by tales of pilgrimages, countries visited, and sights seen. Even the rigours of learning Russian, theological study and debates sounded wonderful compared to rural village life. With an ability to laugh at himself, Nikolaos rubbed his expansive belly and said, 'Oh, and the food we've eaten. You can't imagine the number of ways different cooks create meals with herbs, spices, honey and wine. Thank God I'm blessed with a hearty appetite.'

As if on cue, Irini's mama entered, leading women carrying pots brimming with aromatic stews, baskets of bread and trays of vegetables. No sooner had the women left hungry men to their feast than Mathaios sprang up to move the rug usually hidden by the table. Once he'd revealed a small wooden trapdoor he squatted to rummage in the secret space.

'Aha. Here's the fine French wine I bought in Megalo Kastro.'

He clattered in the dresser drawer to produce a rusty corkscrew. As the cork popped out, he inhaled the rich, fruity bouquet and smacked his lips. Next, he found two good glasses. After tipping the crusty remains of a spider from the largest one he filled it to the brim for Nikolaos and gave the next best glass to the Russian deacon. Two smaller chipped everyday glasses went to the novices. Irini's brother-in-law and Nikos had theirs in tiny, quickly rinsed coffee cups. None noticed how the wine in Mathaios' cracked cup didn't cover its bottom.

With a flourish he twirled his cup.

'Now, let's toast. Best wishes, Nikolaos. Godspeed to Russia!'

Those present sung out, '*Yammas!*' Cheers.

Next, Nikolaos stood.

'Here's to the one I love as a brother, as he becomes a papa.' Men chorused, 'Yammas!'

Still licking his lips, Nikos stood, 'Health to us all, and a pox on those bloody Turks!'

Once again laughing men cried, 'Yammas!' and drained their drinks.

Nikolaos savoured the last drop and clapped his host on the shoulder, 'Ha, your claret is as fine as any I've tasted throughout Europe. You must open another.'

'Po, po! What makes you think there'd be more?'

An uncomfortable silence fell, exposing the chasm between a poor village pappas and rich Russians. Nikolaos spoke first, 'Please accept my apologies. I came without warning and met warm generosity. I'll pay for our bed and board.'

Embarrassed, Mathaios raged, 'You will not. You're my guests and, with the help of my village kin, we'll treat you with the best of our resources.'

Humbled Nikolaos answered, 'No wonder I felt the urge to see you before I set off for Russia. Your straight-talking always did me good.'

Nikos came to the rescue, 'Don't fret, merry lads. We'll never run out of our favourite spirit, raki, there's more in my store. You'll love it, I distil it myself.'

The short time it took Nikos to fetch the raki hung heavy. Nikolaos broke the uncomfortable hiatus, 'Tell me if I speak out of line, but I've been thinking. Can I stand as godfather?'

'Nothing could please me more. It's tradition for the best man to be godfather to the first born. Ah, here's Nikos. Pour the raki, Pa, and lead a toast to Godfather Nikolaos.'

Perched on the sofa's edge, Mathaios tried to ignore rats scurrying between the wooden roof spars. Despite the curfew people flitted to and fro. Each time footsteps sounded in the alley he paced towards the door with his stomach churning then sat again, disappointed to hear tapping clogs or scuffing boots pass. When the knock came at dawn, he woke with a start.

After thanking the messenger and closing the door, the papa knelt to give thanks to God. Mama and daughter thrived.

While Mathaios yearned to enjoy time with Irini and her babe, successive women visited to coo, stroke her angelic face and spit three times to ward off evil spirits. Affronted by pagan customs, the new papa found it too much to bear when Katerina made the sign against the evil eye.

Irini smiled, 'It's the village way. I'm pleased she came. Such a harsh reminder of her lost babes.'

Uncomfortable among women keen to discuss the trials of birth and feeding, Mathaios felt grateful his visitors kept him busy. On the third day, Irini handed him her precious bundle, 'She'll not break. Take her to our house to meet Nikolaos. He can't visit me while I'm abed and he'll leave before my forty days of confinement end.'

*

Nikolaos rose, arms outstretched to greet the proud papa. 'Ah, come to your godfather, precious girl.'

After lifting the child high, Nikolaos chortled, delighted to see blue beads cascade, clatter and bounce. Mortified by the heathen tokens, her papa groaned as if struck.

'Forgive us. Each woman must have thought she alone tucked an amulet inside a swaddling fold.'

In answer Nikolaos grinned at his friend's discomfort.

'Kind folk gifted extra insurance against evil. Here, take your babe, she cries for her mama.'

Eight days later, Nikolaos performed the ceremony of baptism, becoming the girl's godfather and speaking her name out loud for the first time – Rodanthe.

*

At last alone with his family, Mathaios slumped in his armchair. He'd enjoyed his visitors and wished Nikolaos well, but gave God genuine thanks for his Kritsa life. He smiled to see Irini fretting over Rodanthe cocooned in her cradle, hung from a ceiling beam.

'Come and settle in my lap, Irini. I love you and thank you for our precious daughter. I'll protect you both from life's ills, or die trying. Generous Nikolaos gave Rodanthe a baptismal gift of three gold napoleons. He says rich European girls have such fantastic education they choose to marry or have a career.'

'Thank goodness she's Cretan, I couldn't bear her to leave the village!' With a giggle Irini kissed his cheek. 'He gave her another gift, much more to my liking. Promise not to be cross.' She bent over the crib to feel through the folds and then held out a sapphire-blue glass bauble bigger than the baby's fist and painted with a protective eye.

'Nikolaos got this on his travels and thought extra protection for sweet Rodanthe wouldn't go amiss. This makes twenty-five. Use them to help her count when she's older.'

His face a picture, Irini laughed, 'I adore you, Mathaios, and so will Rodanthe.'

He hugged her, then frowned at the ruffled rug under the table.

Later, after he'd straightened the rug, he lit the church lamps and knelt in prayer.

'Dear God, I'll keep my friend's generous hundred napoleons our secret. There's no need to worry Irini. I'll use three for Rodanthe and trust you to show me when to spend the rest. Amen.'

*

The next time Mathaios thought of that Amen was in January 1823 as a suffocating pain in his chest had him struggling for breath in Kritsa's graveyard. Self-loathing shuddered down his spine as he realised his remembered prayer was no such thing. Puffed with pride, he'd told God of his misplaced decision when he should have sought guidance.

At first, memories of his mentor, friends, wife and daughter had brought comfort. Now he suffered feverish agony. His knees hurt, his arm amputation site throbbed, a shoulder wound burnt and a vice gripped his heart, sending waves of pain down his remaining arm to leave him breathless. Remorse drained his will to live. Between breaths he spoke aloud, 'I meant well by diverting her baptismal gift. Now I realise I stole her potential life by spending the gold, no matter how good the cause. God forgive me because Rodanthe can't. Oh Lord, tell me what to do with her gold.'

Part 2

Death and Retribution

12

Burnt Kritsa

Fear comes in different guises, and Kazanis felt his guts churn at the prospect of leading his boy through Kritsa's ruined streets. After patting his weapons to check his armoury, he deemed it time to leave. Fierce eyes sent a silent entreaty to his cousin when he said, 'You lead. Your pace on crutches is plenty fast enough for us today.'

Kostas blinked as the unspoken message registered: he'd act as the decoy.

'Right. Help me load up, Petros. Strap my rifle across my back, and I'll get these hand guns. Put my spare weapons on top of my rucksack. Hang back, it will take me longer uphill.'

'Son, you walk behind with Pappas Mathaios, let him lean on you. If there's any trace of trouble drop him to the ground and flee. Let's go.'

*

Support from the rough crutch wedged under one arm allowed Kostas to lead using an odd step-and-drag motion, his slow pace suiting the debris-strewn cobbled street. On the opposite side of the thoroughfare, Kazanis swung a blade in his undamaged hand, a savage curved *yataghan*, drawn from a dead Turk. At the satisfactory swish of sliced air, he flashed an encouraging grin back at his son and beckoned. Alert for trouble, Kazanis peered into burnt-out ruins, satisfied to see Kostas do the same. Each pace uphill kicked tragic relics of peace – a rag doll, fine silk slippers, tin pans and even an armchair. Where buildings had escaped the flames, doors stood open to show ransacked kitchens, evidence that the encamped army had stolen from resident Turks and Christians alike.

A cat sprang through the jagged remnants of a rare glazed window. Startled, Kostas shot it dead before it landed, his gun's retort resonating among the empty buildings. Kazanis dropped back in case of return fire. A glance behind proved both the pappas and Petros had taken cover. Kostas tossed the cat high then waved the others forward.

*

In the deserted market, where an increasing breeze chased crisp leaves, Kazanis had the weirdest feeling someone was spying on him. He shuddered to feel hairs on his nape stand to attention. Once satisfied no one lurked in nearby buildings, he leant against a tree as he looked downhill where the pappas had fallen. Angry at the setback, he stomped to give aid.

'Sorry to cause delay. A water-filled rut proved deeper than it appeared.'

Despite the sweat across the sodden man's brow, Kazanis offered no sympathy. 'Shall I carry you?'

'No, haul me up, I'll manage. Ha, did you see? That's my empty sleeve. Here have the whole one.'

'No, don't grab me. Hold Petros' arm, and hurry.'

*

Each footstep crushed through drifts of windblown ash from smouldering wood, leather, fabric and furnishings, creating an acrid stink. Dust stung Kazanis' eyes, bringing tears he swiped from the end of his nose. Ahead of him Kostas paused in an imposing soot-covered arched doorway, then hunched over to weep.

By the time the others caught up, Kostas had almost regained his composure. He spoke with a croaky voice, 'Let me tell you of your brave daughter, Pappas. On the eve of battle, Rodanthe set out to gain intelligence and walked along this street disguised as an Arab falconer. A friend of mine owned the falcon and accompanied her as a servant. She overheard the plan to set the village aflame as a diversion and, thanks to her, most Christians escaped to the mountains.'

'Thank you for telling me. Where my daughter gained her courage, I can't imagine.'

Uncomfortable with emotion, Kazanis said, 'From what she told me, the ruling aga used this place as his home. Well, it's not so grand now.'

Busy drawing a face in the soot, Petros asked, 'Pappas, why did Turks destroy their own places?'

'Kritsa nestles snug in its rocky bowl until fierce winds blow, then trapped gusts whirl in a frenzy. Once the blaze took hold, sparks flew in many directions.'

With a coarse snigger, Kazanis adjusted his britches, 'There, I've dampened the embers. I've always wanted to piss on a Turk. Guess that's as near as I'll get!'

Still chortling, he led the way uphill, passing more flame-damaged Turk property.

Saddened at the destruction, Pappas Mathaios whispered as he leant on Petros, 'Only a minority of local Turks joined the fighting. Peasants who knew no other home than Kritsa fled to the south coast to be among others of their faith. Let's pray they carried as much as they could before their army's requisitioning corps made it here.'

'You have empathy for the Turks?'

'The key messages of the Koran, their holy book, is like our Bible, emphasising peace and love. People who kill and devastate for their God are wrong. I'm sure the Koran warns that to spill the blood of one individual is to spill the blood of all humanity. Turks who refuse to follow a killing creed are not my enemy.'

'Although Pa says we need to rid Crete of Turks, I remember several visits to eat with one he called cousin.'

'That isn't surprising. Most Turks here are Crete-born. We rubbed along until the taxes and rules became punitive.'

'When did fighting start?'

'There've often been skirmishes due to misunderstandings or spiteful tax collectors. This big rebellion started on the mainland and spread fast. Folk are keen for freedom, but I wonder if they know what it means.'

Not knowing how to reply, Petros said, 'Hurry, Pa is far ahead.'

*

Each step through rubble sapped Kazanis' energy. He'd not eaten or slept for thirty-six hours, and witnessing huge numbers of deaths without halting the progress of the damned Arab and Turk force crushed him. A child's charred wooden clog caught his eye, and in a heartbeat his boot sent it spinning. His choked yell of anguish echoed through tottering, irregular walls, most ready to collapse with the next vibration. While the projectile arced over forlorn remains a squeal sounded behind him. Bemused and staring at the ruin, it took a moment for Kazanis to realise the wail didn't come from the kicked shoe. As if in a trance, he turned and stared, unable to comprehend the muddle of flailing arms and legs where Petros pulled the struggling man to his feet. Annoyed at his attention lapse, Kazanis waited for the pair to catch up with him.

'Sorry I'm delaying you, Kazanis. Oh, such devastation. Thank the Lord, most people got away. An awful glow lit the night sky, I guessed an intense blaze ravaged our village.'

With no inclination to answer, Kazanis flailed at rats gnawing on the charred remains of an animal. Truth dawned.

'Malacas! Petros go back to the last bend and keep watch. I need to search this building. This carcass was a man.'

Petros clutched his dagger in a sweating fist and tried to ignore pain in his churning stomach as he crept back towards the market place. Mid street, an indistinct call sent him low to a crumbling doorway where a large tree blocked his view. With no alternative he dashed towards the tree, swearing at his stupidity.

13

Rosi

'Don't cuss, Papa.'

To quell a gasp, Petros chewed his lip and peered around the tree.

'Great-Grandpa told me you'd arrive one day.'

A child concealed in branches dropped, breaking her fall against him. Confused by her excited cry, 'Papa! I knew you'd come,' he staggered backwards, arms clasped around the sobbing bundle. His ears filled with incoherent babble while her tears splashed his neck. This unexpected cuddle released pent-up pain and fear, and they cried together. When breathing eased, the girl hiccoughed, and they both used the backs of their filthy hands to wipe their eyes.

Between sniffs she said, 'Great-Grandpa always said you'd come marching up the street to take care of me. Do you want to greet my doll?'

'Hello, doll.'

Movement uphill took his attention. 'Pa needs me. You run to Great-Grandpa. Oh, and thank you for the kisses.'

*

'You're too injured to shift rocks, Pa.'

'Nonsense, I'll shift rubble faster than you and Kostas combined.'

They heaved rocks aside to expose burnt clothing and roasted flesh lain across the remnants of a doorway. It was hard to say why they'd bothered, as the crushed form never had a glimmer of life. Kazanis used his boot to turn the burnt corpse. Petros heaved in revulsion, gaining no comfort from his pa's gruff comment: 'I'd say falling masonry killed him. Who is he?'

'Nikos is my pa-in-law. Help me bury him.'

Kazanis laid a huge arm on the frail man's undamaged one.

'Later, Pappas. We need food and rest.' To underline his statement, he dragged the remains inside the unstable building.

After a few more paces, all enjoyed water from a spring. Wringing out his beard, Kazanis said, 'Which way to your house, Pappas?'

Before the weary cleric answered, an obese man clad in a soot-streaked grey kaftan rushed from a charred kafenion, throwing aside his twig broom.

'Thank God, you're safe.' Despite his considerable weight he dropped to his knees to kiss the hand of his pappas, 'Bless me. Oh, Panagia Mou!'

With the empty sleeve in his grip, he stumbled backwards. Petros leant over to pass the good hand.

'God bless you, my friend. Don't worry, I'll use my other hand to make the sign of the cross.'

Blessing complete, Pappas Mathaios presented his companions. Too rude to bother with introductions, Kazanis aided Kostas inside, grateful for a few usable chairs at the rear. The owner bustled, his high-pitched voice incongruous compared to his bulk.

'I'll put coffee on.' Tinged with hysteria, he continued, 'Where did you find our pappas? How brave of you to fight. We heard the ground-shaking din.'

Bored, Kazanis interrupted, 'Do you have raki?'

'Yes, of course. This saint needs settling first. Excuse me, I'll fetch water. The spring is nearby. Did you notice how grass grows to my door? It's due to overflowing water. I'll never complain of mud again. Damp saved my kafenion from further damage ...' The shrill voice faded as he waddled away.

From the most robust chair Kazanis sighed.

'He prattles more than any woman.'

If anyone answered he didn't hear, asleep the instant his head fell forward, his face obscured by his wild mass of hair. Petros settled the exhausted pappas on the only cushioned chair while Kostas went to the front doorstep to maintain guard, a primed pistol in each hand. Although the place stank of smoke, Petros saw it required little effort to restart trading. Seven chairs, two tables and the compacted mud floor bore little evidence of soot. Not so the walls: they wore a thick black fuzz. A huge woven curtain cordoned off a bed, its once-bright colours now dulled by smoke.

Tumblers of water were soon before the unexpected guests, while coffee brewed in a pair of copper *breki* pots settled in a tray of glowing charcoal. The rich aroma and the slight rattling of a coffee cup woke Kazanis.

'Hey, you promised raki.'

'Yes, and you'll have it before you've finished your coffee.'

Loud grunts beyond the curtain intrigued Kazanis. From under a concealed bed, an arm pushed out a raki flagon, a basket of dried rusks, a sack of beans and a cheese. Kazanis grabbed the spirit.

'Hey Kostas, this kafenion is Aladdin's cave.'

Kostas arrived in time to see a wooden box of potatoes and another of wrinkled apples emerge. With his stomach rumbling, Petros marvelled, 'How did you elude looters?'

Wiping his florid face on a sooty apron, their odd host shrugged. 'This wasn't our first battle, and I vowed long ago never to starve. When Turks swept through, they sought easy pickings. Thanks to my bedframe I can prepare you a meal.'

Knife already carving cheese, Kazanis said, 'Just cold cuts. We don't have time to dally.'

Spanos sat close to Pappas Mathaios and took up his remaining hand.

'Your congregation mourned for you at Rodanthe's disappearance and Irini's cruel murder. We understood why you took up arms. Praise God, you're restored to us.'

'You'll find this hard to comprehend. My Rodanthe didn't die after abduction. Somehow, she escaped to fight alongside these brave rebels, disguised as a youth.'

A moment of joy flashed across the kafenion owner's face, until brought to a swift end when the pappas said, 'We buried her this morning.'

He might have said more had suspicious Kazanis not waved a pistol to demand, 'How did you survive? It's odd you're back home already.'

'Along with fifteen old souls in Afentis Christos; our prayers delivered a miracle. Set apart from other buildings, the fire didn't reach us.'

Paler than ever, the shivering pappas opened his eyes at mention of his church.

'I must visit those in the church. Come with me, Spanos, and ...'

Collective intakes of breath halted conversation. Petros leapt.

'Wait, is your name Spanos?'

Recognising his answer held importance, he hesitated. 'Well, Pappas baptised me Michalis, but I'm known as Spanos.'

His visitors glared at him with an intensity he couldn't fathom.

'Well I'm, ah, I'm not like you. Um … when men realised ...'

Kostas interrupted. 'Are you castrated? Is that why men call you Spanos – beardless?'

Quick to defend his friend against intrusive questions, Pappas Mathaios said, 'Don't focus on his barbaric suffering. He's a fine man.'

Kostas hobbled towards Spanos, who took an uncertain step back.

'Let me guess. You were stolen from your family as a boy, cut and enslaved.'

White-faced, Spanos nodded as Kostas continued, 'Then, because you couldn't grow facial hair men called you Spanos, meaning beardless.'

Spanos sank to a chair.

'Well yes, Kostas, you're right. But what has this to do with sweet Rodanthe?'

'Clever girl realised wearing male garb wasn't enough for us to accept her as a lad. She took your story as her disguise. Once we accepted her as a eunuch no one questioned her soft, pink hairless cheeks. You didn't have doubts did you, Kazanis?'

'I'll confess my first instinct was to laugh and challenge him to reveal he was a girl in disguise. Then, when he shared his story of abduction and gaining the cruellest cut as a youngster, it sounded plausible.'

'And she could speak in the tongue of a high-born Turk, Pa.'

'Yes, Son. His bravery and skills added value.' Kazanis rubbed his frown, 'After the first day I can't say I ever thought about him being anything other than Spanos.'

Kostas groaned as if suffering physical pain.

'Until moments before her death, I thought my attraction for our Spanos unnatural. Each day was torment, wondering why I lusted after such a creature. If I'd known the truth, she'd be alive.'

Drained, Kostas slumped on a rickety chair.

Next to him Kazanis pulled at his beard, picking out debris.

'Ah, but you can't change one thing without changing everything. Remember what I said in the graveyard? Without Rodanthe being Spanos, I'd grieve for a dead son.'

'Yes, that's true. I complain about my lame foot, but I'd have drowned for sure had she not levered rocks to free me.'

Unable to hide his tears, Spanos sat, causing the flimsy chair to creak as he fumbled in deep pockets for his nose rag, 'Rodanthe didn't see me as a freak. She loved me, despite my past.'

Kostas sent his chair crashing to the floor in his rush to reach the pappas, his overwrought words tumbling.

'Your daughter wrapped herself in this man's history. My guess is most of what she told us was a version of the truth.'

Not comprehending, her papa sat white-faced, blinking back tears.

Quick-thinking Kazanis slapped the table.

'That's it! Young Spanos told us he was a slave to Hursit Pasha, the regional ruler. Do you remember the vivid description of rebels breaking into his compound to free an abducted Kritsa lass? It seems Rodanthe killed the Turk and disguised herself with his garments.'

He punched his forehead, 'Damn! Forgive me, Pappas. I should have followed my first instinct!'

Desperate for air, Kostas dragged himself out to keep watch while Petros sipped coffee, the pappas wept, and Kazanis yelled, 'Spanos, for God's sake, raki!'

Even though Spanos had served many hard drinkers in his time, he'd not seen anyone knock back a tot as fast as Kazanis. While pouring another, he said, 'Can I expect more customers?'

'Not anytime soon. Survivors retreated to regroup, and hidden villagers will take time to filter back. You'll not see your close neighbour, flames burnt his corpse.'

Spanos' shaking hand spilt more than he poured, 'Nikos is dead? What about his great-granddaughter, Rosi?'

Kazanis belched on his raki and shook his head.

'We've seen no one.'

Petros spoke, his voice shrill, 'May God forgive me.'

From the front, Kostas called, 'What set him running?'

'Who knows, his voice is breaking, it was hard to understand.'

'It seems he's shouting "Rosi".'

Bemused at his son's concern, Kazanis shrugged and inspected his slashed hand, more serious than he'd acknowledged.

'Hey Spanos, I need a bowl of warm salt water and a cloth.'

Happy to oblige, Spanos set the bowl on the table, 'Oh, Panagia Mou. Don't poke, it will bleed everywhere. Let me dress your hand to divert worry for Rosi.'

Better than a nursemaid, Spanos washed and dressed the wound. After a grunt of thanks Kazanis called, 'Kostas, come for attention. Your jacket sleeves hang in shreds.'

With reluctance, Kostas accepted help. When Spanos failed to persuade him to have his damaged foot cared for, he shrugged and disappeared behind the curtain.

After much puffing, Spanos emerged clutching a cedar chest.

'In earlier times, when my shape was trimmer, I treated myself to a fine set of clothes from a visiting tailor.' He opened the lid with a flourish. 'I'll show you their style.'

Sprigs fell from unfolding garments, releasing delightful scents of rosemary, mint and thyme.

'Try them on.'

After exclamations of admiration, Spanos pulled back the curtain to reveal Kostas, resplendent in black wool britches and two silk blouses, one in dove grey showing beneath the dark blue. Thumbs tucked inside the bright blue waistcoat topping the ensemble, self-conscious Kostas bowed.

Kazanis guffawed, waggling the fingers of his undamaged hand through the rents in his own threadbare waistcoat.

'He'll not want to walk with me. I've more holes than cloth. Good thing hardened mud and gore acts as armour. I've fine boots to tuck my britches in, though, lifted from a fallen Turk. We'll nickname you Adonis, god of beauty. What do you think?'

Before Kostas could speak, Petros yelled from the street, 'Spanos, I need help.'

Kazanis rushed out, gun cocked. His lad struggled towards him carrying a bawling child.

Spanos barged through.

'Panagia Mou! Rosi, my love. Are you hurt?'

'Where's Great-Grandpa? He lost me.'

'Oh, sweet love, he rests in heaven with your mama. Let me find you a morsel to eat.'

As Spanos swept the child into his arms she buried her face in his neck and sobbed, still clutching her filthy rag doll now dangling over his shoulder. Kazanis gulped away the odd lump in his throat and raised an eyebrow at Petros.

'When we met earlier I sent her to search for her great-grandpa.' Without pause the lad looked to Spanos, 'She's calling me Papa.'

'An orphan's wishful thinking.'

Lost in his own thoughts, Pappas Mathaios revived on hearing the child.

'Rosi is her pet name. She's another Rodanthe, nine years old come summer. Nikos cared for her, always praying her pa might return from sea.'

With tears soaking the child's hair, Spanos promised to tend her until a suitable woman returned to Kritsa.

'Bless you, Spanos. She's the image of my daughter at the same age. Now I must go.'

Petros assisted the fragile man towards the door, and in an instant Kazanis remembered the gold. After a final gulp of raki, he followed.

'Wait! Let me ensure your safety.'

14

Bequest

One either side of the pappas, Kazanis and Petros assisted him along devastated alleys, passing tumbledown walls, charred door posts and burnt remains of tethered goats. Wind swirled ash to sting their eyes until light rain settled the motes, adding ammonia to the mix of sickening odours. Four scrawny chickens scratched and pecked through a singed refuse pile, clucking in pleasure at their bounty. At the end of the narrow street, Pappas Mathaios stared at the arched entrance to his home, no longer troubled by a door.

With effort he stretched to wipe soot from the cross carved into the door lintel.

'God knows I live here. Best make it clearer for others.'

Petros flashed a look at his pa. Both recognised the old man's gesture delayed the moment of facing his ruined home. Satisfied no one hid within, Kazanis stood aside. A few painful steps took Pappas Mathaios to his blackened armchair, where he sobbed.

From outside Kazanis called Petros to him, 'Kostas overheard the pappas say he has gold in there. Get him to tell you where.'

'What?'

'Just do it.'

Kazanis shouted in, 'I'll check the path to the church. Petros will stay with you.'

At the doorstep he tripped over Rosi, banging his injured hand on the wall. His profanities echoed along the alley.

While Petros comforted Rosi, he heard the pappas cry out using Turk words: 'My heart! The pain is strong.'

Without pause Petros answered in the same tongue, 'What can I do?'

Still using the foreign language, the pappas said, 'Nothing, it will pass. Oh, you speak as a Turk.'

A flush rushed to Petros' cheeks under the man's incredulous stare.

'I only know fragments. Rodanthe and I considered it a game.'

'Few Turks speak it. Most born in Crete use our dialect. I had fun with Rodanthe's godfather speaking his language while at school.'

With thoughts on gold, Petros picked a jar from the mantelshelf. 'Pa has a similar jar. He uses it for coins.'

'Ah, there's nothing of value. Only blue beads from superstitious women aiming to keep the evil eye from Rodanthe. From our counting games I remember there are twenty-four. Plus, a larger, precious one from her godfather. It is too big for that pot.'

He groaned, either from pain or tormenting memories, and sank in his chair just as Petros realised the likelihood of keeping the valuable trinket and gold together. To soothe the distraught man, he dabbed his own sleeve across the sweat glistening on the pain-furrowed brow.

'Tell me where you keep your largest gem. Perhaps it can bring pleasant memories to ease your pain.'

'Ah, the gift from my friend. It's in …'

Petros held his breath as the man struggled to clear his throat.

A squeal made them both jump. In a spate of tears, Rosi flung herself into Petros' arms.

*

Alert and uneasy on his way to the church, Kazanis checked behind tables and benches stacked under the row of bare mulberry bushes. Hidden claws raked his arm.

'Spiteful cat! Why so jumpy? You hid in a firebreak to live another day.'

Still sucking on the bloody stripe above his bandage, Kazanis barged open the church door to a powerful stink worse than a summer midden, overlaid with frankincense. With daylight behind him, the oldest echelon of Kritsa shuddered at the diabolical silhouette in the doorway.

'Up all those who can. The maelstrom has passed. Between ruins you'll find places fit for shelter.'

Cowed by the apparition, none spoke. Next came news to galvanise them.

'Your brave pappas has returned. He fought and lost an arm. He needs nursing.'

A murmur of prayer and comment filled the sanctuary.

'Thank the Lord.'

'Panagia Mou.'

'Bloody Turks'.

Those who could, rose, most groaning with the effort of moving stiff joints.

A woman enveloped in a hooded black cloak reached Kazanis.

'I'm Katerina, a family friend. I'll be pleased to tend Pappas Mathaios.'

Two men leaning on each other tottered forward.

'How did we fare?'

'Time will bring you reports of those who died; brave men, every one. Lack of munitions and explosive black powder beat us. Now our oppressors can access key routes to coasts and peaks.' A groan of despair met his account but he continued, 'The battle is over; not the war. Our men used the gorge to escape while Turks and Arabs slept. Instead of facing the horde armed only with steel, we've chosen to fight another day.'

Desperate to be on his way, Kazanis said, 'My cousin is lame. I'll send him home to Lassithi and rejoin the fray.'

A reedy voice stopped him at the exit, 'Freedom or death!'

The answering shaky chorus made him turn to old-timers keen to shake hands and wish him well. One said, 'I've a pair of donkeys to assist your cousin. My animals graze behind this church. Take them.'

'Thank you. I'll send my son.'

*

Shrill sobs jangled Kazanis' nerves, even before he walked inside the pappas' house to find Petros nursing the girl.

'What in the name of God upset her?'

'She found a nest of dead kittens in the rag bag by the loom. Hasn't quit crying since.'

Pappas Mathaios said, 'Rosi grieves for her great-grandpa. Those dead kittens released her tears, and I identify with her emotion.'

Lost for an answer, impatient Kazanis barked instructions for Petros to find the promised donkeys, and then raised questioning eyebrows to ask about the gold. A slight, negative headshake brought an angry, 'Damn! Take the snivelling brat with you. Meet me at the kafenion, I need a raki.'

Petros didn't risk delay.

'I'm sorry, there's nothing here I can offer you, Kazanis. This house stopped being a home long before the flames.'

Although filthy with debris, the floor near the fireplace had a much lighter colour. Kazanis rubbed at it with his boot, pondering over hidden gold.

'You stand where my wife fell from dreadful wounds. Women scoured her blood away. As for Rodanthe, people surmised kidnappers took her, with no idea of the culprits.'

Uncomfortable in the face of another's anguish, Kazanis took the few steps to the bedroom where the high square bed still had a mattress and covers to rummage through. He'd forced his good hand behind the bed's wooden steps when a cry sounded from the main room, followed by a thump as Pappas Mathaios hit the floor.

Intent on keeping him conscious, Kazanis lugged the pappas through to the rear.

'See, your bed is usable, although sooty. My injured hand means I can't grasp you. Try to help me.'

By the time he'd hauled him up both men dripped sweat.

'There's a woman to tend you. I'll hurry her.'

A frantic hand caught his arm.

'Wait. I cheated my Rodanthe. Thanks be to God, I bestowed a last kiss and confessed my sin.' For an ailing man, his fever-hot hand had a fierce grip. 'Sit by me. I strove to live as Jesus wanted, but I sinned. I must tell you of Rodanthe's baptismal gift. Her godfather gave one hundred gold napoleons to secure her future.'

'A hundred! Why would a woman need such a fortune?'

'To my eternal shame I deemed it too rich for her. I used much of it to aid the poor here in Kritsa. After her education and dowry, I intended her to have the rest when raising children.'

With his mind racing, Kazanis wanted to keep talking, 'I'm sure she'd have agreed.'

'My sinful pride caused her death. I made poor decisions. Had I done as bid my daughter would be alive. Given the amount of gold, she might have attended school in Europe and found a living there.'

Neither man heard Petros return.

'Or America! She might have gone to America. Pa told me uncles from our village migrated many years ago. She might have—'

'Petros, shut up.'

'Hush, Kazanis. Come closer, Petros.' Between laboured breaths he held their attention, 'I've eight napoleons left. Petros, you and Rosi must share them. Change your young lives for the better.' He wheezed and held his chest. 'I've concealed them in ...' Coughs took his voice, 'Dear God, the pain. I ...'

Pa and son stared at saliva dribbling from Pappas Mathaios' open mouth for several moments before Kazanis shook the lifeless man.

*

A horde of ransacking Turks couldn't have been more thorough. Furious Kazanis kicked at the carbonised table until it disintegrated, covering a rug's charred remains.

'Damned Pappas! What's the point of raising the possibility of wealth?'

Despite Petros witnessing many deaths in the heat of battle, this one brought home the fragility of life. He tried to hug his pa.

'What I've never had, I'll never miss.'

Kazanis shrugged him away. 'Let's go.'

Outside Rosi sat where Petros had lifted her, on the lead donkey, an old jack. She chattered away, scratching between his ears. Petros took the reins from her and struggled to keep upset from his voice. 'I'll act as drover, Rodanthe taught me. Umm, shouldn't we take him?'

Without answering, Kazanis banged through the house, reappearing with an unwieldy sheet-wrapped load. Petros distracted Rosi from seeing the body slung over the second animal, a jenny.

*

Relieved to clasp a raki, Kazanis agreed to wait while Spanos tended the body. Hidden by the bed curtain, Spanos washed his friend, muttering through heartbroken sobs. Frustrated, Kazanis shouted, 'Is he ready?'

'Almost. Wait while I grab another sheet to wind around old Nikos. We can bury both.'

*

Despite the pall of grief, Petros laughed watching Rosi drag a chair, her ambition resolute.

Spanos also smiled through tears.

'Rosi was the reason Nikos lived, he adored her. She rode in his pannier until a Turk soldier stole their donkey.

'Leave the chair, my love, you're not riding today. Phew, you're getting too big for me to hold. Ah, here comes Katerina.'

'Oh, Dear God. I see I'm too late. Who is the other wretch?

'I'm sorry, Katerina. I know you were close to Pappas Mathaios and his family. This is his pa-in-law, Nikos.'

'They were like family to me.' Katerina stooped to cuddle the tear-streaked child. 'Sweet Rosi. What will we do with you?'

'I can spare food for you both if you can foster her.'

'I'll enjoy her company awaiting my husband's return.' To hide her own distress, Katerina hurried inside the kafenion, Spanos in her wake.

Within moments Spanos hurried back to the departing men. 'Here, Kazanis, take this raki flask. You'll need it.'

Busy patting knives and guns to check his readiness, Kazanis found space for the sealed jar.

'Well, cheers to you, fine Spanos. Now hurry.'

'Wait. There's Rosi's doll. Let me take it. Rinsing away grime may distract her.'

As Spanos bustled away, Kazanis said, 'Let me aid you to those trees, Kostas. Might as well get comfortable. You too, Petros. Hobble those donkeys first.'

*

Within the hour another funeral scared away the graveyard birds. This time, Spanos piled leaves over the recently entombed Rodanthe in preparation for her papa's burial. Kazanis and Petros manoeuvred a marble slab off a nearby grave to tip in Nikos' remains.

After they'd replaced the lid, Petros rubbed his strained arm muscles.

'I wonder if he rests with someone he liked.'

'I doubt it makes much difference. See how the shadows shorten? It must be near noon.' He jerked his head towards Spanos and Kostas, 'Let's get this business finished.'

Crouched at the graveside, Spanos delivered a heartfelt eulogy, 'This good man stood head and shoulders above others. Bereft without his wife and daughter, he'll rejoice to greet them on resurrection morning.' Spanos reached in the folds of his kaftan for a tile of wood. His voice shook as he read his etched words.

'Three bodies sleep here, who in their day shed blood for faith and country. Who would not carry the angry pain of their servitude? God bless this Mama, Papa and innocent girl.'

15

Kritsa to Limnes

Human remains, stripped of weapons, boots and clothes, lay alongside dead horses strewn across the churned battlefield. A suffocating stench of rotting flesh and excrement blanketed the traumatised hillside. Several times Kazanis and Kostas drew weapons when confronted by movement or sound, then saluted with wry grins when it proved to be vultures shuffling in a macabre dance.

Sat on the jenny's wooden saddle, it seemed Kostas recognised his trekking days were over. The panniers either side of his labouring mount held an assortment of guns scavenged along the way. Kostas reached behind to open the lid, accepting another.

'Thanks, Petros. When we make camp I'll check these guns and make shot, ready to redistribute them.'

Petros reined up by a trackside body, 'Wait. I heard a sound.'

'Ignore it. Our reduced force found the strength to retrieve Christian corpses. Now they rest together in a gully.' Kostas acknowledged the horrified young face, 'A rough mass grave, I'll admit. At least we didn't abandon them to filthy vultures.'

'Honest, there was a moan.'

'It'll be gas escaping rotting bodies.'

When the next weak groan sounded, Petros stroked his jack's alert ears as they neared the devastated battle site.

'Kostas, is this small ridge all we battled over for two days?'

Kostas paused from rubbing his foot.

'Now they've breached this hill, there's no barrier to prevent a vicious swarm. They'll salvage enough cannon to create havoc. Do you understand? We failed. Troops will scale the mountain trail to empty our barns on Lassithi Plateau.'

Desperate not to expose his tears to ridicule, Petros rummaged in the open pannier before carrying a waterskin to the escarpment. Using pilfered spyglasses, Kazanis made a sweeping search of the steep hillside and green-edged plain.

'Their path is clear enough. See, a dark stripe cuts the plain. We'll use the same route west, then use tracks at the foot of the mountains to reach the long valley.'

'Is that where we muster?'

'Yes, in the area known as Limnes. Homeless Christians moved there to scrape a living by the lakes. From there you can look up to the village of Choumeriakos and the monastery hanging on the cliff edge.' Kazanis couldn't keep longing from his voice, 'It's near our path if we went home to Lassithi.'

'Rodanthe told us her refuge was near Choumeriakos.'

Kostas shuffled to join them to hear Kazanis comment, 'Makes sense, it's where Hursit Pasha lived before Rodanthe killed him.'

Misery sounded in Kostas' voice, 'What a weird thing to hear you say.'

Determined to push on, Kazanis was brusque, 'We can't stand chattering like women at a water cistern. Follow me.'

A steep, stepped path carved centuries ago wound down to Laconia Plain. In springtime oxalis grew in gaps between flagstones to carpet the trail yellow, interspersed with tiny irises and edged by waving poppies. Now, in fear of tumbling, Petros let the donkeys pick their own course over broken tiers crushed under thousands of hooves and trampling boots. With frequent slips and stumbles, the animals brayed their discomfort.

The ravine dropping to the left provided the departing army with a continuous dump. Petros ducked low as a flock of crows rose from the stinking carcass of a huge horse, then grabbed the halter of Kostas' bucking mount.

Petros pointed, 'They stripped the beast of his finery before tipping him, Kostas.'

'Without their cavalry, we'd have stood a chance.'

Puzzled why they'd halted, Kazanis strode back, 'Oh! What would I give for such a horse. No wonder the Egyptian, Hassan Pasha, led from the front, taunting us with white silk flowing from his helmet.'

'See that broken leg, Pa? Poor beast couldn't cope with this terrain. There's so much shit, I guess he slipped.'

'Take it as a warning. Hold your animals away from the brink. Hurry.'

Impatient, Kazanis waited for the riders at the foot of the hillside. He'd watched scudding clouds and was eager to make haste. Once night fell, they'd not gain entry to the lakeside camp by the hamlet of Limnes. None of his bawling could speed their progress west across Laconia Plain, now a quagmire raked by the passing force. A shattered cannon carriage brought the only high spot for Kazanis.

'Ha, a Cretan field beat them!'

He trudged off, not hearing Petros call, 'Pa, a child cries.'

Kostas scoffed, 'You're spooked by every noise. Ah good, he's taking a break in those trees. I could do with a pee. Get us nearer and help me dismount.'

Petros had only taken two paces when a muffled wail halted him. 'Kostas, someone is behind us.'

White-knuckled, Petros gripped his ancient pistol to follow his alert but shuffling cousin around a clump of bushes. When the sound came again, Kostas used his flintlock gun to wave Petros forward and circled his hand to show he'd retrace his steps. On all fours Petros crawled forward, his constricted throat aching and palms sweating. When the pair came face-to-face, each shrugged in confusion. About to move off, a muted cry for help had them both wide-eyed.

Petros pointed to the far side of his jack.

Kostas mouthed, 'Undo the right-hand basket. I've got you covered.'

Clammy hands made hard work as Petros sawed his knife through the leather thong holding bundles on top of his pannier. He sensed the final sinew parting, and darted away as the lid sprung up to reveal a slight form.

'Rosi!'

A cornered wild cat couldn't be fiercer, lashing with scratching claws. With difficulty, Petros lifted the writhing child. He'd sat her on the ground before she saw his face.

'Papa!'

She leapt at him and Kostas stated the obvious, 'Your pa will berate your carelessness.'

'Will you keep me, Papa? Everyone else has gone.'

He watched Kostas struggle to the wood and, dreading his pa's reaction, cuddled her close to answer her teary questions: No, he wasn't Papa, he was Petros. Yes, Great-Grandpa died in the fire. Yes, he'd find Mama in heaven. Yes, everyone had plenty to eat in heaven. No, the Turks wouldn't come today. Yes, she was clever to use a chair to climb in the pannier. Yes, Spanos would cry when he couldn't find her. No, he didn't know what they'd eat for dinner.

Exhausted by the exchange, Petros returned Rosi to stand in her basket then walked towards his pa, keen to protect young ears from expected profanities.

'She thinks I'm her papa, and she hid in fear of Turks. Can we take her home?'

'Give her to the first woman we meet. Let's go.'

Without looking back, Kazanis strode off, covering ground at a speed to belie his bulk.

Later, when he'd trotted too far and too fast without giving the animals a rest, Petros felt cheered to see Pa waiting near a shack by a cluttered yard. Several woodpiles spilt logs and three wooden donkey saddles disintegrated on a crumbling wall. Crushed terracotta pot shards paved the area while two huge pots, each standing taller than a man, flanked the rough stone shack's curtained doorway. Only two clucking hens rooting through the clutter hinted at life.

Petros acknowledged his pa's blade-drawn beckoning gesture.

A click signalled Kostas cocking his weapon. Gun-clenched Petros crept nearer the shabby wooden veranda. He felt momentary panic as Kostas guided his mount away, then realised he'd moved to shield Rosi from return fire. Resolute, he stood tall, desperate to play his part.

The veranda was in a worse state than the yard, littered with fly-covered turds, broken chairs and a pile of rusty tools. Amid this filth a wooden cage kept a small, dirt-streaked child in his allotted space. At the first glimpse of Kazanis, the toddler hauled himself up and banged the spars of his cage with the large wooden spoon he'd been using to ease swollen gums. Unafraid, he gurgled, 'MaMaMaMaMa.'

The child acted as an effective guard, bringing an unkempt child of perhaps six years to investigate. A weak female voice called from inside, 'I'm not decent, but I'm desperate.'

Kazanis peeked. Embarrassed to view a nursing woman without kerchief or dress, sprawled on a mattress, he turned away. 'You talk to her. I'll wait with Kostas.'

*

Even before Petros had covered half the distance towards his pa, he flinched at the bellowing voice: 'Will she accept the girl?'

'Papa Petros. Get on my donkey.'

Kazanis brayed false laughter, 'Ha, look where your kind heart has got you.'

'I didn't ask, Pa. The woman's dying. She's clinging to life and praying her son will return before she passes. He's hunting for food. I won't give Rosi to them.'

At first Kazanis looked shocked at the unprecedented defiance, then said, 'I'll not go slower.'

*

A single shot echoed through the trees and Petros flashed a scared look at Kostas, who primed his handguns within two heartbeats.

'Scout ahead but maintain cover. If your pa has wounds, resist running to him. Report back and I'll plan how to help him. Go.'

Nausea gripped the lad's guts. Twice he tripped over fallen branches as he scurried forward. Now a brazen person came towards him, not bothering with stealth. With his stomach churning, Petros ran for cover. Mid shrubs, he was astonished to see his pa round a bend dragging a goat carcass.

'You must hide better than that. Take this meat to the family. Leave them to butcher it.'

'Pa, you're the best. I'll be back before you've reloaded your gun.'

*

Via rough, tree-lined tracks, Kazanis led the way westward, heading for the Christian enclave of Limnes. When the path dropped towards marshland and lakes, Kazanis stopped. He signalled the others to halt and disappeared under cover of the thicket. After a silent age, Kostas whispered, 'Go to him. He can't risk coming back.'

Each step cracked a twig or kicked a stone, and Petros' heart beat a furious tattoo. He grunted as a huge paw clamped across his mouth to drag him backwards.

'Hush, Son. Someone darted across the path. Tell Kostas. Keep alert, and your weapon ready.'

Petros watched dread flash across Kostas' face and felt a rush of acid bile burn his own throat. He gulped, squared his shoulders and winked at the trusting child.

'Back in your basket.'

'I smell food.'

With a theatrical sniff, Petros was about to say he could only smell cold and damp, except the unmistakable waft of mutton made his mouth water.

'You're right. Someone is roasting. Quiet now, and we'll find out if they're in the sharing mood.'

In the gathering dusk, the travellers rounded a bend. Ahead of them Kazanis pointed to an extensive, cheery glow from beacons by the stagnant lake. He beckoned forward before stepping under cover. Focused on vast quantities of meat set on racks flanking a long firepit, Petros heard his stomach growl, and it took Kostas to jog him from his lip-licking.

'We'll stay hidden. Hurry downhill.'

Pa and son took cautious paces until a shout stopped them.

'Halt. Identify yourself before I blast.'

Chatter around the fireside ceased, and metallic rings and clicks sounded as fifty men drew steel or cocked guns.

'I'm Kazanis. This is my son, Petros.'

Lack of reply sent scowling Kazanis a few strides forward. A lean form hidden in the tree above flew down, knocking Kazanis to the ground.

16

Revels

Terrified, Petros saw a rope twist around his pa's neck. He gripped his gun, hoping he'd hit the right man, as the captor said, 'Get up slowly, Kazanis. Now drop your knife and walk.'

'Don't push your luck!'

'For once in my life I've the upper hand, *malaca*. Now move.'

Relief flooded Petros as he grinned, remembering the thrashing he'd got the first time he'd used the unsavoury term in Pa's hearing. He stood, dusted himself down, stuffed his gun in his cummerbund, whistled to call the donkeys forward and cheerfully followed his captured pa.

As they approached the armed sentry who'd made the original challenge, Petros said, 'Can I enter camp, Hannis?'

'Yes, watch our friend present his captive. Hey there, Kostas, continue.'

Together Kostas and Petros enjoyed the big man's humiliation, joining the crowd cheering the scrawny assailant as he landed a shove behind his victim's knee. Sprawled passive in rutted mud, Kazanis felt his captor's boot on his spine.

'Gather round, gather round. Observe the legendary rebel commander, Captain Kazanis, humbled by your dauntless friend, Falcon.'

Bewilderment silenced the crowd. Confused faces looked at one another. Then, as Kazanis accepted Falcon's outstretched hand and hauled him to an embrace, raucous cheers rent the dusk. Proud Falcon introduced his leader to comrades already settling, and the sentry, Hannis, handed over a full raki flask.

Kazanis jerked his head towards roasting meat, 'Someone cut me a chunk, even if it's still bleating.'

The rebels had slaughtered the free-roaming sheep now roasting along the fires while others found a barrel of excellent red wine plus three clay flagons of raki in nearby abandoned stone shelters. Now, with lubricated throats, battle stories flowed.

'I got too near a Moor's javelin,' said Kazanis, waving his bandaged fist, 'when he made a deadly lunge, I thought I'd breathed my last. Imagine my amazement when the bastard dropped. My Petros saved me by hurling a wooden bucket to smash the brute's kneecap.' Without grudge Kazanis took raki from Falcon, his longest serving lieutenant, and said, 'I thought this hamlet of Limnes was a haven for Christians. Where's everyone gone?'

Falcon explained how six homeless widows arrived expecting to find shelter and companions. Instead they'd found the mean dwellings deserted and took over two of the better stone huts while deciding what to do next. When bloodied and worn men arrived, the women hid until sure they were Christian, then in return for meat they prepared a few greens, potatoes and onions to supplement meals.

Keen to give them due credit, Falcon added, 'They've been tireless in tending injuries and laying out bodies, and I've warned men to stay away from those last two homes.' In response to further questions, he said, 'Refugees from several villages hereabouts have carried what they could to hide in caves above Milatos.'

Hannis caught their attention as he headed towards them, carrying a flaming mass on a pole to illuminate rough, filthy, bandaged and stinking men.

'Here's a torch made from ruined clothing soaked in oil. Bang this flare into the ground, it will burn a good while. Hey, who's this?'

A waif dashed forward, 'Papa Petros! You forgot me. I want food, now!'

'Papa Petros,' echoed Hannis, 'Since when?'

Pulling the youngster close, Petros said, 'This adventurous girl clambered in my pannier to hide. Now she's decided I'm her temporary pa. I'm relieved to hear of women, she needs fostering. First, we must eat.'

After a third huge portion of smoky roast mutton, Rosi licked fragrant fat and rich juices from her fingers with noisy relish.

'I can't manage another bite. Did I eat half a sheep?'

Still chewing, Petros said, 'And I ate the other half.'

'I can cook. Stew is the easiest, you put everything in and stir it sometimes.'

'Well, that's great. You'll make a fine wife.'

Replete and drowsy, he failed to see her dimpled pleasure. His rucksack made a pillow while he relaxed against a tree trunk, listening to rebels tell of narrow escapes and daring deeds with wild exaggerations of numbers they'd killed. None spoke of lost comrades; putting death into words was too overwhelming. This made it more astonishing when Kostas used a lull to share the news he struggled to comprehend.

'Some of you knew our young Spanos. Along with many others, he fell at Kritsa.'

Someone called out, 'A remarkable lad, his cunning saved many.'

Kostas continued as if he hadn't heard, 'This will shock you. Spanos was female.'

Stunned, the group around Kostas hushed.

'Daughter of a village pappas, she hailed from Kritsa.'

This outlandish announcement brought incredulous comments and awkward laughter.

Falcon supported his friend, 'There's no doubt, I was there. I'd fallen, moments from certain death, when Spanos shot my attacker. In return, he … um … she gained gunshot and blade injuries. Spanos had no care for his own safety.'

Those within earshot hardly drew breath, enthralled as Falcon told how he'd carried her limp body to the battlefield surgeon. Overcome, he coughed to clear his throat, hawked and spat before continuing, 'That surgeon wouldn't have yelled more if face-to-face with Lucifer. When he ranted about a girl needing to go to women for decency I hadn't a clue what he meant. As God's my witness, I went to discover why he was shouting and saw her bloodied breasts with my own eyes. For some reason, our brave Spanos fooled everyone.'

Warmed by meat and fuelled by raki, Kazanis lumbered to his feet.

'A toast, my fine palikars. Remember our heroes as we face the next stage of our conflict. Brave men each one, but I've a hunch history will remember this Kritsotopoula, Girl of Kritsa, long after we've turned to dust. Freedom or death!'

Battle-weary hands raised flasks and cups with answering calls of 'Freedom or death!'

Three veiled women carried meagre pots of food to the circle. One scolded, 'We've hidden ourselves for weeks and don't deserve brutes calling an army of Turks to us.'

A voice called, 'We're safe enough here. Local Turks won't come near this place in daylight, let alone the dark.'

Another said, 'Our noise might help guide rallying rebels.'

Yet another answered, 'Even they won't risk a night approach, our sentries will shoot first and question second.'

Kazanis laughed, 'Quite right. Expect an influx of men come morning.'

'More?' She wrung her hands in her grimy apron, 'The tiny graveyard overflows. A distraught pappas keeps vigil by the graves. Let's pray new arrivals have only superficial wounds to stitch and bandage.' Her brow creased, incredulous to see Rosi scamper to a lad, 'Panagia Mou! Why bring a child here?'

Men took this as a cue to turn attention to their meal as Petros explained Rosi needed fostering.

'Give me time to talk to my sister, then bring her over.'

*

Desperate not to lose this papa, Rosi buried her head in his shoulder as Petros carried her towards a domed stone dwelling. Through unglazed windows came flickering candlelight and a tinkle of feminine chatter. A young woman peered from the doorway, smiled and beckoned. Rosi screamed her rage when he tried to leave.

'I need to go with the men. Give me a kiss and I'll go happy.'

There was no reasoning with the wailing girl until the woman eased down to kneel beside Rosi and lifted the child's hand to rest against her stomach.

'In a few weeks when my baby arrives I'll need help. Do you want to be a big sister?'

Rosi's hesitant nod gave Petros his leave, 'I'll collect her when this madness is over.'

'Not here. We'll seek refuge in Milatos caves.'

*

'Her angry cries followed me, Pa.'

Kazanis pretended not to notice the catch in his son's throat.

'Will those women keep her?' Not waiting for an answer, Kazanis shuffled along to make space, 'Sit by me. I remember being your age when your voice goes from squeak to boom. Here, take my flask. These good souls found raki.'

Petros beamed and sipped, determined not to cough as the fiery liquid hit his throat, proud to realise this gesture acknowledged him as a fellow palikar.

Men guzzled raki to drown raw memories of bloodshed and slaughter. Banter increased, and the overloud guffawing of false cheer filled the night. A few men carried precious instruments, lyre and bouzouki, tied up with their scant possessions, and needed no encouragement to strike up a melody. Instead of mournful tunes to fit their losses they sang upbeat accounts of previous victories, as if to raise spirits for future battles. Before long, men danced – in twos and threes at first, with regular slow, swaying steps, then adding harsh foot-tapping actions of the traditional dance of rebellion, each series of hard foot taps mimicking a volley of bullets against the Turks.

Once most men were dancing, the musicians changed to a faster beat, bringing stomping foot movements as if the men were crushing grapes. Energy levels built and soon an undulating chain wound around the makeshift arena, with men swapping places to perform elaborate jumps and kicks at the head of the line. Petros laughed watching men catching Rosi to throw her to the next man in line, keeping time with the music. Miss Mischievous became a hysterical giggling baggage, leaving each catcher with a kiss. He had a fleeting thought about returning Rosi to her carer, until a dancer thrust his girl into his arms. Something melted inside, and he realised men needed her balm.

'Papa Petros! Look at me, I'm dancing.'

Petros hugged the hot, shrieking bundle, swirled her around in circles, enjoyed a peck and passed her to another set of outstretched arms.

Back in line by his scowling pa, Petros picked up the steps of a rhythm and pattern imbibed since childhood. He dipped, crossed his feet in an intricate pattern, stomped, then dipped again. The lead man leapt high, flourishing complicated kicks to loud applause, and swayed away allowing a new leading man the limelight. The huge well-armed bulk of Kazanis wasn't built for a fancy turn, so he mimed the desire to top up his raki flask and pushed Petros forward. Flopped on the ground next to Kostas, he watched with increasing pride.

Higher and faster than any man, Petros soared, helped heavenward by the strong arm of Hannis. Dizzy from exertion and unaccustomed raki, he grabbed Rosi as she darted by, swung her high and caught her with aplomb. Shouts of joy urged him to kick higher and ever faster. The dance ended with him spinning round and around making Rosi squeal with giddiness, just as his pa often did to him when he was a boy. He collapsed with Rosi wrapped around his neck, revelling in applause. Painful panting slowed as he sank in a half-sleep matched by many nearby. A murmured 'I love dancing, and I love you, Papa Petros,' roused him.

'Snuggle close, then. I'll take you back to the women in the morning.'

17

Betrayed

In pitch dark something woke Petros, making him stir and Rosi nestle closer. Murmured conversation took his attention to Hannis, sat talking to a stranger. Next, he heard Kostas making his unsteady way through the night, dragging his leg and grunting in pain. Close behind, Kazanis wove through a maze of sprawled men. When they finally dropped, Hannis made introductions.

'Meet Yorgos. I'd not have recognised him, but he's reminded me his mother lived near mine years ago, in Choumeriakos. He has great news to share.' As an obvious afterthought, Hannis said, 'Ah, and this is Petros, son of Kazanis.'

As the lad extended his hand to shake with Yorgos, a bitter draught woke Rosi. Precocious among indulgent men, she jumped up to wrap her arms around Yorgos' neck. Unabashed, the rascal kissed him.

'I'm Rodanthe. You can call me Rosi.'

Embarrassed, Petros huddled the child within his cloak, and keen to overhear the discussion, he urged her to sleep.

Yorgos only wanted conversation with Kazanis.

'Are you aware of the gruesome murder of the region's previous pasha?'

Cagey, Kazanis said, 'Everyone in these parts heard the tale, it's probably exaggerated.'

'When the replacement pasha took over, he blamed Christians for the assassination so expelled them from the village of Choumeriakos. After this action he moved his troops to a base in the nearby town of Neapoli. My parents overcame their repugnance and converted to Islam to keep their home.' The newcomer faltered in the face of a stony stare, coughed and rubbed his nose, 'Well, the current pasha has fundamentalist principles, so he'll welcome the senior man from Egypt. It's dangerous for me to visit, although I risked it two nights ago.'

Kostas cut in, 'Why tell us?'

The stranger edged closer, 'You'll understand my need to check my parent's wellbeing?'

Kazanis barked, 'Get to the point, man, I need sleep.'

Keen his leader should appreciate the value of this news, Hannis said, 'Yorgos found a huge weapons compound. It seems the Turks overlooked it in their move to Neapoli. We should go tonight.'

Kostas objected, 'Apparently forgotten by the Turks, it might be a trap.'

Kazanis pulled on his moustache for a few moments, 'It sounds worth investigating.'

'It will look bad if more captains show up in the morning and you're not here.'

'Mmm, you're right. Another night won't cause weapons to rot.'

Not hiding his disappointment, Yorgos argued, 'Hannis and Falcon have four mules at the ready. Refresh yourself for your important meeting tomorrow. Besides arms, there's a store of raki I'll bring to aid your discussions.'

Falcon arrived ready for action.

'Hey, you idlers. Hurry, we need moonlight to aid us before it dips behind the mountain.'

In answer Kazanis grabbed his son's rucksack as a pillow and turned his back.

Despite hard, damp ground and a bleak night, Petros slept until dawn when Rosi woke him, demanding a trip to the bushes. Certain his role of temporary papa didn't include such ministrations, he led her to the women. Although the amber eastern sky showed the tops of bare trees, insufficient light reached the glade, and without the drunken snores from scores of sleeping men Petros would have tripped over many more. As it was, loud curses followed him as he headed away with Rosi riding his back.

His bouncing charge leaned to his ear, 'You stink more than a donkey.'

'Well, don't imagine you're scented like fresh flowers, Miss Rosi. No one smells fresh anymore.'

'Only Kostas in his new clothes. Oh, and the man last night. His crispy clean shirt had been with the same lovely herbs.'

A hum of voices inside the main dwelling proved the women had risen. On the threshold, Petros halted in shock.

'S-s-sage t-t-tea? Th-th-thank you.'

Petros dropped his awkward load and ran inside to hug the weary, bedraggled man.

'Rosi, come here. Meet another of pa's cousins, my godfather, Pappas Stavros.'

'Th-th-thank God, I never th-thought to s-s-see you again.'

Sat on a bench, either side of the cleric, Rosi and Petros warmed their hands around wooden cups of sage tea. Between sips Petros confirmed both Pa and Kostas lived and offered to find them. Delighted to see his godson, the pappas stuttered he'd wait until they woke.

After another swallow Petros said, 'They'll wake soon. Pa's looking forward to more captains reaching us with reinforcements. Otherwise he'd have gone with Falcon and Hannis to steal an arms cache from Choumeriakos.'

'Th-th-there's n-n-nothing of v-value th-th-there!'

Colour drained from Petros' dirty face listening to the stuttered tale of retreating Turks taking everything to their new stronghold at Neapoli.

'Out of s-s-spite they s-s-set fire to the place to eliminate Christians.'

Appalled, Petros stood, 'Stay here, Rosi, I must find Pa.'

*

Unkempt Kazanis watched his fellow rebels up to their necks in the murky waters of the lake, intent on washing off the gore of war.

Taunts encouraged the huge man to join them.

'Not me. Ha! You'll develop a chill and die in a fevered heap.'

Proud as a displaying peacock, Kazanis made an elaborate turn to wiggle his rear. Filthy, oversized blouses hung in tattered layers outside multi-folded britches, waterproofed by years of sweat and grease. Only his knee-high, recently purloined boots were new. Even if he had his long-lost turban it would only partially restrain his hair, now frizzed in a woolly halo. A wild beard topped his shabby garb, matted with accumulated meat fat, food crumbs, crusty saliva, blood splatters and snot. It also held his signature tiny knife tied on with a leather thong.

He whooped and twirled.

'I've taken pains to cultivate my dashing style.'

In response to catcalls he preened, showing exaggerated care to caress the long blades in his cummerbund, check the many knives in his waistcoat pockets and point to favourite guns nestled in leather slings crossing his chest. Bellows of laughter filled the air, when Petros arrived shouting incomprehensible news. At first Kazanis stood immobile, unable to grasp what he heard.

'Yorgos is a Turk. Kostas was right. Choumeriakos is a trap.'

'How do you know?'

'Clever Rosi realised he was the only man apart from Kostas to wear clean clothes. I guess he stole them for disguise.' He gulped air, 'Pappas Stavros is here and told me departing Turks burnt Choumeriakos. Dreams of an arms cache is a snare.'

Kazanis sped away, screaming threats of dire retribution.

*

Goats chased over crumbling walls, sending stones tumbling to the overgrown path, while hens strutted to show they owned the place. It didn't take long for Kostas to conclude that wherever Yorgos led his friends, it wasn't Choumeriakos. At the elegant Venetian fountain, water splashed in huge marble basins where Petros led his thirsty donkeys to drink their fill. A snapping twig sent Petros behind a broken wall. In a reflex action, he cocked his gun to give cover to Kostas, who sat rock steady, aiming through the remains of a Roman arch smothered in incongruous red geraniums. By inching along, Petros tried to peer beyond the wall, his ears deafened by pounding blood. Terror tasted acidic in his throat and his trigger finger trembled. While sucking in a deep breath, he prayed for a steady aim.

A bent crone, wrapped in a ragged hooded cloak over a fraying sackcloth skirt, came through the arch. She cowered, dropping an egg from her grasp.

'Forgive me.' They strained to hear her peculiar tone.

'I only dared enter your garden to gather herbs and eggs. If you're moving back, I'll not come again.'

With an impatient snort, Kostas lowered his rifle, placed its ornate stock on his boot, held it by the barrel and beckoned her to pass.

'We're not Turks. Do any live here?'

With her face staring at his feet in modesty, she said, 'Not for months. Folk either bowed down to go with them or set up crude homes by the lakes. In the few times I've ventured here, there's never been a soul.'

Kostas limped off, not hearing her murmur, 'Ah, Spanos' distinctive rifle.'

Instead, he called back, 'Hurry, Petros. Head for Neapoli.'

18

Abominations

Even if Petros lived to one hundred, he'd never erase the vision of his indefatigable pa slumped below the flayed and bloody corpse of Hannis impaled on a barbarous stake.

Crows left tiny red footprints on the hard-trodden mud as they feasted on slithers of flagellated flesh, lying in an arc of cruel torment. Hit by overwhelming dizziness, Petros fell in an awkward heap, caring nothing for physical pain - it was better than the boiling hurt suffocating him.

With eyes tightly shut, Petros refused to rouse himself; he had no wish to view the grisly apparition. A metallic stench of blood combined with the smell of his own vomit set him retching. Kostas dropped next to him.

'Cry, lad, there's no shame. Keep out of sight in those trees. Flee if it's another trap. Live to take word of this abomination to our captains.'

Through his distress, Petros realised Hannis could not suffer such torment without spilling. This martyr's torturers would know of the lakeside force, the cavernous refuge at Milatos and routes to Lassithi. With a gulp he worried about the nearby hanging monastery where he used to work in the hidden mill, mixing saltpetre, charcoal and sulphur to create black powder.

Although Petros heard Kostas' instruction, he secured the donkeys then crept back. From an ornate minaret rising above a magnificent domed mosque, a muezzin sang his midday call. The sound sliced through eerie silence to bring his faithful to prayer.

Now Kazanis stirred as if waking from an unpleasant dream. The second part of the muezzin's cry still echoed when Lucifer leapt inside Kazanis, bringing forth a murderous torrent. In horror Petros watched his pa sprint off, a bundle clutched tight. A piece of black cloth fluttered and Petros ran to salvage the remnant of Hannis' clothes.

A queue of elderly Turks shuffled inside the mosque. The sight halted Kazanis; perhaps it registered that these were not culpable. Within seconds, stomping boots heralded a hated janissary corps: guilty men! Incensed at the thought of heathens seeking comfort in prayer, Kazanis tore away, clamping the rags under his arm.

Foreboding fizzed through Petros' veins.

'Papa! Come back.'

Deaf to the screamed pleas of his chasing son, Kazanis scrambled up a tree beside the mosque. Petros ran forward twenty paces, stumbled and fell. From his knees he watched a frantic figure scale the mosque's elaborate dome.

'Pa, don't. Please, God, stop him.'

Neither Christian nor Muslim God took heed. For an instant, a flaring rag waved aloft, only to disappear down a ventilation shaft. With his vision blurred by tears, he watched his adored pa clamber further up the arced roof to stand like a black shadow puppet against a cloudless blue backdrop. 'Please come down, Pa.'

If Kazanis screamed as he slipped, no one heard it above the cacophony of banging against the mosque door.

Petros spewed.

A solitary cloud passed in front of the sun. Hope flickered as a blazing torch came into view from the far side of the dome. Hope died as a sheet of flame erupted. Kazanis fell again. A rising breeze whipped the flames to consume the cupola. As if stone, Petros didn't even wipe the vomit from his mouth. A dreadful crackle and crash of flaming timbers signalled the dome's collapse to mute the tumult.

For a moment Petros wondered why Kostas dragged himself to aim at the mosque door, then his awful purpose registered. Kostas shot the first two attempting escape. Seared by the conflagration and sickened by the stink of roasting bodies, Petros handed two guns to Kostas before reloading those smoking from hot barrels. Another two men tried to flee. Kostas shot. Terrorised pandemonium must have masked Petros' voice when he told Kostas he lacked further shot – Kostas maintained aim. It didn't matter, bodies barricaded the door.

Direct from Hades, a non-human form appeared from the rear of the devastated mosque. No hair or beard, face blacker than any Moor, with wisps of smoke rising from singed clothing.

Faced by the hideous apparition, Petros took an involuntary step backwards.

This creature rasped, 'Find me a raki.'

'Oh, Pa. Sit here, I'll be quick.'

The sight of a waterskin brought a grimace from Kazanis, his black lips cracking to ooze blood. Slumped on the ground, he spluttered as water hit his raw throat. Kostas berated him for the wrath about to descend. His tirade ended abruptly as another blackened figure hauled a body from behind the smoking ruin.

Under incredulous stares Petros strode forward, offering water. He spoke to the men in the tongue of Turks, albeit with ineptitude. On his return, Petros confirmed there were no other survivors.

'Those high-ranking janissaries were in a separate room and smashed their way out. It seems most people died wedged against the main door, crushed by desperate people.'

Petros faltered under his pa's glazed stare while Kostas sounded bemused, 'How did you ...? Never mind, go on. What else do they say?'

'Despite my limited ability they understood me enough when I promised imprisonment in return for information.'

Kostas raged he'd no right to agree such a bargain, but Kazanis groaned, laying a restraining hand on his cousin's shoulder while nodding encouragement to his lad to continue.

'These men have no knowledge of the lynch mob and no idea what happened to Falcon.'

In a smoke-ravaged whisper, Kazanis said, 'Well done. Tie them behind your mount. Every excruciating step on burnt flesh will teach them not to mess with me.'

His prophesy proved correct: their first few steps brought shrieks of pain.

'Malacas! Serves them right for praying barefoot.'

'Pa, you're a genius. Let me fill the panniers with boots and shoes from outside the mosque. Our men will march better shod in thick leather.'

When they set off again, Petros cried to witness his pa's fallibility – like biblical Samson, he'd lost his vigour along with his hair.

19

Thea's Pool

Kostas realised that initial shock over the mosque's devastation would delay investigation, giving him time to get the injured men away. He knew dire retributions would befall local Christians if there was any hint of the inferno's cause. Once the group was under cover of a huge olive grove below Neapoli, his breathing eased enough for his thoughts to make sense.

'Lead the way, Petros. Stay off the main track and take us along herd paths towards a crossroads above Choumeriakos. You'll know it's the right place if there's a spring with a large pool.'

'And shelter for our patients?'

'We'll hide your pa and take the Turks down to the lakeside. The captains can interrogate them for as long as they can keep them alive.'

Frequent stops to aid the injured trio made the trek interminable. During one pause, Kostas made a shot for his two guns and one for Petros. When riding resumed, Kostas kept both guns primed in case the Turks attempted to flee. In truth, they couldn't run anywhere, but it didn't stop his longing for a flimsy excuse to shoot them and free him from Petros' ridiculous bargain.

After scouting ahead, Petros ran back to confirm they were near the crossroads and spring-fed pool.

'Take the Turks first, I'll keep you covered. Wave "all clear", and I'll follow with your pa.'

Kazanis waded in the pool to ease his burns, turning his back when Petros allowed the Turks similar relief. Soaked through, Kazanis paddled to reach some stone blocks set as seats at the water's edge. Petros saw the comic element when his pa rested his head in his hands, only to jerk in shock to realise his shaggy mane had singed away.

From his hard seat, Kazanis recognised a track rising towards the hanging monastery, named for the way it clung to the cliff. Thoughts of the black powder mill hidden in its vaults made him anxious. Bastard Turks wouldn't know only meagre stocks remained until after they'd attacked. He soon concluded his infirmity put Kostas and Petros at risk. To keep them safe, he decided to let them take the Turks for interrogation while he tried to get up to the monastery to alert Father Abbot.

When he explained his decision, he concluded with, 'Afterwards, take Petros to the caves at Milatos, and I'll join you when I'm fit.' In face of indignant dual protests, he was brusque, 'It's not a soft option. Vast numbers of refugees need men to hunt food and defend them.'

Next came the question he'd been dreading.

'Pa, shall we get Hannis?'

'I missed my chance to cut his body down for burial. When you see Pappas Stavros, ask him to hold a special service. God knows he died a hero.'

To avoid further discussion, Kazanis tottered away to submerge his burns.

To make best use of the stop, Petros refilled the waterskins and was busy retying them to the donkey's wooden saddle when he sensed movement nearby. As he eased round to fumble with the rough holster he'd fashioned on the jack's saddle, a bent, cowled woman emerged from nearby undergrowth. A sixth sense also alerted Kostas, who swung around to level his rifle. As if unaware of them, the figure shuffled forward. When the crone spoke, her odd voice had a familiar tone.

'My guess is you're Kostas.'

'How do you know me?'

'Your gun. It was a gift from the lad you call Spanos. Is he nearby?'

Lost for words, Kostas didn't know how to respond. Petros stepped forward.

'We're friends of Spanos. I'm—'

'Petros, an ally of Spanos.'

Kostas recognised her, 'We saw you in Choumeriakos. Did you find food? We're hungry, and my cousin sits in the pool to ease burns. Can you help him?'

The woman turned for the pool but Petros stopped her, 'Wait, tell me your name.'

'Thea.' She nodded towards thin smoke rising from a meagre fire inside a cave, 'This is my home.'

'Come, Thea, I'll tell you about our special friend.' He took her arm for emphasis, while speaking to Kostas, 'Bring all three to Thea's cave for treatment.'

With limited time for privacy Petros took up the skinny veined hand, ignoring the filth across the knuckles to explain how Rodanthe maintained her disguise until her death in the recent battle. Petros knew the woman wept; her hand crept under her hood to wipe tears. Through sniffles she described how she'd met Rodanthe the day she'd escaped from the Turk compound dressed in male clothing. Keen to learn more of his dear friend, Petros strained to hear every word as Thea said, 'Do you know she killed their leader to escape?'

'We guessed. How did she get to you?'

'On a stolen horse, wearing his clothes. She fell right there and broke her ribs.'

'Lucky you found her. Did Rodanthe stay long?'

'Until her injuries healed, and then she walked towards Lassithi wearing the male garb. The only time I saw her afterwards was when she came for the dead Turk's long gun.'

Petros whistled air through his teeth, 'As you saw, Rodanthe gave the rifle to Kostas, and I'll admit to being envious.'

'When Rodanthe collected it, still in disguise, she hugged me and said she loved a man who deserved the weapon.'

Absorbed in the conversation, Petros hadn't realised Kostas stood behind him until a choked voice joined the conversation.

'By every word and deed she showed her love for me. I stayed blind to the truth until her deathbed.' Awkwardness created a vacuum, amplifying the wind through the trees and trilling birds. After a loud gulp, Kostas demanded, 'Tend Kazanis.'

Thea took control. 'He needs healing dried dittany, I'll fetch some from my store.'

Intrigued, Petros followed Thea, overwhelmed at the size and comfort of her cavern, 'These chambers for storage and sleeping are larger than most built dwellings.'

'This is the only home I've known. Look around, I'll make tea.'

A savoury aroma from rabbit stew drew Petros back from exploration to hear Thea apologise, 'Sorry, Kazanis, this rabbit will not go far between five men. Let me serve you.'

Kazanis rasped, 'Three. Those Turks outside don't need meat.'

'Oh, no, that's not how things work here. I live by my wits and the offerings people make to the Panagia in the nearby chapel. My bounty is for anyone in need.' With a roughhewn wooden spoon dripping in her hand, she deemed her mash ready, 'When this dittany brew cools, I'll wash your face and tend the other two. Your burns are superficial, but sore nonetheless. What you do when you leave here is up to your conscience.'

Rebuked, Kazanis accepted a tin plate of thin stew to eat without his usual gusto, not even licking his plate. As soon as he'd finished, Thea replenished his plate for Kostas.

'When you've served him, fill my empty raki flask with your dittany brew. My wife praised the properties of the mountain herb.'

'Ah, Kazanis. God truly works miracles. The only reason I have dittany is because your wife brought it to honour the Panagia. Dear Rodanthe told me of its medicinal powers when she had vile pus in a hand wound.'

While Kazanis stared in shock through his red, blistered eyes, Petros bounced in excitement, 'You knew Mama! Why did she visit you?'

'She made a pilgrimage to the Panagia three times a year to pray for another child. When I saw her no more, I guessed God had granted her wish.'

'Memories of Mama are hazy. After witnessing the death of Kostas' wife and daughter she fled to the island called Naxos, taking my baby sister.' His pa's lack of comment gave Petros confidence, 'Pa said he'll take me there when Crete gains freedom, even though Mama will throw a fit.'

Thea used a soft goatskin soaked in the dittany liquid to wash Kazanis' burns, bringing groans of pain from her patient.

'Remove your wet rags and wrap yourself in this moth-eaten blanket. Although cold water eased your burns, shock will set in. You need to keep warm.'

She beckoned Petros to walk with her, 'Let me tend those Turks you've left under the trees. Are they for the noose?'

'No, I promised them imprisonment in return for information. Give me a few moments to hobble the donkeys, and I'll bring your patients to you.'

With one Turk secure at the rear of Thea's cave, Petros returned to help the most injured. After a few painful paces, scorched lips said, 'Allah is great. Soldiers march this way.'

A steady thud of marching boots echoed through the trees, and with no time for consideration Petros dragged the wretch inside, ignoring his yelps of pain.

'Pa, Turks head our way.'

Kostas answered first, 'Thea, go to the back of your cave. Take the Turks, we can't afford for them to find their voices. Petros, come back.'

'I'm going for spare guns.'

'There's no time. You've one shot in your gun and mine are both loaded. Hide yourself on the rock face. I'll take cover in the bushes. If you shoot, make it count.'

20

Double Bluff

Petros scaled up to a rock ledge and crouched low, willing his ragged breaths to calm. Caught in an awkward squat, he flexed his leg to a more comfortable position. His boot caught a stone to send a shower of loose shale rattling. Frightened the racket would draw attention, he held his breath until the last stone fell, leaving the clearing tranquil. Water gushed, and insects buzzed in the early almond blossom covering the sapling he grasped. A pinkish-brown bird, a hoopoe with distinctive black and white wings, settled in a nearby tree, close enough for Petros to see it raise the long crest on its head before it called, 'Hoo-Hoo-Hoo.' Infantry boots soon smothered these pleasant sounds.

Yells and laughter proved the troop felt secure. Dirty and dishevelled, they still looked well dressed, their backpacks bulging with provisions. Bandoliers full of expensive pre-made shot cartridges adorned their chests, and each wore a crimson fez set at a jaunty angle. A smart officer rode alongside. With long leather boots encasing woollen jodhpurs, a greatcoat warm enough for any winter and a gleaming mount, he looked ready for the trek up to Lassithi. Thirty men made for the spring and two donkeys brayed a welcome to the horse. Petros' foot slipped again and he cursed as another stone bounced. With one hand gripping the almond sapling, he leant forward as far as he dared, dreading discovery of the boots and shoes.

In a muddle of flailing limbs, cracked head, spinning stones, a scream of surprise and injured pride, Petros landed in a heap on the ground, still gripping the wretched, shallow-rooted tree. Stunned silence met his undignified entrance in the platoon's midst. Then, in a rush to arms, the soldiers drew their blades or guns. Used to strict discipline, the platoon looked to their officer before making a move.

Petros stood, hoping his trembling knees would not fail him, and brushed his hand across his behind. As he went to offer it to the officer, he had a flash of inspiration. He bowed low, and using the Turk language, said, 'Peace be to you.' Then, holding his breath, he stared at his own shod feet, realising his recently acquired boots could be his undoing. Above him Petros heard the bemused, automatic reply learnt by rote, 'And to you be peace, together with God's mercy.'

To stop his smirk, Petros bit the inside of his cheek. Emboldened, he stood tall to continue, 'Hello, brother Turk.'

An irritated voice used local language, 'What in the name of Allah does he say?'

Petros tried again, hesitating as he grasped for the right foreign words, 'From stable. Belong to Pasha. From Neapoli.'

'Search me, Ali, I caught the words Pasha and Neapoli. I know that's a nearby Turk stronghold. Why can't our more recent comrades realise we speak the local dialect?' In frustration the Turk spoke in a louder, slower voice, 'We fight good. Bang bang Christians yes?'

With a disarming smile, Petros realised this man couldn't use the tongue of a high-born Turk, as Rodanthe had taught him. He pretended he had trouble understanding, 'Sorry I speak bad. Slave for good man. Neapoli. Bad men fire mosque.'

Brazen now, Petros beckoned the leader to the jack, opened the pannier and, confident the officer couldn't understand, wailed, 'Shoes from faithful. Burn men. Bad infidels,' as he thrust a much-repaired boot into the man's hand.

Perhaps the officer didn't realise Petros still held his wrist for he followed, barking an order for men to watch his back. Relieved he'd managed to intrigue the man, Petros sent a silent prayer willing Kostas to stay hidden. Near the cave entrance, he pointed to a large, smooth rock: an obvious seat, 'Moment, Lord, wait.' As the force crowded forward to alarm Petros, he gestured they should halt. Without checking they had complied, he dashed inside the cave.

A bemused Kazanis headed towards the sunlight, blinking hard and grateful for his son's supporting arm, 'Turks, Pa. Say nothing, I want them to see your injuries.'

Flustered by the sudden turn of events, the injured man tried to preserve his dignity by holding the blanket closed with hands Thea had bandaged in lengths of wet goatskin.

Astounded by the sight of Petros leading Kazanis, the officer took step backwards as his alert lieutenant barked an order: 'First rank, take aim.'

Petros ignored the guns to maintain eye contact with the officer, 'This my master. Good man. Burn from infidel. Only this man lives.'

On cue, Kazanis lowered the blanket to expose his raw chest. Groans of sympathy met his action. Confidence boosted, he gingerly touched his face, flinched theatrically and gave an elaborate moan. Petros led his pa to the rock and mimed a sitting motion as he spoke the word for sit.

The look on the Turk's face made it clear he had no intention of taking responsibility for a frail patient, and he turned to his troops, 'Continue to Lassithi, his slave will get him back.'

One of his men took a hesitant step forward, 'Forgive me, Lord. Rumour has it the Christians have a holy place near here where the rebels store explosives.'

'If that's true, another force will collect the powder tomorrow.' Annoyed by the soldier's presumption, he saluted. 'May Allah guide your way and heal your sores.'

Uncertain of his next action, Petros sat next to Kazanis and relished the pat delivered to his arm. At a shout of command, the infantrymen came to attention.

'Quartermaster, give them a pack of food, a gun and a pack of six shot. Let's pray Allah allows them to safety before marauding infidels catch them.'

The glade returned to calm. Fear subsided in Petros's stomach, and the hoopoe called, 'Hoo-Hoo-Hoo.'

From his hiding place Kostas sounded, 'Poo-Poo-Poo.'

*

After accepting Kazanis was right not to accompany them, Kostas bid Petros to lead the way to the lakes. On arrival, they discovered improved security at the entrance to the lakeside muster, and now armed sentries held the odd group at bay, demanding to know who inside the camp could vouch for them. Kostas fumed, 'I guess you arrived with a recent influx of men. Call your senior, for God's sake. We've not dragged these wretches for interrogation, only to have them die waiting for you to decide I'm not the enemy.'

Petros didn't hesitate. He slipped past the flustered guard, shouting, 'Let me through, I need Pappas Stavros.'

Aghast to learn of the suffering Hannis had endured, the cleric wept, then cried again, appalled at the dreadful retribution of Kazanis.

'Insanity took Pa. I'm not surprised. The nightmare of Hannis betrayed and tortured will stay with me forever. Pa is a principled man, he'll know setting fire to the mosque was murder.'

Sight of the anguish on Petros' face moved the pappas to clasp him close, 'G-G-God will f-f-forgive.'

Keen to change the subject, Petros said, 'I'll see Rosi in Milatos. I'm going there with Kostas.'

Pappas Stavros stuttered, 'Can I put a few belongings in a pannier? I'll join you.'

The mention of panniers made Petros whoop, 'Hey! Who needs boots and shoes?'

Too many were barefoot or struggled with rags wrapped around remnants of boots; no wonder men hailed him a hero. One man caught up with Petros to shake his hand. 'Thank you. I can't remember the luxury of boots. Before this madness I was a haberdasher, and this length of green ribbon is my remaining wealth. Give it to your maid when you next see her.'

21

The Hanging Monastery

Never before had physical exertion bothered Kazanis. He'd always relished folk calling him Talos, after the mythical bronze giant, for the way he charged from place to place, administering rough justice. As a child his uncle had entertained him with stories of tireless Talos circling the island three times a day to protect Crete from pirates and invaders. Today he puffed up the steep path towards the hanging monastery, desperate for treatment in the infirmary. His face stung from weeping burns on his nose and cheeks, but his main concern was the burn on what had been his undamaged hand. No wonder the novice who answered his weak banging at the door reeled backwards in shock at the tattered apparition. The gatekeeper's scream sapped Kazanis' last speck of energy. He dropped in a faint.

Revived by the stink of a burning feather, he sat bolt upright.

'Rest. I'm in charge of our infirmary. Although I've salved your burns, you'll be tender for days.'

Smoke inhalation reduced the lion's roar to a hoarse whisper, 'I'm Captain Kazanis. Fetch Father Abbot.'

'Rest, you'll get your voice back.'

'Tell him I'm here.'

The monk had heard of the legendary hero Captain Kazanis, but this weak, ravaged fellow was not he. When Kazanis struggled to rise, determined to meet the abbot, his doggedness proved too strong for the infirmarian who agreed to take a message.

Later, murmured discussions on whether this could be the heroic rebel roused Kazanis to offer more credentials.

'My cousin Kostas is lame, he drilled recruits here, and my son is

Petros.'

Father Abbot nodded, sent the others away and pulled a stool closer to listen while Kazanis rasped his account, excluding mention of the destroyed mosque. Afraid for his brethren and dependents, Father Abbot paced the small room, weighing up risks. After kneeling in prayer, the abbot's tension cleared and he called to the infirmarian waiting in the corridor.

'Send our pupils under twelve to the secret school and I'll escort your patient to join them. Brothers and older students able to wield a gun can help guard the powder mill.'

Father Abbot returned to the stool by Kazanis, 'God knows there's insignificant stock, but the Turks don't.' He placed a hand on Kazanis' arm, 'Believe me, many of my fold feel torn between their monastic vows and practical aid. Believe it or not, I'm a good shot.'

'Ah yes, Kostas mentioned you had a truer aim than most who reported for tutelage.'

'I'll set a watch on the wall in case the Turks test our resolve. Come, we must keep you safe, people rally to your name.'

Frustrated by his need for help, Kazanis took the abbot's arm for their walk to the refectory, where dark wood furniture bore the patina of age. Woven cushions, embroidered cloths, elaborate wall tapestries, glazed windows and jars of freesias gave the room a homely feel under the watchful gaze of myriad icons. An upholstered sofa proved irresistible for Kazanis, and he sank in with a sigh to doze.

Six chattering boys hurried in, then cowed at the sight of a bandaged stranger. Huddled together, they kept their eyes on the flagstones, too overawed to speak. Heads rose as several pairs of sandals crunched along gravel. Time hung heavy. While the boys whispered, fidgeted and giggled, Kazanis snored.

An ordained monk who acted as tutor struggled in with a large basket of provisions, and turned to the boys.

'God has asked us to nurse this famous rebel captain until he regains his vigour.'

Six young heads stared at the odd fellow as the monk continued, 'It seems the Turks may visit, hoping to steal our black powder.'

A faltering voice said, 'Will they kill us?'

Certain he had their attention, their teacher adopted a cheery tone, 'No, lads, Father Abbot has a plan. Our part in the defence is to keep this great man safe within our secret schoolroom. If Turks approach, I'll secure the false door and urge you to brave the dark. We can't risk a candle, and our weapon is silence.'

Another boy seemed ready to ask a question, but the teacher shook his head and held a finger to his lips, 'Wander where you wish inside your heads and pray to God. We've bread and produce for a week, although the matter will conclude sooner.'

Opening one eye, Kazanis saw a contagious frisson of fear sweep the boys' faces and coughed to clear his throat, 'Years ago, I hid in your school cavern and used the narrow chamber to escape up the hillside. If I give the word, rush up and out together. Don't wait for me as I might need to entertain Turk scum.'

A coughing fit had him struggling for breath, leaving their tutor to lead through the arched entrance, beckoning his pupils to follow.

A persistent youngster said, 'So, we might die.'

The gruff whisper from Kazanis proved less convincing than he wished, 'The name of this monastery reflects how it clings to the edge of the rock face. None can sneak up unseen, and your abbot is an excellent sniper.' To lighten their spirits, he added, 'One of you, run for a big *kazani* pot. We'll discover who pisses the quietest. Anyone who kicks it over will have to mop the floor.' Nervous giggles heartened him, 'I'm named Kazanis after my grandpa. He won the epithet when Turks shot the church font and a pappas christened him in a kazani. If no one spills our kazani I'll empty it, if you keep it quiet. I don't want people calling me Sloppy Kazanis!'

Hesitant laughter cut off as their abbot appeared, a rifle slung from his shoulder and two knives tucked in his cassock sash. To convey this was a fun adventure, he said, 'What do you think? Will I make our enemies tremble?' Satisfied with their timid nods, he turned to leave.

'You'll have God at your side, Father Abbot. Meanwhile my boys can enjoy extra lessons.' Their tutor ignored the collective groans, 'Help Kazanis from the sofa and bring the cushions.'

Kazanis croaked, 'There's no need to shut out the light until there's an alarm.'

'Indeed. Settle down boys and I'll tell you a Bible story, perhaps David and Goliath.'

*

Monastic life continued, with the brothers taking additional duties to provide an armed watch while the schoolboys lived with their odd guest. Three days resting in semi-darkness gave Kazanis a significant boost, allowing his burns to form protective scabs. With delight he realised movement in both hands proclaimed the damage far less than he'd feared, and as his breathing had eased he concluded it was time to find the rebels. He sought the abbot.

'Thanks to your warning, Kazanis, we'll keep watch from our walls and store emergency supplies in the schoolroom. Leave dressed as a monk; it's the only clothing we have.'

'Thank you, Father Abbot, I'll pause at the kitchen to beg a rucksack of food.'

'Good journey and good month.'

'What month? I've lost track.'

'Today is the first of February. With God's will, this year, 1823, will see the back of our oppressors. Although I thank God for his mercy, I wonder why a band of Turks didn't attack.'

Kazanis sighed, 'I presume they found weaker prey.'

22

Milatos

While Kazanis convalesced at the monastery, Pappas Stavros, Kostas and Petros formed part of a group heading for Milatos. Although the forward party with donkeys used the rough tracks through the forest, those following on foot kept hidden within the treeline. A cloudless sky allowed the sun to warm Petros, and as thermals rose, so did a colony of griffon vultures, wheeling and soaring in lazy circles. One pair took turns to land on a craggy ledge, busy refurbishing last year's nesting site. Rewarded with a crick in his neck from looking upwards, Petros said, 'Must be almost February. Falcon told me it's the month those great birds lay their single egg. I wonder if we'll ever find out what happened to him.'

Distracted from deep thoughts, Kostas said, 'What? Oh, the vultures. They roost high above Selenari Spring. We'll scout ahead. Tell the others to wait for my whistle.'

*

The narrow pass, cut into the rock in distant times, had enough width for two donkeys to walk through together. With dainty steps they climbed up a steep track, staying sure-footed despite the moss hushing their hooves. When the path broadened, the dramatic landscape included charred remains of trees around a small church, untouched by flames. Blackened rock covered in sooty debris rose over tumbledown slabs that once formed an elaborate cistern. Now a new wooden spout set in a fissure enabled refilling of waterskins.

Petros frowned as he rubbed the carved wood, realising it took time to create such a useful spout. His fear that someone lived near here grew when he noticed rubble piled to the side of the clearing. Kostas needed to know but he'd dragged himself out of sight.

Petros shrugged, deciding to share his concern when Kostas returned from private time, and busied himself, not realising his splashing masked other sounds.

A shadow flit across the ground beside him, lifting his neck hairs to make him shudder. Horrified to see a long-barrelled gun protruding from rocks, Petros realised he'd left his weapon holstered on his saddle.

A rough local dialect demanded, 'Why are you here?'

'Umm … for water. Do you live here?'

A familiar voice behind Petros took control, 'F-f-friend, s-s-show yourself.'

The armed man stepped from his hide, lowered his gun and fell to his knees.

'Bless me, Pappas, it's overlong since I met any clergy.'

'May God bless you, Br-br-brother. M-m-meet my godson, Petros.'

Without pause the pappas swiped spittle from his lips with the back of his hand and introduced the recluse who dedicated his life to tending Saint George's chapel.

Kostas returned to find the three of them laughing, and Petros answered his raised eyebrows, 'Pappas Stavros already knows this man.'

'Shake my hand, Kostas. Until now I thought God sent a thunderbolt to blow up my spring and set the hills alight.'

The smirk on Petros' face emphasised his youth, 'I told him you and Rodanthe set the blast. Our friend here says it took the Turks half an afternoon to clear the track.'

In good humour the hermit nodded towards the church and said, 'God forgive me, I knelt, praying for the wind to change direction and smother them.'

Kostas gave a few more details and recalled a lucky escape, 'My friend worked a miracle. Her audacity to delay the troop saved many lives in the port of Sisi.' He slapped his thigh, 'Thanks to her I'm alive.' To avoid further explanation, he gave a loud, coded whistle to bring the rest of their band.

Keen for inclusion, Petros joined the hermit and Kostas on an uphill ledge as both pointed at landmarks and shared information. Although only a few feet above the spring, their perch presented a significant change of view. A steep ravine cut through high cliff walls and a V-shaped gap showed a vivid blue sea to the north, sporting white crested waves. Kostas pointed, 'Look, Petros, several side tracks drop to the coast, but the main route heads towards Megalo Kastro.'

'Which is our way?'

'None. Lead your drove into the ravine; it runs along the bottom before it flattens out to cross the tract to the sea. Rodanthe and I once rode that way and passed the fork leading towards the caves. Let's go.'

Pappas Stavros walked beside the donkeys, picking their way down the boulder strewn canyon. He kept a good pace while sharing tales of his winter, ranging from high plateaus to the coast. Keen to get the facts right, Kostas asked if caves opened on more than one rock face, and seemed pleased with the negative answer. 'Excellent, so much easier to defend if we only need to keep watch in one direction. Ah, what's over there, Petros? Is it an axe?'

When Petros ran to investigate, the donkeys sought the shade of a holly oak, causing prickles to rake Kostas' brow. Crimson with anger, he yelled for help.

'It's not my fault, Kostas! Use the reins to control the beast. You sit up there trying to pretend you're not dependent on your mount. Get over it. Be an excellent rider instead of a poor walker.'

'Shut up, Petros. You're the drover, keep control.'

'H-h-hey you two. I've f-f-found a huge kazani pot for raki distillation.'

For some unfathomable reason, the group of men insisted on hauling the huge metal cauldron, taking turns to drag it along, clanging and sparking over boulders. This wasn't their only treasure. Remnants of precious village life strewn along the way proved their owners carried them until their strength failed. Sharp-eyed Kostas relaxed, enjoying hot sun on his back, and with his height advantage pointed out items others missed. Exhaustion led to abandonment of the kazani; it seemed more important to carry the smaller detritus of earlier travellers.

By the time the steep ravine walls lessened and the dry river bed ran over flatter ground, they had a good haul. Their prizes included a frying pan, a battered tin half full of olive oil, three blankets, a pair of shears and a tatty rag doll – a flash of red fabric had drawn Petros to it.

'Hey Kostas, the Limnes women must have passed this way, I found Rosi's doll.'

Crossing open ground, Kostas pointed out another ravine to the right leading uphill to the caves. After making the turn, trees along both sides of the gully arched to form a canopy. Sunlight filtered through, sending millions of rays bouncing off white stones in the riverbed to create a glinting path. In contrast to the visual beauty, a stink caused Petros to screw up his face, while Kostas fumbled for a nose rag.

Not thinking, Petros called, 'Yuck, it smells of rotting carcasses,' then clamped his mouth shut, afraid he had the answer.

'It's n-n-not f-f-far now. I think you'll f-f-find it's the s-s-stench of overcrowding.'

Petros and Kostas flashed a look at each other and cringed.

At the next bend, increasing wind brought a stronger draught of decay. Instinct packed the companions closer to the riders, all fighting nausea increased by apprehension. One hundred angry beehives couldn't generate the buzz now reaching their ears. A few more paces and a hubbub of voices rose above the bleats of twenty milk goats. They were to discover these desperate folks had eaten the rams and kids weeks ago. Now daily arguments raged; men wanted to kill another goat for food, women wanted a milk supply. A man held a goat by her collar and four women blocked his way. Shrill yells carried.

'One goat won't nourish five thousand souls crammed in this hellhole. Give her back.'

'You need us to haul firewood, bury the dead, dig for water, empty slop buckets, trap rabbits and keep watch. How can we continue with hollow stomachs?'

Another raged, 'Anything edible within a two-hour walk has gone. We need meat.'

Not answering, she grabbed a gun from her cummerbund. Argument forgotten, a united force faced the interlopers. Destined to live another day, the goat darted to join her diminishing herd. Brave Pappas Stavros pushed to the front, signing the cross and calling a blessing as the resolve of the armed party faltered. Next, Petros stepped forward, sensing his age could reduce any perceived threat.

'We're here to assist you. Our group includes skilled marksmen. I turn my hand to many tasks.'

The man who'd been determined to kill the goat hit his head with his hand, 'We don't want more mouths to feed. Go away.'

Kostas asserted his lead. 'The great Captain Kazanis sent us to join your defence, scour the countryside for food and make ammunition for your guns.'

Somewhat mollified, the man relaxed his trigger finger. A brazen woman talking to men without a kerchief to cover her braided hair pointed to the donkeys.

'Welcome, if you'll donate your beasts to the communal pot.'

Petros pulled on a rein, 'No! We can forage, hunt and labour as you will.' Although his high voice betrayed his puberty, he didn't back down, 'These animals offer legs for Kostas. Besides, we'll range further and haul more with the animals.'

To deflect dissent, Pappas Stavros waved to a skeletal man heading towards them, 'Ah, I recognise another pappas from these parts.'

A frustrated male voice yelled, 'We're doomed, he never turns a soul away. I might as well chomp on sawdust.'

Dressed in a rough knee-length shift made from discarded sacking over skinny bare, mud-splattered legs, he appeared the poorest of beggars.

'Welcome.' Without hesitation he took hold of a bridle to lead the way, 'More workers will improve our dire situation.' Their guide halted, 'Wait. Do you have water? Good. Sit on these rocks and I'll tell you what I can.'

Petros helped Kostas dismount, then rummaged for the parcel of wizened apples, cheese and rusks. Polite deference meant he served the clerics first.

'Take this gift from a Turk. I trust it won't choke you.'

'Thank you, but I ate yesterday. We try to give adults a few mouthfuls every other day.'

Pappas Stavros took the food bag from Petros, 'With those rules we're not due to eat until tomorrow. Pass this to your quartermaster.'

Faces surrounding the generous pappas registered shock, resignation, fury, disappointment and, on his fellow pappas, joy. 'Wonderful! We will get on well. Now let me explain. Our tragic group is mainly women and children from villages hereabouts. To avoid confusion, each pappas takes the name of his village. Now you're here we number eighteen. What will we call you?'

'R-r-regardless of what w-w-we decide, p-p-people will call me S-s-stuttering S-S-Stavros.'

Kostas, the only one not to laugh, asked, 'How many dwell here?'

'Well, some say five thousand, I'd half the number. Three chambers give shelter for pregnant women, but of the thirty babes delivered in the past few weeks only five live.'

With no possible answer, the newcomers shouldered their belongings to step towards the living hell.

23

Besieged

Petros once thought his stint as a bucket boy, taking water to exhausted, mutilated men during battle, had desensitised him to cries of pain and the stench of suffering. That was before he experienced this living death. Horror crowded every chamber of the honeycombed cliffs, where crushed women and children generated incredible heat, stink and chaos. Within this subhuman existence, Petros worked alongside other lads removing pail after pail of evil waste. He crawled, crouched and wriggled to reach far under the earth where screams of torment rose from deepest Hades – the maternity section. Twice yesterday his slops included premature babies, tiny hands pointing in grotesque reproach.

Once again, he passed two empty buckets fashioned from powder kegs to a bloody-handed midwife working in the soft pooling light of a single candle set on a stumpy stalagmite. Her screaming patient crouched, her weight supported by two other women. Nearby, five terrified toddlers strained against benign tethers keeping them in place.

Two older girls of eight or nine sat together, one raking her friend's hair with her fingers to make a braid.

'Papa Petros! I knew you'd come.'

In an instant, the awful truth dawned; this woman fighting to give birth was Rosi's carer.

'Follow me, you can't stay here.'

Regardless of shouts in the wake of their stumbling progress, Petros led his girl through the maze. Relieved to stand full height in the largest cave, he rubbed his aching back, happy to see Rosi at the huge opening, enjoying the breeze and knuckling stinging tears brought on by bright sunlight. After steering her from the sheer drop, they sat on the rocky ledge at the cave's entrance to chatter, as if relaxing on a village doorstep. With time to reflect, he fretted over how to keep her safe, and had decided on asking Pappas Stavros to mind her when a hand shook his shoulder.

A weary midwife handed him a grim bundle, 'God needed another angel, take this mite to the midden.'

A glance showed the girl sat mesmerised by the view across the ravine and up mountains.

'Will any of them live?'

'Each babe rests at its mama's breast until one of them dies. Oh, yes, you're horrified, but you've seen the stack of empty water barrels. By tomorrow there'll not even be enough to dab cracked lips.'

'Where did we get water?'

'At first we had plenty. When pools in the riverbed dried, men dug rough wells.' Already walking away, the midwife said, 'We need a prolonged downpour, or a miracle.'

Why was he so stupid? Each donkey could carry four kegs plus several waterskins. Although night came early in winter, he reckoned he'd manage two treks per day to Selenari, and if he set off now he'd pick up the first load today. Elated at the thought, he saddled up and checked his gun.

'Don't leave me. Let me explore with you.'

Desperate to distract the wailing child, he remembered the treasure in his pockets and produced the tatty doll and ribbons with a theatrical flourish, 'Do you know anyone to love this doll?' Squeals of delight made him laugh, 'And these green ribbons? Tame your hair, and with neat braids you'll be beautiful to welcome me.'

Coquettish now, she wound a lock around her finger, 'You'll think me pretty?'

'If I treat you to an extra cup of water to wash the grime from your face, you'll be the most gorgeous girl in Crete.'

'Shall I sit here to wait for you?'

'Find Pappas Stavros. Tell him I've gone to fetch water. Stay with him until I get back.'

*

Exhilarated by success, Petros took jaunty strides, relishing the late afternoon sunshine and clean air fragrant with sage and oregano. Even the donkeys enjoyed good spirits as they hurried along rocky ledges. On his return an hour before sunset, he allowed idle grazing while he searched under rocks for snails. Nearby he found the abandoned kazani, prompting memories of a wedding feast. Two goats had bubbled with rice for hours in a cauldron this size, before seeming to feed the entire population of villages around the Lassithi Plateau.

She'd been watching for him, and as the sentries allowed him through the barrier, Rosi dashed forward to show off her beribboned hair and demand washing water.

'Not today. Desperate people need to drink. When I've filled our barrels you can bathe your face.' Before she could answer, furious Kostas arrived shuffling on crutches.

'Sorry, Kostas, I should have explained. Our friend at Selenari has promised two billy goats tomorrow.'

Determined the lad should not placate him, Kostas made a clumsy turn to trip over Rosi, tangling his hand in her ribbons as they tumbled. His cousin's anger and the youngster's distress left Petros undecided over which to follow as one limped away and the other darted to Pappas Stavros. Certain both would yell at him, he shrugged and unloaded.

With one hand in that of the pappas and the other clutching her doll, Rosi feigned indifference to the men praising Petros for his initiative.

'T-t-thank God f-f-for your in-in-inspiration.'

'Thank you for supporting me. I'll start at first light. Meanwhile, let's put this full moon to good use. Help me retrieve the huge kazani we abandoned. Come with us, Rosi. It's not far, and women can stretch food further as broth. Ha! Two meat goats tomorrow

132

will be more welcome than my eight snails!'

*

Busy stowing empty water containers the next morning, Petros sensed movement behind him, 'I told you yesterday. You're not coming, Rosi.'

Her throaty little voice said, 'I'm Yannis.'

A flush-faced boy gripped the hand of her favourite pappas, who didn't hide his amusement at the way she'd hacked her hair and wore boy's garb.

'Pappas says I'll make you a fine companion.'

'Where's my favourite girl with the fancy hairstyle?'

Sneezes took her breath, leaving Pappas Stavros to explain she'd loaned her ribbons and rag doll to a friend.

'It's my fault. Too many stories of Rodanthe's brave exploits in disguise.'

'Take her, it will benefit you both. Let me walk a short way with you.'

Not waiting for a decision, Rosi picked up some waterskins to tie to a saddle.

'Yannis, wait, you can't journey with me. You lack proper equipment.'

Her face crumpled as her hero placed his rucksack in a cleft between boulders to delve through its contents, 'Take this silver knife to tuck in your waistband. Palikars don't venture unarmed.'

'For me?' With exaggerated care she ran her thumb over the exquisite silver filigree handle. 'It's fantastic.'

'Rodanthe's papa gave it to her mama as a betrothal gift.'

'And now it's mine?'

'Look how Yannis' big eyes shine, Pappas.'

'Well done, lad. Let's go.'

*

The air became sweeter with every step. Sat atop the jack's wooden saddle, Yannis rubbed her throat and sneezed.

'Do you hear her splutters, Pappas? This fresh air, scented with

133

winter blossoms, sun-warmed earth and breeze from the sea annoys Yannis' delicate nose.'

A natural with children, the pappas tweaked the cute nose on a filthy face.

'Our young are so adaptable. Unlike us. We realise the grimness of our condition.' To keep his companions amused, the pappas pointed out birds and flowers until beaten by the steepness of the gully, 'Time for me to turn back. Go with God.'

*

With his faced creased in amusement, the Selenari recluse shook hands when Rosi introduced herself as Yannis, 'It's a secret, but I'm not a boy.'

She might have said more had violent sneezing not taken her energy. A desperate search for a nose rag through unfamiliar clothing proved unsuccessful.

'Use my rag, child, and I'll brew us herb tea.'

By the time Petros went to say goodbye, she lay snug in the hermit's humble bed, shivering with a film of sweat across her forehead. After flashing a look of concern at the caring man, he gave her a reassuring smile. As he dropped a kiss on her burning forehead, Rosi sneezed, spraying his face. Fearful, Petros stepped backwards.

'Oh no! Bloody flux killed ten cave dwellers yesterday.'

'Don't fuss, your lass has a chill. A few days cosseting, and she'll be fine. What do you say, Yannis, my lad?'

A paroxysm of sneezing answered for her. As she quietened, the distinctive sound of whinnying horses reached them. Wide-eyed in fear, the old man clasped her to his chest, attempting to smother her next bout of spluttering.

Petros mouthed, 'Troops?'

With a nod, the hermit said, 'We'll both fare better further up the mountain, in a cave I use during wet weather.'

Fully understanding what his friend didn't say, Petros nodded, 'Take the donkeys, I'll join you when I can.'

Hidden in a rocky nook, Petros clenched his jaw, not daring a noisy breath to escape as a joint Arab and Turk platoon clustered at the spring. Horse dung disguised tell-tale donkey droppings, bringing a smirk to brighten his face. His luck held when loud shouts sent the cavalry off on horses adorned with brightly coloured quilts and heavy leather breastplates. Riders, resplendent in fine costumes, guided their mounts with ease. Infantry followed, weighed down by bulging rucksacks, rifles and full bandoliers. At the rear, two officers sporting scarlet-plumed helmets chivvied an artillery section struggling to move cannon carriages. Those heaving to turn wheels grunted and shoved until momentum moved the weight to crunch through loose gravel, sending sparks as axles hit larger stones.

Petros leant forward, praying the force turned towards Megalo Kastro, their major stronghold. Instead, they took the minor track towards Milatos, and the moment the last artilleryman passed from sight, he bolted.

*

When two sentries yelled at him, demanding the password or they'd shoot, he kept sprinting. Ragged breaths burning his lungs prevented his answer. He collapsed, blowing hard, and a guard knelt to give support.

'Deep breaths. And again. That's it, now what's the rush?'

It took Petros several attempts to get out coherent words to send both guards speeding towards the cave complex, yelling, 'Turks head our way.'

*

Hand over hand, Petros hauled himself upwards. Hampered by his lame foot, Kostas struggled on a second rope. At each outcrop and rocky indentation, Petros halted, ready to aid Kostas. After weeks of praying for rain to replenish water supplies, it seemed ironic that they started their climb in a chill, grey drizzle. Now hammering rain pelted them and they felt sure it caused equal delay to the approaching enemy. Hit by a constant shower of loose stones,

Petros clamped his mouth against squeals of pain to concentrate on his climb.

Both climbers had reached the safety of a small overhang, when an avalanche of shale swept down.

'Don't look at the ground, Petros.'

Without waiting or testing that the rope remained secure, Kostas resumed his laborious challenge. Even though cold rain drenched him to the skin, Petros felt sweat running down his back. He'd long since given up wiping the stinging rain from his eyes, and now prayed his blistered, bloody hands could keep grip.

At last they reached the sniper's eyrie, littered with spent shot, waterskins, spyglasses and a basket of shrivelled apples. As Kostas and Petros slumped in the muddy hollow, the two current occupants stood, massaged their aching legs and prepared to descend.

One of them said, 'I wonder if either of you should be here; a lad and a cripple.'

Even though the barb stung Kostas, he hadn't enough breath to respond. With a light touch on the man's arm, Petros said, 'Best not pass comment on what you don't know. There's no finer shot for a sniper's lair. Go below to those who'll appreciate your strength. Take care, there have been many rockfalls.'

With an attempt at bravado, Kostas shrugged off his drenched rucksack.

'With due modesty I'll say I'm the best shot in Crete. I've no need of legs up here. Go with them, Petros.'

'No, I'll stay with you. I'm a fair shot.'

As if he'd not heard, Kostas continued speaking to the man about to disappear over the ledge, 'When you reach the bottom, tie on the basket I left at the base. I'll haul it aloft to make a good stock of shot. Take the lad down with you. Once the basket reaches me, I'll cut one line free. Men are piling mattresses against the rock face to absorb the shock of cannonballs. They'll be glad of this rope.'

'I don't want to leave you alone.'

Kostas already had a gun out, checking its sight, 'Do as I ask, Petros. Climb back to help me once this is over.'

Unable to think of an alternative, Petros helped a departing man to wrap the line around his waist to aid his descent.

'Listen lad, there's a way you can add more value. Take the goat track rising behind those shrubs. Follow the escarpment east. You'll see Neapoli and Choumeriakos down on your right, then drop to the plain and head for Limnes. My guess is men will regroup there. Tell them our plight.'

Petros knew Kostas would stop him, so he shouted his goodbye from the ledge to make it seem like he'd descended, then doubled back up the track to the summit.

24

Brother Kazanis

Three days later, Kazanis paused on the hillside to survey the rustic scene, a lifestyle unaltered for centuries. Almond blossom buds thickened on songbird-filled trees, and two lowing oxen led by a monk tilled a strip of thin, stony earth followed by cawing crows. He inhaled a lungful of sweet, fresh air and spoke without realising, 'This life's worth defending.' Early sun streamed along the valley to reflect off the lakes, drawing his attention down to Limnes. A hard gulp hit his throat as his gaze turned left to Choumeriakos. Further along, the dominant landmark of the mosque's dome no longer troubled the skyline of Neapoli. Sickened by the memory of Hannis and the blaze, he lifted his head to look beyond where the mountains became hills to block the north-western view. He knew Petros had used the rocky pass at Selenari to access the ravine towards the Milatos caves, and presuming his boy rested out of harm's way brought relief.

In this brief pause, Kazanis decided against climbing to Lassithi Plateau; any attack there had already put folk beyond his help. If Turk artillery had heaved their cannon to Neapoli forge for repair, he reckoned on nearby rebels plotting to wreak havoc. Determined to rejoin the fray, he straightened the skirt of his uncomfortable habit over his own knee-high boots, punched the air, and with a still croaky voice proclaimed, 'Freedom or death.'

*

Invisibility was a new experience for Kazanis as he passed among Turk villagers about Neapoli market; their worries were scant supplies, not a hooded monk. He guessed soldiers and clerics toiled in gruesome wreckage on the other side of town, trying to work out what caused the catastrophic fire. Today, traditional religious tolerance between ordinary folk who'd grown up in mixed communities served Kazanis well. Unchallenged, he walked the dusty track leading to a forge set alongside a strong winter stream, where the compound gates stood wide open. Deep ruts gouged through the road gave evidence the cannon and associated troops had long gone.

At a loss as to his next move, Kazanis went to an ornate Venetian fountain spilling water through tiered marble troughs. As he bent to sup, he heard, 'Keep drinking, Brother.'

His head jerked.

'Please drink. Touch your hood as a sign you hear.'

Not turning strained his will. As directed he made a swift movement, then held a drinking pot chained to the font while feigning a sip and taking a sideways glance at a veiled woman filling a series of water jars.

'My husband insisted we bow down as Muslims to keep our home and feed the children.'

Kazanis started to turn.

'Don't engage with me.'

With effort he resumed his task, refilling the overflowing cup.

'Brother, can you take a message to the rebel leaders? Troops head for Milatos caves. The huge number of refugees embarrasses our new Egyptian leader, Hassan Pasha. He sent his trusted lieutenant with a strong army to flush them out.'

The ancient vessel in Kazanis' grasp shattered – he didn't flinch. 'What news of the Egyptian himself?'

'The bulk of his force went to a place called Kastelli. He's moving them to meet troops descending from Lassithi, before turning south to the fertile plains.'

Drops of bright blood swirled in the water. 'How do you know?'

'I'm married to the smith following the army.'

'Why should I trust you?'

Already walking away, she said, 'My Christian sister and nieces shelter in Milatos.'

*

Slumped beside the fountain, Kazanis realised no trace of conflict at the forge meant the rebels either came too late or had news to divert them. To help think through what to do, he scratched a rough map in the dirt, estimating when the cannon might reach the caves and pondering his comrades' location. Next, he drew in the peaks, convinced there was only one route for the Turks to descend on the far side if they intended to join the major route south.

'She's right, the flat lands of Kastelli are an excellent meeting place.'

As he stepped his fingers along an imaginary trail, he figured his fellow captains had formed the same conclusion and taken the two-day trek around the mountain. There wasn't time to find them and urge them back to Milatos. In frustration, he kicked his sketch to oblivion. A black cloud moved in front of the sun. In the sudden chill, a dreadful realisation struck him, along with the first rain drops – he'd sent Petros to peril.

*

Long before Kazanis reached the tree-clad hills of the caverns, the ground trembled beneath his feet, each dull boom signalling a tremor a few seconds later. Rain fell in slanting sheets, blurring his glimpse of the distant caves, and the lee of the steep hill blocked sight of the cannon. Hampered by slow-healing hands, Kazanis struggled to open his rucksack to rummage for the spyglasses. A protruding rock acted as a rest to train his sight on the cave openings, where he nodded approval to see mattresses and bedding piled around to absorb cannon shot and debris. As rain rendered his spyglasses useless, he stowed them and wiped rain from his sore face, then ran, forcing through undergrowth for a better view. A disgusting miasma brought stinging tears to mix with the rain. Nauseated, Kazanis coughed, overcome by a stench from the catacombs.

'To what hell did I send you, Petros?'

Fuelled by rage he charged through dense foliage, heedless of tugs to skin and cassock, until an abrupt sheer drop halted him. Defeated, he slumped at the edge of the chasm; he'd chosen the wrong route. Helpless in the face of calamity, fatigue hit hard. Even if he descended to tackle the hated force, he'd be like a flea on a dog – after causing momentary irritation, they'd crush him. Rain didn't dampen the assault. A puff of smoke rose from a hidden cannon. When the boom sounded, its echo bounced long after the impact shook the rock edifice. Within moments tumbling rocks obliterated one cave entrance. Desperate for a glimpse of life, Kazanis fumbled for his spyglass. In a flash of dreadful certainty, Kazanis realised the commander of the hated force had no need to press their attack. Periodic blasts could hold the poor wretches besieged for days – or weeks.

Adrenaline spent, he trudged uphill, hoping to locate the course he needed. When he found the correct fork, he hit his forehead, rebuking himself for missing such an obvious turn, 'Oh, great Kazanis, how did you miss this?' He pointed uphill towards Selenari, 'Even a child walking from the spring would have— oh, visitors. Friend or foe?'

Glasses focused on the small force, he sighed in relief, realising their lack of uniforms and sparse arms proclaimed them Christians. To gain attention, he laid two rifles to form a cross in the path. The descending captain raised his arm to halt his men and cocked his rifle. On hearing the resonating click, Kazanis stepped forward, hands high.

'State your business, Brother.'

'Despite my garb, I'm no monk. You're speaking to Captain Kazanis of Lassithi.' He extended a bandaged fist, 'I'm recovering from burns, but keen to return to the fight.' He winced despite the gentleness of the handshake, 'I head to Milatos. Turks besiege a multitude.'

'Ah, we're heading there.'

'You know the place?'

'No, we rested by the lakes. A lad hurried to rally our men. He said he'd spied on a group of Turks at Selenari Springs and overheard their plans to empty the caves at Milatos.'

'Which one? Let me question him.'

'He's ill. Disappointment at finding so few of us sent his temperature soaring to a fever. In fact, he's probably still sleeping. We'll fall in behind you.'

'Good, I intended to race in alone. It makes more sense in a group. Hurry now, we'll take their rearguard by surprise.'

Fortified by improved prospects, Kazanis turned on his heels.

25

Massacre

Kazanis feigned death under a crush of bodies. His brain throbbed to remind him how he'd used his forehead to smash a Turk's nose. With cautious movement in the ominous silence, he rose. Crushed helmets, boots, clothing, weapons and bodies littered the rutted track. He shook his head to clear a red fuzz from his vision. Two dogs scampered nearby. They stopped to squabble over a dismembered arm until one raced off with his prize. Still knuckling his eyes, he watched the dogs chase uphill. Now the silence made sense; he alone survived. Without a thought for the men who'd fought with him, he set off to find Petros.

*

Nothing he'd faced before prepared him for this horror. Stomach churning, he kicked at hooded crows feeding on a grotesque heap of babies and boys, tossed as vermin beneath the remains of three crucified men. When he screamed, 'God, you're sick!' the birds hopped to feast on the next heap. In anguish, he wondered if he should try to deal with the massacre or leave nature to take its course. A bird settled on a babe still trailing its umbilical cord. At Kazanis' shot, a cawing mass flew to settle on the cliff top. In the relative quiet he heard a feeble sound.

'H-h-help.' It took a few heartbeats for him to realise the cruelly staked men were clergy.

Kazanis shoved the flimsy structure, cursing how recent trials had reduced his bulk. Encouraged by splintering he braced to heave, and with a primeval scream lunged again, not flinching as spars tumbled around him.

Of the three clerics tipped on the cushioning mass of death

below, only Pappas Stavros lived to bear witness. Kazanis supported his cousin's torso with one arm while reaching to free his waterskin. Pappas Stavros pawed the air, his need for water greater than the pain from three severed fingers. Kazanis swung his head to glance at the other clerics; only bloody stumps remained of the fingers used when signing their cross.

'Drink your fill.'

Without interrupting the dying man's laboured stutters, Kazanis learnt how the brutes had raped women and girls, killed many and led the younger ones away, bound as slaves. After a pause, Pappas Stavros managed to describe how the besiegers had set a fire inside the cave entrance to smoke people out. Later, they stoked the flames as a pyre.

'T-t-tell people to k-k-keep some remains in t-t-there and s-s-sanctify the place. W-w-without evidence f-f-folk will be like S-s-saint T-T-Thomas and not b-b-believe without s-s-seeing.'

After gulping more water, Pappas Stavros assured his cousin the thirty men defending the refugees fought as heroes to the end. Exhausted, the tortured man paused. On hearing ominous rattling breaths, Kazanis steeled himself for the answer he dreaded.

'Cousin, what of my Petros?'

'G-g-gone ...'

Kazanis closed the dead man's eyes, wanting to believe that if he lived, albeit for a short time, others might be alive too. Against all odds, he searched for Petros pulling bodies from pile after macabre pile, careless of where they fell. At the mouth of the major cave, charred remains formed a grim barrier. Many of the women had died in a crush, attempting to flee smoke. At first, he didn't comprehend the grey blanket covering a woman; then, sickened by the plague of feasting rats, he reeled away.

Down the slope, he found the most defensible spot and realised it more probable for Petros to have been here. Kazanis tore through the devastation until he slumped against a boulder, exhausted. When his breathing eased, he saw a familiar woollen rucksack in a

144

rock cleft.

Heedless of tears he stroked the distinctive design, crafted by his wife in happier times. When his sobs eased, he fumbled with the drawstring, then slit it open to reveal his boy's treasure. He tossed away a precious pack of cards, oblivious of them scattering, incongruous with the devastation. A sheepskin cap band held a miniature goat horn-handled knife, the first he'd made for his son. Faced with irrevocable evidence, Kazanis rocked back and forth, the precious rucksack clutched to his hurting chest.

'I failed to keep you from harm.'

Aghast, Kazanis stared at his burnt hand. An eye for an eye, tooth for tooth, hand for hand, foot for foot, burn for burn ... he punched his head. Could this slaughter be retribution for his calumny against worshippers in the burnt mosque?

'Oh Petros, forgive me.'

When rocks tumbled, bouncing close, instinct sped him under cover. At another flurry of stones, he shouted, 'Show yourself. Hold your weapon high.' In answer, a watermelon-sized rock kept him squatting under the burnt skeleton of a single tree while scrutinising the cannon-ravaged cliffs. Was that a slight movement, up high near the ridge? Now sight of bright blue cloth waving from a length of stick galvanised him.

His hands lacked elasticity, causing splits and tears as he grabbed protruding rocks to scale the precarious cliff. One point threatened to beat him, until he wedged the hook of his crook over a protrusion and trusted it to carry his weight as he hauled himself up. At last he crouched on a narrow ridge, grateful for the opportunity to catch his breath. Dark shadows passed overhead. This, coupled with the indignant cawing from the multitude of crows below, meant one thing. A macabre image of griffon vultures feasting on Petros delivered stabbing pains deep in his guts. He spewed. Grateful for a physical reaction to his grief and revulsion, he didn't bother to wipe his mouth as he reset his sight on the fluttering pennant.

A mess of broken rock and shrubs rendered movement treacherous. Kazanis lost his footing to send loose rocks clattering. With every sinew taut, he grabbed a protruding ledge caused by cannon shot. His foothold crumbled, almost jolting his arm from its socket. Still clinging, he sought a toehold, causing one disturbance too many. The rock ledge above Kazanis sheared off, bounced right over him and dislodged an avalanche of rocks from on high. Dazed, bruised and bleeding, he thought he heard a scream.

Not one to trust angels, Kazanis later conceded there could be no other explanation for the success of his crab-like movements in getting him to the sniper's hide. An emaciated body lay at an odd angle against the wall of the cavity, with a mound of rocks where his legs should be. The trapped man must have sensed someone was nearby, as he tried to reach the rifle settled in a cleft where a piece of tattered blue waistcoat acted as a rough flag.

'Kostas?'

'Panagia Mou. I need to die.'

Frenzied, Kazanis sent rubble in all directions until Kostas dragged his legs free.

Cracked and bleeding lips whispered, 'Thank you, Brother'.

'It's me, Kazanis.'

'Who ...? Where's your beard? Why wear monk's rags?'

'Never mind that now. Take my waterskin, you need it.'

Three gulps finished the water.

'No water for days makes a slow death. I even lacked strength to hang myself over the edge with this rope.'

Busy undoing the knot under Kostas' chin, Kazanis didn't look up when he heard, 'I should have kept a last shot for my head. Pass me one of yours.'

It took deep breaths before Kazanis dared to speak, 'I'm pleased the cliff face is disintegrating, it means I can't get you down. I've no wish to see the bloodbath again.'

'Their screams remain etched in my brain.'

'You'll give testament to their sacrifice. They slaughtered babes and crones. I guess they took women and captured men to God knows what fate.'

'From this height I saw them lead young women and girls away. Those heathens tied them together with their braids ...'

A spasm of coughing left Kostas whispering his confession, 'May God forgive me, I used a shot against Rosi. Her green ribbons bouncing in the distance wiped out sensible thought, she'd already passed out of my range. At least the poor child still carried her rag doll. Do any live?'

'No, it's carnage. Although sadistically maimed, Stavros lived to tell me I've lost Petros.'

Unable to form a response, Kostas closed his eyes and fell back. In despair, Kazanis accepted the inevitable: they'd succumb to cold and hunger together. Hours later a vulture landed on their ledge and they lashed out against its indignant flurry of wings. It seemed the flash of energy gave Kazanis heart. He peered up, weighing the chances of ascent.

'There's a rough path to the top. Hold my crook and I'll tie you to my back.'

26

Moving On

At Selenari, Petros gulped from the bubbling spring, relishing how the icy water numbed his sore throat. A distant donkey bray reached him.

'Poor beasts, now I feel sorry for you chewing on thistles.'

Two days' hiking with a high fever and little rest had taken him beyond exhaustion.

Elation at reaching the crest above the sniper's eyrie delivered a short-lived spurt of energy to hurry him eastward along a ridge of hills. Energy drained, he slipped more than scrambled down steep slopes towards the lakes. By the time he arrived, burning with fever, he found it difficult to lift one foot in front of the other, and his disappointment at finding so few men encamped hit hard. Between fierce sneezes that threatened to tear his chest, he described the plight of those in Milatos. When the incensed men shouldered arms, Petros wanted to join them.

'Not in your state, lad. Besides, you'll do more harm than good if you pass on your illness. God bless you for alerting us.' He searched through a stuffed rucksack, 'Here, it's only a thin, holed blanket. Rest and live to fight another day.'

*

After a brief sleep, Petros set off for the hermitage with dogged determination. When a chill wind threatened to bowl him over he leaned against the sheer wall of the narrow path, where despite his shivers he mopped sweat from his forehead. With aching limbs crying out for rest, he pushed onward, knowing he couldn't steal up on anyone as splutters broadcast his progress.

At the top of the track a fallen tree formed an irresistible seat. A loud 'achoo' attracted his attention and he headed through the trees, holding his nose to delay his own next explosive sneeze. Petros discovered the hermit huddled under a sheepskin in a cave's entrance. Nose streaming, the old man pointed at the sleeping girl and mimed she'd passed the worst. After another loud sneeze, the girl's carer curled up in a space behind his charge and settled to sleep.

Although Petros longed to rest, he overcame hot shivers to light a fire to make a tin pot of tea with herbs from the hermit's store. Without realising, he turned the tinderbox over in his hands. Since mislaying his rucksack he'd worried how to obtain another. He shrugged and replaced the box near the rocky hearth. His movements roused Rosi.

'I knew you'd find me. I'm ravenous.'

'It's a sign you're on the mend. Doze and I'll scavenge.'

Aromatic herbs boiled with a few greens made a weak broth. Warmed by the scant meal the pair drowsed, relishing the afternoon sun on their backs, until the damp of a grey cloud blanketing the mountain sent them to shelter. Rosi snored, the sick man coughed and sneezed without pause, the donkeys brayed and Petros slept.

Waking, he saw fear in her eyes. She smiled and washed his brow with a cool, wet cloth.

'I've made sage tea. Can you skin a hare?'

Tea soothed his raw throat as her words registered, 'What hare?'

'The nice man who looked after me trapped two the day you left. He cooked one and left this hanging in a tree.'

'Ask him to help you.'

'His breathing made rattling noises, and now he's asleep.'

'I'll do it, I'd like to taste your stew.'

Sneezes sapped his energy and made his dizzy head spin while he prepared the hare, with frequent stops to wipe his sore nose along his sleeve.

'Here's the meat, Rosi. You cook while I wrap up in my cloak next to the hermit.'

On the verge of sleep, he felt a kiss on his hot cheek.

*

Slanted fingers of bright morning light woke Petros to a savoury aroma.

'Rosi, I need food.'

'You two are horrible, I ate alone last night. You're lucky there's lots left, it's warming.'

'Give me a few minutes to stretch my legs.'

A fast-rising sun brought welcome heat as he sat against rocks.

'Did you take stew to our host?'

'No, he sleeps even more than you, his portion will keep for later.'

A meal and a mild February morning allowed pleasant rest. A gliding vulture cast a shadow to jolt Petros, sending him into the cave to reappear with a bundle of blankets.

'Here, stow these in a pannier.' The moment she'd turned her back, he lifted the hermit's precious tinderbox to stuff in a deep pocket.

Back at the pot, Rosi asked, 'Does he want stew?'

'Err, no ... no, he's not hungry. Hurry, I've told him we're going on an adventure.'

Intoxicated by the heady scent drifting from a canopy of almond blossom and sun-warmed oranges, Petros' spirits soared as they rode the westward track. Rosi lobbed an orange.

'This is how my hands smell in olive picking season. Fruit trees grow between Grandpa's olives, and we peeled oranges as a treat every time we filled three olive sacks.'

'Lassithi is too cool for citrus fruit. Let's fill spaces in our baskets with oranges.'

With panniers full and bellies satisfied by the glut of juicy fruits, oranges became missiles thrown at crows, rocks, and each other. When their laughter echoed Petros fell silent, staring across the sweep and on out to sea. Guilt absorbed him; he wished he'd joined the group heading to relieve those in peril. Lost in his nightmare,

Rosi had to tell him twice about two men ahead.

'Thanks, my gazed lingered in the wrong direction.'

Both men sat, exhausted from catastrophic injuries. They licked their lips, 'Water?'

One had lost an eye and an arm; both had gunshots to their chests. Rosi dispensed fruit and dabbed wounds with a rag. With the blunt honesty of a child, she said, 'Are you trying to get home to die?'

'Yes, lass, I want to kiss my wife.'

The older man recognised Petros.

'You spoke to our captain at Limnes. Thanks to your tip-off we fought at Milatos.' He shook his head, 'We tried to reach them from the rear.'

Petros went for blankets to cloak the men, 'Did you see my pa, Captain Kazanis?'

'Your pa? What a fighter.'

From the pannier Petros said, 'Where did the survivors go?'

'Sorry, there were no others. May his memory be eternal.'

He spoke to the nuzzling jack, 'Dead? Should I have sensed something? Impossible.' His thoughts flashed to the Kritsa battlefield, remembering how he'd lost count of the dead. Yes, it was possible. After rubbing his eyes, he returned to hand over blankets, keeping his face averted, 'Here, you'll need these.'

Neither man commented on his distress.

'Come, Rosi. I must update my other godfather, Zacharias.'

From the jack's saddle, Rosi looked at the injured men, 'Can we give them a donkey?'

'Good idea, it might mean survival. I'll help them mount the jenny.'

*

First stars of the evening winked their approval as Kazanis heaved his crushing load over the ridge. He cut Kostas free, then rolled away, struggling to force air into his burning lungs.

'You're heavy for a starving man.'

151

Kostas curled in a shivering huddle. While rubbing arms and legs to ease their aching, Kazanis realised a few dwellings in the hamlet of Sisi on the coast offered their best chance.

Countless falls later, Kazanis stumbled, and unable to take another step, he fainted. Kostas reached over to shake him.

'Look there. Let's crawl.'

A circular shepherd's hut stuffed with stinking fleeces provided a miracle. Near dawn, a noise woke Kazanis. He shoved away the warm pile covering him and listened, hand on a blade. The noise came again.

'My stomach growls, we must eat.'

Shepherds often left supplies in their huts, never knowing when dire need might arise. This hut's clutter included milking pails, a cauldron for making cheese, one full tinderbox, a heap of kindling, three logs, a cask of brackish water and a chipped oil lamp without a wick. Kazanis ignored all this and went to the mound of rocks at the back of the hut, sure they covered the traditional coolhole used for storing cheese. He tore the rocks off the wooden lid and groped around the space below, swearing as clumps of thorny bushes, kept inside the dark space to deter mice, pricked him. While ruing the lack of cheese and sucking drops of blood off his fingertips, he realised the dry, thorny brush would burn well, and soon had a blaze in the small hearth set outside the doorless opening of the stone shelter. Once he'd set water to boil, Kazanis scratched around for something to cook. Within a few paces he found eight snails and a mix of edible greens. Back at the shelter, he noticed the goatskin wrapped around Kostas had a clump of dried flesh on its edge the size of a fist. A sheen of sweat covered his cousin's face, even though he shivered. This was no time for niceties; a quick flash of a knife sent the dried meat splashing in the pail. After a brief walk, he added thyme and oregano to the mix.

'You're trying, cousin, but no herbs will make it palatable.'

'Ha, I'll be thankful if it fuels us to the next settlement.'

Renowned for bullish ways, Kazanis dithered. Should he leave

152

the frail man sheltered while he searched for food, or haul him through the countryside until they both died? He watched Kostas shiver and reached a decision.

*

The downhill walk, half a day for a fit person, took two days of stumbling falls for Kazanis to haul Kostas over uneven ground. On reaching the tiny port of Sisi they collapsed on some heaped fishing nets. Once rested, they found the place deserted except for three hens scratching in a vegetable patch, one of whom proved too inquisitive. After Kazanis moved oddments strewn from ransacked homes to the most robust dwelling, he made sure they enjoyed a warm and comfortable night, sustained by roast chicken, potatoes, cabbage and oranges. Later, Kostas cleaned their guns and made more shot from a satchel of cartridge paper and black powder found under a bed.

After a day of recuperation, Kazanis rummaged in abandoned kitchens hoping for raki. Although unsuccessful, he discovered clothing to replace his rags and now wore a hooded cloak to keep out the most severe weather. Kostas was brighter and remarked how his numb foot was easier to bear than the constant pain. He'd fashioned a pair of crutches and padded the armpit supports with linen scraps.

Now he grinned as he stomped, 'These are great. Race you to the boat.'

'The boat?'

'Yes, there's a craft tied at the wharf. I can't walk any distance.'

'Neither of us has set foot on a boat. Poseidon, bad-tempered god of the sea, will claim us in minutes. Let's sleep and decide in the morning.'

*

On waking, Kazanis donned bandolier, guns and knives before he bent through the arch to the storeroom where Kostas rested.

'I'm not asleep.'

'Don't leave your bed. It's bleak out there. A cloud of steam rose from my piss.'

'Time to leave?'

'Stay warm. Build your strength.'

'It makes sense. I'll tend the two hens to live off eggs. Where will you head?'

'Ah, there's the rope. I'll gift it to Zacharias at the homestead.' Choked with emotion, he concentrated on winding the line around his waist, 'My boy spent more time with Zacharias than anyone. He'll be heartbroken.' Kazanis cleared his throat, 'First, I'll head around the mountain to Kastelli Plain. It's where Hassan Pasha went to meet his troops descending from Lassithi, and I'm hoping our force won't be far away.'

'Hey, don't forget your crook. God speed your feet and strengthen your arm.'

27

Revenge

Near noon the next day, Kazanis slurped a long draught from a gushing spring as it rushed to its lush green course, ignoring the water drenching his boots. Habit sent his hand to wring his beard.

'Pah, my Petros had more fluff on his chin.'

With light, tentative movements he felt his face. Satisfied with regrowth along one jaw, he spoke to his vanity, 'It will regrow. Now, where are my spyglasses? Strange no other captains have mustered here, it's an excellent vantage spot.'

He panned from side to side. A galloping rider charged far ahead of a dozen followers. When trees on the uphill path swallowed the rider, Kazanis turned his glasses to focus on the brow of a hill, where he glimpsed a flash of white. He guessed the Turk rode a known circular route, with no intention of stopping before Kastelli.

Furious the enemy should enjoy leisure, he sped downhill. Untroubled by paths, he sprang over boulders, ignored barbs from tangled shrubs and leapt streaming runnels. Guns and blades jiggled and clanged to flush out hare and partridges.

*

Shocked and splayed, he spat mud from his mouth and shook his head, trying to fathom what had felled him. Glad no one had seen his fall, he knelt to free the trailing rope from his ankle, then whooped as inspiration struck. After gathering the length he sprinted downhill to a track.

His fingers fumbled to fasten the rope to a tree. When hoofbeats told him there was no time for a second set of knots, he ran across the path, pulling the line taut. With the strong cord wrapped around his waist, he hid behind a tree, leant against it and braced.

Jerked as if cut in two, Kazanis' pain-filled bellow became a jubilant cry as the terrified horse catapulted its rider. Screams from the somersaulting man ended abruptly, leaving frightened neighs resounding through the trees.

Used to men, the stallion didn't baulk at Kazanis' cautious approach accompanied by steady chatter.

'Lucky a studded leather breastplate covers your quilt. Are you wounded? Let me see.'

Relieved to see its heaving flanks steady, Kazanis rubbed the horse's withers.

'Well, you're a splendid beast. Stand still. That's it.' As they both gained confidence, Kazanis stroked the stallion with a gentle rhythmic motion, 'You're worth a fortune. Shame I can't take you.'

Rewarded by a head dip and turn, Kazanis moved his palm.

'Ah, you like your nose smoothed. Well, it's a fine one. Mind my foot. Where are you going?'

After a couple of paces, the horse sniffed the crumpled corpse then snickered as if talking. Kazanis used the distraction to remove a weighty sabre from its ornate saddle scabbard. He lunged and parried an imaginary foe.

'Step aside, handsome. Good idea: crop grass.'

Kazanis' booted toe turned the bare-headed man. No blood oozed. He relieved the body of its rifle and was admiring the gun's silver-inlaid stock when flapping material, caught in a bush, intrigued him. He lifted an ornate steel-capped turban and reeled in the length of white silk, issuing a shrill whistle through his teeth, 'The Egyptian malaca Hassan Pasha wore such a helmet.'

In his mind's eye he saw the cavalry ranged against Christian forces at Kritsa. Despite the flowing silk distinguishing the wearer in the mêlée, no rebel had shot him.

'I pray I have the pleasure of addressing Hassan Pasha.'

Before his glob of spit hit the corpse, a shudder of realisation drenched his back in a cold sweat and he dropped the helmet as if it were aflame.

'I'll not make you a victim of robbery to bring retribution to poor wretches.'

With a stab of disappointment, he replaced the sabre and fine gun.

'Come here, my beauty. Time to go home.'

A hefty slap to the horse's rump sent it galloping along the track. There was no point going on towards Kastelli; he couldn't risk an encounter with the pasha's men. With no better plan, he trekked towards Lassithi, each step a reminder of his bereavement.

Part 3

Worlds Apart

28

Diverging Paths

Petros pointed across the ravine, 'See that round cap of rock? It's such a distinctive landmark, I know we're on the right track.'

'I'm tired. Can we stop soon?'

'Further on up here we'll find a church where we can spend the night.'

He noticed the child didn't look impressed, so added, 'I bet I'll be the first to see it.'

It had the desired effect. Rosi sat taller in her saddle, determined to shout out she'd seen the church before him.

Tough as the path was, the donkey trudged on, not even flinching when Rosi's high-pitched shriek rang out, 'I'm first! Look, I can see a white cross. It must be on top of the church. Lift me off, I can run up from here.'

'Well spotted, Rosi. Hey, don't dash too far ahead.'

By the time Petros reached the church, Rosi stood with her hands on her hips in the doorway.

'It's all broken and dirty inside.'

Frustrated and worried, Petros ducked inside.

'Yuck. It's horrible. Well, I can't think of anywhere else, and there's enough roof left to give us some shelter.'

Busy kicking rubble to make a clear patch on the floor, Petros swung around when Rosi said, 'Ugh, why would anyone leave a long plait of hair here in the church?'

In the few paces it took Petros to reach the dilapidated iconostasis where the braid hung, his brain whirred.

'I wonder if Rodanthe came this way. As daughter of a pappas she may have thought it fitting to leave her hair as a tribute.'

Later, when Petros was on the edge of sleep, he regretted

mentioning Rodanthe in connection with the church.

'Do you believe in angels, Petros?'

'Archangel Gabriel?'

'No, people who die then help us.'

At first, he thought the frescoes of Christ and his angels disturbed the child.

'Sorry, you're frightened.'

'Rodanthe doesn't scare me.'

He feigned sleep.

'Did my cousin have short hair and a kind voice?'

Caught by surprise, he answered, 'Well, yes she did.'

'That proves it. When I was ill, Rodanthe visited me. I saw her angel face, and she bid me to be brave. I was too young to know her, but Grandpa said we looked similar. Now it makes me feel warm inside to think she was here before us.'

'I expect—' He swallowed, not wanting to tease her for confusing the hermit's voice. A mention of the kindly soul might bring difficult questions – he'd died before they left him.

Unaware of his pause, she continued, 'Rodanthe says she'll always watch me.'

'Let's pray she helps you sleep. It's a stiff trek to Marmaketo, my village.'

*

Kazanis, loud, brash and bullish, perched on a jutting rock sculpted by centuries of weather to form a prominent head. Here, on the edge of his domain, he gazed across a ravine, knuckled his eyes and shook his head. For a moment, he imagined people stood near a ruined church on the far side of the wide chasm. No, even before he searched for his glasses he realised wishful thinking mixed with hunger had tricked him. With eyes closed, he lifted his face to the light pine-scented breeze and late February sunshine, relishing the morning's peace broken only by cawing crows. Subdued, defeated and bereft, Kazanis wept.

Calm and resolute, he stepped the two paces to the precipice, not daring a backward glance towards home. Although the shale-lined chasm below looked impassable, he knew different. Many a time he'd led his men whooping and hollering downhill on the safe track, exhilarated by speed and their echoing refrain. On his mountain, he'd feared no man. A crow flew by, urging him to hurry. Eyes screwed shut against the grey pit of oblivion, he raised a foot.

*

Seated on her wooden saddle, Rosi swayed in rhythm with the jack's footsteps until the steep zigzag path became loose and narrow, causing the beast to falter. Ahead of her, Petros slithered down a steep length before regaining his foothold.

'Dismount, Rosi, and walk from here. Let our jack make his own way up behind us in case he slips. No chattering, you'll need your breath.'

In a lee of the cliff he waited for her to catch up, impressed with her determination.

'Do you see the large head-shaped rock at the top? Pa told me it was Great-Grandpa Kazanis, King of the Mountain.'

Tired and hungry, she hadn't spare energy to look.

*

Winded, flat on his back and confused, Kazanis clutched his throat.

'Sorry! I dragged you back with this crook. Better a torn hood and a bruised neck than a fall. Give me your hand.'

Each man recognised the other's fear. Uncertain, they stared until a crow's caw broke their reserve.

'Kazanis!'

'Zacharias!'

In the older man's close embrace, Kazanis felt safe, 'Thank you, my friend. I stood nearer the rim than I intended. Why are you here?'

'You piqued my curiosity near Marmaketo. I watched you start the path towards me and was surprised when you turned back. What was in your mind?'

'I'd made the turning for home when I realised I didn't deserve such comfort.'

Zacharias stood on tiptoe to hug Kazanis, 'Don't be ridiculous. Whatever ails you, a few nights at home will sort you out. Come, we'll walk together.'

'How did you know it was me? My bulk has halved since we last met.' Kazanis scratched his bare chin, 'And, I'm hairless as a lad from standing beside a burning mosque – the best sort.'

'Ah, I recognised your gait, and was sure when you dropped your crook by the spring. Your distinctive carving on the handle gave you away. I couldn't shout, I needed my breath to climb after you.'

'Do you have raki?'

'Your place is too high to bother marauding Turks. Thirty people have taken refuge there. Don't worry, your raki is under a barn floor.'

'What a wise decision I made appointing you overseer.'

Arm in arm, they headed down while Kazanis brought Zacharias up to date with dreadful news.

*

Disappointment showed on Rosi's face. After struggling up such a steep path, she'd expected more than a patch of scrub with the skeletal remains of a single walnut tree, even though she'd enjoyed the gushing spring.

'Did a Turk burn this tree, Petros?'

'No, it was a lightning strike. You should have seen it years ago. A thick gnarled trunk with ridges acting as a stand for long guns. Pa always lolled in its shade with his palikars, all guffawing as they drank raki, plotted and schemed.'

When his sigh gave way to tears, Rosi had enough tact to refill their waterskins. On her return, he was crouching.

'What are you doing?'

'I'm planting a walnut. See, it's already growing.'

'You're still crying.'

'When the tree is big enough, I'll ask Zacharias to cut Pa's name on its trunk. He's an accomplished carver.' He dabbed his wet cheeks, chuckling at a sudden memory, 'I almost killed Pa when I lobbed a stone at ripening walnuts. I missed the nuts and hit his head.' He gave his backside a subconscious pat at the memory of a thrashing, 'Such a long time ago. Give me a moment to water this before we leave.'

*

Like anyone first glimpsing the plateau, with its winter lake shimmering in early morning sun under a ring of snow-topped mountains, Rosi stared in awe. The same view filled Petros with heartache; several smokeless chimneys gave poignant evidence of emptiness. An established track allowed fast descent until they turned to trudge through the rubble of lower Marmaketo.

'Is your house up there?'

When he didn't answer, she took his hand to lead him forward. Outside a trashed building, fronted by huge overturned pots of pink geraniums, Petros groaned, doubled over, retched and choked on acid bile.

'Is this your home?'

'No, it's Zacharias' house. Ours is higher.'

'Look at the grass growing through the cobbles. It looks as if someone walked there.'

'Fierce winds struck. I've seen gusts flatten more than grass. There's no point walking further.' Unable to bear the destruction, he mounted, 'Let's go.'

Annoyed she didn't follow, he turned, 'Hurry!'

'There might be houses with food further up the path.'

'Children should throng this street. Zacharias never grumbled when we chased after pigs and chickens to make a right babble. I'm going, hurry.'

His white-knuckled hands gripped the reins as he cantered downhill.

'Don't leave me. You promised not to leave me.'

Contrite, he waited, then held her close until her sobs eased.

163

'I'm sorry. The ruins of Marmaketo emphasised my loss. Hush now. There's a lambing enclosure along the track. We may find rations in the shepherd's rest.'

She smiled, delighted as he kissed her forehead, wiped her eyes with his thumb and lifted her onto the saddle. 'Let's race to blow the cobwebs away.' Galloping on two legs, he whooped, 'Come on, catch me if you can!'

*

Unexpected aromas hit Petros as he crouched at the entrance to the low, domed stone hut. A wooden rack hung from the ceiling, keeping a treasure trove of food out of the reach of mice. Not caring he'd bumped his head on the low rack, his mouth watered to find apples not yet wizened, a gauze-wrapped cheese and a crate of sprouting potatoes. Two rusty hooks also hung from the ceiling: one holding a net of rusks and, beyond his wildest dreams, the other, an enormous smoked ham. A tin pot stood ready in the hearth outside the shelter, and this became Rosi's domain.

A steaming broth made with greens, enriched with thick slices of meat and thickened with potatoes, provided a feast. Either side of the pan they dipped rusks and speared meat with knives.

'Zacharias must have reckoned this remote place safe from Turks, and stowed supplies.'

Through her mouthful, she said, 'I love potatoes. Great-Grandpa baked them in ashes.'

'This crop comes from potatoes I planted last year.'

'Great-Grandpa explained potatoes came from a faraway place called America.'

'Really? Before my birth, two men from these parts set off for America. Pa explained how men made their fortune sifting river stones to find gold.' He mimed panning before spearing a chunk of potato, 'Hey, what's this? A gold nugget? I'm rich! When Crete is free, I'm off to America.'

Her giggles tinkled, like music in the night, 'Will you take me?'

'Of course, and you shall have a new dress every year, whether you need one or not! Now, let's finish this fine supper with cheese and a couple of apples.'

29

Lassithi to Kritsa

Petros woke in fear, clutching his cloak closer to his throat. Nearby water churned, tumbling and foaming from Katharo to the nearby winter lake. Frogs chirruped like daytime songbirds and a scops owl screeched while the donkey munched on knee-high grass. The unknown noise came again: a metallic, scraping noise. A silver pool of light illuminated a dark figure rummaging through a pannier. Knife in hand, Petros ducked through the low entrance.

'Rosi!'

'Sorry to wake you. I used the pan lid and a rock to scrape embers into the tin pot. There's half a blanket here. Pick up the pot and carry it inside to warm us, and I'll fix the blanket over the entry to trap the heat. Grandpa did similar with the alcove under his bed where I slept. It kept me toasty warm.'

'You're a genius. Hurry though, it's a frigid wind.'

Curled together and feeling content, Petros kissed the back of her neck.

'Thank you for cooking a tasty supper and having a great thought to keep us warm. You'll make a wonderful wife.' He didn't sense her smile.

'I'll empty the ashes from the tin in the morning and fry you a slice of bacon.'

'Good idea, I'll leave oranges in exchange for food we take.'

'All the way to America?'

'Oh, very funny. Let's concentrate on getting you home.'

'How? We've travelled so far.'

'Tomorrow we'll climb the mountain to Katharo and locate a descending path to Kritsa.'

'Clever! Have you walked the route?'

'No, Rodanthe told me.'

'Ah, my angel is looking after us. Goodnight, P— Petros.'

Already asleep he missed her giggle as she cancelled the papa.

*

Defeated by winter's erosion, Petros conceded he'd never coax the braying jack up the steep gradient now rockfalls obliterated the track. Rosi stroked the silky nose of the donkey, hobbled in abundant pasture.

'Will he survive on his own?'

'It won't be long until someone finds him.' He coughed to disguise his emotion, 'Perhaps Zacharias will come this way.'

After a final glance at Lassithi, he hoisted a pannier and followed Rosi, who laboured upwards lugging a saddlebag.

Once on the track above the rockfall, she raised a triumphant fist, 'Race you to the top.' Not waiting for his answer, she ran ahead. Full of vitality she darted back and forth, making light of the slog. Red cheeks and breathless laughter soon made her the carefree child she should be, 'Take this lucky pebble, it has a hole.' After a few minutes, she reappeared, 'Have this goat horn. Carve a handle for a walking stick.'

Petros puffed up a steep length to leave the pine forest. Where pockets of black-edged snow gave way to larger tracts, he stopped to catch his breath, expecting Rosi to dash back with more treasure. Worried at her disappearance, he hurried up the tough incline shouting her name. Ahead, tall grey rock formed a narrow pass and he laughed, realising she'd hidden to surprise him with a snowball.

Squeals of delight met his returned snowball. Bent to mould another handful of snow, he spotted a wide, muddy quagmire sectioned off with stone walls and littered with wooden troughs. He dropped the snow.

'Well, Miss Kritsa, I need your help.'

'Why? What do you mean?'

'If I've guessed right, this is Alexaina Bend, where shepherds from Lassithi and Katharo trade stock. Have you heard the story of Alexaina?'

'Tell me.'

As he led her away, Petros enchanted the girl with a story he learnt from Rodanthe.

Many years ago, a high-born Turk took a young woman called Alexaina from Kritsa to his harem in Constantinople. Out of his many wives, she alone bore him a son. Overwhelmed with joy, he promised her heart's desire and he agreed to her choice of returning to Kritsa, on condition she waited until her son was old enough to leave. Years later when her grown son visited, she hung out red carpets in his honour. When she took him up the herd paths to Katharo, he found it enchanting. Here, his mama complained of constant feuding between Kritsa herdsmen and those from Lassithi who vied for the fertile Katharo Plateau. Called on to settle a current dispute, Alexaina's son decreed only Kritsa folk had the right to use Katharo.

'Vouch for me if we meet anyone as we cross Katharo. Or they'll banish me to Lassithi.'

'I'll tell them you belong to Kritsa now we're betrothed.'

'What? Oh, be careful, it's slippery here.'

*

Hunched over, they slogged up the narrowing trail, bracing against roaring blasts of stinging sleet. Where scant shelter under a soaring limestone edifice gave brief respite, they heard crashing water make its hasty descent. At last they had their first view of Katharo, a long, snowbound plateau flanked by mountains. In a burst of fun they slid downhill, their laughter ringing loud. Under a clear blue sky, they crunched across crisp snow blanketing the plain, breathing out plumes of white breath while squinting against the sun's reflected glare sparkling from a myriad of crystals. On reaching softer snow, free of the mountain's shadow, the going got tougher. From here on they tripped over snow-covered boulders, tangled their feet in hidden bushes and broke through to muddy puddles. Saturated boots offered no protection and stumbling on numbed feet sapped their energy. When the trail churned to oozing mud along a river, they trudged in grim determination. At an obvious ford point, Petros realised they had no choice.

'Even though our boots are sodden, we should carry our britches and cloaks across or we'll freeze to death. I promise not to peep.'

Stiff fingers made undressing difficult and Rosi had tears chilling her face by the time she'd stuffed her clothes in the saddlebag. Through chattering teeth, she said, 'Give me your clothes bundle, you'll need both hands to lift your pannier high.'

Unable to muffle shrieks of freezing fear, they splashed across the shallows. Although smooth boulders marked the way, Petros lost his footing midway. In his panic to stay upright he rocked, arms flailing, sending his pannier splashing to spin away in the current. Horrified, he watched her wade away from the ford.

'Leave it. It's not worth the risk.'

Ignoring his shout, she lunged in a futile attempt to grab the pannier.

'Stupid girl. If you slip, they'll find your stinking carcass in Lassithi.'

'Don't call me stupid.'

Anger brewing with each shiver, he clambered out to watch her paddle cautiously to the bank. He reached out and caught her arm too hard, 'Yes, you are stupid. Not as stupid as me for traipsing across this barren place.'

'It was your idea.'

'If I freeze, it'll be your fault.'

She flung his clothes to the ground, 'Go back, Lassithi farmer. You don't belong here. I'll fend for myself.'

In silence he donned his britches, and as he pulled his boots, heard her sniffles, 'Don't use tears on me. You're sly.'

'Why call me sly?'

'You hid in our pannier to lumber me. I should tend goats, not a child. Since I must, do as you're told.'

When searing pains signalled blood returning to his numbed feet, he knew Rosi would be in similar straits. Good, it served her right. At the foot of near-vertical hewn steps cut into the rock, he waited until she drew close, then delivered a curt, 'This way,' his first words since the river.

Collapsed on a fallen tree at the summit he realised darkness loomed, and his loss of another tinderbox along with their food was a calamity. Laboured breathing sounded behind him, and full of anger heightened by fear, he strode off, not giving her time to rest. At last, the snow thinned and as the terrain dipped his boots scuffed over a reassuring cobble path. In a clearing, he headed for boulders set in a semicircle under trees and dropped to rest. When something in a deep pocket bruised his thigh, Rosi lagged too far behind to hear his joy.

'Hooray, I've found the hermit's tinderbox.'

A dig in the firepit delivered charcoal, and he lit a small fire to have snow melt steaming in a dented tin pot, when she collapsed by his side.

'Someone left this pot.'

Huddled in her cloak she didn't answer, asleep in a moment. An hour later he woke her.

'Drink this, I found herbs to make tea.'

Desperate to get her to talk without apologising, he tried again, 'Those stars seem within reach. Did you ever try to touch them?' She blew on her tea.

'Pa lifted me up when I was small and laughed when I reached out.' She sipped.

'Patterns made by stars have names. Do you know any?' She drank.

'What's that?' He pointed east towards a faint outline of the Thripti Mountains. She concentrated on the dregs.

'Can you see a strange light?'

'It's the moon.'

About to laugh at her notion, Petros snapped his mouth shut. A mere glint of light sparkled. Seconds later, a silver wand drew an outline of rounded mountain tops. In the next heartbeat, a crescent gleamed. Entranced, they watched the luminous globe rise. A chilled hand sought his as the moon sailed free. Neither spoke as the shimmering moon rose, sending a beam of light across the distant bay. A chill wind brought realisation that they needed to move, or die of exposure. Hand in hand, the pair forgot their squabble and descended the moonlit path.

*

'All right, I'm coming.'

Bare feet slapped across the hard dirt floor, 'What a time to bang my door.'

Before Spanos gathered his wits, Rosi launched herself at him. He carried her inside the kafenion, smothering her with tears and kisses. Petros stood, awkward; he'd not thought through their arrival. Should he follow?

'Hurry in and shut the door. My baby girl's like ice.'

Spanos produced a feast, and between each mouthful Rosi garbled her version of events. As another plate of beans appeared in front of Petros, he felt a squeeze on his shoulder.

'Eat your fill, lad, then use my bed. The minx can use the sofa. I'll sit outside to tell customers my happy reason for not opening.'

'Folk have returned?'

'Yes, many women and older men seek to rebuild their lives. Most goatherds took what's left of their stock to the hidden village above Kritsa Gorge.'

Too excited to sleep, Rosi heard their conversation from the sofa, and the mention of goatherds made her animated, 'My brother Nikos is there?'

'A brother?' For some reason the thought of her brother caring for Rosi saddened Petros.

Spanos ruffled Rosi's hair.

'Your Nikos hides safe with his goats. You can stay with me, I never want to lose sight of you again.'

'Only until I'm grown up, then I'll go to America with Petros.'

She didn't notice the questioning eyebrows Spanos raised to Petros, nor his answering, confused shrug. She accepted Spanos' kiss and snuggled under a blanket.

Hours later, a wonderful aroma brought Petros awake, 'Can I smell real coffee?'

'Yes, lad. Let's sit outside while you tell me the hard facts.'

Spanos proved a good listener. He asked questions for clarity, provided a comforting hug when Petros choked on grief, and handed over a clean nose rag when tears fell.

'Sorry for the loss of your pa. Be my apprentice and I'll teach you to read, write and reckon. It will hearten me to know my business can pass to safe hands.'

30

Distant Shores

Positioned on the prow of the small sailboat, Kazanis made an unlikely figurehead. With numb fingers around the shaft of a split oar, he poled through a shallow lagoon. Stomach churning with each swirl, he gritted his teeth against griping pains. Silt stirred in the narrow channel, marking the craft's progress through a necklace of flat islands, its ragged sail making no contribution as tatters fluttered in a light breeze. The stink from rotting seaweed made him gag; he didn't have enough saliva to spit, let alone enough stomach content to spew.

Gulls swooped, shrieking indignation at the lack of fishing scraps. He cowered low, breathing out in relief as they wheeled over the wide grey expanse of water in front of them. As a swirling mass, the gulls clustered over six huts built above the lagoon on stilts. In a heartbeat, the flock turned in unison to screech over a sleek anchored vessel. This craft sported two masts, and with several small boats bobbing alongside, it made Kazanis think of a duck clustered with her ducklings.

Angry at their predicament, Kazanis yelled to the skipper at the rudder, 'Hey, malaca, we're in shallows. You should have steered nearer those boats.'

From the stern the skipper used the moment to pause, using one hand to rub his eyes, 'Look ahead, I can see buildings. There's bound to be a wharf.'

'What's the purpose of those odd shacks on stilts?'

'No idea.'

Kostas proved he was awake, 'Someone's on the nearest one.'

Kazanis spun round to look where his cousin pointed. A splash from thrown nets signalled opportunity to the gulls. Their chaotic screams drowned other sounds as the battered craft continued towards shore, its bright green edge signalling a dangerous marsh.

At last the skipper shouted, 'Hey, paddle to moor on the empty pontoon nearest us.'

A bare-chested stevedore stood among dozens of feral cats, all eager to greet a new catch. Relieved he'd survived, Kazanis tossed a rope to the outstretched hand. Without pause he snatched one of three knives from his cummerbund and dropped to slash at the bindings securing Kostas to the mast.

'Rouse yourself. No, don't fuss, your rifle is secure.'

The vessel owner said, 'Do you want me to help you with Kostas?'

'I'll manage. What will you do now?'

'With my load of carob overboard, I've nothing to trade. I'll find a seaman's rest to ask where we are. Some old sailor will stand me a drink in exchange for a tale of survival. It's the best place for news of a charter. Are you two sailing with me?'

'No. With our fortune overboard, one port is as good as the next. I saw salt pans as we sailed in, I'll seek work there.'

In an awkward moment the skipper stared at Kazanis, who hadn't paid a fare. As far as Kazanis was concerned, the wrong location annulled their bargain and he made it plain by reaching for Kostas.

'Grab my arm and I'll get you off this stinking flotsam. Whoa, this bridge bucks. There, dry land.' His foot squelched, 'Ah, almost dry.'

Three crunching paces across a shingle rim and two steps up took him to the busy harbourside. A quick glance took in a handcart at the top of the neighbouring pontoon. Six multicoloured ducks clustered around their feet, broadcasting annoyance as Kazanis kicked them out of his way. Panting with exertion, he hauled Kostas atop the cart.

'How far do you think we'd get if I trundled you on this

contraption?'

'More importantly, where are we?'

'God knows! I don't. Did you overhear my conversation with our hapless skipper? He's keener than me to discover where we've landed. With his load overboard, he needs another cargo.'

'What about the state of his boat?' Kostas rubbed his soiled waistcoat as he spoke, in a futile attempt to reduce the vomit stain, 'Only people as desperate as us will hire him.'

'Not my problem. Have you seen those towering buildings the other side of the dock? I've seen nothing similar. Makes me worry this is Turk land.'

A shrill voice yelled from a nearby deck, 'Get your arse off my cart!'

'I'm only resting my lame foot. We'll move.'

Less polite, Kazanis grunted and hawked a glob of phlegm into gentle lapping waves. After wiping salt water from his nose along his sleeve, he checked his guns and knives nestled secure in his ragged cummerbund, and then hoisted Kostas.

*

'Slow down, Kazanis.'

'Shut up, malaca!' His cuss may have been for Kostas, or the vendor forcing through the throng with a cry of, 'Fish! Landed this morning.'

Through a fleeting lull in the press of people on the cobbled esplanade, Kazanis spotted an arched gateway. Its wrought-iron gate swung on oiled hinges, allowing access to a tunnel beneath a multistorey building. He dragged Kostas through, and within a few paces the hubbub behind became a distant hum.

A tranquil, alien world, with flowers in brightly painted tubs scenting a paved courtyard, brought them to a stunned halt. At the edge of a tidy kitchen garden, a wooden bench nestled under a shady mulberry tree.

Kostas found his voice, 'We died, and this is heaven.'

'If I spot a fountain spurting raki, I'll agree. Meanwhile, the seat looks inviting.'

Exhausted from their traumatic voyage, they both slumped. Grateful the solid ground didn't sway and buck beneath him, Kazanis vowed he'd never step on a boat again. He added, 'A bout with angry Poseidon churning the sea was worse than a slow death at the hands of a Turk.'

'Shame I didn't follow my crutches overboard, I'd give anything to be free of pain.'

'Is this a palace? The sultan can't have a grander home.'

'Don't distract me. Leg pain eats my will to live.'

A woman stepped from the nearby door. One glimpse of the two dishevelled strangers sent her armful of wet laundry to the ground, her scream stuck in her throat. Keen to sooth her fears, Kazanis stepped forward. Faced by a filthy peasant, she shrieked and ran. Desperate to avoid a furore, he sighed, and turned to collect Kostas.

The beast stopped them.

31

Lyon's Den

Not one to avoid confrontation with any man, it took two heartbeats for Kazanis to run. Huge white paws knocked him flat. Trapped, Kostas screamed, attracting snarling attention. Kazanis scrambled up, knife drawn. With a growl the brute sprang, gripping Kostas' boot in its maw.

'Kill it. It's pulling me to its lair.'

Kazanis chased the beast, judging a space for his blade. A shout froze his arm mid thrust. He watched aghast as two foreigners laughed and called encouragement to the drooling mouth tugging at the boot. Successful in moments, it rested the boot between its great paws to lick and chew.

One laughing man raised Kostas, supporting him to stand, while the other spoke gibberish. The one holding Kostas said, 'My employer wants to know why you've invaded his garden. You've frightened his dog.'

Although neither Cretan fully understood the dialect, they grasped the sentiments. Kostas yelled, 'Dog? That damned bear tried to eat me.'

Incredible as it seemed, the employer was unafraid and he hunkered down before the lathering animal, using meaningless sounds. 'Lyon, heel. Lyon, drop it. Good dog.'

Still gripping Kostas, the Greek speaker said, 'Lyon's no bear. He's from a place my lord calls Newfoundland. Be fair, you're trespassing.'

'I needed to escape the turmoil.'

'Kostas is right, we meant no harm. After a traumatic voyage, we needed rest. Ask your master to hold his brute while we leave.'

The elegant gentlemen, garbed in strange skin-tight, ankle-length grey leg coverings, looked confused. Kazanis stared at the man's odd red and gold boat-shaped slippers, one twice the size of the other. When he forced his gaze higher, his jaw fell. Fascinated, he fought an urge to touch the striking, translucent white face. The younger man, dressed in equally strange clothes, at least had Mediterranean features.

'Ah, we thought you sought him on purpose. He asks what faction you support.'

Kazanis rubbed his brow and frowned, 'Perhaps our dialect interprets words with a different meaning. The only faction I support is a wish for freedom from Turks.'

'But which leader do you follow?'

'I'm my own man.' Kazanis edged towards the tunnel, dragging single-booted Kostas.

'My name's Lukas. Where are you from? Stand still, Lyon wants to be your friend.'

Furious now, Kazanis jerked Kostas away from the growling beast, 'From Crete. Across the sea.'

Relief when the creature dropped the boot was short-lived. Now it tugged at filthy foot wrappings.

Lukas ran up to grab the animal's leather collar, 'Lyon! Leave his foot. Apologies for the dog's behaviour. My employer has more questions. Who leads Christian opposition in Crete? Oh, Lyon's fetched your boot. Good boy.'

Kazanis grabbed Kostas, opting to leave the boot in the great mouth. Then, determined to retain his pride, he held his head high and said, 'I captained rebels against the joint Turk and Arab army. Circumstances beyond our control led us here. I saw salt pans by the lagoon, I'll seek shovelling work. In fact, I'll work at anything to earn enough to return to the fray.'

He propelled Kostas forward.

The employer shouted a word that probably meant wait and hobbled forward, leaning on a silver-handled cane, slobbering dog at heel. He handed the chewed boot to Kazanis and then shuffled to bar their exit. Kazanis freed a gun from his tatty cummerbund, then looked from man to man as the employer and Lukas exchanged a garbled conversation.

Lukas jerked his head towards the house.

'Come, my master wishes to serve you food.'

In an uncomfortable pause, Kazanis frowned at the two smiling men while trying to discern their motives. He sensed he had little option, so said, 'We'll go, Kostas, although I hate to do his bidding. Your boot is under my other arm.'

A curtain twitched. Embarrassed, Kazanis guessed the maid watched their humiliation. Sun reflected off the windowpane, bringing more confusion – if they could afford to glaze, why have curtains? Their interpreter opened the door.

'Sorry for such a stink. It must be the dog.'

Their host pulled out a chair to make it easier for Kostas. After speaking to his servant, the man paused, waiting for translation.

'My master wants me to explain how I learnt Italian working on transport ships and met him on his journey from Kefalonia. He's from England but speaks Italian, studded with a few Greek words. Trust my interpretation, I attend his important meetings.'

Lukas noticed a kerchiefed woman cowering in the pantry, 'Ah, Popi, we've guests. Bread and cheese will be welcome.'

Not wanting to take refreshment as a stranger, Kazanis proffered a hand to his host. Lukas' fast translations made it as if the men could talk directly with each other.

'Good to meet you, Kazanis from Crete. And I'm sure I heard you called Kostas. Welcome to Missolonghi. Now, what do you drink?'

'Thank you. We'll take raki with pleasure, with plenty of water. We're parched from seasickness.'

Kostas tried moving his filthy bandaged foot away from drooling jaws.

The foreigner noticed, 'Lyon, heel.' With a firm grip on his pet's collar the man sniffed, wrinkling his nose. Now their host looked uncomfortable and talked to Lukas, pointing first at Lyon, then Kostas, disgust on his face. Kazanis sprung up, sending his chair clattering across the floor.

'Yes, he stinks, he's dirty, flea-ridden and has lice.' With a theatrical flourish, he scratched deep in the folds of his britches to underline he too housed such pests, 'This stink, good Lord, is months of blood, sweat, and yes, I don't mind admitting it, tears. We'll not defile your home any longer. Thank you for your hospitality.'

The gist of the angry outburst needed no explanation. Popi broke the resulting silence.

'Excuse me, I lived in Crete before Papa fled here to Missolonghi. They've asked for raki, a spirit distilled in Crete.' While lifting the chair, she addressed Kazanis, 'You'll not find raki here. Try ouzo. After the third sip you'll enjoy it.'

The Englishman said something else and Lukas nodded, 'We'll take Lyon away. Popi will see to you.'

Morose, the Cretans concentrated on their hands, their awkwardness hidden by Popi's chatter as she cut bread. 'Well, you're lucky. Larders are full again after the siege. Ah, you'll not know about it. Ottoman forces had the town pinned down from Christmas Eve to New Year's Eve. It seems Mr Turk underestimated the loyalty of a Greek in their employ. Thanks to his warning, we coped. City dwellers here believe the besieging Turks gave up because they knew Lord Byron headed this way, him being such an international figure.'

Kostas sat upright, 'Lord Byron?'

'Yes. Some say they might pronounce him King if we gain independence.'

Now she had Kazanis' attention.

'Independence?'

Popi placed a full tray on the table, 'Lord Byron talks with senior Turks. Now, eat.'

The two men devoured their meal, too hungry to care for manners. Popi must have expected her master's return, as the second tray she set out held four flimsy white china cups with tiny handles. She poured fragrant sage tea and smiled when she saw hesitation.

'The cup looks fragile, I'll grant you. Don't worry, drink.'

After testing his finger on the rim, Kazanis sipped.

'Who is this Lord Byron?'

Popi grinned, 'You are enjoying his hospitality.'

Kostas grabbed Kazanis' arm, 'Rodanthe told us! It meant nothing at the time. A secret organisation to free Greece. English Lord Byron is one of them.'

A cough sounded behind them, 'Indeed, he is.'

Lukas explained to Lord Byron what he'd overheard. He nodded, translating for his employer.

'Apologies, gentlemen. I forgot to clarify my name and purpose. Please call me Byron. I've sent dispatches to London begging financial aid to establish a Greek government. Despite unpleasantness here in Missolonghi, tensions have eased. I arrived in January after the Turks lifted their blockade. In February I fell ill, so I've yet to scour the area for information.'

His guests sat open-mouthed. A thread of saliva dripped from Kazanis' lip and he swiped it away with the back of his hand, angry to feel himself overawed.

'Are we free?' he asked.

'No. International cogs grind slowly. Forgive me, I know nothing of Crete. I beg you, bide a day or two. I've much to learn from you.'

Kostas realised the opportunity, 'Tell him of the oppression we suffer. It's your golden chance to influence.'

Another man entered the kitchen to whisper with Lord Byron. At a nod from his master, Lukas took a seat next to Kostas.

'My Lord empathises with you. He's suffered lameness since birth. Will you let his physician amputate your foot? Lord Byron believes the dreadful smell, so attractive to Lyon, is foot rot.'

On the edge of sleep, Kazanis twitched awake at his own snore.

'Now I agree with you. If we drowned in the storm, this is heaven.'

No answer. He assumed his cousin slept. Kazanis lay rigid trying not to sink in the down mattress, longing for a hard slab of Cretan limestone. Hot and pink, he felt sympathy for a boiled lobster. He blamed the bathtub. They'd both protested at Popi's expectation they should wash – all over. Now clean, and shrouded in fine white, lavender-scented sheets, they shared a room with two beds. Wide awake, he stared through the glazed window, focusing on a bright star and remembering Petros as a toddler, reaching out as if to pluck a star from the heavens. Kostas broke his pleasant reverie, 'Freedom comes for me tomorrow.'

'Lying flat out and coffin clean is a bad omen.'

'Don't be angry with the physician. One way or another, he'll free me.'

'Huh, you're looking forward to the brandy Byron donated,' said Kazanis. Then he mimicked the translation Lukas had provided earlier, 'Not the spirit you'd choose, but I'll wager you'll find it agreeable.'

32

Crisis

Before dawn Kazanis wandered along the deserted wharf. He'd feigned sleep when Popi crept in with the damp clothes she'd boiled clean. In the moment the door closed, he scrambled to dress. After a long look at Kostas, he touched his shoulder in farewell and dashed from the house. Brave in battle, he'd no stomach to witness butchery.

Sat on a low handcart, he gazed east across the lagoon. Fingers of light probed the horizon, heralding sunrise. An ethereal rosy glow within dark clouds mesmerised him. First the colour intensified, next a chink in the cloud freed a golden beam to fire the sea, creating an illusion of a stairway to heaven. Could it be true? Did Petros wait for him? How he'd marvel at those long-legged flamingos stepping through the shallows. An apple core stung his neck.

'Oi! Get your arse off my cart.'

About to deliver an opened palm insult, he froze. A weather-lined face, wreathed in a faded red pashmina, issued a cloud of smoke from a pipe clamped between broken teeth. His brain turned a somersault as the echoed insult from the previous day hit and he recognised her voice.

'Bouboulina? Hey, you're Bouboulina.'

'Yes, and that's my cart. Move yourself. Here come my stevedores.'

'I'm Kazanis, from Crete.'

'Really? Wait.'

As the unprecedented female captain jumped ashore, he said, 'I pray you've raki aboard, you owe me.'

'You're as slim and neatly bearded as the day I collected your wife and girl babe from Crete. When I later saw the hairy oaf you'd become, I applauded her judgement.'

'Ha ha, hilarious. I heard you have a great ship. Where is she?'

'Ah, my elegant two-masted ship is my pride and joy. She's anchored deep, outside the lagoon. I use this tub to ferry supplies across the shallow basin.' With stumpy, blackened teeth, her grin looked like a grimace as she added, 'Come aboard, I've remembered a raki flask.'

Three men, who'd been hauling supplies, stepped backwards to let the pair pass.

'Ha, you've made my boys gawk.'

Although the flimsy gangplank bowed beneath Kazanis, causing his guts to heave, he decided it wasn't the moment to voice his vow not to step on another vessel. A wave slapped the boat, making it bounce against its fenders. Almost jolted from his feet, he gulped and gripped the brass handrail, feigning ignorance of bellowing guffaws behind him.

No better than a wooden hut on the rear deck, Bouboulina's narrow bunk filled the cabin. She fished in an overhead locker.

'Ladies first,' she said, flourishing a raki flask before taking a swig. Not bothering to wipe its neck, she passed it over.

'Panagia Mou! Ambrosia from the gods.'

As the liquid level fell, their words tumbled, each vying to tell of daring escapades, until, belching rancid breath, Bouboulina said, 'Enough, Kazanis. What brought you here?'

When his voice faltered recounting the horrors of Milatos and she placed her calloused hand on his arm, this small kindness broke him. Once he'd regained his composure, he talked fast to reach more recent events.

'By the time I returned to Kostas, a homesick fisherman had discovered him and was content to share. This old salt knew the folk who'd escaped from Sisi port a year before; they'd set up on an island offshore. Right under Turk noses.'

Even when he tipped the empty flask over, Bouboulina didn't take the hint.

'Get on with it, man, I leave at noon. By the way, you smell odd.'

'It's too long since you lived as a woman. Don't you remember the light scent of freshly laundered clothes?'

Her answering punch proved his words, 'You mean the island opposite Megalo Kastro.'

'Yes, I figured you'd know it. I volunteered for raids against Turk merchant boats.' He rubbed his nose, adding, 'Kostas made shot and cleaned guns,' to avoid confessing how his new comrades jeered at his seasickness – although their teasing soon stopped once they appreciated his strength in a fight.

Bouboulina brought the conversation up to date, 'What boat are you from? Even my crew found it nigh impossible to make headway in the tempest.'

'We were aboard a ketch loaded with carob which the skipper intended to trade in Kefalonia. We went along, hoping to procure arms with stolen loot. Those gales blew us here. Kostas bides further up the quay.'

'It really is your unlucky day. This is the third time the city bought my entire stock of cannon shot, black powder and guns.'

'Cannon shot?'

'I can't imagine how they did it, but the city walls boast cannons.'

After whistling through his teeth in admiration, he admitted, 'We can't buy as much as a meal. Our trade goods rest in Poseidon's watery depths.'

'Fetch Kostas and sail with me.'

Kazanis felt blood drain from his face.

'He lies in the home of the English lord, but he'll not last until evening. A foreign physician will roll up his sleeves, and then …' He formed a macabre sawing action across his calf, 'At least it will release him from foot rot.'

Her eyes widened, 'Stupid man. Why didn't you say? Follow me.'

She sprinted through the narrow gangway, 'Peggy! Where in God's name is Peggy?'

*

With one hand Peggy clutched the bouncing handcart, determined to stay aboard as Kazanis sped him over rough cobbles. His other hand clutched a precious sailcloth roll to his chest, while the staff of his wooden leg drummed a furious beat. Bouboulina raced ahead, batting folk aside to clear the path. Kazanis bawled, 'Turn left.'

Between gulping breaths, she yelled, 'I met Byron yesterday. The customer who bought my stock has loaned his mansion to him. Hurry.'

'No, stay on the quayside. There's a gate.'

When he sped to lead through the tunnel, a barking frenzy heralded their arrival. Despite their haste he enjoyed her squeal of fear.

'Don't mind Lyon, he's friendly.'

In the laundry, the physician, Lukas and two other men bound their victim to an armchair. Mouths gaped as the door burst open to admit an odd trio: a small one-legged man, a rough woman and Kazanis. Without preamble Peggy took control, speaking the physician's tongue.

'I've lopped more limbs in twenty years than I care to recall.' In Greek, he added, 'I need a bucket of hot embers from the kitchen.'

Lukas recognised the woman, gave a brief nod and hurried to a hearth.

With a flourish the interloper unrolled his sailcloth bundle, setting its precious contents out of the patient's line of vision. Peggy pointed to each instrument in turn.

'Capital knife, to make the deep cut. Bone saw, clamps, nippers, skin hooks, cautery irons, sailmakers' needles and waxed thread.' With a wink at the stunned physician, he said, 'If you've tools and experience to match mine, I'll quit.'

'Umm. Oh, indeed not. I've had a leaflet on amputations in my medicine chest since I left England. I read it last night. This morning

I arranged for these men to help me: a butcher and a carpenter.' He handed over a brandy bottle, 'Lead on, I was about to administer this. Coals are a good idea, I'd not thought how to cauterise.'

Peggy snapped the stopper, took a swig, wiped his mouth on his sleeve and handed it back, 'By God, it's good. Take a drink to restore colour to your face. That's it. Now, give a single tot to our patient, no more.'

As Peggy worked up from the distorted black foot, stabbing rotting flesh with a needle, he explained strong drink would make the patient heave his guts long before it dulled pain.

Kostas cried out.

'Good, now I know where the live flesh starts.' Safe in the knowledge his victim couldn't understand, he said, 'His knee is safe, if not his life.'

Peggy flipped from Greek to English without pause for breath. 'Which of you is the butcher? Run for a bladder. The freshest you have.'

'I am. Why a bladder?'

'Tsk, there's no time to explain. Go.'

As Peggy stroked the marble draining board, he said, 'Untie him, Kazanis, the slab will serve us better. When I'm ready, hold his arms. You there, I guess you're the carpenter, I'll not need your saw. Place yourself across his torso.'

He bowed to the physician, 'Oblige me by affixing these clamps when I say.'

With a cold pipe between her lips, Bouboulina grabbed a sheet to rip into lengths, 'This is the best place I've ever seen for a lopping. A sink for the blood, and bandages aplenty.'

She relit her pipe, then, haloed by a fragrant cloud, leant over Kostas.

'Here, blow smoke while we prepare.'

Fear strangled his voice and brain; he'd not even questioned Bouboulina's arrival.

Lukas panted, 'Where do you want this bucket?'

'Here, bury these iron rods among the embers and put the bucket in the doorway where the draught will make the coals glow. Wait – are you squeamish?'

'Probably. How can I aid you?'

'Find rags to handle the rods, and then apply a firm touch with a hot rod to the left of my finger when I call for you. Hold it to the count of three, then stick the rod back in the heat, ready to go again.'

When a glance at the ashen-faced physician told Peggy the man was ready to bolt, he gave a toothless chuckle, 'My first time as loblolly boy was on a warship. You'll spew, right enough.'

'My remedies are bloodletting and strong cordials. I never aspired to surgery.' He blotted his sweating brow with a pristine handkerchief, 'How did you get your fine instruments?'

'A gift from a grateful Turk. After years chained to galley oars, I earned my freedom when their captain took a hit. I knew enough of their language to risk an offer to lop and sew.'

Fighting an urge to flee, Kazanis broke in, 'For God's sake. You chatter more than women on doorsteps!'

Before Peggy could answer, the butcher reappeared, with a bloody parcel.

'In a pail of water please, quick as you can.' Rolling his sleeves up, he added, 'Move there, we can use your weight.'

Bouboulina saw the signal and rescued her fragile pipe, replacing it with a wad of rolled cloth. Peggy touched Kostas' shoulder and, as if to reassure him, said, 'Let's go for neat, with a single flap.'

33

Byron

An unfamiliar waterside din of screeching, flapping and honking roused Kazanis. His stomach churned. Predawn wind whistled through the rigging of moored boats. Shrill gulls fought for scraps tossed by men sorting their overnight catch. His first thought had him wide awake; he needed to get away. With a stealthy hand, he groped for his britches. The bunk groaned as he bent for a boot. She was many years his senior and weather-raddled. What had he done?

Her laugh rang overloud, 'Any port in a storm, eh?'

What could he say? Strong drink, grief and anxiety responded to her sympathetic kiss. Bouboulina helped him, 'Hurry, discover if Kostas lives.'

Balanced on one booted foot, he bent to pull on the other, keeping his eyes on his task, 'You meant to sail yesterday. Whatever the outcome, thank you.'

'We depart at noon. If he's dead, come with me. If not, God willing, I'll pass this way within two weeks.'

She saw him struggle to form an answer, and guffawed, 'Don't fear a repeat performance. We need muscle aboard, nothing else.'

Relief flooded his face, 'Well, thanks. I'll test your boast you've the finest ship afloat to get me back to the action.'

'In a full wind she flies on fourteen sheets. And, if you promise not to tell the Turks, I'll show you how we disguise our cannon. Now go.'

*

Apprehensive, Kazanis hurried through the marble maze, frustrated at yet another wrong turn. After the empty kitchen and pristine laundry, he sought stairs to their bedroom. In a corridor lined with

189

ornate panelled doors, his heels clacked on marble to broadcast his progress. One door stood ajar.

Smooth plastered walls carried strange emblems, flags and paintings of pale men in odd dress. When he looked closer, Byron, at different ages, appeared in each of them. One, as a youth, pictured him with a huge black dog, the same breed as Lyon. Another had the man in a green and red checked kilt, topped by a cap of similar material and the odd slippers he wore yesterday.

A veritable armoury lay in disarray across every flat surface. Guns in styles he'd never seen, ornate daggers and long curving blades favoured by Turks. Although he lusted after the weapons, the number of books astounded him. He replaced a book on a pile, not comprehending how people made sense of those black squiggles. Scrawl on a whitewashed wall caught his eye. Lukas spoke from behind him.

'My Lord wrote those words. It says, "Give Greece arms and independence before learning; I am here to serve her, first with my steel, and afterwards my pen."'

Without turning, the Cretan said, 'A true friend of Greeks.' With his eyes still fixed on the wall, he gulped and asked, 'What of Kostas?' He held his breath.

A kind hand clutched his shoulder, 'He lives. Our kitchen maid, Popi, has responsibility to follow the odd fellow's instructions. The sailcloth binding will stay on for three days. After another three days she'll soak off the bladder.'

With a hissing breath, Kazanis turned, 'Bladder?'

'It catches pus from the stump.'

'Can I see him?'

'Popi says he sleeps. I hear my lord in the hall. Wait while I learn his needs.'

Byron entered wearing a white kilt with many pleats, a white blouse topped with a blue jacket embroidered with gold thread, and white leggings down to his mismatched slippers. Embarrassed to be where he shouldn't, Kazanis turned to leave. Lukas fell to translating.

'Good morning, Kazanis. This chap will paint a likeness of me in the costume of my Souliot platoon. I'll send it to London. It helps with fundraising.'

'Souliot?' said Kazanis, raising his eyebrows at Lukas, 'Check what he meant.'

After clarification, Lukas explained the fierce Christian Souliots hailed from Albania. They'd fled oppression and now fought with passion against Ottoman oppression. Lord Byron counted himself lucky to have them at his disposal.

While the artist organised his easel and paints, Byron settled on an elevated cushion. Once comfortable, he pointed to a nearby chair. 'Stay to talk.'

Kazanis needed little prompting to regale tales of bravery and fortitude against tyranny right through to mid-morning, when Popi delivered refreshments. Her progress report on Kostas left him distracted when the debriefing resumed.

'Don't fret. My deformed foot has been with me since birth. At school the boys called me the limping devil. It didn't stop me doing things, I'm an accomplished boxer, horseman and swimmer. Newfoundland dogs have provided friendship all my life, and the one I had as a youngster always rescued me when I tired from swimming too far.'

'A deformed foot is a better proposition than no foot.'

'Lukas explained that the surgeon you found only had one leg and manages on a wooden peg. You've told me Kostas is an excellent sniper and shotmaker, he'll find a way. Now, advise me about Crete. It holds such a tactical position I'm not surprised the sultan offered it to the Egyptians to maintain hold. No matter what such a move costs his exchequer, he will deem it worthwhile.'

With an opening like that, Kazanis couldn't resist, 'With due modesty, I'll tell you how I killed the Egyptian pasha of Crete.'

Byron listened enthralled and cheered long and loud, 'I'd say you made the right decision to leave him and the horse intact. A mystery will have cast a veil, whereas theft would have brought severe retribution to your people.'

*

Once the artist was content, he turned the completed portrait to Byron, who laughed and clapped the man on his back.

'He says you looked like a fierce warrior as you shared your tale. Sit here. He wants to paint you.'

Intrigued by the notion, Kazanis only made a half-hearted argument. Next on the easel the artist stood a regal portrait of a man sitting proudly, complete except for the face. Lukas explained, 'My Lord Byron is a fidget and won't spare the time to pose. Sometimes his artist gets ahead by painting men in various poses and completes the face later. This one will have your likeness and name, Kazanis.'

'I wonder if you should put "Emmanuel Rovithis"? Kazanis was Grandpa's nickname, earned when a pappas baptised him in a kazani pot to foil Turks who shot the font. It seems my angry baptismal wails matched Grandpa's, so I shared his nickname. On the other hand, some call me Talos.'

This excited Byron, 'Ah, from mythology. If I remember rightly, Talos was a mechanical bronze giant.'

'Yes, able to circle Crete three times a day to protect her from invaders while administering his own form of justice.'

Byron waited for Lukas to draw breath, then added, 'I expect the fair ladies of London will dig deep in their purses at the sight of such a fine warrior. We can talk while he paints.'

With a rueful tug on his wispy moustache, Kazanis said, 'Ask him to paint me with a grand pair of moustaches. Mine haven't been the same since I lost them to flames. Oh, and can I have a fine red fez? I swore to buy one if I ever had coin to spare. With such an elegant symbol of a gentleman, I'll opt for Emmanuel Rovithis.'

*

At dusk, both the light and Kazanis lost strength. Byron had his scribe summarise the key points and expressed admiration over the pair's voyage to continue their fight for freedom. Kazanis didn't confess the mischance of their arrival in Missolonghi, even though their original plan to bargain for weapons had once been a sound idea. Byron said something to Lukas who nodded.

'Kostas can join the Souliot division. They'll welcome him for what he can do.'

A weight lifted from Kazanis and he went to shake hands, but froze wide-eyed, mouth gaping as Byron passed him two bags of coin. A flashed look to Lukas brought good news.

'Take them. One is advance wages for Kostas, to make sure he gets fit. The other is for the information you've given today, and to fund your return to the fray in Crete.'

34

Busy Hands

'If I dress as a boy you can take me.'

'No, Rosi. Herding is not for girls. We had the same argument last spring. Nikos and the other shepherds need my help. Girls never go to Katharo.'

'That's not a reason. Take me.'

Petros was about to scold Rosi for her tantrum when he recognised anxiety on her face, 'What's the matter?'

She poked out her tongue, then flicked tears from her cheeks.

'Move along, I'll sit on the sofa with you. Why are you upset?'

Between snivelling breaths, she explained her fears.

'You once told me Kritsa men meet Lassithi shepherds to trade at Alexaina's Bend. News of home and your Zacharias will tempt you away from Kritsa.'

His guts churned. Immediate pain in his chest made Petros struggle for composure, 'When I trekked with your brother and the other shepherds last year, I met men from Lassithi who had dreadful news. Zacharias died defending the monastery near Pa's homestead. Hassan Pasha's forces set it ablaze.' He kept his gaze down when her instinctive embrace threatened to unman him.

'That's tragic. I'm truly sorry for your loss.'

Lost in thought, he didn't hear her sigh of contentment as she nestled against him, happy to spend the rest of the day beside him on the sofa.

'Before the end of summer, your brother helped me take a few weaned lambs for the Lassithi boys to tend. This season, he's taking me to another mountain village to bargain for rams, and two of those will go to Lassithi to strengthen their bloodstock.'

Mollified, Rosi sat still, enjoying their closeness, 'I remember the night you came back, carrying cheese and delicious pears. It must have been hard for you being unhappy when everyone else was laughing and drinking. Katerina took me away, she said a night of raucous revelry was no place for a child.'

'Well, if you didn't hear my sad news, you missed the mystery too.'

'Don't tease, tell me.'

'Our fortunes depend on the sultan in Constantinople and the pashas he appoints. When the rebellion stretched his forces right across his empire, he gave Crete to the Egyptians who sent a senior pasha to quell us.'

'I know, Spanos told me Hassan Pasha had a shock when our brave force opposed him outside Kritsa.'

'Well listen to this – the Lassithi men we met told us that within weeks of that battle he fell from his horse, stone dead.'

'Panagia Mou!'

'Muslim converts told their wives, who gossiped in market places with Christian kin.'

'What happened?'

'No one knows. His lathered stallion galloped to the corral wearing full tack. It seems the stable lads expected their master to ride in on a borrowed horse. Not so. When his officers rode in a good while later, they expected criticism for not keeping up with their leader. Once they realised the pasha was missing, the rebels took the blame – ha! – perhaps I should say credit. Anyway, forces rushed in all directions, keen to return with the culprit's head and claim a substantial reward. After three days they found Hassan Pasha in some undergrowth. With no wounds on man or horse, they declared his death their God's will.'

'Good, so now we are free?'

'I wish it were that simple. What made us laugh was the dead man's officers fought with more enthusiasm for ownership of the stallion than to become pasha. It seems Cretans are more rebellious than the Egyptians imagined.'

As Petros guessed, the story drew the girl's mind off their Katharo argument. Before she had a chance to start again, Spanos came to his aid by shuffling in with an armful of wet linen.

'Rosi, you've been daydreaming. I met Katerina who was bringing this bundle you dropped at the cisterns. Come on, help me sort it.'

Relieved by the distraction, Petros scooted across the track to collect his rucksack from the bedroom he shared with Nikos.

Rosi spent most afternoons with Katerina, learning traditional skills of crochet, sewing, embroidery and cooking. On the day Kritsa men set off for Katharo, Rosi arrived in tears. Her patient tutor waited until toiling with difficult stitches had calmed her.

'Have you measured that waistcoat against your brother to make sure it fits?'

'No, he'd wear it to shear sheep. When I started this, it was for Petros. Now I hate him, so I don't know why I'm bothering.'

Bent over her delicate work, now spotted with hot tears, she didn't see Katerina's knowing eyebrows rise.

'Whoever you gift it to will appreciate your effort. No need to decide now. Sew on my front step to enjoy the air while I feed the rabbits.'

Too distracted to sew, Rosi stroked an inquisitive cat.

'Hello, you're brave. Guess you saw Katerina leave, or she'd chase you with her broom.'

Relaxed by its contented purring, the girl felt disappointment when the cat scurried off, probably to tend her kittens. Spanos was the only person she knew who allowed a cat indoors, and as he still mourned his last pet she thought he'd welcome another.

By the time she'd placed her needlework indoors, the cat had disappeared inside one of six ruined houses beyond the cosy home of Katerina and her husband. Wind chased down the street to whistle through broken masonry and disintegrating timbers, making it impossible to hear soft mewing. At the open gap between houses and the forsaken church of Afentis Christos, barefooted Rosi decided against crossing the huge puddles. After turning back, she stooped at the first dwelling.

'Ah, there you are. Go on, show me your babies.'

*

A shiver chilled her spine the moment she stepped over the threshold.

'Hello? Is anyone here?' As Rosi stepped around a sooty loom, she couldn't shrug off the feeling she wasn't alone. To bolster her confidence, she spoke to the cat winding around her ankles.

'I didn't expect to see a comfy armchair. Ha! Look at this hair, I guess it's your favourite seat.'

Two paces took her to a fallen wooden chair. After righting it, she rubbed dirt from her fingers. Her whispered words sounded overloud, 'Who lived here?'

Someone had ransacked the house after nearby flames had caused smoke and heat damage. Broken crockery felt sharp underfoot, ransacked dresser drawers lay where they'd landed, and a carpet of leaves and pink bougainvillea swirled in the draught. As she turned to leave she saw a twig broom in the corner. Without thinking it through, she knocked grime and cobwebs off it and swept up the mess.

A sense of someone being in the room remained, and although she wasn't frightened, she chattered as she worked. Clouds of dust soon stung her eyes and made the cat sneeze.

'Sorry, cat, I'm making things worse. Tomorrow I'll bring rags to mop.' The word rags made her spin around to face the loom, 'Oh, the rag bag of dead kittens. I remember now. This is your home, Rodanthe.'

*

Within two weeks, three plates and four cups, one without a chip, stood on the scrubbed kitchen shelf. On the floor, round quern stones needed only a replacement wooden handle to grind grain, while tinder, kindling and logs in the grate awaited a spark. In the rear chamber, recently polished steps led to the bed. Rosi smiled at the two tabbies and a ginger tumbling over each other trying to catch tails.

'Oh, you three are funny. Well, I'm not putting the clean bedding on until you've moved out.'

She placed her basket on the bed and lifted out a patched sheet, a lumpy pillow and a thin blanket. As Rosi turned she smiled to see the kittens already sniffing the strange object. It only took moments to place the linen in a cedar box by the wash stand, both treasures she'd found in a nearby house. When she returned, the ginger kitten was already snug.

'Ha, I guessed one of you would go in my basket. Come on then, Spanos will love you.'

On the doorstep she turned back and called, 'Keep watch, Rodanthe. Our house is ready for a guest.'

*

Excitement bubbled in Rosi's tummy as she returned Katerina's welcoming wave. Everything was prepared, mint sprigs poked from her apron pocket, and even the heavy water jug didn't stop her skipping.

'Good morning, Katerina. Will you have mint tea with me?'

'Good idea, the kettle is above the fire.'

'No, not here. Come with me.'

Bewildered, Katerina took Rosi's sweaty hand to walk the few paces to a scrubbed step, 'Welcome to my home.'

Rendered speechless, the woman stroked her palm along the clean but unstrung loom.

'Sit there, Katerina. Sacks made good patches for the chair, and when I have time embroidered covers will make it pretty. Give me a moment to light the fire. Don't be cross when the kittens come out, their mama lived here first. Abandoned houses gave me these cups, a kettle and that narrow table. Next, I'll find sacks to sew curtains for the doorway. It's a constant battle to keep dirt and pink bougainvillea petals out.' Katerina stood transfixed, her mouth open.

'Are you angry with me?'

'Oh, sweetheart, I've not been here since we cleaned away the blood after Irini's murder. Come here, let me kiss you. What a lovely job, you've created a home once more.'

'I'm not in trouble?'

'Only your Nikos has a claim on this house. My guess is he'll have no intention of settling in this quiet part of the village.'

'Rodanthe wants me to be here. Sometimes she sends a message.'

'Whatever do you mean?'

'She's my angel. One day, I asked Rodanthe if she minded me in here, and right away my foot broke through the flimsy board covering a hole.'

'Sorry, I don't understand.'

'Rodanthe showed me her treasure as a sign she wanted me to live here.'

'Don't talk in riddles. What treasure?'

Without further bidding, Rosi knelt, pushed her table along, fished in the space and took out a small box. Then, ignoring the bag of odd metal discs lining the box, the girl held out the large sapphire coloured glass bead with a white painted eye.

'There's a jar of small blue beads on the mantelpiece. As Rodanthe hid this one, it must have been special.'

'I don't know about dear Rodanthe being pleased, but I am. Now you've cleaned away the film of soot I can see the fire didn't take hold in here. My husband will fix a door. I can restring the loom. You'll be a delight to teach.'

Rosi wanted to dance and sing with happiness. Instead, she remembered her role as hostess, so replaced the blue sphere and said, 'Thank you, I'd like that. The first rug I make can cover this hole. But now, I'll make the mint tea.'

*

Overjoyed with her first visitor, Rosi giggled as she rinsed the cups, 'Did you hear, Rodanthe? Katerina will teach me to weave. I must learn well and make a rug to top our bed before I marry Petros.'

35

Reluctant Sailor

There was enough bright sunshine to set Kazanis blinking as he emerged from trees on an August evening. He rubbed his eyes and then stared at men spaced at intervals on a wide, flat grassy patch.

'Why are those men dressed in strange white clothing?'

When his host continued, unperturbed he shrugged and followed. Within five paces he leapt aside to avoid a speeding missile. In the instant he felt a draught pass his face, a man in the odd uniform lunged at him. Alarmed, Kazanis dropped to the ground, yelling 'Hey, malaca!' as the stranger snatched the object from mid-air.

With an exultant, 'Howzat?' the man jumped high then submitted to a swarm of cheering men who rushed to lift him as if he were their hero.

Breathless and still prone, Kazanis demanded, 'Was that a grenade?'

His companion Angelos looked surprised, 'What? Oh, the ball. They're playing a game called cricket. A gift from our English rulers.'

'What are you talking about?'

'Come, I'll explain about the Ionian islands while we walk.'

Angelos pointed to a dockside *ouzeri,* 'We'll enjoy a warm welcome and a bite to eat here.'

Wary of strangers, the owner stood, before giving a shout of joy, 'Welcome, cousin. Sit by Grandpa. Only last week he wondered if we'd ever see you again.'

'Hello, Grandpa. Yes, it's really me. Meet Kazanis, he rescued me from a band of Turks in Sisi, Crete when they objected to me liberating one of their boats.'

Chairs scraped as men shuffled along to make room; visitors meant news and an excuse for an extra flask or two. Kazanis shook hands with all present and accepted a seat, pleased to relax among good company.

'Your grandson did well to get us here. Although I'll confess I'd not heard of your island, Kythira.'

Grandpa grinned, 'I guess that's what keeps us safe. Look in the morning. With the rising sun warming your backside you'll see the south-eastern tip of the Peloponnese peninsula.'

'So, if we sailed across, we could minimise time afloat and trek overland before finding another boat to cross to Kefalonia?'

Angelos mimed frustration to his audience, 'Boats are much faster, and as we aim for Kefalonia to join the navy, you must get over your seasickness.'

Most of the men sniggered, then laughed aloud when Angelos added, 'I don't know why I thought him brave. He cowered in the bottom of the sailboat day and night all the way from Crete, and then took fright crossing our cricket pitch.'

Kazanis laughed too, 'How could I imagine men with leisure to play a game? Your habits are so different to ours in Crete, even though my island is little more than two days away. When I met Lord Byron, he forgot to tell me the British held seven islands under their protection.'

The men spluttered ouzo, guffawing at his tale, and one cried, 'Met Lord Byron.'

Another winked at Angelos, 'Ha, your friend tells a good story.'

Kazanis shrugged, he'd not waste his breath. He poured and said, 'Let's raise a drink to brave rebels. Freedom or death.'

Glasses chinked, and all present still cheered when Angelos rose, pointing to a vessel nearing the jetty, 'Drink up, Kazanis. The quicker we unload her, the quicker we set off.'

Grandpa tottered forward, 'I'll shake your hand, Angelos. I envy your opportunity.'

'Thank you. Now pray my friend gains his sea legs on our way to Kefalonia, or we won't aid our navy to victory.'

Kazanis slapped the youth's back, 'He'll return a hero. As for me, I've sworn not to set foot on Crete again until she is free.'

*

By September 1825, Kazanis' honed muscles bulged thanks to hauling stores from ship to shore. Bountiful supplies of pilfered food from damaged crates resulted in a level of fitness not enjoyed for years. Despite this, frustration irked him; he'd signed up for action, not labouring. With filthy thumbs he wiped stinging sweat from his eyes, and saw a crowd of men gathering around a uniformed officer. He nudged Angelos.

'Let's find out what's drawn their attention.'

'Although the siege of Missolonghi holds fast, we're confident in our numbers to risk sailing close.'

Kazanis should have kept his mouth shut, but instead he blurted, 'The water is too shallow for your ships. Much of the lagoon barely covers marshland.'

'You're right, and I need volunteers to take a chance with thirty small commandeered boats. You've biceps to row. Step forward.'

Three nights later, Kazanis fought to keep the contents of his stomach in place as his flimsy craft lurched and yawed on successive waves. He used his forearm to wipe his brow, swallowing hard to realise he'd not make headway rowing against a stiff wind while ten rice sacks stacked behind him caused the prow to rise. Full of misgivings, he decided to manoeuvre three sacks forward. A wave caught his small boat broadside, drenching him again.

'Bastard weather!'

Thrown down on his plank seat, he raged, 'Turks couldn't kill me. Damn you, Poseidon, you'll not drown me.' Teeth clenched, he strained an arm backwards to reach a sack. When his fingertips scratched the tarpaulin, he jerked his hand away, 'Argh, I can't let the rice get wet.'

Another wave hit and the boat lurched, knocking him to his

knees. With no choice he crawled to the stack, expecting the next pitch to toss him overboard. After sacrificing three sacks to the mercy of the waves hitting the prow, he felt more confident he'd save the rest. Even then, his awkward rowing sent him in a curve. By the time he coordinated his pulls to push forward, he trailed the brave flotilla, swearing aloud each time the craft dipped and bucked to saturate him.

*

In the early hours, he didn't know what hurt most: his strained back, blistered hands or his throat, raw from spewing. In a lull, he tore a length from his undershirt to bind his palms, failing to notice Angelos skilfully bringing his boat alongside.

Angelos had to yell several times to get his voice to carry above the howling wind and waves. 'Good try, my friend. Step aboard and we'll tie your craft to mine.'

With little breath to spare, Kazanis yelled, 'I've come too far to give up,' before pulling on his oars to head towards several of the other returning boats. How he wished these seafarers could see him in his own element, running through mountains.

*

As the dark veil of night lifted, steady drum beats signalled a vessel heading his way, and he guessed the regular strikes kept the chained wretches in a multi-oared galley pulling together. Desperate to hide, he realised the nearest spit of reed-fringed land offered his best option. Spyglasses round his neck, pistols under the bench and a knife between his teeth, he slipped overboard. His frenzied heartbeat sent blood pounding through his ears, drowning the drums. With one arm clutching hold of the boat's rim, he sighed in loud relief to feel shifting silt beneath his feet. Half-swimming, half-paddling, he beached his boat, and even without spyglasses, saw the enemy ship turn away.

'Sail to Hades, you bastards. You've made me miss my rendezvous with the ships.'

It salved his pride, although his lack of prowess had long since removed any possibility of him getting back. Determined to pull across the lagoon at dusk, he hid his boat in a reed bed before crawling under the cover to sleep through the day.

Awake and refreshed by mid-afternoon, he scanned the deserted wharf and noticed the huts on stilts had gone, limiting the supply of fish for the besieged. No boats vied to unload. Even the pelicans and long-legged flamingos had deserted the salt pans. Distant smoke rose beyond the town walls, evidence of the besiegers' camp. From his vantage point he thought it best to wait until dark to punt to the dock wall, where, if his memory served him right, he'd be near Byron's building. In no hurry, he settled again to enjoy a drowsy state.

Footsteps crunched through dried seaweed, and in the instant Kazanis reached for his weapons a high-pitched voice ordered, 'Stop! Put your hands in the air.'

36

Uncle Kazanis

Kazanis calculated the odds lay in favour of the three armed youths and tried to seize the initiative.

'Who are you?'

'Why are you here?'

'My boat is full of rice for Missolonghi.'

Bravado shone as bright as the angry pustules on the young inquisitor's face. He jerked his head at two companions.

'One of you, check.'

'Well done. Don't take my word.'

Despite his youth, the lad's resolution didn't falter; the gun remained aimed at the unexpected visitor until he heard, 'Yes, there's rice.'

After shaking hands, the senior youth pointed to the island nearest the shore.

'Unload on the quartermaster's isle, it's out of the Turks' sight.'

'Is it possible to reach Missolonghi? I've a message for a citizen.'

'Authorised men row out at night to replenish their stock. Get them to ferry it for you.'

'Right, I'll bid you good evening, and commend your vigilance.'

*

Despite bleeding hands, Kazanis' eagerness for news sent him rowing past the designated island to moor at one of the empty pontoons. Once he'd hauled his cargo over the side and dragged the rice sacks against a wall, the emptiness of the dock unnerved him. He'd expected a challenge but there wasn't even a cat on guard. With no sign of activity, his small craft looked conspicuous. Inspired by his period of rest, he rowed a short distance to hide the boat in nearby reeds. Now he'd no option other than to wade through the calf-deep water. His attempt to lift a booted foot from the sucking mud almost toppled him.

'Urgh, my boots are filling with water.'

He hoisted his britches and tightened the cummerbund, hoping his pockets were above water. After two attempts he turned back for an oar, sucked in a breath, and drove the spar deep. With the pole bearing his weight, he wriggled and pulled until a foot freed with a belch and a splash.

'Damn marsh. It'll take me an age.'

Dusk loitered as he rattled the chained gate at the far end of Byron's tunnel. He peered through the grille.

'Pah, nothing but weeds.' With a final kick at the gate, he turned away. In a different mood he'd have barged at the gate until the links broke. Tired, wet and hungry, he set off to find the front of the house. At last he met a challenger.

'Halt. State your business.'

'I've unloaded rice on your wharf but missed my rendezvous. Truth is, I'm a better fighter than sailor.'

'How do I know you speak the truth?'

'Do you remember Kostas, the man who had his leg amputated? I'm his cousin.'

'Ah, he'll be with Popi. Take the second lane from here. You'll find them in the first cottage after the church.'

'The rice?'

'I'll send a boy to inform the quartermaster.'

'One more thing. Why no sentries on the dock?'

'Ah, that's where I'm heading. My bowels caught me out.'

'Better to shit yourself, I could have been a Turk.'

*

About to rap on the robust wooden door, Kazanis swatted mosquitoes away from his face. In those seconds he heard a happy, shrieking child.

'You're a whirling wind, Manos. Stand still.'

'No, Papa. You'll tickle me. Mama, help.'

Caught off guard by the trilling voice, Kazanis rubbed away prickling tears. Next, a light laughing voice.

'Ha ha, I've caught you. Will you go to bed, or shall I pass you to Papa?'

Kazanis clicked open the latch. Three faces froze. He knelt on their rag doormat, holding out roughly bandaged fists towards the stunned tableau. In the seconds Kostas fumbled for his pistol, the child hid behind his mama's legs, and Kazanis registered the meanness of the dwelling. What sort of home was this? A wooden kitchen table their only furniture?

'Come, say hello to Uncle Kazanis.'

'If you're a Turk, I promise to go to bed if you don't eat me.'

Kostas stared open-mouthed as the intruder continued, 'I'm no Turk.' He showed his bloody, blistered palms, 'Do you think your mama can make my hands better?'

Popi recovered first.

'How did you get here? Greet your cousin. I'll get you a cushion.'

In those moments, as Kazanis took in the gloomy room lit by a single oil lamp and scant flames in the hearth, he wondered how gaunt, hungry people still loved and laughed. When Kostas groped for his crutch, Kazanis noticed his cousin was sitting on a bolster with a bright, woven cover.

'What's this lounging, Arab-style?'

Before Kostas gathered his wits, Popi said, 'Here, use this cushion. The quartermaster's committee confiscated all wooden furniture. It's doled out as firewood.' She nodded to the weak glow in the fireplace. 'See, we enjoy a roaring blaze.'

'Can I put my wet boots by your fire, Popi?'

'Oh, you're soaked. Go to the back chamber. Take a blanket to wrap around you, then bring your clothes to dry by the fire. There's enough heat to warm water so I can bathe your sores.'

Snuggled in Kostas' arms, the boy listened in awe to hear this huge man had brought a boatload of food.

'Other men rowed ahead of me. They must have unloaded on your storage island.'

Reaching for the pot heating over the meagre fire, Popi said, 'No one has their own food store. Our quartermaster keeps communal supplies under armed guard.' She poured steaming water into cups, adding, 'I eat something every second day. Those engaged in physical work eat daily.'

Proud of his physique, Kazanis felt uncomfortable in the face of obvious need. A quick rustle in an almost dry blouse pocket produced a horn-hard carob bean the length of his hand.

'Here, Manos, chew this next time you're hungry.'

With the curious brown pod held across two open palms, Manos looked to his mama.

'Yes, take it. The sweet taste will be a treat. Keep it safe under your pillow.' The smile in Popi's words seemed as if he'd bestowed great treasure, 'Bless you, he'll love it.' She handed over steaming cups, 'Hot water satisfies for longer.'

Kostas bristled at Popi's embarrassment when the poor lighting didn't mask Kazanis' frown.

'Sorry, it's poor reward for your labour. Fresh water remains abundant. You do your best, don't you, Popi?'

She nodded and reached for her boy, 'Say goodnight, Manos.'

Kazanis drained his drink in one gulp then padded to his wet britches to rummage in their folds. With a flourish, he waved his flask, 'I trust ouzo will suit you?'

As if unwilling to broach recent events, both men concentrated on the spirit in their cups, while rats scratched along roof beams, mice searched corners and cockroaches scuttled along the wall edge.

Kazanis broke their discomfort, 'Why did you stay?'

'Lord Byron trusted me. I accept his coin. Who else would employ a one-legged sniper?'

'He proved a generous benefactor.'

'It's thanks to him I'm welcome in the Souliot garrison. See, I wear their kilt with pride.' He flapped his pleated skirt, 'Makes for easier movement with my peg leg.'

'Ah, Byron. I gather he'd died of fever after a storm drenched him.'

Popi sat next to Kostas, 'His useless physician bled him to death. I'd have tended him.'

'The fact I'm alive is testament to your nursing skills. Come here.' Not showing a hint of unease in front of their guest, Kostas pulled her onto his lap. Laughing, she dropped a kiss on his forehead.

'I thank God daily for sparing you.'

When a cry sent Popi to her son, Kazanis watched her go, then fell to urgent whispering.

'Among constant skirmishes on Crete we had news of worse persecution on the mainland. I met a lively lad intent on joining our navy in Kefalonia and travelled with him.'

'That's a surprise, I never imagined you a sailor.'

'I'm not. I hauled stores off ships before heeding a call for volunteers to row the final distance to Missolonghi.' He poured again and gave an odd snort, 'Now I realise they didn't expect many to get back before the fleet sailed.'

In the glum pause, Kostas accepted another tot of ouzo.

'By God, it's good.'

'I admit I thought you'd perished in a second siege. Your city elders must lack sense to remain if the town endures a third time.'

'Our walls house nine thousand souls. Too many to flee. The bastards trapped us last April the eleventh, in 1825, according to the Souliot's chaplain.'

Two rats fell from the beams above to take bold steps towards the men. At Kazanis' swipe they dashed away, bringing a hollow laugh from Kostas.

'They'll be back.' He drained his cup, 'The food shortages make them braver now we've no cat to give chase.'

Kostas didn't say more; he knew they'd both savoured similar stews when hungry. Kazanis pulled on his moustaches, watching the rodents scuttle up wooden wall supports to reach the safety of the rafters. Decision made, he poured from his flask.

'Our sparse loads won't hold off the inevitable. Come with me. I've a boat hidden.' To emphasise the urgency, he padded towards his boots, 'Hurry, I can get us further along the coast. We can row away by night.'

About to sip his ouzo, Kostas' hand trembled, splashing the liquid.

'My life is here.'

'No, your death is here,' Cowed by the glare on his cousin's face, Kazanis dropped his eyes. He poked his toe in the pool of liquid, 'then, I'll say goodbye ...'

Manos ran in squealing, chased by his protesting mama.

'Uncle Kazanis, I didn't kiss you goodnight.'

Defenceless against the sudden onslaught, he stiffened, hoping Popi would lift her child away. Instead, she thought it amusing.

'He's found a new hero, Kostas. Settle down, Manos. If you want to sit with Uncle Kazanis you mustn't wriggle.'

Kazanis flashed a glare at Kostas, who wore the grin of an imbecile. The words, 'Take your child, I'm leaving,' spun through his brain but couldn't reach his mouth – perhaps because his face gained a covering of light kisses. Small hands stroked his moustaches.

'Carry me to bed.'

Once again, his words got stuck. He felt sure he wanted to say, 'No, ask your mama, I'm leaving.' Instead he rose, with the child wrapped close, 'Promise to sleep and I'll show you my knives in the morning.'

He'd only taken five paces when a resounding explosion sent him to the floor, shielding Manos.

37

Kazanis Explores

Thirty filthy men, clad simply in loincloths, toiled beneath a reed-thatched canopy over a wide ditch. Others hauled buckets to pile earth on a ridge above them. When Kostas shouted, 'Engineer,' several men glanced up at their visitors. One man shielded his eyes against the sun, while the rest resumed digging.

'He's the architect of our defences. Without him, they'd have overrun us months ago.' Kostas tapped his peg leg, 'Come up to meet my cousin.'

The engineer gave a broad toothless grin, 'Well, thank the good Lord.'

With his makeshift shovel stuck under his arm, the architect scaled a ladder of reed and twine, ignoring the way its swinging motion threatened to tip him off again. He glanced at his filthy hand, rubbed it across a mud-caked thigh and offered it to Kazanis, while speaking to Kostas.

'Where did you find this prize specimen?' Without waiting for an answer, he continued. 'I praise God he brought you to us. Come down, join our tunnellers.'

'I'll give him a tour of your handiwork first.'

Instead of answering, the human mole saluted and dropped to his trench to resume scooping soil alongside his gang. No mean feat for undernourished men in the sweltering August morning.

'Why do they dig here?'

'They aim to carve an escape route under the shallow moat to exit the far side of the ground the Turk soldiers use for daily drills. If they succeed, folk can escape to those nearby mountains. Meanwhile, we've excellent defences. Climb those steps in the wall and I'll explain.'

By the time Kostas clambered alongside him, Kazanis had his spyglasses trained on an Arab cannon atop a nearby mound.

'The bastards built those earthworks to gain a better firing angle against you?'

'Yes, their enslaved men worked day and night. After just one day our engineer guessed their intention and designed improved defences.'

'This city must rival Megalo Kastro in Crete.'

'Not as large, but secure. We're at the furthest point from the sea. Keep the mountains behind you to face across the city rooftops towards the harbour. Now, what do you notice?'

'I see this right-hand wall edges the river you termed a moat. The back wall curves, as I can't see the end. It must join another wall running to the sea.'

'We'll walk the ramparts, then you can observe our full defences. The same engineer built a canal from the lagoon to feed the moat, and created our seventeen projecting bastions. In the second siege we fought with only forty-eight guns, plus the four cannons taken from a ship in a dry dock along the coast. Cowardly Turks fled when they heard a defensive army had mobilised. We couldn't believe it when they rushed away, leaving eight cannons.'

'Ha, I bet your men seized them.'

'I doubt the dust had settled before they'd hauled them inside our walls. Now, the interlocking pattern of fire from the bastions keeps the malacas at bay.'

'What about the nightly explosions?'

'They hit the same site relentlessly. It's closest to their tented compound and we think seeing the demolition gives them heart. The truth is, their focused attention allows us to concentrate on our tunnel.'

'Why don't they access via the harbour?'

'Our snipers fire down, so they don't get close.'

'Clever. Why is there such a gap between the city and the walls?'

Kostas pointed. 'Look at the reed-thatched houses; only the multistorey buildings by the wharf have roof tiles. The distance between walls and homes reduces fire risk.'

'Ah, I see the top of Byron's mansion now, overlooking the lagoon. Missolonghi is well-armed and defended; it's surprising the Turks had stomach for a third siege. Lead onward.'

Kostas nodded to one of two men guarding the first triangular bay. This guard responded with a raised eyebrow; the other kept his vision trained down the cannon barrel peeking out of the wall's embrasure.

'This is my cousin, Kazanis. I'll warrant he's seen nothing to match our defences.'

Kazanis stepped within the stone enclosure to stand next to the square-based pyramid of thirty heavy balls next to the cannon, as Kostas continued.

'These men are from a twenty-man squad called the Lord Byron set. Two stay on guard while the others sleep, exercise or work the bellows to make shot.'

Without lifting his gaze, the lookout used odd, accented Greek to say, 'You can tour our defences all day, but Benjamin Franklin, William of Orange, Lord Sheffield and the others can't match our standard.'

Kostas laughed at his cousin's confusion, 'Ha, your ears will soon catch his accent. Our cannon emplacements are all named after heroes who fought for freedom in their own countries. We've many friends here from across Europe. He's from a place called Switzerland.'

The second man stood and held out his hand. 'I'm from England. Once a navy gunner. As my colleague said, we've named our bastions after famous men, and this one is known as Lord Byron.'

Kazanis puffed his chest, 'Well, perhaps there will soon be cause to name one after me.'

'You don't change, cousin. Come, I'll show you more.'

When Kostas halted in front of a pile of rubble covered by men, women and children hauling debris, Kazanis' voice registered shame, 'This couldn't be further away from your home. What must you have thought of me when I hit the floor? Even Manos told me not to worry.'

'I'd have done the same at one time. It seems they're short of munitions. They use the least needed to keep us besieged.'

Loud, stomping feet heralded a platoon of Souliots marching from their barracks, and Kazanis stroked his moustaches while watching them take up position on the wide strip of ground before the city. He nodded his approval as they started their drill.

'What an excellent engineer and tactician to leave space for troops.'

An unexpected voice came from behind them.

'We want our noise to raise lots of questions for the Turks.'

Both Cretans swung around to face a dapper officer, who continued, 'It keeps them guessing how many soldiers we have.'

This soldier's neat grey moustache and a crisp white kilt over snow-white leggings showed his determination to keep standards high. Sunlight glinting off the red tunic's brass buttons caused Kazanis to squint in discomfort.

'General Botsaris, allow me to introduce my esteemed cousin from Crete, Captain Kazanis. Yesterday he ferried supplies from the navy. He's decided to stay.'

Filthy and dishevelled, Kazanis had no option but to grasp the white-gloved hand extended to him. The general didn't even glance at the inevitable stain.

'Tell the quartermaster you'll count as part of my Souliot battalion now.'

Kazanis felt his eyebrows rise as a question formed. He'd no need to voice it.

'With only four hundred soldiers against a force I reckon to be over fifteen thousand, I need every man I can get. Our engineer will welcome you at the shaft head. Kostas, show him to your empty berth in the bunkhouse.'

Botsaris hurried away, chortling at Kostas' shocked face.

'Damn, he knows I've been lodging with Popi and her son.'

'What? I thought Manos was your son.'

'No, although I confess to loving the scamp as if he were. Popi's husband died in the second siege. Manos is four years old.'

'He looks younger.'

'As do all malnourished children. Follow me.'

Despite the loose debris, Kostas had impressive speed and agility. He pointed towards the nearest rifle emplacement.

'Four such stations intersperse the cannon. I provide ammunition.'

Snipers must have recognised the distinctive tap of Kostas' wooden peg leg heading their way, as one man stepped forward.

'Ah, Kostas. We've plenty of shot. Our sector is quiet.'

'Good. See you tomorrow.' Kostas led on, explaining as they walked, 'Byron's landlord, Christos Kapsalis, stashed away a huge powder store underneath his house.'

'What about paper? Have you resorted to Bible pages as we did in Crete?'

'No need. People hereabouts take learning letters in their stride. Another Swiss resident publishes a newspaper. When he delivers a new copy, he takes back the previous one, and then I get them. I can't read a word, but the paper quality is excellent for making ammunition. Popi reads aloud sometimes and threatens to teach me.' He stopped at the next pair of marksmen, 'Meet Kazanis. I've told him our men only shoot if they can make it count.'

'When we see the heathens heading towards us with ladders, we cheer. Easy enough to hit them with debris. I didn't catch your name.'

'Kazanis. I'm to join the Souliots.'

The other sniper, still focused on activity seen through the narrow aperture, said, 'Don't let their superficial welcome fool you.

Born Souliots consider themselves superior. Can't deny they're excellent combatants, though. Step forward, take a look.'

'By God! Their trenches are so close.'

The first marksman agreed, 'Now you know why Botsaris says our tunnel is so important. He aims to lead our exit. Look to the right.'

Kazanis put his head as far in the gap as he could to increase his span of vision. With a sharp intake of whistling breath, he saw the besiegers had a tented city.

'They must be hard put to find enough food. I'd wager they send more men to rob and pillage daily than look towards our walls.'

He felt Kostas touch his shoulder, 'As usual, you're right. Sometimes we let a man or two scale the height to daub a crescent on our battlements. If we're sure they're rag heads, we knock them off the wall. If we guess they've sent Greek slaves we pull them in for interrogation. It must suit their warped nature to think they'd trick us to kill our own.'

'You let them live?'

'Such men prefer to dig our trenches instead. In fact, thanks to them we know Turks and Egyptians make better fighters than engineers. They excavated trenches too near the marsh and abandoned them once they filled with water.'

The other lookout agreed, 'My wife wades out each morning to collect seaweed and haul in our fishing nets. Now they've abandoned their lower trenches, she goes further through the dock to take mussels from dangling ropes.'

As the shadow of boredom covered his cousin's face, Kostas said, 'Come this way to my shot workshop. I employ boys and injured men with nimble fingers.'

38

Calamity

With back-breaking monotony the days merged, until Kazanis felt as miserable as his comrades, and like them, he tied his cummerbund tighter each day. Engaged in physical labour, he had one of the larger food rations; even so, his meagre portion brought nothing except fish broth thickened with seaweed. His joy the time he found a few grains of rice and a mussel in his bowl made him recall the brief snippet of conversation on the rampart when he'd first arrived.

'Kazanis. Stop daydreaming. Help me with this door.'

It took a moment to register that a fellow excavator was speaking.

'Sorry. Hey, that door will help shore up yesterday's crumbling tunnel work.'

'Our engineer had the idea when he realised many women were burning doors for fuel.'

'Ah, I guess the two deaths yesterday made it an easy choice. Raw food might prevent more of us being crushed to death.'

'According to my wife, the chief of the cooking committee refuses to burn the last four tables in the communal kitchen.'

Without further comment, Kazanis hefted the door to his back and crawled through the tunnel. As he reached those working to repair the previous day's damage, he realised the trickle of dusty earth had become a constant flow, making conical piles on the ground. Other men seemed oblivious to imminent danger.

'Get away. Hurry! It's about to collapse.'

Regular pounding sounded from above, and five grimy faces stared in horror as earth tumbled. By rising on his knees, Kazanis forced the door aloft to cover the space above him. Adrenaline surged through his veins, giving him more strength than his diminished frame expected.

'Tell someone to bring forward a powder keg. Let's make the malacas think we are attacking them. I'll take the strain.'

Blood vessels bulged in Kazanis' biceps as sweat-drenched men strove to pass him. Now the muffled sound of troops marching sounded closer, and his arms trembled against the strain. Each stomp sent more earth spilling, making breathing difficult. With numb limbs and wheezing coughs, Kazanis had accepted the inevitability of entombment, when movement sounded behind him. A surge of determination strengthened him; he'd push a while longer. Unseen hands thrust a keg past Kazanis, then the chief engineer squeezed through the gap.

'A little longer, Kazanis. I'm as far forward as the shaft will let me.'

With no breath to spare, Kazanis didn't even grunt.

'Right, it's done. I'll shout when I'm clear. I've sent for armed backup. They'll spill out to attack even before the dust settles. When the fuse burns past you, flee. You'll have seconds.'

Crackles and sizzling neared Kazanis and he scrunched his face. Sparks stung his bare legs as the burning line passed. Above him, parading Turks stamped to attention a heartbeat before the powder keg exploded.

Regaining consciousness in absolute dark, Kazanis tried to rise unsuccessfully, prevented by a great weight of earth covering the door on top of him. By turning his head sideways, he sucked in a breath before snorting hard to dislodge dust. Coughs turned to choking, causing red knives of pain in his lungs. Desperate for relief, he tried to move his hand out of its dirt covering, taking several attempts before he clawed some space around his nose and mouth to free it of cloying mud, and struggled for air. A wet, warm mess gummed his face, and he struggled to get a fingertip up to wipe it away. Without a glimmer of light, he listened to frenzied beats and pounding.

'Help! Is anyone there? Help!'

Dust clogged his throat and he retched, gagging on bile. A wry thought flashed through his drumming head – how lucky it wasn't a food day, as an empty stomach couldn't spew enough to drown him. Now chaotic sounds beat a furious tattoo, and he allowed himself to hope it signalled men were seeking him.

'Hurry. I'm being crushed.' Those words exhausted his oxygen supply.

Raw hands uncovered his face, bringing choking air to fill his burning lungs. Bright morning light flooded the now roofless pit, illuminating the backs of two men digging like dogs to free him.

'Well done, lads. Hurry, the blaring row means trouble.'

One man half-turned, mouthed something and resumed excavating. Dirt clogged Kazanis' mouth. Too dry to spit, he mumbled, 'Water?' This time the lack of answer brought a chilling certainty, Turks had dug him out. He'd seen the remains of too many tortured wretches. Desperate now, he felt through earth and folds in his clothes for his knife. A faster hand wrenched the blade from him before he'd got it near his throat.

Now his lifesaving shield became a stretcher as his bearers rushed him over torn ground littered by shattered bodies, dismembered legs, arms and feet. Crows picked at winding entrails. Sickened, Kazanis clamped his eyes shut against the sun's glare and stopped his ears with his hands, unable to bear a drumming din of incomprehensible sounds.

*

When Kazanis next regained consciousness, he found himself propped against cushions with Popi spooning thin broth.

'Ah, the Turks didn't get me.'

He knew she replied; her mouth moved.

'I can't hear you above the dreadful noise. Is their attack gaining ground?'

With the spoon hovering near his mouth, she spoke. He grabbed her hand, heedless of the hot liquid splashing his chest.

'Speak again.'

Her lips moved.

'Louder, Popi.'

She tried again with exaggerated mouthing, 'Nothing seems broken. You've bruises from head to toe and a nasty gash on your forehead. Our physician will call when he can.'

Popi fed him another spoonful.

'Pass me the dish. Wrecked ears won't stop me feeding myself.'

He'd only taken a few sips before he needed to chew.

'Meat? Am I so ill?'

She pointed up, winked, and mouthed, 'We've no more rats.'

*

After a few days he developed limited lip reading skills. Thanks to Popi's patience, he learnt the ruse had partial success. Believing the Greeks were attempting an escape, the parading Turk force gathered around the chasm. Fifteen Missolonghi men got through the crushed tunnel. They exited, throwing grenades and shooting to force the enemy backwards, until more Turks came to their senses and rushed for arms. Although two men rescued Kazanis, only four others made it back inside the city walls. An army of citizens hauled debris in a desperate hurry to refill the remnants of the shaft.

Still pondering the heroic sacrifice, Kazanis watched Popi rub the small of her back. Although there was no noise he saw her sigh of relief, then she gave her stomach a light pat and eased down to sit on the floor.

'Does Kostas know he's becoming a papa?'

Her head swung to face him, and he read her shocked lips. 'What? Um … no.'

'Kostas deserves to know.'

Neither heard Kostas step over the doorless threshold.

'What do I deserve to know?'

39

Wedding Gift

News of a wedding emboldened most women, who were determined to lift spirits with a feast. Wives of local fishermen nagged their husbands to punt across the lagoon to Klisova Island in their flat-bottomed skiffs to beg the few remaining islanders to raid their fish farm. Not one husband agreed, as it made more sense to keep their boats hidden. Undeterred, ten women waded out to the immense sandbar to walk the distance to Klisova. Other women scrutinised the chickens kept under guard to ensure a constant supply of eggs, and sent a deputation to the quartermaster, who donated a dozen old hens, judged past laying. February rain had boosted the communal allotments, allowing a harvest of greens, peas, beans, tiny courgettes and undersized peppers to form a sparse but welcome dish.

Between late afternoon showers, men carried Kostas on their shoulders towards Popi's home. Many cheering men raised empty glasses, play-acting toasts they'd have shared had a single drop of alcohol existed within Missolonghi's walls. Others sang rhyming mantinades to poke fun at the groom.

'Make way for Groom Kostas, so nimble on his peg,

His poor bride trembles to fear his member is wooden, just like his leg.'

Despite the raucous assembly, the cheerful men had no reason to care about their noise. Outside of the city walls, the Ottoman forces strove all day to rescue their sodden armaments, tented dormitories, stores and trenches. Inside the walls, the Christian leaders gave thanks to God when they realised their effective drainage was delivering torrents to feed the quagmire outside their walls.

Excited, Manos also rode aloft, hoisted on shoulders above the throng.

'Papa. This is fun. Why are we up high?'

Kostas leaned towards him to shout above the commotion, 'Because today you become my son.'

A reveller called out, 'Why isn't your cousin best man?'

'He stands in for my bride's pa.'

Another called, 'You must trust he lets you steal her away.'

Popi's friends hung a red blanket in place of the missing door to allow the bride and her attendants their modesty. Kazanis shrugged the curtain aside, grinning at the resulting squeals.

'Is my daughter ready?'

A neighbour, busy fussing with the bride's white apron woven with red geometric designs, stood aside, eager to gain compliments for her handiwork. To his surprise Kazanis found his voice gruff, 'You're such a beautiful Cretan woman, I've a mind to refuse your groom and take you for a wife myself.'

Pink-cheeked and smelling of rosewater, Popi hugged him. 'You'd be so mean?'

'For all I know, my wife lives on the island of Naxos, so I'll let you go.' Then he coughed to disguise a sudden catch in his throat.

Popi twirled to give him the full effect of the red-backed skirt as it rose enough to show the white leggings trimmed with lace at her bare ankles. Her friend tutted, catching her arm, 'Be still, you make me dizzy. This fine woollen kerchief is taking an age to set right.'

Popi kissed her friend and stood motionless to explain.

'Mama wore these clothes when she married Papa in Crete, long before they came here. When I was growing up, she often lifted the lid of her cedar chest to let me see them as we daydreamed of my future husband. Mama put on a brave face when I chose local silk finery for my first wedding.'

'You will delight Kostas.'

'Papa had a generous build, and I'm sure the white blouse on top of the chest will fit you. Take it, as a gift from me.'

A volley of gunshots signalled Kostas arriving with his groomsmen. Kazanis rubbed his ears, grinning at her raised eyebrows.

'Yes, my hearing improves daily. I heard most of what you said. Now, Daughter, take my arm and I'll hand you to your groom.'

*

Another volley of overhead shots greeted the married couple as they left the church. The smoke hadn't even cleared when a lad bolted towards Kazanis.

'You're needed by General Botsaris in the main gun emplacement.'

Pride suffused his face, and once again mimicking the legendary Talos, he raced away, delighted it hadn't taken him long to gain high regard. Once in the lookout point, he shared Botsaris' puzzlement.

'Why are six men hauling a dead donkey?'

'I guessed it a trap, Kazanis, and value your opinion.'

Both used spyglasses to peer through the cannon's embrasure. All six wretches, dressed in nothing but tattered, mud-spattered shifts, held their hands up, signalling their lack of weapons.

Botsaris called for ropes, then said, 'Find something white to lower as a signal we'll talk.'

Kazanis felt his mouth twitch as he pointed at his commander's flowing kilt, knowing full well he wore a clean one daily as an emblem of pride.

'We could use that.'

To emphasise he spoke in jest, Kazanis stripped off his new blouse.

Tied to the rope and weighted with stones, the white bundle swung back and forth as Kazanis lowered it from his awkward position atop a cannon. Emboldened by the signal, a man outside the walls walked forward to cup his hands.

'I'm slave to the artillery section. Why your fusillade of gunshots?'

Kazanis looked to Botsaris, not trusting his own hearing. The general clapped his hand on Kazanis' arm, reporting, 'We've unnerved them.'

Then he too cupped his hands to amplify his yell through the wall's gap, 'We're celebrating a wedding.'

Through their spyglasses, they watched the man return to the odd group. They waved, slapped each other on the back, then hauled the grey corpse forward. It took an age.

'What do you make of it, Kazanis?'

'I can't imagine. I'd find the way they're slipping and sliding through the swamp comic in other circumstances. Perhaps they've stuffed the ass with black powder.'

This odd group made slow progress until at last they reached the moat edge and their spokesman shouted, 'Throw me a line. I'll prove my integrity.'

Botsaris reached a quick conclusion, deciding to let the charade play out. With a nod of agreement Kazanis hauled in the rope, before using the wall's rough stonework to climb until he risked his head above the rampart. In full view of those below, he threw the bundle weighting the line. As it arced beyond the moat, Kazanis jumped down, determined not to let go of the rope's end. Vibrations soon told the story.

'They've tied something.' Blade between his teeth, he climbed again. 'Haul it, General. If it appears dangerous, I'll cut it free.'

The shirt-wrapped package splashed through the water to bounce against the wall. When Kazanis reached out to grab it, the distinctive shape brought the broadest smile.

'What is it?'

As he cut the bindings on a stone jar, Kazanis couldn't resist, 'Get your wish ready in case a jinni pops out.'

With due caution Botsaris opened the stopper, releasing sweet fumes to crease his face with joy. 'No need. The jinni guessed my desire. Here, smell.'

'Brandy!'

'Do you think it's poisoned?'

Dutiful as ever, Kazanis risked a sip, 'Better than ambrosia.'

'Dare we hope this a truce?' Botsaris peered out. 'They've moved back where it's easier to see them.' He yelled, 'What do you want?'

Paraphrasing the answer for Kazanis, he said, 'One of them wagered our noise was a wedding celebration. Although I've no idea why, it seems this won him the right to bring us the dead donkey. It drowned in a trench this morning.' Botsaris licked his lips, 'It will make a fine roast. Keep watch. I'll organise men to haul up our odd load.'

*

Later, wearing a damp shirt, Kazanis explained their fortune to an enthralled throng.

'Wary of a trap, we insisted on lifting our messenger on the donkey.'

A pappas called out, 'I'll minister to him.'

'He's gone. Their artillery would line up his comrades for target practice if he didn't return.'

Botsaris stood forward.

'He gave us intelligence about their earthworks and the problems caused by the sodden ground beneath their camp. Food for thought tomorrow. He can't share information about us, we blindfolded him. Now my only worry is how far a jar of brandy will go.'

When the cheers subsided, Kostas paused before his sip, 'Our first toast should go to the brave slave.'

Kazanis said, 'I agree. Our visitor's last words were, "Long life to the happy couple".'

40

Flotilla of Fire

To give Kostas a few hours of wedded bliss, Kazanis took his early shift to deliver supplies of shot to snipers. Now, in the predawn chill, he walked the walls, chaffing his hands and trying to ignore griping pains in his bony, stiffened joints. A clamour carried from the army waking in their dark, tented city outside of Missolonghi. A Swiss gunner recognised him.

'Morning, Kazanis. Their lamps cast dark shadows as men flit to and fro. Been at it since their cockerels first sensed the night lifting.'

'Keep watch, and I'll check again from the next bastion. It might be preparations for an onslaught.'

'The fact we've been expecting it won't make it easier now we're so weak.'

'I'd hoped our navy would have success and get rations through to us. Men in the Lord Byron redoubt have a daily debate about the ethics of eating human flesh.'

The gunner shrugged, 'Rumours are the undertaker's men are better nourished. I'll volunteer next time there's a vacancy.'

'Well, anyone is welcome to my carcass. Shame, they've missed the years when I'd have provided a feast.'

With a grin, Kazanis hoisted his britches and pulled his cummerbund tighter, then patted two pistols nestled in its folds. He shouldered his rucksack of shot, saluted and marched off as fast as his scrawny legs could carry him.

*

Kazanis leant out from the seaward parapet for his daily habit of watching the sunrise. Without realising, he inhaled a great breath of tangy salt air, then exhaled in a slow puff as if enjoying a smoke. A cloud with a bright orange rim caught his attention as beams of light forced their way between chinks to illuminate distant snow-capped mountains beyond Patras on the far side of the Corinthian channel. He pushed his tatty turban up from his eyes, unaware he mused aloud, 'What would I give for a draught of crisp mountain air?' He never found an answer, for the widening span of sunshine flooded the sea, attracting his gaze, 'Panagia Mou. What manner of flotilla is that?'

He bellowed to the nearest dockside guard, 'Fetch General Botsaris, and a pappas. Hurry.'

*

With spyglasses in one hand and a knife in the other, Kazanis scored a mark in the stone battlement for every boat heading down the channel from Patras.

Word spread, and shouts, cheers and blasphemy soon filled the air as men, women and children ran to the dock. Speculation buzzed. Had the navy come to rescue them? A pappas counted Kazanis' marks. 'Pray to God those eighty boats are sailing to aid us.'

Without answering, Kazanis focused on a hated star and crescent ensign fluttering from a large galley's stern. Botsaris ran up, pulling his clothing straight and gripping his spyglasses.

'What's your guess, Kazanis?'

'Those ships are acting as a decoy to capture attention. There's unusual activity outside our walls.'

Shoulder to shoulder, Botsaris and Kazanis watched large-sailed vessels, long galleys and small oared craft congest the channel. After lowering their glasses, they looked at each other with raised eyebrows. Both had seen the first small boat thread its way between islands to enter the lagoon. As one, they lifted their glasses again.

Bright flames caught a hut on the most distant island. Screams rang from the watching crowd as a breeze whipped the fire. Fear and wailing increased as two more boats entered the lagoon under sail. Botsaris prevented pandemonium with four clear instructions.

'Bishop Joseph, lead your flock away. We'll need plenty of prayers. Quartermaster, take your punts and salvage what you can from the supply island. Don't leave one grain of rice. Lieutenant, double the guard on the walls. Fire at will. This is not a day to conserve shot. Kazanis, round up those with fishing rights on Klisova. Hurry with them to organise their defences. Tell them an infantry captain with thirty men plus a squad of gunners will march along the causeway as support.'

He knew the fishing community lived in reed-built, thatched shacks alongside the river now carrying foul refuse from Turk middens into the sea. With fishing reduced to wading in the shallows, most fishermen spent their days making cord from reeds or weaving fishing nets in preparation for the return of normality. A dozen men huddled around a brazier. How did they bear the stink from the polluted water? Behind them, a fleet of twenty punts rested upside down on poles driven in the shingle, all in excellent repair, ready for the day when fishing and trading could resume.

'Up. Get your boats in the water.'

One man walked forward, while others hesitated before rising to their feet. Bent double, hand on hip to relieve the sharp pain in his side, Kazanis gasped for breath with a hollow thought: Talos had deserted him. A hand reached his shoulder.

'What is it?'

'I'm Kazanis. Sent from General Botsaris to tell you Turk forces attack the islands.'

'I'm Titus, captain of the fishing fleet. Come.'

*

Long and thin, the punt had a triangular tarpaulin canopy over the front, designed to keep hot sun off baskets of fish. Today Kazanis sat hunched in the first craft launched, the tarpaulin's frame a sturdy headrest. His waterman used a long spar, resting in a tall Y-topped shaft at the stern, as both pole and rudder. Although cramped, Kazanis felt thankful he was the only passenger; other vessels were ferrying four.

229

Titus pointed, 'My brethren are wading for the sand bar. They'll match us for speed.'

With wind muffling sound, Kazanis realised the man's lips moving beneath a trimmed moustache helped his improving hearing. His own booming voice carried.

'Our troops are hurrying behind them. Shout at me, I've damaged ears.'

'They'll offer target practice for the Turks as they pass by the edge of their camp.'

'Perhaps not. There's something afoot with Lord Turk this morning.'

As the craft cut through the water, among gulls sweeping and squealing over what they hoped was a fishing fleet, Kazanis gripped each side with white-knuckled hands, immune to the beauty of the vast blue shimmering lagoon. A wave hit the boat broadside to jolt his eyes open in time to spot a flare on an island near the city.

'Bastard Turks are ravaging our food sheds. Let's hope the quartermaster rescued their meagre contents.'

'Where are the enemy boats heading now?'

'Still busy with their current target.'

Waves splashed over the side as the wind increased mid lagoon. With his teeth clenched in determination, Titus sped his punt along, causing his passenger's stomach to heave. At the midway point, Titus called out, 'I'm worried about a deserter last week.'

'Who?'

'A cousin led his widowed daughter and her three sick children out to sea.'

'Drowned them?'

'No. They waded ashore on the Turk's side of the wall.'

It didn't take a genius to form a conclusion.

'Ah, the malaca bowed down.'

'Let's pray the cost of his conversion wasn't information about our defences.'

'You fisherman never go near our walls.'

'But he knows about the two cannons and other arms stashed in Klisova's church.'

For a moment Kazanis' mouth opened and closed, mimicking a landed fish. With nothing helpful to say, he turned to watch the distant cavalry forming up on the shore. His stomach lurched and he swallowed hard as familiar sweating nausea threatened to expose his seasickness. With a dry mouth he gulped air, and forced himself to view the island.

'They've seen the danger. Six men are hauling a cannon.'

'They don't know how to use it.'

'We must learn. Fast.'

'I'm heading for the rear, to get inside the protective dam. You'll be impressed. We build it at low water each autumn, it protects the island from winter storms.'

'A malaca is aiming at us.'

'Good. For all he knows, we've stolen these boats. Stand up and face him. Put your hands in the air to reassure him.'

41

Klisova Threatened

Sweat stood on Kazanis' brow as he crouched to grip the tarpaulin's rim. The craft wobbled at his movement, turning his legs to jelly. He spat bile. Fear drenched his back as he forced himself to stand. He'd lifted both hands to shoulder height when the next wave sent him to the narrow deck. When he'd struggled up, they were in hailing distance.

Titus shouted, 'Gangway?' Not waiting for a response, he answered his own question, 'Ah, they've dismantled the pontoon. Makes sense.'

An armed man yelled, 'Titus?'

'Yes, our fleet follows.'

Still clutching his rifle, the man walked atop the harbour wall of reed caging filled with pebbles to reach the gap left as an entrance.

'Throw him a rope, Kazanis.' Titus made it obvious he'd seen his passenger's suffering, by adding, 'Don't worry, the water's only knee-deep.'

Kazanis lurched off the moment the boat beached. Frantic to alert the islanders of impending trouble, he didn't spare time to investigate the cache in the thatched church, surrounded by another reed-framed, stone-filled wall. He bolted past the single thatched home to send six hens rushing from his kicking feet in a flapping, squawking fury. Two milk goats looked up, blinked, bleated, and returned to chewing dry reeds. When Kazanis stopped at a rough sledge hauled by four sinewy men, he realised they'd seen unusual activity and were preparing their defence.

'Titus ferried me from the city to help you.'

One man held out his hand, 'Welcome, friend. We've taken the cannon forward. This is powder and shot.'

'Heave away, lads. Armed support follows.'

His stomach and chest boiled with energy, sending blood pumping as he reached the men pushing an empty sledge back towards the church.

'Bring forward another cannon.'

Not waiting for an answer, he raced onward. By the time he arrived at the tip of the island, he appreciated the fine workmanship of the dam encompassing the perimeter. Here, he found six men puzzling over the cannon, and between harsh, panting breaths he became their leader.

'I'm Captain Kazanis.' Heads swung to face him, 'Folk and troops from the city are rushing to aid you.' He waved his spyglasses aloft, 'The spirit of your forebears, who defied cruel elements to raise families, will sustain you.' The rookie gunners stepped nearer, 'Everywhere I go in Missolonghi, men talk of your delicious eels and flathead mullet. I long for the day I taste your smoked roe speciality.' Men punched one another on the arm, 'Today, you'll become heroes for your kin.'

As one, the Klisova men raised their fists and cheered.

His bellowed 'Freedom or death' brought such an answering cry, a nearby flock of gulls wheeled away shrieking in competition. As the cry subsided, a woman clad only in a knee-length sackcloth smock and conical reed hat arrived, carrying a water jar. Entranced by her unrestrained black hair, Kazanis stared. When a breeze sent a loose strand fluttering across her face, his hand ached to stroke it. She smiled, shaking her head as if aware of his thought. After a second swallow, the significance hit him.

'Fresh water? But how?' He couldn't resist a third gulp.

With a smile to melt his heart, the woman said, 'A solar still. It came generations ago, with a bride from an island in an Italian lagoon near Venice.'

Loath to admit his lack of understanding, he said, 'Do other women live here?'

'Mama and my sister. Mama tends the still's glass dome. Two

brothers live here too. Since trading ceased, our communal living has been a strain.'

She blushed under his gaze, 'What is it?'

He stepped forward, reaching out to caress her face, raising emotions he'd not bothered with for months.

'I can't remember when I last saw beautiful plump cheeks.'

Her hand clasped over his and her eyes twinkled.

'Well thank you. Fish is plentiful, but monotonous. It's company we've hungered for these past months.'

'Your husband?'

'Long dead,' Three excited boys dashed by and her face softened with an indulgent smile. 'The middle one is mine. Eleven years old.'

'The other two?'

'One a year older, the other a year younger. My widowed sister's boys. The sea is a cruel master.' She pointed. 'There's my fish farm.'

For the first time, Kazanis noticed circles of reed staves.

'Fish farm?'

'We push thick reeds in as far as we can before tying on fine mesh nets. The fish live a natural life until they're big enough to eat.'

'Do you have more reed spars?'

'Of course.'

Kazanis pulled her close to deliver a smacking kiss. Then he winked at her shocked face and pushed her away.

'Work with your sister. Embed spears in the seabed. No pattern; the more random the better. You might be our secret weapon and spear a horse or two.'

Without turning to check she did his bidding, Kazanis punched a fist in the air and hurtled to find her mama.

*

'Madam, what water stock do you have?'

'Our barrels are full. We store it against cloudy weather when we can't distil. We've plenty.'

'I'm relieved to hear it. Fill every portable container. Thirsty work beckons.'

He ran off, muttering under his breath, 'For I know too well, water is a man's last request.'

As each new group of fishermen arrived, Kazanis directed them, 'You six, wade out to the sand bar with a length of rope. Stand firm to create a safe trail for our troops to wade ashore. Hey, you four. Get that sledge unloaded. You two, race for more powder and shot.' He noticed a lame man leaning on a cane while struggling to carry three rifles from the cache, 'Grandpa, can you load a rifle?'

'In my sleep.'

Kazanis pointed to the shade thrown by the cottage, 'Sit there. Load as many as you can. Don't stop.'

Three boys scurried by, halting at the stranger's call. Kazanis enfolded them in his arms, 'I've an important job for you brave lads. Take rifles and bags of shot from Grandpa. If a soldier drops his gun, pass him a loaded one.' Wide-eyed, they nodded. 'To tell the truth, you'll see men die. Don't pause to aid the fallen. We'll tend the injured after we've sent the Turks back.'

His eyes moistened as the trusting trio bowed before him. He thought of Petros, hauling buckets during the Kritsa battle. No matter what you tell a boy, you can't prepare him for the horror. His voice had a gruff tone when he barked, 'Make me proud, lads,' as they ran to do his bidding.

With his inner Talos back, Kazanis flitted everywhere, ordering, chivvying, backslapping and bawling. Heartened when the first gunners from Missolonghi paddled ashore, he hurried to meet their captain. He found him sitting one leg either side of the dam.

'Good to see you, Kazanis. This dam is a great defensible barricade. Let's get organised.'

Once the Klisova force had taken their places, they focused on the distant shore. Beyond the coast, mountains stood proud in their bright livery of leaf-clad trees. Puffy white clouds dotted the azure blue sky, while waves rippling the lagoon shimmered like gold cloth. Rank after rank of horses wore bright-coloured quilts, and sunbeams sparkled off helmets and wicked curved blades.

Knelt side by side, Kazanis and the infantry captain steadied their elbows on the dam wall to focus their spyglasses.

'Hey, did you ever see such colours? I'll bag a quilt for my wife.'

'Take my advice, pray not to get close enough. See the malaca with the tall hat? It has a metal dome above a flowing length of white silk.'

'Yes, the sun's glint is blinding.'

'I've seen similar in Crete. I'd say the pasha of these parts rides for glory.'

'Pah. What honour derives from this soft target? The sultan must scorn him for not taking Missolonghi.'

'Who cares about the sultan? Pass word to your men: aim for officers wearing helmets. The reflected sun provides clear targets. Ah, meet Titus, captain of the fishing fleet.'

'I thought you should know, boats are heading across the lagoon.'

As if he hadn't heard, Kazanis said, 'Titus, can you reckon?'

'I'd be a poor businessman if I couldn't.'

'Take my glasses and get on the church roof. Try to estimate the force heading our way. Afterwards, take six of your brethren to guard your boats. Any survivors will need an exit route.' With a hollow laugh, Kazanis added, 'And keep my glasses safe, I'll need them tomorrow.'

*

Heart thudding and dry-mouthed, Kazanis took his place. Gulls screamed overhead, diving for bounty as fish leapt from the water in their dash from splashing hooves. Hot sun burnt his forehead, a voice to his right whispered prayers, and his nose wrinkled at the pervading odour from pre-battle bowels. He called out, 'Focus on a single target and don't shoot before the cannon blast. Those bastards are out for sport.' No one replied.

He braced his weight against the dam wall. When the knives and pistol snug in his cummerbund dug into his stomach, he felt reassured; he was ready. He shut his mind to everything, except his

236

chosen Turk.

Seconds later, the cannon boomed and recoiled. As the ground shook, acrid smoke belched out and the ball arced high in the sky. Somewhere in the mid ranks, a gory shower of broken limbs and horse flesh stained the sea red. Alongside their pasha, the leading cavalrymen continued to splash towards the island's defenders. Christian gunshot flew, most splashing harmlessly into the sea. Kazanis drew in a long breath and held still, concentrating on his target sat on an expensive silver-trimmed saddle above a bright yellow quilt. He squeezed his trigger, not exhaling until red exploded his chosen forehead. Now his self-control burst and he waded forward, ramming home another shot, bawling, 'Freedom or death'.

Another cannon blast delivered destruction, and in its gory wake Kazanis paddled through pink foam, cursing his dragging britches and water-filled boots. Unsteady in the shifting silt, he stopped to shoot, reloaded, took a step and shot again. His accuracy in the odd circumstances astounded him, and still they came forward, herded to death.

An angry rider charged across the phalanx with wet trailing silk from his helmet wrapped across his face. This officer was grappling with the blinding material when a hot metal ball struck his arm, sending his scream of pain-fuelled fury above the bedlam. A jubilant trooper whooped, 'I hit their pasha!'

Kazanis' mouth hung open in disbelief as the wounded rider turned for the distant shore. At first, he dared not believe the pasha sustained injury; then, astounded by the sight of the withdrawing cavalry teeming after their leader, he joined his cheering comrades.

*

Jubilation died at the sight of four men laying in a row. After checking for life, Kazanis dripped and squelched to the mama.

'Are your daughters safe?'

'Yes, thank God. In the church.'

Busy bandaging, the women looked up when his arrival blocked their light. The one he'd met earlier blushed; the other jerked her head back and said, 'Three men are before you. Rest on the floor.'

'I'm not hurt. I came to count your patients. Oh, and to thank you for your spears. Several horses floundered. If you can, rescue floating staves to replant them.'

Next, Kazanis found Titus still guarding the boats to share the good news.

'They've turned tail. I don't believe our luck.'

'The Turk boats are withdrawing too. From here I can see two large ships patrolling the main channel. It seems the smallest craft head to join them, and the rest are following the cavalry to the shore.'

Weary now, Kazanis sat on a rock, elbows on his knees and head in his hands.

'I don't trust them, Titus, they didn't expect resistance.'

42

Klisova Heroes

'By my reckoning, Kazanis, we faced two thousand mounted men.'

'Sheesh! They'll not tell the sultan how few we number.'

'They misjudged things by using horses. From my vantage point on the church roof, I saw the beasts suffer. Without local knowledge, the Turk leaders must have presumed the lagoon had a solid base. Many animals floundered well before our range.'

'Stay on guard, Titus. I'm going to the foreshore. Hand me my spyglasses.'

*

Wet clothing had dried as stiff as salt-crusted boards, adding to the discomfort of the men labouring to haul the second cannon. Two of the injured men declared themselves well enough to help Grandpa make shot. Alas, Kazanis carried the third to join the tarpaulin-covered bodies now resting in punts.

Once confident he'd accomplished the necessary actions, Kazanis climbed to the church roof. He spared a moment to view the city, where he guessed Botsaris maintained a careful watch on Klisova. After what he hoped was a reassuring wave, movement on the far shore claimed his attention.

Titus followed Kazanis to the roof.

'I thought you'd be up here. How many this time?'

'Can't count beyond twenty. A horde is my description. Those large boats delivered troops further up the coast.'

'How do you know?'

'Big upheaval in their camp this morning before the ships sailed along the channel.'

'You think the pasha put on a show for incoming reinforcements?'

Kazanis guffawed, 'Well, if I'm right, Lord Pasha's pride will hurt more than his wounded arm. What set out as a rout backfired in spectacular fashion. Now they come again.' Kazanis passed his glasses to Titus, 'Take a look. They're marching on the causeway, following the route of our troops.'

'Ah, a different mix.'

'There are fewer Turks this time. They ride large horses with bright quilts beneath their saddles. Most of those on smaller mounts wear brownish uniforms, and my guess is they're Egyptian mercenaries.'

Titus didn't answer, although his lips moved as he counted. He handed back the glasses.

'How will our force of a hundred and thirty-six fare against three thousand?'

False mirth set Kazanis chuckling, 'And three women. Believe me, I've seen what an angry woman can achieve in battle.'

He'd not reached the ground before Titus shouted, 'Boats. Twenty are heading our way.'

The first of two cannon booms had Kazanis racing. Loud cheers met each new puff of smoke heralding the next arcing ball. The gun captain shouted instructions to alter aim, and then walked to meet Kazanis.

'Look at the mess we've made of the causeway. The gulls swoop for the food glut.'

'You genius!'

'We need practice, and we've lost the surprise.'

'Good work. Malacas floundering in a mud bath is a sight worth seeing.'

A pile of boots and clothing showed men had learnt from their earlier bout. Kazanis stripped off, and naked except for a weapon-stuffed cummerbund, stepped over the wall. Now the noon sun refracted through waves to create a shimmering gold net to ripple over the sandy bed. He kicked out at some grey striped fish darting for his toes, then scratched his balls, enjoying the caress of sun-warmed water.

'Ha! At least my lice will drown.'

The first wave of Egyptians halted as the compacted sandbar became a churned swamp. With successive ranks still marching behind, they'd no choice other than to wade forward, where deep pools, excavated by cannon shot, took their feet from under them. Scores of bodies floated together, making progress difficult for the following soldiers. Those on the island picked off their assailants as they came within range. The wind stopped, bringing further hindrance to the advancing force as a growing island of corpses bobbed together.

Kazanis chanced a shot at a mounted Turk officer wearing an elaborate red jacket trimmed with gold-fringed epaulettes. He missed. Enraged, the officer urged his horse forward, determined to carve a path through the dead. An infantryman fired. The resulting splash gave those on Klisova strengthened resolve, and turmoil culled the front line. Those not drowned turned back to face a crushing death. Mounted Turk and Egyptian officers rode through the debacle, trying to regain order. When Kazanis yelled, 'Shoot the officers,' the islanders' answering chant rose to a crescendo.

'Shoot the officers, shoot the officers, shoot the officers.'

A volley of gunshot from the east alerted the Christian infantry to approaching troops, and their captain spread his force to meet them. At the same time, Kazanis saw Egyptians attempting a landing on the far side, and spread his Klisova men westward.

With rifle and pistols emptied, Kazanis swung round, cursing the absent ammunition lads. His moment of inattention brought the swish of a mounted Egyptian's sword to send him splashing under the water. Desperate to get upright, he grabbed a stirrup. Towed by the horse, he looked up, horrified to see the curved blade rising for a fatal strike. Dripping water stung his eyes. Blinded, Kazanis reacted by instinct to plunge his dagger deep in the horse's belly. Flailing hooves churned the sea and a falling blade struck his arm. His screaming mouth filled with brine.

A crush of the dead held him underwater. Fear opened his eyes. Through murky swirling sludge he gauged the surface. Bubbles escaped from his nose, his lungs burnt with the need to gulp air, and the searing agony in his arm added colour to the swirling red water. Kazanis used his good hand to push human debris aside, creating room to first kneel, then stand. Dizzy, he gripped his slashed arm and coughed stinging saltwater from his throat. Another horse charged towards him through increasing waves. He braced himself, unsteady in shifting silt, and with blood dripping from his open bicep he hefted his knife in his other hand. Prepared to swing in close if he had a chance, he stood ready for death.

To his astonishment the approaching horse reared, screaming in pain, hooves flailing. With another glance, he realised a spar once planted in the seabed now punctured the stallion's underbelly. Its rider splashed, and Kazanis seized the opportunity to wade.

Somehow the Arab still clutched his long blade, and shrieking for his God's help he lunged towards the foulmouthed Christian taunting him. Without hampering clothes, Kazanis had the freer movement. They circled, each gauging the best response. Both made unsuccessful thrusts. A huge stallion splashed near to distract Kazanis. His glance registered the rider's arm nestled in a white sling, matching the silk billowing from his steel-capped helmet. Two against one. Kazanis faced death as the pasha's victim. Hampered by floating carcasses, he backed away, focusing on the vicious whip carried by the Turk. As his foe's hand rose, he flinched, expecting searing pain. With a crack as loud as gunshot, its length uncoiled.

In shock, Kazanis realised it was the Arab's face that took the slice of the whip. Startled by the turn of events, Kazanis fell backwards. He broke surface coughing water. In disbelief, he watched the bleeding Arab raise his blade towards the Turk on horseback, who once again lashed out with the whip. Blood flowed from a second lesion. Arabic screams rent the air as the enraged man splashed after his superior, who sped away. For a fleeting moment Kazanis wondered what this pasha hoped to achieve by whipping his own men. Then, loath to stab a man in the back, Kazanis yelled, only letting his knife fly as his whiplashed victim turned.

With no time to still his ragged breathing, Kazanis became a target again. He paddled through the churned silt, luring an Arab towards firmer ground; then this opponent stopped, his barbarous blade mid-air.

Ululation from grieving throats sent shivers chasing down Christian spines. Man by man, fighting stopped as the Arab multitude reined in their mounts to follow the horse bearing the corpse of the senior Egyptian. Desperate now, the screaming Turk pasha flailed his whip at the departing force while his stalwarts rallied to his side, then escorted him away.

Shocked Klisova defenders looked at each other, hardly daring to believe the turn of events. To a man they were incredulous to see Turk boats speed away, leaving the lagoon littered with corpses. Inclined to leave their attackers as fish food, Kazanis realised most wore bandoliers. Keen to get his wound bandaged, he yelled, 'Hey, rake ashore as much rubbish as you can. Rescue arms.'

In the gathering dusk, vast numbers congregated on the dock to cheer their heroes home. Botsaris listened to the hurried report, his concerned frown clearing at the news. Elated, he clapped the two captains across their shoulders, not noticing how the jolt made Kazanis wince. Determined people should hear him, Botsaris climbed up the sea wall, and as he cleared his throat people nudged each other and fell quiet to hear his historic announcement.

'Brave people of Missolonghi, God knows we struggle. Now take heart and cheer. The battle for Klisova Island will go down in history. Today, the sixth of April, 1826, a small but determined force won the most victorious battle of Hellenism. We mourn with the bereaved families who gather to bury twenty heroes. We rejoice for the safe return of most defenders and for their prize booty of two and a half thousand Arab guns, many with bayonets.'

With cheers still ringing, Botsaris led the captains away for a proper debrief. His first question was, 'What of the powder stock? I dread those bastards going back for our stock tomorrow.'

Within seconds, a boom took everyone's attention to the island. Another blast lit the sky. 'What the—?'

Kazanis winked.

'Seems Titus sped a mound of Arab martyrs to paradise.'

43

10 April 1825

The next morning, after Popi redressed his arm, Kazanis ignored his aches and pains as best he could. Crouched on her scrubbed doorstep in an awkward pose, he worked with a prize Egyptian knife. Snug and warm, Popi sat across the street in a pool of sunshine, wrapped in a bright yellow horse's quilt, a recent gift from Klisova.

'You winced in pain. Let me look at your arm again.'

Heat suffused his face as he mumbled, 'Don't fuss, I'm fine.'

'Well, you don't look comfortable.'

Not answering, he pulled a wad of his britches to act as a cushion.

'Oh, have you wounded your backside?'

Determined not to admit to a sunburnt arse, Kazanis stood and ignored the question.

'Here, look at these. Leather braces made from Arab bandoliers. They'll keep my britches in place, and provide a good supply of ammunition.'

While stroking her unborn babe through deep folds of her cosy quilt, she squinted to view his handiwork.

'How ridiculous, you've pulled them so high you've no need of an underblouse. Mind, you're so skinny these days, I guess anything to keep your dignity is positive.'

'This set is for Kostas.'

'No point, he'll not wear britches again. Give me the leather to boil in the broth pot.'

'Yuck, every time I sup that foul liquid I try to think of a good mutton stew.'

'Ah, Kazanis, you should have heard us last evening, tormenting ourselves with memories of favourite foods. Kostas tells me nothing beats a Lassithi potato.'

'Well, I agree, but I dream of biting a crisp Lassithi apple. That's if I escape here with any teeth in my mouth.'

Popi's lip trembled, then she gnawed it to choke back a sob and used a bony knuckle to wipe a tear from her prominent cheekbone.

'Watching children fade away is torture. My friend, two houses down, lost her third daughter yesterday. Now she's at her wits end trying to tend her young son and a sick husband. Kostas says with two Turk ships patrolling the gulf, there's no chance of our navy getting through with supplies.'

About to speak, Kazanis heard bare feet slap the swept earthen floor. He reached around, winced as the movement tore his cut arm and pulled Manos to sit on his lap. Shocked at how his clothing swamped the small, rickety frame, he hugged the boy. With a calloused finger he traced over the weeping sores, so bright on the pale, drawn face looking up at him with adoration. On impulse, he landed a kiss on Manos' forehead before he ruffled the boy's hair.

'Look after your mama, and I'll let you polish my gun later. Now I will meet with the ruling committee.'

*

Kazanis peered through the gloom and waved to Kostas, already sitting on the mosaic floor of the church where the senior men assembled. Christos Kapsalis, owner of the house once rented by Lord Byron, beckoned and pointed to an empty seat. Since they'd first met, the older, seasoned fighter enjoyed hearing about the resistance in Crete.

'Sit by me, Kazanis, Oh, you've spilt blood.'

'A scratch I'd not have noticed in burlier days.'

Chatter ceased as Bishop Joseph stood to offer prayers, before inviting the quartermaster to give an update. It didn't take long. Their depleted rations would last three days; no more. On cue, bellies rumbled. Botsaris took to his feet, looking distinguished in an elaborate red jacket trimmed with cream braid stripes, and topped with an oversized, floppy red fez. All this finery was at odds with his muddied, white pleated kilt and holed leggings.

'Gentlemen, this morning an emissary under a white flag brought a formal invitation to negotiate.'

A collective intake of breath left the chamber silent and alert.

'I scrambled over the walls to meet the pasha, charged by the sultan himself to clear us from Missolonghi.'

A lightening charge zipped through the gathering.

'Through his interpreter, the pasha offered congratulations to the brave men of Klisova. While ashamed of the force deployed against us, he assured me he has thousands of competent men keen to prove their prowess. Now the pasha urges us to surrender and offers each man a choice. Convert to Islam, or spend a lifetime chained to galley oars. His army will provide husbands for unmarried women, unless they choose an alternative life as slaves. Male orphans under the age of twelve will enjoy his funding. After this age, they must join his ranks.'

Botsaris may have expected clamour; he got frigid silence. Kazanis felt his patron's eyes on him and tried to fathom what he wanted. Under the full scrutiny of the assembly, he rose, coughed and bowed.

'General Botsaris, what response did you give?'

'The keys to the city dangle from our cannon.'

Loud cheers brought relief to the general.

As the clamour quelled, a man who almost matched Kostas for accuracy with gunfire stood.

'I propose we seek volunteers to shoot our women and children.'

A collective gasp showed none expected such a proposal. Focused on the bishop, this brave papa said, 'Send the innocent to heaven with a sure shot to protect them from horror.'

'Oh, no. There must be another way.'

The quartermaster, who suffered constant abuse from desperate women, risked another unpopular opinion.

'Don't be hasty. Consider the offer. We're not living, not even existing. There's not even a mouse alive in this hellhole. Every living thing has gone, except for a few scrawny fowl kept under armed guard. Fish soup boiled with seaweed and leather fools our stomachs for moments. Undertakers bury scores daily. More drop dead in our streets than die defending the barricades. Perhaps it's sensible to consider their terms.'

Botsaris overrode the whispered buzz to ask Bishop Joseph, 'What did your census tell?'

'Of the seven thousand souls who say they'll fight, four and a half thousand are women and adolescents.'

A senior military man snorted.

'Women? How can they help our cause?'

The representative from the guild of commerce jumped to respond.

'My wife and daughters can shoot, and we'll take our chances as a family.'

Determined to make a proper address, Kostas accepted a helping hand to stand tall.

'Friends, I'll not presume to add weight to your decisions. But, know this, I'll lead a rearguard until my end. So help me God.'

Under the cover of cheers, Kazanis whispered to Kapsalis, 'God seems a fickle fellow. Those ragheads outside our walls believe him to be on their side.'

Instead of condemning the blasphemy, Kapsalis nodded, as if distracted by his own thoughts. Opinion went back and forth during the impassioned debate. At last, a summons went out to the Swiss newspaperman. Although Kazanis couldn't read, it pleased him to know that printing the outcome might give history a chance to learn their fate. Bishop Joseph invited the editor to read what they'd agreed.

'In the name of the Holy Trinity we beseech you to see how the army and the citizens, young and old, have no hope. All necessary items for life are absent. We have fulfilled our debts as faithful soldiers of the country in this tight siege. We recognise we will all die unless we make a bold decision. We can't expect help from land or sea. In light of this, we declare victory over the enemy. Our triumphant exit will be at two o'clock in the morning of the tenth of April, heralding the dawn of Palm Sunday.'

In the ensuing hush, the editor left to attend to his press.

With a bow, the quartermaster gained everyone's attention. 'Now there's no cause to harbour scraps, my team will visit every home tonight.'

Christos Kapsalis stood, 'Kegs of black powder fill my cellars.'

A puzzled voice asked, 'Do you aim to feed us with it?'

'Those too young, too old or too ill can join me to laugh, sing and pray. When our enemy draws close, I'll light the fuses.'

A timid voice admitted, 'I'll stay with you and pray for courage. Death scares me.'

Kazanis stood, 'Pah! What's the worry? We're already experiencing worse than anything Hades has in store. I've seen lingering deaths from illness, and torturous deaths when souls screamed for release. For me, death in battle is freedom.'

A thrilling rush of energy punched his stomach as all eyes turned to him.

'I prefer to live one more day as a free Cretan than two days as the sultan's vassal. I'm ready for my freedom.'

Careful to gain eye contact with as many men as possible, he waited three heartbeats for maximum attention. Fire shot up his raised arm to his clenched fist as he yelled, 'Freedom.'

As one, all present took up his refrain. 'Freedom!'

*

Later, Kazanis objected, 'No, Kostas. Enjoy some special family time.'

'What, you'll leave me to the rough edge of Popi's tongue? She'll not forgive me if you stay in barracks. You're right, it's family time. Join us.'

Sat cross-legged before a blazing fire, Kazanis accepted his bowl.

'Thank you, Popi. What a treat, I can't remember the last time I felt warm.'

For a moment, his mouth watered at a sliver of meat. He stole a glimpse in the other bowls. Neither Popi nor Kostas had chicken, while Manos had three tiny pieces.

'Here, child, eat my meat.'

'Really?'

'My loose teeth can't chew.'

Popi returned from settling Manos under his blanket.

'Are the plans made, Husband?'

'You muster in front of the fourth gate with the final group. Sorry, the nimble go first.'

She dabbed her eye with her apron and forced a smile.

'What about you, Kazanis?'

'Behind Botsaris, charging from the main gate with the decoy group. We'll draw fire, allowing our key fighting force to surge through gates two and three. They'll engage the enemy from the sides. Men are clearing the barricading stonework as we speak. Mothers with young will escape once we've cleared the way, then head for the mountains.'

Kostas picked up Popi's hand to hold to his cheek, 'It's difficult to imagine how you will live. Perhaps you'd better go to Kapsalis.' He stroked her belly. 'Neither of us can flee.'

'Both my babes deserve a chance, I must try.'

With eyes locked, he fumbled behind his neck.

'Here, Mama placed her crucifix around my neck before she died so I'd know her love when it moved against my skin. Feel my love.'

In that moment, Kazanis realised his place was elsewhere.

*

Before dawn on Lazarus Saturday, Kazanis recognised the limping gait of Kostas heading his way. After quelling his cough, Kostas said, 'I could use a hand to make manikins.'

'That's a good ruse. Fake heads in our watchtowers will buy us time.'

'As long as they don't burn as fast as a stuffed Judas on Easter morning.'

'How many lifetimes ago did we collect discarded clothes to create our figures?'

'Ah, I remember your pa belting you the time you stole his best shirt.'

Clouds chased by a brisk wind scudded across the sky, revealing the morning star to the east. Deep in their own reverie, the pair worked side by side. Finally, with their task complete, Kostas looked seaward towards the first glow of sunrise.

'It's so clear, we'll be able to view the distant mountains beyond the main channel. I miss our mountains in Lassithi.'

'We'd be selecting the Easter lambs for roasting now.'

'I thought I'd die on Crete.'

'We carry her with us, Kostas. Embrace me, I'll not look for you later.' With forced cheer he added, 'See you on resurrection morning.'

He'd taken only six brisk paces when he heard, 'Will you take care of Popi and Manos?'

Bile rose in Kazanis' throat. He swallowed hard, and without turning, said, 'I can't make an empty promise. Who knows what the turmoil will throw at us?'

44

Exodus

Folk buried valuables under their floors with little prospect of reclaiming them. Many women sewed coins in hems, while the men stacked the few remaining doors at regular intervals, ready to bridge trenches. Other women, many in male garb, piled mattresses, pillows and blankets against the walls, ready to fill fissures and ditches. Uninitiated folk had brief lessons on how to fire a gun. Unlike any other battle preparation, none tore sheets for bandages.

By mid-afternoon, Kazanis had leisure to join the throng in the cobbled city square, where tavernas once traded. To whip up a carnival atmosphere, musicians played rousing songs of ancient heroes as folk danced with passion. Children ran wild, chasing and screaming; no parent had the will to quieten them. At dusk, a distant muezzin called his faithful to prayer and Christians made for their churches. Lost for something to do, Kazanis wandered to the main watchtower where a cadet, puffing with exertion, found him.

'Botsaris wants you.'

*

'Ah, Kazanis. My men are wearing their best uniforms. Take your pick.'

Fine silk blouses, thick woollen kilts and snow-white hose lay on the mattress beside a row of burnished boots. Kazanis fingered a pair of red-tasselled pompoms; a glance showed the general's boots wore similar decorations.

'Do you mind if I say no? I've lived and fought as a Cretan peasant.' He grinned at his friend, 'God won't recognise me if I turn up wearing this finery. Thank you for the thought.'

Botsaris, resplendent in an elaborate costume with a bejewelled breastplate, forced a cheerful reply, 'Humour me. Select something as a memento.'

Kazanis remembered a tale about small, hidden knives. He toyed with the pompoms, his disappointment clear.

'Lift your boot. I'll fit them. Now wait.'

Botsaris lifted his own foot to rest it against the wall, and fiddled a moment. Turning back to Kazanis, he held out a thumb-length blade, a gem in its hilt, 'Now you know the rumour is true. Let me fix my knife for you. The ruby will pay your passage to Crete.'

'I once had a knife this size. I kept it tied to my beard so I'd never be without a weapon.

'Ah, same reason for our little knives. I always knew you were a Souliot at heart.'

Brusquely, to hide his emotion, Kazanis said, 'You should go. Bishop Joseph awaits.'

'And you. You've earned your place for communion.'

On bony knees, in the swathe between city and walls, Kazanis dreaded the service being overlong. Bishop Joseph reminded everyone that today commemorated the miracle of Lazarus, who thanks to Jesus rose from the dead, and assured his congregation they too would rise on resurrection morning. After psalms, Bishop Joseph shared communion, passing along each line with his treasured silver chalice filled with water instead of wine.

When Kazanis felt the bishop rest his hand for a blessing an unexpected heat suffused him and he jerked his head up in surprise. Love shone from the bishop's eyes.

'Go forth with the certainty God goes with you.'

For all he decried religion, Kazanis experienced a cocoon of calm as he watched the bishop pass through his flock. Afterwards, Kazanis had no task to occupy his final hours, and on impulse decided to keep Popi company.

*

Horrified screams ended his mellow mood. Wails from the crowd near Popi's house galvanised him. He dropped to cradle the lifeless woman, tugged a dagger from her stomach and closed her eyelids, thankful he didn't recognise her. Another man lifted her child, and the growing assembly cried out as blood from the boy's slit throat puddled the dusty street. Righteous voices raised a clamour the moment the men carried their sad burdens out of sight.

'Her husband should have stopped her.'

A man's emaciated corpse, not yet rigid, lay on the bed.

'Now she's damned for ever.'

They laid the mama next to her husband.

'How could she?'

They placed the boy in his mama's arms.

'Cold-blooded murder.'

Both men kissed the serene face.

'It's a sin to end your own life.'

Livid now, Kazanis burst out of the house.

'How dare you judge? Your brave neighbour gave her son a final gift. A swift, clean end.' He waved the bloodied dagger aloft, not caring who it splattered, 'How I wish I could have spared my son his dreadful death. I'll never know if I'd have had the nerve. Are you brave enough?' Stunned silence provided his answer.

*

Later, enemy cannon blasted as expected, shaking the city walls as the defenders returned fire. One by one, stuffed heads appeared in lookout points, releasing men for the muster. Direct hits on city walls went unattended, as the chasms would aid the Christian exodus. As usual, the cannon bombardment ceased in the hour after midnight.

Botsaris and the senior officers saluted to bring their forces to attention. Never was a multitude so hushed. Flag bearers swirled new embroidered standards in soundless tribute. As the first gate swung wide, the leading pennant dipped. The end had started.

Shoulder to shoulder with his comrades, Kazanis squeezed through to leap over the rough, shaking bridge. Botsaris led the charge with screams to rouse the dead. On reaching the centre of the enemy camp, Botsaris halted in confusion.

'Where are they?'

Bewildered, Kazanis spun to see the swarm spilling unchecked from the second gate. Kazanis stooped to free his boot from a torn carpet, and as he slashed at it with a dagger, he realised he stood in a cleared area of the compound where tents had dotted the ground before dark. Shouts and gunfire swallowed his angry howl, 'Those mongrels expected us.'

Sickened, he witnessed the Ottoman forces stand aside to funnel the human tide. Their first artillery rank fired with appalling precision. Cavalry took a slow, deliberate ride to close the trap. Against the flow, Kazanis jostled for space to witness the final gate open. Mounted troops waited until women and children rushed out, then rode at them, hooves scything through the soft target. Fury sped his feet and fuelled his arm. He shot, hacked and stabbed, while horses pranced through a swelling mound of bodies. When a Greek voice called retreat, their doom became inevitable.

Frightened beyond thought, the multitude headed towards gaps in the city walls. Converging folk fell where they died, blocking the exit for others. Such a winning tactic brought shrieks of glee from the triumphant pasha.

The bright moon broke free of the clinging clouds, and in its silver flare Kazanis saw smoke-enveloped fighting on the walls. As a rebel flag fell, his yell of rage mingled with the pandemonium. He reached a breach at the same moment as a Turk wielding a curved sabre.

Kazanis stepped forward as if the blade didn't exist. He ignored his opponent's rising hand and fired without flinching. Not checking his foe had died, he seized his weapon and leapt on the board bridging the rubble-filled moat. Determined to hold the flimsy pass, Kazanis knelt to refill his pistols. A looming shadow won his hasty shot. Powder sparks stung his eyes. With no time to reload, he grabbed a blade from his cummerbund. It spun towards the next screaming harpy flying at him. Acrid smoke billowing to mix with an incoming sea mist caused Kazanis to cough and wheeze. Desperate for air, he gripped his prize blade and braced himself against the swipe of his next attacker. His stomach lurched as the plank splintered. He backed up, a movement that allowed the Turk foothold. Their blades sparked with each clash and parry, delivering reverberating pain. His heart pounded, his lungs wheezed, and he sensed imminent freedom from this life.

The strained timber folded, its crack drowned by the din. Kazanis felt the lurch, and leapt. Satisfied his opponent was drowning in the disgusting water, he hawked and spat, then sprang up the pile of rubble with the ease of a mountain goat. Now, with a height advantage and an inexhaustible supply of ammunition, he bowled rocks at each aggressor. A sudden memory of his friend Angelos gave him frenzied strength as he yelled, 'Howzat,' pelting the oncoming horde. A sickening crunch as his ankle turned on loose debris sent him backwards.

After breaking his fall on a corpse, he tumbled down piled rubble to land near an abandoned gun emplacement. Winded, Kazanis sat gasping. Not trusting his foot, he crawled to a cleft, too dark to see people sheltered there.

'Mama, be quiet. Turks will find us.'

'Manos? What in God's name are you doing here?'

'Mama keeps yelling. I hold her hand, but she won't stop.'

Curled in pain, Popi's next birthing scream chilled him.

'It's Kazanis. Can you stand?'

Ankle and head throbbing, he looked around. Fires burnt bright the Turk side of the wall, making black silhouettes of those battling on top. Huddled at the base, they didn't seem in immediate danger.

He made a rapid decision to join those sheltering with Christos Kapsalis. To gain the safety of the city alleyways, they needed to cross the void. Ah well, no matter if they took a shot in the back. Although Popi resisted his efforts, he pulled her up and half-dragged her along, limping in pain. Scared and confused, Manos grizzled but followed down a cobbled lane between houses. Here, flickering light from candles and lamps behind unglazed windows lit their path, and Kazanis blessed the fleeing women who created the illusion their house remained a home. At last, they reached the grand facade of Kapsalis' house, and he hammered on the solid wood door without wondering why this house still had one. Inside the house voices rose in song, blanketing his noise.

'Uncle Kazanis. The fighting is getting nearer.'

'Follow me. There's a tunnel where your papa and I had an adventure.'

Shocked by the volume of Popi's screams, Kazanis paused in case Christos Kapsalis came to investigate. With a false grin at Manos, he said, 'I once hid a boat in reeds. If it's still there, I'll take us away.'

His ankle seemed stronger, and thoughts of the boat delivered a surge of energy to haul Popi. Although he worried she'd not screamed since they left Kapsalis' house, he left her on the gravel near the tunnel.

'Stay with Mama. I'll be back, I promise.'

Moonlight illuminated his problem. He shook the chained gate, cussing how this single piece of metal had missed the meltdown for cannon shot. Although reluctant to use the last knife in his cummerbund, he had no option. He drove it between the rusty links and twisted until his biceps strained and the recent cut burst open. Slippery blood dripped off his fingers to make things worse. A resonating boom brought urgency.

The link broke as his blade snapped. Propelled forward, Kazanis hit the path leading to the docks. He scrabbled for the pieces of broken knife, held them with disbelief then flung the bits away, his howl of dismay echoing down the tunnel.

Even under stress, Kazanis recognised Popi had to go with him while he sought the boat. When the cold water on her bare legs brought whimpers, he closed his ears and waded forward, cursing he'd not removed his boots. Manos rode on his back, gripping tight. Three times Kazanis slipped in shifting silt, and he expected to drown if he went down again. God must have been on their side, for the craft lay safe among the reeds. Kazanis tipped Manos in, dragged Popi over the side and reassured himself as much as her.

'You're safe now.'

Kazanis welcomed the initial queasy turn, proving they were indeed afloat. With no means of propulsion, the craft bobbed and drifted while Kazanis caught his breath. Then came the most chilling sound, 'Will you deliver my babe?'

He hugged her close, still staring at the flashes, fire, and shadows of battle.

'Easy. I must have delivered a thousand lambs.'

Inspiration sent Kazanis scrabbling around his wet, booted ankles.

'Thank God for Botsaris. Now, Manos, hold this tiny knife and Mama will show you the magic of life. Tonight, you become a brother.'

*

All four drowsed as the craft drifted in the lagoon. Kazanis planned to use his hands to paddle out to sea once dawn came. A blast direct from Hades woke them. A swift series of explosions sent great draughts of hot air rushing across the lagoon to rock their small vessel. Forlorn and helpless, they watched in awe as the blazing remains of Kapsalis' house sent debris high.

In a gruff whisper, Kazanis prayed, 'May their memory be eternal.'

45

Dreams

A draught, resulting from Rosi's vicious slamming of the door, wobbled a chipped jug of early fresh freesias, wafting their heady scent. Those inside the kafenion stared, wide-eyed and open-mouthed at the door. It trembled in its frame long after her furious clacking clogs had dashed away over cobbles. Katerina, who sat prim and veiled, found her voice first.

'Don't be so soft with her, Spanos.'

'No use trying to work out what fires her. Only the other day, Miss Opinionated stated that if she owned my kafenion, she'd encourage women. I'd have thought she'd delight in serving you. What do you say, Petros?'

His companion, Nikos, laughed, answering for him.

'We chatted about the bride Katerina proposes for me. With my sister unmarried, I can't consider it.' He clapped Petros' shoulder, 'I suggested my friend takes the bride instead.'

The hum of conversation around the warming brazier resumed as if uninterrupted. Spanos wiped the spilt water from the table.

'Let me fetch more water to go with your coffee, young Nikos, it's an easy price. Last time Rosi lost her temper, I ducked to avoid a flying plate. Good job it was tin.'

Katerina stood, pulling up a rabbit fur hood, 'Consider the offer, Nikos. To use your sister Rosi is a flimsy excuse. Everyone knows your great-grandpa Nikos raised her until his death, and Spanos has fed, housed and clothed her these past years. I'm shocked you claim responsibility.' She winked at Petros, adding, 'Better save to offer a dowry big enough to attract a groom to accept such a testy girl.'

Spanos picked up a jug and accompanied Katerina over the rain-sodden track to the spring.

'Her rudeness is inexcusable. You're always so good to Rosi.'

'She'll tell me the cause sooner or later. What these lads don't understand is young women overheat every month.'

Later, Petros swept a pile of crumbs round and round the floor. Spanos snapped him from his daydream.

'She'll come back before dusk.'

'What? Sorry my thoughts wandered.'

'Rosi won't stay angry. Meanwhile, I'd prefer that mess in our fire.'

'Why does she get so cross these days? Everything I say is wrong.'

'Most men find women complicated. Here, take a raki. Let's celebrate a good session this morning.'

'If any of them pay.'

Spanos eased down onto his bespoke wider chair, and puffing with exertion, said, 'You've learnt to reckon numbers. Now learn to value the other ways men repay me. Take Katerina's husband. True, he has a long line in the tally book, he'll never pay. Now, who made Rosi's clothes until she became adept? Katerina. Who helped Rosi understand the way her body changes? Katerina. Who taught Rosi a wider range of recipes than I ever could? Katerina.'

When Petros tried to interrupt, Spanos raised a hand, 'No, let me finish. Those widowers who eat here each evening don't come for our raki, they can get similar elsewhere. No, our girl's fine pies, stews and bakes keep them loyal.'

With a nod and a wry grin, Petros said, 'Ah yes, customers even bring the wine, raki and meat we serve them.'

'Exactly.'

'Where does Rosi go most afternoons?'

'Katerina used to collect her; now, I confess I don't pry. She enjoys more time to herself than a normal family allows. Admit it, we've an odd set-up here.'

'It works though, and Nikos enjoys sharing my bedroom across the street during the winter.'

Flames flared and crackled as Petros added his sweepings.

'Stoke the fire, so I'm cosy for my sleep.'

'Look at your cat, ready to snuggle with you.' As he spoke he lifted a woollen cloak off the sofa, 'When Rosi flounced out, she left this. Rest, and I'll search. She'll be too proud to return, even if chilled to the bone.'

With no sign of Rosi nearby, Petros walked into the maze of alleyways at the top of Kritsa. Only a few determined souls lived up here, and as he neared an open door, he sniffed, appreciating the tempting aroma of stew. Petros didn't notice the dark shadow on a doorstep.

'Do you seek your maid?' It was Katerina, 'Ha, ha! I made you jump.'

'Um, how do you know I seek her?'

'When she strutted past, I asked if she was well. Rosi shouted back she hated you and never wanted to see you again.'

Petros studied his boots.

'Don't fret, lad. The cloak will be welcome. You'll find her at home. Can't miss it, old Nikos carved a cross in the lintel.'

'Oh, Rodanthe's house. I've only been there once, the day her papa died.'

'I've a hunch there's a great deal you don't know. Best get yourself up there, but don't tell her I told you.'

Petros clutched the cloak and strode off, the woman's laughter bouncing along the crumbling walls of the narrow alley behind him. Now his anger fizzed and sped his feet. How dare she play in a deserted house and put herself at risk?

Even without the carved cross, he'd have known he'd reached the right place. A sad lament in her light, tuneful voice reached through the unglazed window, setting time for the rhythmic thrum of a shuttle. Dry-mouthed, he noticed the scrubbed doorstep flanked by pots of the same freesias scenting the kafenion. A peek through the grille registered a cosy fire blazing in the grate. With a glance at the cloak over his arm, he hesitated – this unknown Rosi appeared to have everything.

In response to his angry knocking, the door opened a crack.

'Go away. If you want a hearth, check what your new girl can offer.'

His boot wedged in the small gap, 'Here's your cloak.'

'She won't want you fussing after me.'

'Don't be silly. Let me in.'

The gap increased. He stepped in, banging against a loom, and stood confused by the sight of a proper home. Behind a much-repaired armchair, Rosi crossed her arms tight against her chest to issue a terse invitation to sit. Without realising, he rubbed a sweaty hand on the chair arm, then stopped, anxious not to soil its exquisite embroidered cover.

'I didn't know you could weave.'

Rosi went to speak, choked on tears, then tried again, 'Katerina taught me.'

'Why here?'

'This is my play house.'

'No, it might have been once. Now it should be a family home.'

Eyes narrowed as her fists clenched, 'Katerina bid me ask Nikos if he wanted this house. My brother scoffed, saying he had no wish for a heap of stones too far from the village heart.'

Petros cast an appreciative glance round the neat and tidy room, noticing a new door in its stone arch frame, grey from ingrained soot.

'Katerina's husband fixed it for me.' With a blush, she added, 'For privacy in the bedroom.'

'You plan to leave us?'

'No, it's for time alone. Unless Cousin Rodanthe joins me.'

'Oh my, it's time you grew out of hearing voices.'

She took a pace towards him, hands planted on hips and hair unbound, 'Don't laugh. Rodanthe's my friend, and she gave me the idea to make a home for my husband.'

'Why be sly and not tell us?'

'Where else could I practice what Katerina teaches me? Anyway, you're sneaky, talking about a wife when you're already betrothed.'

'What? Who said anything about betrothal? Be sure, when I marry I'll find a gentle soul, not a harpy.'

As she snatched a jar from the mantelpiece, he ducked just in time as it shattered at his feet, sending blue missiles bouncing. She screamed as if in pain, dropping to the floor.

'Sorry, Rodanthe. Now he's made me spill your beads.'

Her distress cut him.

'Don't cry, I'll help you collect them.' He knelt next to her, 'Spanos will spare you a jar. How many must we find?'

Through sobs, she said, 'Twenty-four.'

Petros stopped scrabbling, 'I remember now. Rodanthe's papa explained his embarrassment when her godfather held her as a baby. I'm sure he mentioned twenty-five talismans.'

Through sniffles, she said, 'Yes, there's a bigger one. Hidden in a box, with metal discs.'

Frozen, with one hand reaching under her loom, Petros felt his stomach lurch.

'Please show me the box?'

Rosi changed back to a giggling girl.

'Help me move this table. The rug was the first thing I wove. This hole looked dreadful when I trod on the remains of its lid.' She reached inside the space, 'Ugh, spider's webs. Here's the box.'

His breath hissed in release, 'Open it.'

Unaware of his anticipation, she prised the lid and held up a sapphire-blue glass bauble with a painted white eye.

'It wards off evil. Take it.'

He held the ornament up to the light and tried to sound nonchalant, 'What else do you keep in there?'

Rosi passed him a faded red velvet bag with a worn drawstring, and eight gold coins clinked together as he tipped them in his hand.

'My clever girl.'

Keen to put their quarrel behind them, he bent to kiss her cheek in the same moment she moved her head to speak. Their lips held a kiss. Pink and coy, she smiled. His blood raced. Joined in another kiss, he stroked her hair. Shocked by his passion, he tried to hide transgression by whirling her around in the tight space until they were both dizzy.

'Rosi, don't you realise? You can have whatever you want in life.'

Back on her feet, Rosi staggered, 'Oh, I'm giddy and happy. Sit there. Make yourself at home.'

'Rodanthe's papa told me he hid gold coins in here and said we should share them. Pa helped me search. We thought we'd looked everywhere.'

'Ah, so they've value?'

'Remember how Spanos gives us a few coins to spend in the autumn market? Well, one of these could buy everything in the place. With four each, we're rich. You can choose a new direction for your life.'

He should have noticed her smile fade.

'Oh. What do you intend?'

'Spanos won't hold me to his kafenion, he'll understand ...' His eyes closed against her glare, 'America! That's it. I'll seek my future where my dreams lead.'

The chill in her voice passed unrecognised. 'I suggest you go. Break your news to Spanos.'

Thin-lipped, Rosi handed four napoleons to Petros.

*

If only he'd stopped to think; but no, he raced to the kafenion.

'Spanos! We've found the gold coins left by Rodanthe's pa.'

Although he panted for breath, not making any sense, men waiting for Rosi to cook their dinner heard the word gold. Questions came thick and fast.

'What gold?'

'Where is it?'

'Who has gold?'

Petros poured a large jug of raki with a trembling hand.

'Here, my friends. Drink. Share my excitement. For the first time, I'll treat you.'

Still confused, the odd assortment of widowers, bachelors and henpecked husbands accepted their drink with a happy, 'Yammas.'

Spanos, the only person who knew of the bequest, slumped on his special chair as if his bones turned to jelly. Not returning Petros' smile, he stated the obvious.

'You'll be leaving us.'

On dancing feet, Petros leapt to hug his patron, 'I knew you'd wish me well.'

An ancient gent lifted his glass, hinting for a refill.

'Where will you go, lad? You must know the Turks still restrict travel.'

Conscious he had everyone's attention, Petros stood, 'Restrictions? Pah. Since when have restrictions held back a man of wealth? Once I get to Megalo Kastro, I'll be one more traveller thronging the port.' He looked to Spanos for support, 'Remember the men who drive carts of olives to the soap factory? Every year they urge villagers to ride with them, saying there's plenty of work in the docks.'

Revived by this news, Spanos sat straighter, 'Wonderful, I can visit you in the big city to see its huge fort at least once before I die.'

'Travel much further to visit me, Spanos. Refill the glasses and I'll tell you where I head. Get ready to toast my good fortune and wish me a good journey.'

After flourishing his own full glass, Petros gulped, wiped his mouth on the back of his hand and grinned.

'Friends, I am going to ... Am.Mer.Ri.Ca!'

46

Kritsa, January 1830

Flies buzzed around oil lamps. Flames crackled in the brazier. A cat mewed. Boys chased each other outside. Blank faces stared at the lunatic. Confused by the silence, Petros turned to Spanos, who sat with a glass frozen before his lips.

'You've heard of America, Spanos? It's the place where rivers hold gold nuggets.'

A chuckle broke from the stunned ranks.

'Aye, lad. Go to the moon afterwards. Some say it's made of cheese.'

One hungry man said, 'Hurry to the moon. Get me a slice of cheese to go with this raki.'

Customers returned to their chatter, laughing at the crazy ideas of youth, while Petros tried in vain to get someone to understand. Spanos dabbed his eyes with the end of his sleeve, only looking up when Katerina stomped towards the kitchen, untying her cloak as the room hushed.

'I'll cook supper for your customers, Spanos. Meanwhile, Rosi sleeps near me.' With a venomous glance at Petros, she said, 'Remember, the love of money is the root of all evil.'

*

Daylight woke Petros long past the usual hour. As he forced himself to sit upright, he realised he'd slept through Rosi's routine knock. A bemused glance took in the empty windowsill; no steaming cup of herb tea. Odd. She invariably left him and Nikos a drink. A glimpse at the still form on the second bed showed her brother had overslept too. As he reached for his boots, the sole item removed before bed, he remembered she'd stayed with Katerina. He groaned. His head hurt from drinking too much raki; coffee was the only remedy. Snores from Nikos continued as Petros left their bedroom, heading to the spring to wash.

As he walked towards the kafenion, customers poked fun in voices chiming over each other.

'Ha, Spanos, do you see how our great adventurer even finds it difficult to cross the track this morning?'

'It's so late in the morning, we thought you'd already gone on your travels.'

'The wild wind of last night was strong enough to carry you overseas.'

'Sit by me, youngster, and I'll give you directions to leave Kritsa.'

'My old grandpa told me tales of Pegasus. Guess you'll need the mythical winged stallion to whisk you to your paradise.'

'Ha ha! You are all comedians this morning. Let's pray you still see the joke when Spanos gets my letter saying I found gold.'

Spanos was the only one not laughing.

'Such a journey needs preparation. Will you delay until the next visit from our pappas? I'd be happier if you leave with a proper blessing. Meanwhile, drink this coffee.'

With his first sip, Petros realised his mentor wanted to delay his departure, and always grateful for the home Spanos provided, he nodded, 'When do you think the pappas will visit?'

'Who can be sure? With clergy numbers depleted, our pappas ranges a wide parish.'

'Yes, Spanos, that sounds good. Whenever he next visits us, I'll leave the day afterwards.'

As the men drinking coffee resumed their chatter, Petros glimpsed Rosi's apron over the back of a chair, bringing a delicious recollection of yesterday's kiss. Sudden heat suffused his face. When did Rosi become a beautiful young woman? Not wanting his blush questioned, he hurried to milk the goats tethered behind the kafenion. Later, and each subsequent evening, Rosi served men with quiet efficiency before leaving. Everyone assumed she'd moved in with Katerina.

The next day Petros found Rosi in the kafenion's kitchen, sawing at a rabbit with a huge knife.

'Hey, I always chop the rabbits.'

'I must grow used to managing, now you're leaving me.'

Ouch, Petros hadn't expected that. 'Ah, well let me do it today.'

She swung around, gripping the blade as if holding an attacker at bay, 'Spanos says you must hunt strange animals for food, unless they kill you first.'

'Um, I hadn't thought of meals. I guess Americans must have something sorted out.'

Chopped onions already in the pot caused Rosi to sniffle.

'Pass me the meat.'

Wiping her nose along her sleeve, she lifted the bloody carcass.

'Go away. I don't need you.'

Her rejection made him awkward. Free of a kerchief, her hair tumbled down her back, and a sudden memory of their embrace gave him the urge to stroke the tantalising locks. As if reading his mind, she brandished the knife again.

'Chop some firewood. Spanos asked you yesterday, but you've been busy talking of gold to anyone who'll listen.'

'Why does every girl become a shrill nag?'

'Why does every self-centred man expect women to wait on them?'

'I offered to help.'

'Interfere, you mean. It'll be good when you've gone.'

Shocked at her venom, Petros stalked out.

That night's stew brought comment from the first customer to dip his rusk. 'Hey, Spanos, why no chunks in my stew? With these shreds you should name it rabbit soup.'

*

Two days later, Petros was sweeping debris from the veranda when Rosi emerged from the alley, weighed down by a heavy basket of prepared food.

'Hey, I'll carry that.'

268

To restore her circulation, Rosi rubbed at her sore wrist.

'It's not too big, I can manage.'

If Rosi noticed he met her to carry her basket every morning, she didn't mention it.

Today Petros walked as far as Katerina's without meeting his girl, and at Katerina's open door, he called, 'Have you seen Rosi?'

Slow movement brought the woman to her threshold.

'My husband is ill in bed. Rosi has been a godsend bringing warming broths, and she went to feed our rabbits earlier.'

'Do you want me to tend your milk goat?'

'Thank you, but no. These days there's plenty for her to eat between the cobbles. When I came to Kritsa, every wife in this street worked hard to bring daily greens as goat feed.'

'She's doing a grand job munching overgrown weeds and shrubs. When do you expect Rosi?'

'Not until tomorrow.'

'I thought she lived here.'

Even as he spoke, Petros knew the answer, and ran to Rodanthe's house.

Back in a hurry, Petros stepped inside Katerina's home.

'Sorry to disturb you again. Where do you keep your rabbits?'

*

After the muddy patch between the last houses and Afentis Christos church, Petros strode the uphill path to reach the hutches full of rabbits munching on piled fresh greens.

'Rosi! Rosi, where are you?'

Dread chilled him, then anger spurred him forward through the crushed grass proving someone had walked this way. How dare she not answer.

'Rosi, show yourself. This is no time for games.'

'Petros? Help me. I'm in a hole.'

'Call again, I can't see you.'

'Here, I'm shaking a bush.'

Her kerchief tangled among thorns made an effective signal. For a moment he halted in shock. Her blood-streaked face poked out from flattened grass, and her mud-caked hands clung to some woody thyme.

'Hurry. If this last clump breaks, I'll splash down.'

In a heartbeat he saw the sheer-sided pit overgrown by shrubs, and threw himself down to seize her under her armpits. 'Grab my blouse. I'll wriggle backwards to draw you out.'

It was easier said than done. His arms strained, grasses tickled his cheeks and thorns raked his legs, while a pesky cat mewed at his side.

'Wait, I'll kneel instead, then pull. Try to climb.'

The sodden earth collapsed, sending Rosi backwards. When the blouse fabric tore, she squealed in fear and grabbed another handful. The leverage Petros gained by kneeling did the trick, and he soon cradled a drenched and slimy Rosi in his arms.

'Don't cry, you're safe now.'

Through chattering teeth, she said, 'How did you find me?'

'You weren't by the rabbit hutches, then I saw your track through the grass.'

Not heeding his own wet and muddy state, he clasped her close to carry her, kissing her lips when she tried to speak.

'Shush, such a fright. You need to get warm.'

Without considering an alternative action, he raised the latch to her door and set her on the floor before the fire. Thankful a kettle stood in the hearth, he used a stick to stir the embers.

'Have you any clothes here?'

'Spanos has my spare set.'

He picked her up again and ducked through the arch to place her on the bed.

'Strip off and wrap yourself in a blanket. I'll make you a hot drink then go for your clothes.'

Her stare unnerved him. 'Do you hurt?'

Flushed under her mud streaks instead of ashen white, she bit her knuckles to smother her giggles. Unsuccessful, she snorted then laughed. Petros grinned, 'Well, that's not how I expected to find you.'

Convulsed with what Petros saw as tears of laughter, she said, 'The way you've carried me to this room wasn't my dream.'

Not understanding, Petros shrugged and handed over an almost-clean nose rag.

'Wipe your eyes and get cosy while I fix your drink.'

*

Despite his bulk, Spanos rushed to Rosi, Petros at his heels. Not until he'd clambered onto her bed to kiss her did Spanos believe Rosi safe. Concern and cuddles drew more tears as she explained how she'd chased a cat running off with a snatched baby rabbit. In a split second she'd fallen through undergrowth to a hidden water trough. By the time she'd realised she could touch the bottom, she was choking up foul water and panicking at blood dripping from facial scratches.

'It was so scary, Spanos. When I tried to climb out, the mud sides broke away, tipping me back into the hole.'

Spanos held her close, 'It makes me sick to think what might have happened, had Petros not looked for you.'

'I'd have drowned.'

Red-rimmed eyes turned on a smiling Petros, 'If it happened after you left Kritsa, I'd be dead, and you wouldn't even know. Don't pretend you care.'

Petros' smile died as his chest tightened, and his lack of reply passed unnoticed as Spanos marvelled at the house and how hard she'd worked. He gave Petros a wink, 'Katerina swore me to secrecy until our lass was ready to show us your home.'

A frosty 'My home' passed unnoticed by Spanos; not so, Petros.

'Stay here tonight, Spanos. Use the armchair by the fire. I'll tend our customers.'

*

The three men, sitting huddled in their cloaks on the veranda, welcomed Petros' arrival.

'Ah, thought we'd die of exposure out here.'

'Thought Pegasus had whisked you and Spanos off to America.'

'Perhaps he did, and the lad has popped back with a sack of gold.'

'Great, he can treat us to raki.'

Frustration burnt at the teasing, 'A word of encouragement wouldn't go amiss.'

Not bothering to lower their voices, the taunts continued while Petros brewed coffee. Although he didn't realise it, each of his tormentors was in awe of his audacity to even consider such an adventure. None of them had been beyond the church of Panagia Kera, or Katharo.

Slops splashed as he banged the tray.

'Drink up and go. There'll be no food tonight. Katerina tends her husband, and Rosi is in shock from an accident. Spanos is tending her at the top of the village. I'll take them a basket of food before catching a shooting star back to America.'

Damp and uncomfortable, he stomped off, feeling sick and drained of energy. As soon as he was out of sight, he slumped on the doorstep of an uninhabited house. Overwhelmed by a sense of loss, he wept. His sobs couldn't have choked him more had Rosi died; she was dead to him. Once he'd composed himself, he set off along the alley. Nervous at his potential reception at Rosi's, he smiled at Spanos, waiting in the doorway.

'Here's food to see you through the night.'

'Bless you for knowing me well.'

'There's cold stew in this pot, and cheese and rusks to make a meal. How's Rosi?'

'Asleep. It turns out she fell in the old Epiphany pond, dug by Pappas Mathaios with best intentions. You look white. Are you ill?'

'No, I'm fine. I'll borrow a pick tomorrow and fill that pit.'

'So … um … I've had time to think and want to say something.' Spanos coughed to clear his throat, 'I'm loath to interfere, but I'll never forgive myself if I don't speak my mind. Do you realise no one will think worse of you if you decide against America?'

Relief surged, catching Petros off guard. Desperate to prevent his friend seeing his face, he stared along the alley. What he wanted to say was that he loved Rosi and couldn't bear the thought of leaving her; instead, he said, 'I should have gone before I went soft.'

47

Goodbye Kritsa

Life resumed its awkward pattern, with Rosi spending as little time as possible at the kafenion while Petros contrived to be in the right place at the right time to lift and carry. Every day he longed for her to soften and chat with their previous easy familiarity. Each night he punched his pillow in frustration at her continued aloofness. Since he'd pulled her from the pit, he realised he didn't want to live without the love of his life. He even woke in the night to rehearse telling her of his wish to spend a lifetime together in Kritsa.

*

A few days later, two boys ran in, breathless with exertion, each vying to spill their news. Spanos laughed, 'Stop! Now you, you're the tallest, tell me.'

'We were behind Panagia Kera church collecting lemons, and we saw the pappas at rest. He bid us to tell folk to be ready for him tomorrow.'

Rosi paled. She dried her hands, untied her kitchen apron and smoothed her kerchief.

'Katerina will need help to prepare food.'

By the time the pappas arrived at the now popular Church of Saint George, people had packed the grassy knoll for a fine holiday, thanking God for delivering one of the renowned warm, if short, January days. Several men tended a sizzling firepit issuing delicious wafts of roasting mutton. Each woman contributed what she could to the plank tables groaning under the weight of potatoes, olives, eggs, chicken stew, spicy rice pilaf, bean stew, pasta, assorted fresh greens drizzled with oil and lemon, nuts, cheese, and rusks dampened with water and sprinkled with precious salt. Some men gained cheers of appreciation by producing wine to wash down their splendid meal. By mid-afternoon the children were playing and the women were tidying up, while the men were lounging in a group, laughing, joking and passing raki flasks.

Content with his reception, the pappas circulated, blessing the faithful and baptising babies. Several villagers loudly pointed Petros out with a taunt, and each time, he forced a grin or a quip in response. As the crowd thinned, Petros couldn't avoid a direct conversation with the cleric.

'Well, young man, you're off travelling. Nothing to hold you in Kritsa?'

'I've never belonged, Pappas.'

'Spanos seemed to make you welcome.'

'No man could have been more generous.' From the corner of his eye he saw Rosi, and a sudden lump in his throat threatened his ability to talk. After a swift cough, he continued, 'I'll get to America and relish adventures along the way.'

'Do you know how to find America?'

'No idea! My plan is to walk to the port at Megalo Kastro to seek a passage.'

'Have you heard our navy won a major battle back in 1827?'

'No, Pappas. News reaches us slowly.'

'God willing, the seas should be safer for your enterprise. Now, let me bless you.'

As Petros knelt, his eyes levelled on Rosi sitting nearby, her watching face a mask of anguish. The pappas moved on, not recognising the great unhappiness engulfing Petros. Blessing received, Petros could no longer fake a cheerful response when teasing men barracked him. He wandered away, feeling confused and in need of time alone. At the edge of the happy gathering, he finally concluded his best action was to set off without delay.

Confident no one saw him, Petros rushed up the steep bank between the pine trees, leaving the cheery revellers behind. As he topped the mound, he saw Katerina resting on a log in a patch of sunshine. A different resolution hit him like a lightning bolt, and full of optimism, he requested permission to sit beside her.

As soon as his brief conversation with Katerina concluded, Petros sped away and charged into the kafenion, desperate for a hiding place. Startled by the cat leaping from Spanos' great bed, Petros chuckled.

'Thank you, cat.'

Even as he pulled the bed curtains closed, heavy footsteps sounded on the veranda. Spanos groaned from hauling his bulk and dragged his favourite chair.

'Missed me, have you? Sit still and keep your claws to yourself.' Contented purring, then a clink as Spanos poured raki. 'No! What have you done? Pesky cat. Move so I can mop this puddle. Ah, here comes our lass. She'll not want raki.'

Petros heard Spanos bustling in his kitchen, followed by vigorous stirring, then familiar footsteps.

'Sit by me, Rosi. We'll have no customers while most men are tidying the churchyard.'

'Soumada? You've not mixed me an almond cordial for months.'

'I turned and saw you today as a stranger might. My precious girl has blossomed to a delightful young woman. We'll enjoy a last treat together.'

'Why? What do you mean?'

'We need to discuss serious matters. No, don't look so worried. The choice is yours and I'll love you no matter what.'

'Don't scare me, Spanos.'

'I had a visit from Katerina, in her role as matchmaker today. A crazy lad wants to know if I'd accept his proposal to marry you.'

She gasped.

A fly buzzed near Petros' ear. He couldn't swat it because he'd clasped his fingers in prayer.

'Now I've money, I'll finish repairing Rodanthe's home, ready to care for you if your kafenion gets too much. I'm not the marrying kind.' She might have said more, had she not bitten her trembling lip as she knuckled hot tears.

'Tell me if you change your mind. Meanwhile, I'll find Petros and advise him he must travel alone.'

'Petros!' Her shriek sent the cat running. 'Why didn't you say? In my mind, we had betrothed to each other years ago. Look, I thought this silver knife was his token. I was crushed by the thought of losing him.'

Behind the curtains, Petros coughed.

'Can I come out?'

Within seconds he held his girl in a close embrace, both crying, giggling and kissing.

'I love you and don't need America. My treasure is you.'

'Ah, but you promised to take me to America. You said I could have a new dress every year, whether I need one or not.'

Not embarrassed at their lingering embrace, Spanos said, 'What about your hard work on the house? You've made it such a lovely home.'

Petros held his breath for her answer; it would shape their destiny.

'As long as I'm with Petros, our home can be a hollow tree for all I care.'

Joined in a kiss, they didn't hear the door open.

'Rodanthe! Have you no shame? Pull your kerchief straight, and hurry. We've only got one night to prepare you for your wedding.'

Katerina paused as she steered Rosi towards the exit, and spoke over her shoulder, 'Your wedding is mid-morning. Go to the pappas, Petros. He wants your pledge to treat her as a maid until she turns fifteen.'

Word spread overnight, and Spanos employed two lads to keep up the steady demand for raki and mezes. Katerina's husband arrived carrying a large jar of honey filled with walnuts, a symbol of fertility.

'This will be a treat, Petros. Although my wife is bemoaning the lack of many wedding traditions, at least the pappas can feed you newlyweds sweetness. I'm happy to stand as Rosi's pa if you want Spanos as best man.'

As men pushed forward to dip fingers in the jar, Spanos snatched it away, 'Get back to the raki. I'll save this jar. I'll be proud to act as your best man, Petros, but I couldn't love Rosi more if she were my daughter.'

'My almost brother-in-law Nikos can earn the raki he's supping by standing for me. Go to Rosi. Hurry, I hear lyres tuning to lead my procession.'

Loud brays from three donkeys made their presence known. Hoisted aloft, Petros rode the lead donkey to pass by men and lads raising glasses and shouting ribald mantinadas, while small boys clamoured and chased the groom's party.

Halted by a press of crones, women and girls singing of the bride's beauty, Petros dismounted to push through to the doorway blocked by Spanos.

'Stand aside, dear friend Spanos, your daughter I'll wed, do you hear?

Bring forth my bride, I'll love and cherish her forever, have no fear.'

Keen to appear fierce, Spanos crossed his arms for emphasis.

'Away, callow youth. You'll get no blessing to wed my dear daughter.'

For the second line he wagged a finger, allowing a hint of a smile, 'Unless you vow to keep her safe from distress and deep water.'

A low bow gave Petros a moment to think.

'True, we're away over land and seas, searching rivers for gold,

Wherever we wander, my love will stay true. Dearest Spanos, I pray you're consoled.'

The exchange continued through several more rhymes, until Katerina called for silence by banging a saucepan with a wooden spoon.

'I present my sweet Rosi, a beautiful bride. Take her, dear Petros, you make quite a pair.

Almond blossom bloomed early so here is my gift, two woven rings to crown your fine hair.'

Cheers greeted the blushing Rosi. None who saw the look of adoration pass between bride and groom doubted the rightness of the match. Used to seeing her clad in rough, woven everyday garments, Petros gasped at her elegant beauty, then smiled as he stepped forward to claim his bride.

By searching hidden trunks, the generous Kritsa women had delivered up a good selection of finery. Under a skirt woven with intricate red and black designs, Rosi wore white leggings, only slightly yellowed with age. A rich red silk waistcoat emphasised her elegant white cotton blouse. When Katerina came to tie on the matching red kerchief, she had grumbled.

'This isn't big enough to restrain your long, lustrous hair.'

Rosi had laughed and said, 'It's hard to remember how short I cut it when pretending to be a young boy to accompany Petros.'

Katerina hadn't answered, as the girl's words sent her thoughts spinning while she pushed unruly strands of hair under the silk.

Three abreast, arm in arm with Spanos between them, Rosi and Petros led the procession out of the alley, across the patch by the spring to pass the closed kafenion, and down the main thoroughfare. The lack of Turk businesses had led to the street's decay, causing them to weave between ruts and puddles, while behind them the loud cheery cavalcade drowned out the noise of banging shutters on abandoned balconies.

Well-wishers lined the knoll in front of the small church to cheer at the first sight of the bridal party. Decked in a clean cassock, the smiling pappas awaited them.

*

Afterwards, the crowd melted away as folk knew the feast of yesterday meant nothing today. Instead of being subject to a ribald escort to their marital home, the bride and groom halted at the kafenion door to wave their goodbyes. Once all well-wishers had gone, they enjoyed a kiss, before moving indoors to see Spanos emerging from the hidey-hole under his bed.

'I've had this flagon of wine hidden away for years. No, sit down, Rosi. Let me serve you.'

Breaking from a kiss, Petros said, 'Four glasses, Spanos?'

'Katerina will arrive with a plate of yesterday's leftovers, so we can relax while we toast your dreams. Oh, do you realise she expects to take Rosi home with her tonight?'

'She's determined I should keep my oath.'

Rosi giggled and blushed, 'I'm fifteen before autumn, but Katerina suggests saving the risk of babies until our travels are over.'

When Petros put his head in his hands to feign loud wailing, the cat fled.

*

Early the next morning, a bag chinked on the table next to Petros' hand.

'Here, this is overdue wages.'

'I don't need your money, Spanos. I owe you more than I could ever repay.'

'Take it. It's full of small coins. Hide it in different places, and always behave as if you're poor. Keep those napoleons sewn inside your boots. Convert them to cash one at a time.'

'Here, exchange a napoleon for your coins.'

'Tsk, no. You have both worked for me without due reward.' Spanos gave his nose a loud blow, then croaked, 'I'm a richer man for having enjoyed your company.'

Petros hugged his benefactor, feeling warm tears on his neck. With no comforting words, their embrace continued until the door crashed open. A lad with overshort hair ran in, waving a small silver knife.

'Ha, look at me. I'm Yannis again, ready to journey with my hero.'

Both Spanos and Petros stared open-mouthed. In the pause, Rosi faltered, 'Oh, are you cross? Katerina made me promise to wear this disguise until we reach America.'

'Ah well, I guess that's for the best. It will keep my thoughts from the beautiful girl I married yesterday. Bid farewell to Spanos. I'll tend the goats one last time.'

48

Piraeus

Popi cried when selling Kostas' crucifix, consoling herself he'd have agreed to it funding her dockside ouzo bar, mean as it was. A glass and a few mezes were all she could afford, although she nursed a dream to offer more. No wonder the kafenion next door was much busier. As usual, Kazanis still lolled in his cloak with an empty ouzo flask near to hand as she tiptoed out to wield her broom in the first rays of sunlight. Busy sweeping, she stopped to pick up a discarded newspaper. To read, even if it was old news, reminded her of better times in Missolonghi. Today the headline made her frown.

Even though Popi routinely avoided Kazanis until he roused himself, she hurried towards him, certain he'd want to know of events before the newsprint fuelled their brazier. Her filthy toes prodded him awake.

'Lift the awning, I need light.'

Slow to absorb her words, he attempted to focus through bleary eyes. Frustrated at how he couldn't cope with a simple request, she snapped, 'Oh, move, I'll do it.'

With a yawn he rubbed his face, hunched to a sitting position and winced as daylight hit his eyes.

'Careful, woman. You'll bring the whole side of the awning tumbling on our heads. Out of my way, you wanted me to do it. What's the hurry?'

'Don't flood the place with sunshine. Give me enough light to share this shocking news.'

She sat cross-legged with the paper spread out before her and used a finger to trace under the words.

'The European powers signed the London Protocol on 3 February 1830 to declare Greece an independent monarchical state under their protection ...'

At the closing paragraph, Kazanis leapt up, stamping his foot to emphasise his words, 'Really? This is peace? We've battled and bled. Lost countless lives. For what? Yes, I'm proud Greece is to have her own king. But it's not good enough. The great powers are carving up the world to suit themselves. Despite our suffering, Crete is still vassal to the Turks.' Diatribe exhausted, he crashed down on a half-barrel stool before a plank table, 'For God's sake, bring me ouzo.'

As she crouched to pour from a cask, Kazanis scowled at their wretched conditions.

'Pah! Free indeed.'

Their rough, tented ouzeri formed part of a shanty town on the dubious fringes of Piraeus port. It gave Popi a meagre living to supplement the intermittent coin Kazanis earned as a stevedore. Manos acted as pot boy, until he curled around his sister to sleep in a newspaper-lined wooden crate.

Popi pushed lank strands behind a grimy kerchief, sighing as she set down a tot of ouzo and a chipped water jug.

'At least we're alive to hear of it.'

He thumped his table, 'This is no life.'

'Shush, keep your voice down. Many evenings after Missolonghi I thought we'd be dead by dawn. Truth to tell, I'm content.'

Kazanis fought the urge to shake her. Why couldn't the woman understand? Even during their days on the edge of death he'd been more alive. Chance had saved them when a fishing boat towed them ashore, but his determination to walk to Piraeus, living on scraps, stolen chickens, sneakily milked goats and trapped hares, had got them here. Even while recognising his sulky tone, he bawled, 'What, crammed in this shack? This is surviving; nothing more. Now men flood in, the days I work a shift get fewer.'

'Don't shout, you'll wake Manos. Both children have dreadful coughs.'

As if on cue, the undersized girl cried out. Kazanis huffed, 'Don't fret. Brats are tougher than you realise.'

Instead of arguing, Popi bustled to tend the child, with her own hacking cough taking her breath. Realisation hit Kazanis; he needed to live a man's life again, and he rushed after Popi, determined to convince her it was time for a fresh start. While the mama clasped her daughter, soothing with kisses and smiles, something jolted deep inside him. A long-subdued memory of his wife cradling his baby girl as she boarded a boat for Naxos made him clamp his eyes shut. Anger at his wife's decision to return to her family continued to hurt his pride. Clench-fisted, he remembered how he'd snatched Petros away at the last moment. Now, seeing Popi nurse her fretful daughter, he realised a courageous mama risks everything to protect her babe. It hurt him to admit Petros would be alive if he'd gone with his mama. Kazanis scowled at this thought at the same moment Popi looked up. He saw her wariness and recognised she had cause; he'd often cast angry blows.

Decision made, he smiled.

'After surviving so much, I refuse to stay in this pit until we succumb. Boats leave each evening. Your children deserve fresh air, you need a husband, and I must regain my pride.'

Popi paled and swallowed, 'Poor mite, she's almost asleep. Wait for me outside. We must talk.'

*

A regular merchant from Crete moored his craft against the wharf and Kazanis walked forward, hoping to help unload. After a few paces he stopped, disappointed to see two lads on board had earned the task. The taller one caught Kazanis' attention, and with his heart beating fast he groped for his spyglasses. Then he made an abrupt turn, annoyed with himself for acting out of habit – he'd sold those glasses for food long ago. As he returned to the timber bench outside their ouzeri, he shook his head at his sentimentality.

Determined not to watch others earn his coin, he sat with his back to the water, then relaxed as warmth from the morning sun chased his chills away. Popi joined him and took up his hand to cup it between hers.

'Both children need more sleep.'

'What do you say, Popi? Shall we leave? Let's take advantage of this current mood of change.'

'Dear Kazanis.' She patted his hand, then kissed his cheek, anxious he should understand, 'We owe you our lives and I thank God daily for your bravery. No, let me finish. If you've realised now is the time to seek more from life, then I'm happy.'

Kazanis became animated, such a change from his usual glum countenance. 'There are a few things to sell, everything else can fit in our pockets. Let's sort through while the children sleep.'

She laid a palm on either side of his face, 'My other daily prayer is never to flee again. Go, you've too much heart to settle for a miserable existence.'

Excitement flared and possibilities flashed through Kazanis' mind, creating a pause more truthful than his words, 'You three can't fend for yourselves alone.'

'You don't see what goes on under your nose. Our neighbour, the widower in the brick-built kafenion, asked me to marry him.'

'What! When?'

'His daughter plays with my girl most days and we often chat. At Christmas, he asked the truth of the rumour we sleep apart. When I confirmed you're my dearest friend, and not my spouse, he proposed marriage.'

Dumbstruck, Kazanis' mouth gaped.

'My answer until now was no. I'd never leave you homeless.'

Kazanis' brow furrowed, finding this news hard to comprehend. Popi held his gaze, tears sparkling on her eyelashes.

'The plot our shack covers will give space to extend his kafenion. He wants a mama for his girl and a cook for his customers.' Silent tears fell, 'And, I'd have a permanent home for my children – with food every day.'

*

In Megalo Kastro the crush of people had overawed Petros and Rosi, adapting to her role as Yannis. Here in chaotic Piraeus they clung to each other. Shouts rang out in many languages. Huge carts towed by enormous horses rumbled past lines of ragged men trailing across the concrete dock. Bemused, they watched a man in a peaked cap and odd, tight clothing walk along a row of men, pointing at the fittest among them. As each man stepped forward to join a growing group, the line shuffled to close the gap. When the capped man led his chosen workforce away, those still in line groaned, shrugged and moved to another column.

'Oi, move, you two. You're asking to get crushed.'

Jolted from his staring, Petros took Yannis by the arm and steered towards a savoury smell wafting from skewers of grilling pork. After sorting through unfamiliar coins, Petros paid for breakfast.

'Do you know where the ship for America moors?'

'Never heard of that island. Next, please?'

*

By noon, Petros had trudged around the huge port with Yannis hitching an overlarge rucksack from one shoulder to the other. The pair had dodged cranes, refused beggars, ignored curses flung at them for breathing, and braved flimsy bridges. Harder to bear was the constant ridicule that met Petros's pleas for information about America. Tired, but conscious of not looking feminine, Yannis heaved her bag onto a pile of stacked carob sacks and slumped to sit, legs splayed.

'What now, big brother?'

'Sorry, I can't think straight. Look at that man. Does he remind you of anyone?'

'Who? Men are milling everywhere.'

'See there, with a similarity to my pa from the rear. Apart from us, he's the only one wearing baggy Cretan britches. I'll ask him for advice.'

After helping Yannis hoist her bag, Petros sprinted after the probable Cretan. Perhaps a shift had ended, as men swarmed from side alleys to throng the wider cobbled road rimming the harbour.

Pain in his heaving side halted him, and by the time Yannis caught up, a rowdy multitude covered the path ahead.

'Sorry, Petros, I dropped my rucksack. Which way did he go?'

Hit by overwhelming sadness, Petros pointed, 'Most of the horde left the port by the first gate, but he might have hurried down there. Come on, I want to find him if I can.'

'Why does it matter? One man telling us we're crazy is as good as another.'

'Daft, I know. A Cretan seemed a good omen.'

*

Opposite the trading boat they'd arrived on, Petros and Yannis rested in the shade of a tumbledown ouzeri. A chesty cough signalled the approach of a sickly lad whose bare ricket-bowed legs protruded from a coat several sizes too big.

'If you want a drink, I'll fetch it. Mezes will need to wait until Mama returns from visiting our neighbour.'

Before Petros could decline, a whiny, snot-nosed girl in a sacking shift appeared, stinking of pee.

'Uncle is angry. Tell him where Mama went.'

*

'Petros, is America a real place?'

'Of course! A Lassithi man once broke farming tradition to become a sailor. Years later, a message telling of gold finds encouraged two others to leave for America. I remember when Pa first allowed me to spend a night in the mountains with his men. Sheltered under the walnut tree, they shared raki and dreamed of gold.'

'Are you sure it's possible to make the journey?'

'Do you think we should give up?' Not trusting the potential answer, Petros hurried to the water's edge to meet a vessel heading to the berth.

To open conversation, Petros caught a rope.

'Can I unload?'

'You're no stevedore.'

'My brother, Yannis, can help me.'

'Today we take on merchandise. If you can pay, I'll take you to Naxos.'

'It's years since I heard of Naxos. My mama lives there. We're heading to America.'

'Ha ha, that's a good joke.'

With bravado, Petros waved to Yannis before focusing attention on the rope, blinking fast against stinging tears. After stepping ashore, the boatman took his line.

'You new here?'

'Arrived this morning from Crete, on the cargo boat next to yours.'

'Best get back on it.'

Disheartened, Petros had turned back towards Yannis when shouts drew his attention to a nearby crew preparing to sail. Not wanting to let any chance pass, he went to speak to the sailor on the gangplank.

'Excuse me. Do you know how I can sail to America?'

'I don't know, but wait there and I'll see if our captain will speak to you. I've heard him talk of America.'

*

'Hurry, Yannis, we're off to Malta. Our captain says from there we can take a ship to a country called Gibraltar, where we'll get passage to America.'

Settled in the stern, Petros chose to keep Piraeus in sight for as long as possible.

'Oh, look. There's the fellow I tried to follow along the wharf. He's in a hurry.'

On the waterfront, a lone boy chased behind the Cretan. Enthralled, Petros witnessed a tableau rich in childhood memories as the man stopped, stooped to face the boy, and then lifted him to spin round and around. As if dizzy, Petros felt tears prick as the pair embraced. Placed on the ground, the child crumpled to his knees, imploring arms outstretched to his hero who dashed away without a backwards glance.

Spasms of dreadful loss made Petros clutch his chest, then gripping the boat rail, he swallowed fast to quell rising bile, fearing derision for being seasick in port. Emotion threatened to choke him; he'd not felt such pain since Pa died.

The absurdity of his imagination brought a headshake insufficient to erase the magnetism of the familiar figure. With a squint through tears, Petros focused on the man paused between the boats bound for Crete and Naxos. Petros sucked in a breath; it mattered which he chose.

A foaming wave caught the departing boat and the resulting splash made Yannis squeal. With a swipe at his sweaty brow, Petros smiled to reassure her. When he turned back seconds later, he'd missed seeing which vessel had gained a passenger.

Tears streamed down his face.

Bereft, he raised his arm to wave. Shrill gulls masked his cry.

'Goodbye, Papa.'

Author's notes and acknowledgements

Thank you for reading Rodanthe's Gift. As an independent author I rely on word of mouth to introduce new readers, so I'll be delighted if you add a review on Amazon. You don't have to have bought the book from them, and even a few words make such a difference to potential readers. If you wish to give direct feedback you can contact me via my website, https://kritsayvonne.com or by email, kritsayvonne@talktalk.net

As with my first book, *Kritsotopoula, Girl of Kritsa*, I owe thanks to my husband, Alan, for his support during the research phases and for embracing my wish to visit Missolonghi, Greece. While in Missolonghi we had the pleasure of visiting the Museum of History and Art, which has wonderful displays focusing on Lord Byron and the sieges the city endured. Here, we met the curator, Ioannis Paraskevas, who gave us a guided tour and privileged access to exhibits. My ability to write the chapters set in Missolonghi are thanks to Ioannis' generosity, and the quality of the exhibits in his museum. If you'd like more information about Missolonghi, I recommend https://www.discovermessolonghi.gr/

I am incredibly lucky that Chris Moorey, author of *A Glimpse of Heaven*, read my draft novel and used his expertise to make sure my references to the Greek orthodox religion were correct.

My friend Maureen Ramsay and I once sat in the dark caves at Milatos, and, lit by the light of a single flickering candle, we tried to imagine the horror of so many confined there. I'm thankful that one of her thoughts stayed with me, when she said, 'Imagine not even having enough water to dab a baby's dry cracked lips.'

My thanks also go to Jerry Flint, who calculated the sailing time from Sisi to Kythira.

Modern-day place names are used to describe locations in the novel, using either the most widely used or my preferred spelling/transliteration, with the exception of Megalo Kastro instead of Heraklion.

Emmanuel Rovithis, born in 1793 in Marmaketo, Lassithi, Crete, was a rebel leader widely known as Captain Kazanis. He died on the island of Naxos in 1846. For more details visit http://www.marmaketo.gr/ I love their statement about the village of Marmaketo: 'A small village, but it has a divine grace. A small village, but she gave birth to a big lad.'

Among a wealth of internet information, I'd particularly like to acknowledge the excellent material gleaned from the website, https://www.cretanbeaches.com/en/
Don't be fooled: this website contains information beyond beautiful beaches.

Serendipity was at work when I 'met' my editor, Nicky Taylor, on social media, and found she had even sailed into Missolonghi Lagoon. This led to a very pleasant and thorough editing experience that I look forward to repeating. You can contact Nicky via her website https://nickytayloreditorial.com. My dramatic book cover was produced by Luke Harris at Working Type, http://www.workingtype.com.au – yes, in Australia! Finally, my thanks go to Ian Yates, of Black Bay Publishing for pulling everything together.